Redemption Mountain

Redemption Mountain

A NOVEL

Gerry FitzGerald

Henry Holt and Company
New York

Henry Holt and Company, LLC
Publishers since 1866
175 Fifth Avenue
New York, New York 10010
www.henryholt.com

Henry Holt® and 🏛® are registered trademarks of Henry Holt and Company, LLC.

Distributed in Canada by Raincoast Book Distribution Limited

Library of Congress Cataloging-in-Publication Data

FitzGerald, Gerry, 1949–
    Redemption Mountain : a novel / Gerry FitzGerald.—1st ed.
        p. cm.
    ISBN 978-0-8050-9489-3
    1. Housewives—Fiction.   2. Businessmen—Fiction.   3. Mineral industries—West
Virginia—Fiction.   I. Title.
    PS3606.I8786R43 2013
    813'.6—dc23

                                                                                2012034073

Henry Holt books are available for special promotions and premiums.
For details contact: Director, Special Markets.

First Edition 2013

Designed by Meryl Sussman Levavi

Printed in the United States of America

1 3 5 7 9 10 8 6 4 2

For Robin, Tom, and Jo.

No one deserves to be this lucky.

Redemption Mountain

CHAPTER 1

July 2000

T HIS WAS HER TIME. THE QUIET TIME. BEFORE THE SUN AND THE
kids and the rest of McDowell County rose to demand her attention. When she could run and be alone and pretend to be someone else,
living a different life in a different place.

The young woman slipped quietly out of bed and picked up the small
pile of clothes and her running shoes, which she'd set out the night
before. She heard her husband before she saw him. Buck's labored snoring
told her he'd probably spent the evening at Moody's Roadhouse again,
which was more routine than not these days. The sliding door that led to
the trailer's narrow hallway rumbled and squeaked, causing a furtive
look at her husband to see if he'd awakened. She reminded herself for the
hundredth time to oil the track.

The small bathroom had a folding door with its own set of noises as
she carefully drew it shut behind her. It was still dark in the trailer at
five-thirty, even at the end of July. She turned on the small light over the
mirror and slid on the baggy khaki shorts, a sports bra, and a faded black
T-shirt she'd pulled randomly from the drawer the night before. It was
the Pittsburgh Steelers T-shirt that Buck had brought home for their son
a few years earlier, the only gift she could remember him giving the boy.
A glimmer of hope at the time.

The shirt was cheaply made, a size medium, snug to begin with and
after many washings now too small for a twelve-year-old. She pulled it
over her sandy-blond hair and leaned on the sink to find the insides of

the running shoes with her toes. She never wore socks when she ran. As a child, she rarely wore shoes, and ran on rougher ground than she would this morning.

She brushed her teeth, splashed water on her face, and stared into the mirror. Her hair was getting long, almost to her shoulders now, the curly permanent from four months earlier, which Buck hated, now hanging limp and lifeless. *Have to get it cut before school starts in the fall.* Maybe she'd just cut it all off like her mother did to her when she was in elementary school, when she was more often than not taken for a boy.

The woman leaned in closer to the mirror and examined, as she always did when she was alone, the faded two-inch scar that ran horizontally just above her left eyebrow. Another, shorter scar started at the edge of her upper lip. Both scars were nearly invisible now, to everyone but her.

Her broad shoulders stretched the T-shirt a little more tightly across her chest than she preferred, while it hung loosely at her small waist. Two pregnancies had enlarged her breasts to at least a noticeable size in relation to her small frame. Her mother complained that she looked bony at a hundred and ten pounds, but she felt good physically and she was finally beginning to feel good about herself as well. At thirty years old, Natty Oakes was finally ready to admit that maybe she wasn't so plain and ordinary anymore and that some men might even find her attractive now.

So why had Buck been losing interest lately, she wondered. Only once since the beginning of July had Buck visited her side of the bed. The few times that she'd tentatively edged over to initiate activity, she'd been rebuffed. *Probably the alcohol.* Buck had been drinking more lately. She hoped that was the reason.

In the small kitchenette, she turned on the gas burner and shoveled two heaping teaspoons of instant coffee into a large steel mug. Bending low to look out the small window over the sink, she could see that the stool at the corner of the trailer across the gravel road was unoccupied. She glanced at her watch. Still a few minutes early.

She went back up the short hallway to the smaller bedroom. The room was cramped enough without the mess of clothes, books, toys, stuffed animals, and the Nintendo game, with its wires and controls and various game cartridges spread between the beds. *Damn, this room sucks.* It was too small for one child, let alone two.

She looked down at her son, lying on his back, wearing only Jockey shorts that were too tight. He was snoring lightly, his mouth slightly open. She could see his irregularly spaced teeth—beyond the scope of orthodontics, she had been told, but it didn't matter. They couldn't afford it, and the Pie Man was never going to be popular for his looks anyway.

In the other bed, a small girl lay on her side with her thumb in her mouth. Natty pulled the sheet up over her, gently extracted her thumb, and brushed away the strands of matted blond hair covering her face. She sat on the edge of the bed and ran her hand down her daughter's pencil-thin arm. Cat was a tiny girl, small for her age—scrawny, some would say—but with boundless energy and a streak of stubbornness that Natty made allowances for because she knew where it came from.

Natty thought about Cat's seventh birthday coming up in September. *Seven.* The same age Natty was when she first came to McDowell County, West Virginia, with her mother and her sister Annie. It was 1977, the year her father was killed in the mine up in Marion County. The year they came to live with her grandparents at the farm on Redemption Mountain because they had nowhere else to go. The year the joy went out of her mother's eyes.

Natty could still feel the icy chill of the rainy day in November, when they stood all morning in front of the tall wooden doors, surrounded by the miners' wives who'd quietly drifted in to stand vigil, like they had for a hundred years. And then the screech of the elevator cables—a sound she could never erase from her mind—bringing her father up from two thousand feet below. She walked back up the hill in the rain to their empty house, holding Annie's small hand, following their sobbing mother, who was never the same after that day.

Sarah DeWitt wasn't from West Virginia. She didn't know coal mining and couldn't understand how a man could go off to work in the morning and be brought up the mine shaft in the afternoon, lifeless, covered with black dust, and wrapped in a dirty blanket. She'd listened to some of the old miners' wives telling stories about the day in November nine years earlier, when the earth rumbled and the Consol Mine No. 9 in Farmington, just a few miles up the road, exploded in an underground firestorm, killing seventy-eight men, burning so hot that the mine was sealed off, with no attempt at rescue. Sarah had passed by the monument many times and always assumed that was how men died in coal mines, in big catastrophes that happened only in the past because mines were safer now, Tom had told her, and technology was better. But her husband died the way most men die in the mines, one at a time, miles down a dark tunnel, the lone victim of a relatively minor occurrence in the business of coal mining, leaving Sarah alone with her two girls in a strange land.

Natty stroked her daughter's moist forehead and heard the distant whistling sound of the blizzard winds piling the snow against the windows of the farmhouse. She looked down and saw three-year-old Annie sweating and delirious from the fever. *It all would have been different if Annie had lived. Mama had talked about moving back to Wisconsin, where she grew up, to a city called Waukesha, with parks and streets with big houses and green lawns and modern schools.* Natty could hear shouts. *Natty! Natty! They were yelling at her because it was her fault for letting Annie play outside too long in the stream, breaking the thin ice with their shoes and getting their feet wet. She knew Annie's pneumonia was her fault, with the road down the mountain impassable with the snow, but why were they yelling at her now?*

"*Natty, get that fucking pot!* Nat, you out there?" Buck was yelling from the bedroom over the whistling teakettle. *Dammit! How long had he been yelling?*

She bounded out of the children's room. "I got it, Buck. Sorry, honey. Go back to sleep," she called out, as she yanked the kettle from the burner. She poured the boiling water over the coffee crystals, watching the dark steaming liquid swirl and bubble as she thought about her daydream of Annie. It surprised her. She rarely thought about Annie anymore, only when they went up to the farm. The nightmares had stopped years ago. She reminded herself that they needed to visit her mother soon.

Natty added an ice cube to the coffee, and a straw that hinged in the middle, and carried it outside. She stood on the small wooden deck that was their front porch and breathed in the ever-present scent of pine in the air. The sun hadn't yet made it over the Alleghenies, but it was light enough to see that nothing was stirring in Oakes Hollow.

She looked up the hill toward the *big house*, where Buck's parents, Frank and Rose lived. The house was surrounded on three sides by a wide covered porch from which Big Frank would look down over his domain, where his three sons lived with their *sorry-ass wives and too many kids to bother with all their names.* Under the porch, one of the old coonhounds lifted his nose to Natty and barked twice before lying back down.

She had to giggle, looking over at Ransom and Sally's house, at the overturned plastic riding toys, rusted bicycles, a broken swing set, a collapsed kiddie pool, and probably a hundred other toys that had been scattered about all summer. It wouldn't look much different inside. Housekeeping would never be one of Sally's talents.

Natty wondered if Ransom was still working at the cement job he talked about bringing Buck onto. She'd begun to notice his truck parked in front of The Spur, the dingy little gin mill in Old Red Bone, most afternoons when she drove through town. She'd seen Buck's truck up there on occasion, but she knew if Buck was drinking in the afternoon, he preferred the pool room at Moody's Roadhouse.

A light went on in the trailer directly across the road. That would be Amos. With his dead left side, it would take him a while to pull his pants and shirt on. He was careful not to awaken Yancy or especially Charlotte, who was a bear when the old man woke her up in the morning, and *heaven forbid if he woke the girls!*

Natty felt sorry for Charlotte, because she was fat and dim-witted and mostly disagreeable, but she was still too young to be trapped in the mountains with two babies and an out-of-work miner for a husband. They had a lot in common. But Natty had never warmed up to her sister-in-law, from the first week that Charlotte and Yancy moved into the trailer across from theirs and Charlotte let her know *that little mongoloid boy'd be better off in a home somewhere.*

They'd had it out then. But it wasn't just about Pie. Later, it was about her grandfather Amos whom, after his stroke, Charlotte considered a burden. Beyond providing a small sleeping space and a place at the supper table, she largely ignored him. That wasn't fair, Natty thought. He deserved better.

She heard the old man shuffle slowly through the gravel and watched him feel his way around the corner of the trailer. He couldn't turn his head, and his eyesight was failing, so he wouldn't see her until she stood right in front of him. She would wait until he was ready for her.

Amos Ritter was a hard, wiry little man with short-cropped white

hair and a perpetual stubble of white whiskers. Up close, you could look
into the deep creases in his forehead and the pockmarks of soft skin
under his eyes and see the tiny black gritty remnants of more than four
decades spent underground in the coalfields of West Virginia and Kentucky. His gnarled left hand was missing the last two fingers, taken off so
long ago he could barely recall the mine he'd lost them to.

Every morning when Natty went out to run, Amos was sitting on his
little stool, waiting for her. As she brought his coffee over to him, his mouth
twitched into an unsteady smile, the best he could do. He slowly raised
his right arm in a kind of half wave, with his fingers pointed at her, and
blinked his small, cloudy eyes in an effort to tell her that, *yes*, he was still
alive and that she was someone special to him.

"Morning, Amos." Natty squatted down and set the mug on his knee
until he could get his arthritic fingers through the handle. He'd spill some
getting the straw to his mouth. She stood and kissed him on the forehead.
"Sun's going to be hot today, Amos; you'll need your hat," she said as she
started down the hill to begin her run. She turned around briefly, walking
backward, and smiled. "I'll fix you an egg when I get back." Amos blinked
and squinted and twitched his mouth. He bent his head forward slightly
in a slow nod and watched until she disappeared down the road and
around the corner of the woods.

If Amos could speak, he would tell Natty how much he loved her.
He'd thank her for being his friend and making him feel like he mattered. For helping him forget the pain for a while. And for being such a
good mother in a hard situation. He would tell her how beautiful she was
and that if he were a few years younger, he'd beat the living piss out of her
worthless husband until he straightened up or, even better, just went off
for good. And if Buck ever hit her again, he'd take a pickax handle to his
head so bad you wouldn't know which side his face was on.

But Amos knew he'd never say any of these things to Natty or do anything to Buck. All he could do now was enjoy the sunrise and the sunsets,
the smell of the woods, and his visits from Natty.

CHAPTER 2

CHARLIE BURDEN FLEXED HIS RIGHT HAND AS HE DROVE. IT didn't feel broken, just bruised a little, in need of some ice to keep the swelling down. He knew what broken fingers felt like, and this wasn't it. He'd caught the kid flush with a couple of good ones and had probably broken his nose, from all the blood on the ice. "*Dammit*," Charlie said, as he eased the steel blue Lexus out of the rink parking lot onto Route 1. *This was turning out to be one piss-poor day already, and there was a good chance it was going to get worse when he picked up Ellen.*

He shook his head in disgust, but he also had to laugh. As bad as he felt, he could still enjoy the irony—a forty-eight-year-old professional engineer, a partner at Dietrich Delahunt & Mackey, one of the most prestigious engineering firms in the world, a member of several charitable boards, et cetera, et cetera, getting thrown out of an over-35 hockey league for fighting.

He thought about how his friend Duncan would react to the news. *He'll have a lot of fun with this one.* Charlie could see it coming, at an important meeting in the luxurious boardroom of the OntAmex Energy building in Toronto. Duncan McCord, one of the most powerful men in the utility industry in North America, would rise to his feet to address the meeting. *Before we get to today's agenda, a round of applause for my old line mate at Michigan, Charlie Burden, the only middle-aged guy to ever get tossed from a recreational hockey league for fighting. What a dickhead, aye?* Yes, Duncan will enjoy this. Duncan, who, in college, was always ready to drop the gloves and start pounding away before the opening face-off.

Charlie headed west out of Stamford toward New York. The Saturday noontime traffic was heavy, with the usual crush of shoreline tourists, shoppers, and minivans full of kids headed for what had to be the world's busiest McDonald's. It would be faster if he took I-95, but he had plenty of time, so he'd just stay on Route 1 all the way down to Mamaroneck and then head up to the country club to pick up Ellen.

The road to Hickory Hills Country Club ran through some of Westchester's most prized real estate, past the lush, verdant meadows and white fences of the tony riding academy, through expansive neighborhoods of manicured lawns and large, stately homes. The neighborhoods were beautiful, quiet, and tranquil and had a naturally calming effect that made you slow down and bask for a moment in the warm glow of exclusivity. It was a contagious feeling, easy to catch around the country clubs of Westchester County. Ellen Burden had caught it, and along with everything else, it was part of the rapidly growing crevasse in their marriage.

A few miles before the club, Charlie decided to take a short detour to have another look at the home Ellen had set her sights on, her new obsession. He was an hour early and didn't want to hang around the club now that he was no longer a member.

He turned off Old Colony Road and drove through some woodsy middle-class neighborhoods, then onto Dowling Farms Lane. Here, the woods gave way to the gently rolling former fields of one of Westchester County's oldest farming regions, reclaimed over the years for more-profitable use.

Charlie turned down a driveway through an 1800s-era stone wall backed by a thick stand of well-trimmed arborvitae. He drove a short way down the long driveway, turned off the Lexus, and sat gazing at the surroundings. The house had been empty for four months, but the landscapers had obviously been busy. The driveway had puddles from the sprinklers, and the shrubbery had been recently trimmed. *Yes, for this kind of money, Ellen's realtor, a close friend from the country club, would make sure the grounds were in pristine condition all summer.*

Charlie got out of the car and sat on a wrought-iron bench that was part of the front garden and faced the house. *A magnificent old English cottage-style home, with every conceivable amenity and feature for gracious country living*, the four-page brochure had begun. Built twenty years ago to look two hundred years old, the house was much bigger than it appeared from the outside. An architectural deception, Charlie knew, due to the long sloping roof descending to the first floor and the oversize fenestration throughout. The latticed windows were large, and the front entryway was wide, with large oak double doors. Even the truncated cupolas poking through the slate roof on the second floor were larger than the overall scale of the home made them seem.

And the inside of the house wasn't small, Charlie recalled, with four bedrooms, two family rooms, a library, and a study. The interior definitely wasn't two hundred years old, either, with its Viking kitchen, Jacuzzi in the master suite, and state-of-the-art sound system.

Charlie strolled down the long driveway to the rear of the house to look at the *real* features of the property—pages three and four of the brochure. Between the curving driveway and a large enclosed porch with green-and-white-striped awnings was another perfectly coiffed lawn, garden, and patio area. Crossing the driveway, Charlie walked down a wide, gently sloping stone stairway to the pool. Beyond the pool was a pool house with attached tiki bar worthy of any Caribbean resort, and on the far side, a tennis court surfaced in dark blue, surrounded on three sides by closely planted evergreens.

He walked up a curving gravel path to the stable at the end of the garage. Next to it there was a half-acre riding area, now overgrown. The stable doors were open, and Charlie could smell the rich aroma of old hay. There were no horses, but he knew that would be their next *discussion* if they were to live here.

Charlie leaned back against the sun-baked fence of the corral and let the warmth soothe his back, aching from the morning hockey game. He looked up at the house and the garden patio and down at the pool and tennis court. He could see why this had become Ellen's dream home. It fit perfectly with Ellen's need for status and social power. And it certainly wouldn't hurt her campaign to become the first woman president of Hickory Hills Country Club.

But Charlie knew that the home was about more than status, gracious country living, and the Hickory Hills crowd. He knew it the first time they looked at the property. He saw it in Ellen's eyes, how they came alive when she moved around the grounds. *This was where Ellen grew up. The life she was born to.* Smaller certainly than the estate in East Greenwich, Rhode Island, with its expansive colonial farmhouse, acres of meadows and woods, stables, and the barn with the loft apartment where they had first made love, the summer after his junior year at Michigan, the night they met in the bar in Newport. Three months before the federal prosecutor indicted her father, Augie D'Angelo, and it all disappeared. Charlie knew that the house was as much about vindication as it was about stepping up to the next level of Westchester society. And that would make it all harder.

Charlie disliked the opulence of the house and what would become their lifestyle in this neighborhood. It was everything he was trying to escape. And it was wasteful, moving into a bigger home now that Scott and Jennifer were out of the house. He knew they could afford it, even though it was stupid money. But it was a huge, irrevocable step in a direction he didn't want to go.

He drove back out to the main road and headed north toward the country club. Seeing the house again reminded Charlie of his larger problem, the problem that had been festering for three months, since the Thursday before Easter, when he received the call in his office in the city from his friend Dave Marchetti. The call about Ellen's affair.

"So, Linda's got a big mouth anyway," Dave began. "But the other night she gets all lathered up on vodka tonics and . . ." Linda Marchetti was Ellen Burden's best friend. "I hate to . . . but I'd want to know, Charlie." Marchetti hesitated. "Name's Morgan, Phil Morgan. Used to be a member of the club, few years ago. Played in our group on Saturdays. Maybe you remember him." Charlie didn't. "Quit the club, then quit golf, I heard. Too bad—he was, like, a three handicap. Made his money on Wall Street, a pile of it. Retired and started a foundation to build schools in Africa. Mostly all his money." Marchetti paused again. "Ellen was on his board a few years ago." Charlie vaguely recalled Ellen serving for a short time on the board of an outfit dealing with African children. "Lost his wife to cancer last year," Marchetti said softly. There was a long silence between them until Marchetti spoke again. "Linda tells me it only lasted a month. Over before it started."

"Okay, thanks, Dave. I appreciate it," said Charlie, anxious to get off the phone and take a deep breath and be alone. "Anything else?"

Marchetti sighed audibly. "Charlie . . . he's a very decent guy."

Outside Charlie's windows, the Park Avenue traffic six floors below was heavy and slow, as it always was before a holiday. It was only Thursday, but, with tomorrow being Good Friday, the weekend had already started. *It was going to be a bitch getting out of the city and back to Mamaroneck.* Charlie thought about staying in one of the corporate apartments on the second floor. He'd used them more often over the past year, staying in the city overnight after an extended workday, or to get an early start on some project in the morning. The call to Ellen had become routine, most often a message left on her voice mail.

Charlie pulled off his tie and tossed it on the chair across from him. Whether he spent the night or drove home with the traffic, he wasn't going anywhere for a while. Right now he needed a drink and a cigar. One of Lucien Mackey's big Cubans would be perfect.

Charlie left his office, suddenly aware of the quiet. It was just after seven o'clock—past quitting time on the partners' floor. The staff engineers and architects would still be working down on the fourth and fifth floors, where Charlie had worked when he first joined the firm, putting in the happiest years of his career. In the executive lounge, he went behind the bar and poured a small glass of Canadian Club. As he made his way around the massive mahogany table, he gazed at the display cases lining the interior wall, showcasing Dietrich Delahunt & Mackey's greatest projects.

The largest and most impressive display was also the most recent project—the first of two giant hydroelectric dams the firm was building in China. The two dams together were by far the largest project the company had ever undertaken. Charlie studied the model of the dam with its cutaway section, showing the intricate details of the massive turbines inside the huge wall of concrete and steel that would be holding back a body of water the size of Rhode Island. While Charlie sipped his whiskey and gazed enviously at the model of the dam, a germ of an idea began to form. An idea that might salvage his career—and now maybe even save his marriage.

"Hard to believe we can build something that big, isn't it, Charlie?" He was startled out of his thoughts by the commanding voice of Lucien Mackey and turned to find the managing general partner of Dietrich

Delahunt & Mackey coming toward him around the conference table. "Working late? Saw the light on in your office. Everything all right?" Lucien extended his huge hand, as he always did. He insisted on shaking hands with everyone he came in contact with, holding on for a few seconds while locked in intense eye contact, in a sincere effort to glean some insight into his subject's state of mind. Charlie was glad to see him. Lucien's presence in a room was magically uplifting. He was tall, silver-haired, and, even at sixty-eight, had the physique of a linebacker.

"Lucien, hello. Yes, I'm fine. How was China?"

"Got back this morning. Oh Charlie, you've got to see it; the model doesn't do it justice. It's spectacular, and what beautiful people. Charlie, do you realize that the first phase of this project alone is going to bring low-cost dependable electricity to nearly a *hundred million* people, so they can finally stop choking on coal soot, nitrous oxide, and sulfuric acid. . . . You know all about it as well as anyone, I guess." He put a hand on Charlie's shoulder. "Come on, Charlie, let's go have a cigar. Not too many guys around here to have a smoke with anymore. All those kids downstairs want to do is suck on Tic Tacs and drink bottled water."

"As a matter of fact, I was just on my way down to your office to steal one of those Cubans," admitted Charlie.

"We'll have a nice cigar together, Charlie, and you can tell me why you're not on your way home to be with your beautiful wife for the Easter weekend."

Charlie always welcomed the opportunity to sit down with Lucien Mackey, and, *yes,* he certainly had things on his mind, things that were weighing him down, that had changed him and changed his relationship with his wife, and now it was all coming to a boil. *Where should he start? How about, Why does life without children in the house feel so pointless? Or, Why does my job get more and more boring and my career feel so unfulfilling as I get wealthier and more successful?* And what had become a constant theme in Charlie's introspections, *Why, as everyone I know gets wealthier and wealthier, do so many others continue down the road to poverty, losing hope of ever improving their condition in life?*

Charlie was genuinely troubled over the polarization of the classes in America and where it would lead. The rich were getting richer much quicker than at any other time in history, and the numbers of the poor were growing, with little relief in sight. Life had been good to Charlie, but what family was going hungry because his stock portfolio had nearly doubled in value in a ridiculous three years? He wasn't an economist, but he knew there was a connection. And he knew that he'd long been part of the *winning team,* the side that had the corporations and the politicians, the lawmakers and regulators, the lobbyists and the lawyers, bankers, and venture capitalists. He was on the team that made the rules, and he wasn't sure he belonged anymore.

No, he wouldn't burden Lucien with his personal whining, problems with no solutions. But he would tell his boss about Ellen. He needed to talk to someone, and Lucien certainly had some experience with marital discord. When he was fifty-one, after his two children had left home for college and career, Lucien had informed his wife of thirty years that he was gay and moved out of their palatial home in Bergen County and into the apartment in Manhattan where he still resided. For many years now, Lucien's partner was a slender, light-skinned Jamaican named Carlos Marché, the owner of an extremely successful women's salon in the elegant first-floor retail shops of the Dietrich Delahunt & Mackey building.

In Lucien's office suite, they relaxed on oversize leather chairs and filled the air with billowing clouds of cigar smoke. Lucien rambled for a while about the merits of traveling first-class on international flights, while Charlie searched for the right words to describe the phone call from Marchetti.

Ellen's been fucking some hedge-fund guy—no, that's not fair, that's not how it would have been with Ellen. Charlie took a long pull on his cigar as he reflected on his marriage. *Ellen has had a brief relationship with . . . who? An old friend she respected, who was there for her when she needed someone after her husband told her suddenly that the life they'd been working so hard for just wasn't working out for him. . . .*

Charlie thought about Ellen and how it had become harder and harder to share her interests and ambitions. The last few years, with the kids gone, had been so different from the first twenty years of their marriage. They'd been gradually growing apart, developing new interests and priorities and discarding old ones, and now they were on different paths, leading away from each other. They were still husband and wife, a couple at parties, caring parents of successful children, good neighbors. They talked, though not as often as they used to, and discussed things, though not as intimately or intensely as before. They still had sex but more physical than emotional. They never fought about anything. But, more and more, life seemed to be happening to them separately. Charlie envied Ellen. She was so certain of what she wanted, so at ease with her enjoyment of life.

Charlie knew that he had changed over the last few years. The more successful he'd become, the less certain he was about what he wanted in life. Since becoming a partner, his job had changed. Working as the OntAmex account supervisor was much more about money, influence, and connections than it was about building things. He hadn't become an engineer to sit in meetings with lawyers and accountants.

And he knew he missed his children—his young children, not the successful, confident young adults he now spoke with on the phone or saw on holidays and the occasional ski weekend at the house in Vermont. He missed everything about the early years of parenting—their first house, in Windsor, Connecticut, a little five-room ranch, with the huge backyard, and the flowering crab tree, and the little hill they would all roll down in the kids' overloaded wagon, crashing in the grass at the bottom. He missed the stories—the Roald Dahl years—the vacations, the wide-eyed wonderment of so many Christmases and birthdays, and the celebration of so many excellent report cards.

He still had vivid memories of the kids' sports and the many teams Scott and Jennifer had played on, the T-ball, softball, baseball, and soccer games that he and Ellen had dragged their folding chairs to, and the basketball games at the rec center in the winter—pretending, along with the other adults, that they didn't really care who won.

"Charlie, you still with us?" Lucien's voice got Charlie's attention. "What's up?"

Charlie looked over at his friend and blew out a cloud of smoke. *No, Ellen's private life was her own. She didn't deserve to have it discussed by two men smoking Cuban cigars, like they were debating whether the Yankees had enough starting pitching. And it wasn't Lucien's problem.* Charlie would use his time with Lucien for another purpose.

"Lucien, I've been thinking about going outside, about building something. Being an engineer again."

Lucien Mackey leaned back in his chair and smiled. "Happens to all of us, Charlie. But you're pretty damn important to the company right where you are. OntAmex is a huge account, and you're the one who makes it happen."

"OntAmex isn't going anywhere, Lucien. It doesn't need me anymore."

Lucien raised his eyebrows and shrugged. "It's *your* bonus, Charlie. We'll give it some thought. Maybe we can find a good project for you."

CHAPTER 3

NATTY USED THE DOWNHILL RUN TO SOUTH COUNTY ROAD AS her warm-up, jogging easily until she turned east toward Old Red Bone. Then she picked up the pace. Her first two miles were always her fastest, then slower for the steep climb up to Main Street and around the long tail of the mountain that would bring her back down to the top of Oakes Hollow. Today she planned to take a detour, which would add about a mile to her regular five-mile circuit.

Natty Oakes loved to run, and she loved to run fast and hard. When she got her wind and her rhythm just right, she felt as if she could run forever. After a while she'd enter a runner's trance, conscious of every muscle and joint, feeling the inside of her rib cage as her lungs expanded and contracted, the blood and oxygen coursing through her body. The trance would clear her mind and allow her to enter a fantasy world far away from West Virginia.

Today, Natty couldn't daydream. She didn't want to miss the turnoff on the north side of the road halfway to Red Bone. She was surprised to see a pickup coming toward her. It was unusual to find anyone out this early. The truck slowed down and made a right-hand turn onto the road Natty was looking for.

She followed it down the narrow road, which, like most of the local roads in McDowell County, was cracked and rutted from years of use by overloaded coal trucks. There was no sign of the pickup, but it could only be going to one place, which made Natty uneasy. This was the road to the new electric-generating plant being built by OntAmex Energy. It was the biggest construction project in McDowell County's history.

Two years earlier, Natty, Buck, the kids, and the rest of the Oakes clan, along with several hundred other residents of Red Bone and surrounding towns, came down this road one Saturday in late June for a public picnic and a rare visit by the governor. A joint announcement was to be made with officials of the OntAmex Energy Company regarding a project that would have a *monumental impact on the future of McDowell County.* It was a show that the people of Red Bone would long remember and a day that Natty Oakes would never forget.

The picnic took place at the site of the new plant, a two-hundred-acre plateau hidden from view by a ring of heavily wooded hills. The site had been a surface mine, leveled down to the bedrock in the early seventies. The celebration was scheduled to start at noon, and it was obvious that an army of people had been working since early morning to get the site ready. Two large trucks were parked off to the side of the field, behind a stack of cargo boxes from a Charleston catering company. A huge three-masted circus tent had been set up to shelter several long buffet tables filled with food of an endless variety.

Behind the tent was a battery of aluminum-framed charcoal stoves, manned by several dozen white-clad cooks. Half chickens and pork chops, along with hamburgers, hot dogs, and sausages, covered the smoking grills. At each end of the tent was a complete bar and a large cooler filled with ice and bottles of several types of Molson beer. It was a mystery why only Molson was on hand, but it was ice-cold and there was plenty of it, so no one complained. Uniformed bartenders mixed and poured, while some obviously imported waitresses circulated to take drink orders. It only took a little while for the Oakes brothers and the rest of the crowd to get comfortable with the idea that the drinks were actually free.

The show really got started when a man from a public relations firm in Charleston mounted a stage at one end of the field and started talking over a huge loudspeaker system. He welcomed everyone and made a little speech about what a great day it was for McDowell County and how some very important people would soon be dropping by. He was still talking when he was drowned out by a deafening roar coming straight toward them through the woods. The ungodly noise sent the adults out of the tent and the children jumping around in circles, wide-eyed with both fright and glee. The PR man yelled something over the microphone and pointed up in the air. Suddenly four helicopters appeared just over the treetops. One after the other they flew over the tent and banked into a sharp left turn before landing, one by one, in a roped-off area at one side of the clearing.

The crowd burst into applause. The helicopters were magnificent twelve-passenger jet-powered Bell 430s, finished entirely in high-gloss black with dark-tinted windows. Silver lightning bolts adorned both sides of the cabins, over the distinctive logo of ONTAMEX ENERGY.

Natty sat at a picnic table, eating lunch with her sisters-in-law Sally and Charlotte and Buck's mother, Rose. Cat had scrambled up onto her lap at the first sound of the helicopters, holding a ketchup-covered hot dog in one hand and a can of orange soda in the other. Pie was running around with Sally's boys, trying to get close to the helicopters.

Buck and his brothers and a half dozen of their buddies had found a comfortable spot inside the tent. They'd moved one of the picnic tables inside and kept one of the young waitresses on a continuous circle between them and the bar.

Natty nursed a Molson Light, engrossed by the show unfolding before her. She'd never seen the governor before, and was eager to see the people arriving on the helicopters, but she couldn't help taking a quick glance every few minutes over at Buck. He always enjoyed himself so much when he was drinking with his friends. It wasn't about being drunk; he could be plenty miserable when he was drunk. It was about rehashing the old times with old pals, recalling past adventures that men loved to talk about with a beer bottle in hand. Buck became animated, gesturing with his hands, laughing, always at the center of attention—just like he was as a child when Natty first saw him, when he was in sixth grade and she was in fourth, many years before he even knew she existed. She wished he'd bring some of that good nature home occasionally and share it with his children.

The helicopters unloaded their passengers. Natty picked out the governor right away, from his distinctive silver hair, and thought she recognized a few other county officials. One of the helicopters unloaded a television crew. On her mother's lap, Cat was wilting in the hot sun and had rubbed her ketchup-covered face against Natty's white tank top.

The passengers from the third helicopter were introduced as OntAmex executives. There were five men and a very attractive professionally dressed woman, who carried a leather notebook and was talking on a cellphone. One of the men from OntAmex was obviously in charge. He looked to be in his midforties, with black hair combed straight back. His charcoal suit was perfectly cut to his athletic build. The governor made his way through the throng to lead him to the stage, the woman with the notebook following closely behind.

The man at the microphone welcomed the passengers from the last helicopter, introducing them as representatives of an engineering company from New York and a law firm from Charleston. Natty watched as another group of expensively dressed men joined the others near the stage.

The governor went to the microphone next and prepared to make the big announcement. Sally returned from the bar with a half dozen bottles of ice-cold Molson, attracting a lot of attention in her skintight halter top and short shorts.

The governor described the new billion-dollar coal-fired power plant to be built on the site and all the new jobs it would create. He received polite applause from a crowd that had been let down before by smiling politicians and knew well the history of abuse the counties of southern West Virginia had suffered for so many years at the hands of companies that had come for the coal.

The governor ended by bringing Duncan McCord, president and CEO of OntAmex Energy, to the microphone. He thanked many of the same people the governor did, then explained how big the power plant was going to be and how important it was to his company.

The last speaker was Kevin Mulrooney, an executive of Ackerly Coal of Pittsburgh, the largest mining company in West Virginia. Mulrooney was well over three hundred pounds, with a red face and a head that sat directly on his shoulders without the assistance of a neck. He spoke with a strong Irish accent about the quality and purity of McDowell's low-sulfur coal. Finally, he got to the point and announced that Ackerly Coal had just signed a contract with OntAmex Energy to supply the coal for the new power plant. The amount of coal the new plant would require was a minimum of eight thousand tons a day, bringing hundreds of new mining jobs and millions of dollars to the local economy. Mulrooney received about as generous a welcome as a mining-company executive could expect in McDowell County, no matter how good his news.

As Cat ran off to find the other kids, Natty looked around for Pie and saw him on the stage, jumping up and down, waving to her with his big *happy face*. She stood and was waving back when she noticed Duncan McCord walking down the path between the tent and the picnic tables. He was with another man, who, like McCord, had a lean, athletic build. She saw he had a rugged handsome face, with a crooked nose that made him look like he might've been a boxer. Both men were holding Molsons and strolling in the direction of Natty's table. She sat down quickly, suddenly feeling a pang of self-consciousness.

She didn't want to stare, but she couldn't keep herself from watching the two men out of the corner of her eye. The woman with the notebook approached McCord, holding her cellphone out to him. With a quick shake of his head, he declined the call, and she retreated immediately.

At one of the tables, McCord and his friend stopped for a little chat with some old miners, laughing over somebody's quip, and walked away smoking fat brown cigars they'd begged like a couple of street people.

Sally had just turned her head and noticed the two men getting closer. She inspected McCord's friend unabashedly, then turned back to Natty with her eyeballs rolling. "Get a load of this one coming; he is *beautiful!*" She turned for another quick look as Natty pretended not to know whom she was talking about.

Natty looked back at the stage to see if she could engage Pie in another wave and so avoid any eye contact with the two men, who were almost beside the table. She wished she hadn't just pinned her hair up hastily. She must have looked like she had a pile of straw sitting on top of her head. Natty was moving her head back and forth with squinting eyes, looking for her son in the crowd, when she felt the men stop at the end of the table. Sally was saying something about having a good time in West Virginia, and then the CEO of OntAmex Energy was standing directly in front of Natty on the other side of the picnic table. The man who could make a decision to spend a billion dollars was saying something to her. She was forced to turn her eyes to him and saw a look of concern on his face.

"Are you all right, miss?" he asked.

Natty wondered how he could tell. She tried to smile. "Well, I'm a little buzzed, I guess. I don't usually drink in the—" He cut her off with a smile.

"No, no, I mean that," he said, gesturing toward her chest. Natty peered down at the front of her tank top and gasped at the bright red stain left by Catherine's face. The red blotches looked like dried blood.

"*Oh, fuck!*" she cried, without thinking, reaching for a napkin. "Oh, I'm sorry, I shouldn't have said that. It's only ketchup from my daughter's hot dog."

McCord smiled. "Well, I'm glad you're not bleeding to death."

"Yeah, me, too." Natty thought about pouring some beer on the stain, but it was obvious that there was nothing to be done. She'd already made an ass of herself, so she just smiled. "Thank you, but I'm okay."

"I'll get you something to wear," McCord offered, as he turned to find the woman with the notebook. At his gesture, she was instantly by his side. She listened intently to McCord, then left at a quick pace toward the helicopters. He turned back to Natty. "My assistant will get you something to put on."

"There's no need for that, really," Natty protested. "I look like this all the time."

"It's my pleasure. I'm Duncan McCord," he said, holding out his hand.

"Natty Oakes," she replied, wiping her palm on the thigh of her blue jeans before reaching out to take his hand. "Thank you," she added. "Thank you for coming to West Virginia and building your . . . thing in Red Bone."

"You're welcome, Mrs. Oakes." He let go of her hand but continued to study her face. Natty looked away, embarrassed. "You know, Natty, you have very beautiful eyes." Before she could say anything, he added, "It was a great pleasure to meet you." Then he turned and walked off to rejoin his friend.

Natty smiled weakly at Sally, who hadn't missed any of what had gone on. Normally she would have had a sarcastic comment for a situation like this, but this time she let it pass and looked away, having seen the drop of moisture in the corner of Natty's eye.

The woman with the notebook returned with a package wrapped in plastic. "I hope this will do," she said, handing it to Natty. She was very attractive, with a lot of makeup, perfectly applied.

Natty pulled open the plastic covering the soft package and unfolded a beautiful jacket, which was exactly like those the helicopter pilots were wearing. The black nylon shell had silver rings at the ends of the sleeves and at the waist and a soft tan lining. On the left breast, embossed in silver, was the OntAmex logo, with the words ONTAMEX ENERGY in a circle crossed by a lightning bolt.

"Holy shit," she whispered. "I was thinking maybe a T-shirt. Wait 'til Pie sees this." She was startled by the sound of the helicopters firing up their turbines, the big rotors beginning to spin. A few minutes later they were airborne, quickly becoming distant specks as they rose over the mountains toward Charleston. Natty watched until they disappeared in the deep-blue sky to the north, carrying all those rich, beautiful people.

She thought about Duncan McCord and his handsome friend, who seemed so much more genuine than the politicians. She wondered if it was true, what everyone said about big utilities and coal companies always screwing the common folk. McCord and his friend were probably headed straight home to be with their beautiful wives in their expensive homes and wouldn't even remember their afternoon in Red Bone, West Virginia.

A noise from the tent reminded her of Buck. One of the men had fallen off the edge of a picnic table and was having trouble getting up. The rest of the group laughed hysterically, in the typical drunken overreaction to any alcohol-induced mishap. The men were getting louder by the moment. Natty could pick out the harsh rasp of Buck's liquor-soaked voice. She hated it when he got this bad; he was unpredictable and uncontrollable. Better to leave him be and take the kids home, batten down the hatches, and wait for the coming storm. This was going to be a bad one. She'd seen the warning signs before.

NEAR THE END of the road, Natty could see the framework of steel girders rising beneath a huge crane. OntAmex had paved a road around their site, which was said to be an after-hours racetrack for the teenagers. Up ahead the new road branched off, running through the large sliding gate to the grounds. Inside the fence was a long building with a dozen windows. This was the main administration building, the object of Natty's search.

"Damn," she said under her breath. In front of the building, several dozen cars and pickups were parked in the unmarked lot, and at least forty men lingered outside the building. *The ad in the paper for construction workers said apply in person at nine a.m. Hell, by nine o'clock there'll be two hundred men lined up. Buck won't even get out of his truck when he sees that mob.*

Natty darted into the woods, down a narrow path that led to an old logging road and back to South County Road. Halfway to Old Red Bone, she saw another runner coming toward her at a good clip. Natty knew instantly who it was. She'd seen Emma Lowe run before. Natty slowed her pace and wondered how many other thirteen-year-old girls were out doing roadwork at six-thirty in the morning.

They walked toward each other, both catching their breath, then hugged in the middle of the road. "Damn, Emma, you've grown about three inches already this summer. Look at you, you're taller than I am now." Natty put an arm around the girl's waist. Emma was several inches taller.

Emma smiled self-consciously, her thin arms crossed in front of her chest. "I guess I growed some, but I needed to, Mama says." Emma Lowe was painfully shy and spoke in a barely audible whisper, even to Natty, who, outside her family, was the adult Emma was most comfortable with. She had thick, coarse black hair tied in a ponytail and heavy eyebrows that would someday join in the middle. Her eyes were small and dark, set closely together. A wide nose and full lips were the most visible gifts from her black grandmother, Ada Lowe.

"How're Mama and Papa and Ada doing?" Natty inquired. It had been at least a month since she'd seen Emma.

"They're all fine, 'cept Papa's shop ain't doing too good, he says, 'cause o' that new gas station out at the crossroads. But Mama's okay, and Mawmaw Ada's real good."

"And how about you? What're you doing out here so early? Getting in shape already? Season don't start 'til September, you know."

"Naw, I ain't worried about that. I just like to run a couple of times a week, sometimes more. Makes me feel good. It's like, you know, the only thing I'm good at." Emma spoke so softly that she always sounded sad.

Natty understood how she felt. "Well, we both know it's not the only thing you're good at, but I know what you mean, it does feel good." She gave Emma a long hug and told her the first soccer practice would be the last week in August and that she'd post a schedule on the bulletin board in Eve's Restaurant. She watched as Emma loped off down the road with long, graceful strides.

Natty saw so much of herself in Emma—the insecurity, shyness, and the need to withdraw into physical exertion. But Emma, Natty knew, was much different from her. Emma had a gift, an immense talent that would transport her out of McDowell County one day and make up for any shortcomings she might have in the way of looks or intelligence or personality. Unlike Natty, Emma would never be considered pretty or anything more than an average student. But, at thirteen, Emma Lowe was without argument the finest soccer player for her age that anyone in southern West Virginia had ever seen, boys included. Not just an excellent player, the best on the field at any one time, but an extraordinary player with near-magical ability in every facet of the game.

Natty let out a giggle when she thought about how good Emma would be this year. She was noticeably taller and looked stronger, and she knew that Emma continued to practice her soccer skills year-round.

As Natty came into Old Red Bone, she looked over at the soccer field off to her left. What grass there was on the field was at least a foot high, surrounding large bare patches of earth where not even weeds would grow. It was a mess, as always. The worst field in the league by far. Before the season started, Natty and Pie would come out and fill in some of the holes and ruts.

At one end of the field was a small L-shaped building with a gray-shingled roof. A plain white sign said RED BONE CHILDREN'S LIBRARY. Natty saw that the sagging roof had gotten worse. She made a mental note that, before any serious rain came, she'd have to move the rest of the books into the storeroom at the dry end of the building.

A voice above her interrupted her thoughts. "Morning, Mrs. Oakes. Little late this morning. Sleep in, did we?"

Natty looked high up, toward the back porch on the fourth floor of the old brown stone building that stood on the corner of Main Street. She found P. J. Hankinson where he was most mornings, leaning over the porch railing, wearing only his boxer shorts and a wide-brimmed straw hat, his teacup resting on the wooden railing. "Hey, Hank. Just getting slow in my old age, is all." Natty gave the old man a wave before she disappeared from view, going up past the building and turning right onto Main Street.

On the first floor of the building was Barney's General Store, which was actually a hardware, grocery, bakery, liquor store, and gift shop rolled into one. Natty looked through the big windows of the restaurant section and waved to Buck's sister, Eve, who was sweeping the floor. The widow of the late Barney Brewster, Eve smiled as Natty ran by.

A quarter of a mile down Main Street, Natty left the road and picked up the trail that ran along the long southern flank of Red Bone Mountain. The path ran through the dark woods and out into the sunlight, along rocky ledges where the view was spectacular.

At around the midpoint of the trail, Natty came to a stop and began a laborious climb through the rocks and trees, up a steep, narrow goat path that few people would even notice. She hadn't been to her spot in several weeks, and today she thought she deserved a few minutes on the rock.

The trail ended in a thicket of pine trees on a high outcropping that dropped off precipitously on three sides. Natty walked through the trees, as she had done so many times in her youth, to a mammoth rock formation that jutted off the side of the mountain like a huge nose. The top of the rock was smooth and gently curved, like an inverted saucer. She sat down and rested at the edge of the rock, her legs dangling over the edge. She leaned forward and looked down at the tops of the trees and the rocky cliff side several hundred feet below, instinctively pulling herself a little farther away from the edge.

Next to the farm on Redemption Mountain, this was her favorite spot in the world. The mountains stretched as far south as the eye could see. When the sky held wispy white clouds, it was difficult to tell where the mountains ended and the sky began.

Natty came to the rock with her friends in high school to smoke cigarettes, pot when they had some, to drink and talk about boys and sex and share their dreams about what they would do when they all left McDowell County. The other girls were gone—to colleges, jobs, husbands, new homes in Ohio, Pennsylvania, and North Carolina, and only Natty still came here, alone, to enjoy the view and the serenity, to daydream.

But not today. She didn't have time to get into a good daydream. She stood up on the rock and looked out toward the southwest. Beyond some of the smaller hills, she could just make out the peak of Redemption Mountain. Her mother was probably up, working at some farm chores, thinking about Natty, and wondering when her little girl was coming to visit. Natty stood on her tiptoes, cupped her hands around her mouth, and shattered the morning stillness. *"Hello, Mama. I love you, Mama. I'm coming to see you on Sunday."* She laughed and wondered if any mothers living on the other side of the Heavenly River might have been cheered by her message.

CHAPTER 4

CHARLIE WAS FEELING MORE UNEASY AS HE GOT CLOSER TO THE club. He wished Ellen hadn't asked him to pick her up after her tennis match. He wished her Volvo wasn't in the shop. He wished it wasn't a beautiful Saturday afternoon in July. The clubhouse and the patio bar would be crowded, and he was sure to run into old friends anxious to discuss his defection from the club. And to subtly take his temperature on the health of his marriage, no doubt.

Hickory Hills was a beautiful country club and a wonderful golf course, but Charlie felt enormous relief in his decision to leave the club. Beyond the time he now had for running and hockey, his liberation from the country-club lifestyle produced in Charlie an emotion close to euphoria. He was tired of the displays of wealth and status and the conversations endlessly devoted to the benchmarks of success—stocks and the market, big houses and summer homes, exotic vacations, good schools and fast-tracked children, and, of course, the politics that supported it all. Charlie couldn't pretend any longer that these things interested him.

For his wife, though, the country-club lifestyle was something she had set her sights on from the first days of their marriage, living in a squalid three-room apartment in Cambridge with its permanent odor of Asian cooking. This was the life she was raised in. It was all she knew of how adults were supposed to live and socialize, and Ellen had been aghast when Charlie told her he was quitting the club.

Eventually Ellen embraced the club's activities as a single member, with enthusiasm and energy. At home they simply didn't discuss the club, although she did enjoy chatting about the results of her tennis matches, and Charlie was always glad for the opportunity to share in some part of her day. They'd reached a truce over the issue, but the fissure in their marriage remained.

The outside restaurant area was crowded, as Charlie had feared. Every linen-covered table was occupied with lunching, drinking, and gabbing golfers and tennis players, eager to get on with the main sport of the club, which was watching and talking about each other. Charlie wore khaki shorts, his favorite faded University of Michigan T-shirt, and a pair of well-worn running shoes. He left his sunglasses on to hide at least part of the shiner that had darkened around his left eye. When he was a member, walking around the grounds in this outfit would have brought a reprimand and some penalty points from the membership committee. It felt good not to have to deal with the petty aspects of the club anymore.

He stood at the edge of the patio, hands in his pockets, trying unsuccessfully to look inconspicuous while scanning the tables for Ellen. Charlie Burden had the muscular build of a defensive back and the kind of rugged, permanently weathered face that women were universally attracted to. His nose, broken more times than he could remember, had a slender S-curve shape. At forty-eight, Charlie was actually ten pounds lighter and in better physical condition than when he played hockey at Michigan. It was difficult for him to be inconspicuous anywhere, and he could feel the eyes upon him.

As he was about to wade into the murmuring crowd, a familiar sight caught his eye, off to his right at a small table against the garden wall. He immediately recognized the wide grin, the trademark black beret, horn-rimmed glasses, and the long dark cigar. He hadn't seen Mal Berman in months, and he instantly regretted it. If there was one person at the club he truly missed spending time with, it was Mal. Charlie postponed his search for Ellen and went over to see his old friend.

"Well, hellooo, Charlie," Berman cooed, as he half-rose and extended his hand. "Come sit with me and have a beer, like the old days."

"I'd love to, Malcolm, since it'll have to be on your number now, not like the old days. So, how have you been? Break one-fifty today?"

"Ha! Oh, I miss you, Burden. Golf isn't as much fun without you, and, yes, I damn near broke a hundred today, wiseass!" Charlie took a chair next to Berman at the small round table, his back to the garden wall, looking out at the crowded patio. He would enjoy a few minutes with his old friend.

Berman was a senior partner in a small but extremely prestigious and profitable law firm specializing in international banking and finance. Dietrich Delahunt & Mackey was his oldest and most important client. There were few big-league bankers in London, Zurich, Paris, Hong Kong, or Tokyo whom Berman didn't know on a first-name basis, and no American lawyer was more respected or feared in contract negotiations.

Semiretired, Mal loved golf and loved playing it with his friend Charlie. He had been disappointed when Charlie told him he was leaving the club, but, unlike Ellen, Malcolm could empathize with his friend's decision. Malcolm wasn't a country club kind of guy, either, but he *did* love to play golf.

Berman folded up his *New York Times* and stuffed it into a canvas tote bag by his chair, coming back up with a long silver cigar case. "I know this is what you're really after, Burden. It's the only reason you ever played golf with me."

Charlie laughed and accepted the twenty-dollar cigar. He'd taken plenty of Malcolm's cigars over the years while playing golf. It had become a ritual of their friendship, and he would enjoy this one. He slid the long cigar out of its silver sleeve. "I'm here to pick up Ellen. Have you seen her? She's playing tennis."

"What else would the lovely Mrs. Burden be doing but playing tennis?" Berman beckoned over a young waitress, one of the attractive college girls the club was known to hire in the summer. "Bring us two Heinekens, and run down to the tennis courts and inquire as to the score of Mrs. Burden's tennis match. And very quietly, at an appropriate moment, you may inform Mrs. Burden that her husband is on the patio, enjoying the stimulating company of Mr. Berman and Mr. Castro, and she needn't hurry through the next set."

The girl flashed a quick, flirtatious smile at Charlie before hurrying off on her assignment, stopping in the kitchen only long enough to report to the other waitresses that the gorgeous and dangerous-looking stranger in the sunglasses was none other than the husband of the elegant Ellen Burden.

"So, you gave up golf to take up boxing, or is that eye shadow you're wearing?" Malcolm gestured to the darkening bruise visible from the side, behind Charlie's sunglasses.

"Rough game this morning." Charlie gave Berman a brief synopsis of the fight at the hockey game.

"The kid should sue the shit out of you," Berman said, taking out a ballpoint pen. "Maybe he needs a lawyer. Got a name?"

They shared a laugh just as the waitress arrived with the bottles of Heineken and frosted mugs. "I'm sorry, I didn't see Mrs. Burden anywhere down at the courts," the waitress explained, as she put the beer on the table. At that moment, Ellen Burden and her entourage of three other women, an older man with a towel around his neck, and the club's tennis pro emerged from the stairway that led up from the courts.

The buzz level on the patio rose as the group made their way toward one of the large tables near the center of the floor that, almost by design, opened up as they made their entrance. Greetings, waves, and radiant smiles were sent around the patio as the women and the tennis pro unloaded their equipment on and under the canopied table. This was a group with star power within the club's social spectrum, and the group's leader was clearly Ellen Burden.

Tall, tanned, and elegant, Ellen radiated confidence and charisma. Her jet-black shoulder-length hair shone as she quickly brushed it out of its competition ponytail. Her dark eyes and brilliant white smile sparkled like the jewelry on her hands as she moderated the discussion of the day's match with animated enthusiasm. Her companions coveted her attention, which she would bestow by leaning forward, raising her eyebrows and the intensity of her smile as she listened to her subject's contribution, followed by a hearty, guttural laugh or a clap of the hands to show her pleasure. *Compete hard, relax hard.* Few people could match Ellen Burden's intensity in the pursuit of life's enjoyments.

At fifty years old, Ellen D'Angelo Burden was easily one of the club's most attractive females. Large-boned at five foot ten, with the figure of a twenty-five-year-old, Ellen had been accustomed since adolescence to the subtle peeks and sideways glances that beautiful women detect like sonar. She also enlisted whatever outside assistance she needed in pursuit of her image. Several hours every few weeks at the Carlos Marché Salon preserved the deep sheen of her hair and eyebrows. A visit to a noted cosmetic surgeon in Boston several years earlier, followed by a recuperative stay at the Boca Raton Resort & Club, effectively erased the creases around her eyes.

Ellen worked hard at her appearance, but anyone who got close to her soon came to know that her dominating characteristic was relentless ambition. Ellen Burden craved success and status and recognition the way others needed alcohol, sex, or money.

Mal Berman motioned the waitress over and pointed his long cigar in the direction of Ellen's table. "Darling, run over and tell Mrs. Burden—"

Charlie interrupted him. "No, no, let her enjoy her time with her friends. And we'll have two more on Mr. Berman's tab." He clapped a hand on his friend's shoulder and smiled. "We don't get this chance too often. I'm in no hurry, and it looks like they're getting something to eat."

"You know, Charlie, Ellen's going to be the first female president of this club very soon," said Berman.

"And no one deserves it more, Mal." Charlie gazed over at his wife's table. Ellen was in her world, enjoying herself, having fun with her friends. And there was nothing wrong with that. She had always been a woman who needed substance and craved status, and she'd never pretended to be anything different. This was the life she was born to. It was he who'd changed, who'd altered the small print of their marriage without warning or explanation, and he was determined not to let his confusion about life distort Ellen's clarity.

"In fact," said Berman, "I pity the two fools who are running against her." He blew out a cloud of smoke and chuckled. "They don't know what they're up against."

Charlie smiled. "No, I'm sure they don't, Mal," he said, peering through the haze of cigar smoke at Ellen as she presided over the center table. He knew his wife well.

The fire of determination was lit within Ellen during her senior year at Wellesley, when word spread across the campus that Ellen D'Angelo's father, a Providence car dealer, had been indicted for racketeering and loan sharking, along with a group of other Rhode Island businessmen known to reside on the fringe of the Providence underworld.

Years of mob activities, including old contract hits, soon surfaced, leading Augie D'Angelo to plea-bargain his way to a twenty-year sentence in a federal prison. His daughter's humiliation at the hands of the high-society Wellesley elite that she had so recently been a part of was deep and permanent.

The family had enough money for Ellen to finish college, but the estate in East Greenwich was gone, along with the stocks, the house at Sea Pines, and the A-frame at Killington. After graduation, Ellen had virtually nothing but a degree, her clothes, and the Karmann Ghia convertible her father had given her when she left for school.

She also had Charlie Burden, the handsome Michigan hockey player she'd met the previous summer in Newport. Even though Charlie came from a lower-middle-class background, the son of a train conductor for the New York and New Haven Railroad, he had future success stamped all over him. He was a brilliant engineering student, an outstanding natural athlete, and the most sensual lover she'd ever had. Charlie Burden was going somewhere in life, and Ellen D'Angelo was determined to be there with him.

When Charlie was accepted into graduate school at MIT, everything began to fall into place. Ellen's suggestion that they get married and squeeze out enough from her teaching salary to pay for Charlie's tuition seemed like the most natural thing to do. She was a beautiful, sexy, and intelligent woman, and in spite of her family misfortunes, Charlie felt fortunate that she'd marry a penniless grad student like him. She was also employed, and there was no avoiding the fact that Charlie needed a source of income if he was going to attend MIT.

"So, Charlie, any chance of joining the club again?" Berman asked. "I'm sure Ellen could get you a better locker this time."

Charlie laughed and shook his head. He gazed across the patio at his wife, at her friends, and then around at the other tables, at all the wealthy, successful, contented members. All the white faces enjoying each other's company. He couldn't help but flash back to the sour memory of two summers earlier, to the day he'd invited his lifelong best friend, Cecil

Thomas, to play in a member–guest at Hickory Hills. The events of that day became a catalyst in his decision to leave the club and still festered in Charlie's mind.

Charlie couldn't remember a time before he and Cecil were best friends. Their mothers brought them home from the hospital only weeks apart to the old house on Western Boulevard in New Haven. The Thomases lived on the second floor, one of several black families in the handful of three-decker houses on a street that was gradually giving way to an expanding industrial zone.

That Cecil was black or in any way different from him was never a concern to Charlie. He knew Cecil long before he ever met any other white children. From elementary school through high school, the best friends were a curious pair: Charlie, strong, athletic, and only marginally interested in school; Cecil, overweight and uncoordinated but gifted academically. Cecil was often called on to help Charlie with his homework, and, more than a few times, Charlie had to put his fists to work to protect his buddy.

After turning Charlie down for several years, Cecil finally accepted the invitation to play. Charlie had no reason to suspect that Cecil wasn't ready to play in a real tournament, on a real golf course. He also had no reason to suspect that Hickory Hills wasn't ready for Cecil. But Cecil knew it—the moment he stepped into the dining room for the luncheon, looked around for Charlie, and saw a sea of white faces staring back at him, an overweight black man in basketball sneakers and an Izod sports shirt a size too small. Cecil had been there before.

It didn't help that they played with a member with a five handicap and his guest, who had a Westchester Country Club bag tag. They would have had little patience with a white man's whiffs, shanks, and wild slices, let alone this clearly out-of-place black man, who looked like he could very well be picking up their trash next week. After a few holes, the member and his guest played as a twosome, standing well off to the side of the green or heading on to the next tee while Charlie and Cecil finished the hole.

It took Charlie a while to fully grasp Cecil's discomfort at being the only black man on the course, the only black man on the grounds of the club not working in the kitchen. Then he began to notice the sideways glances and the cupped-hand-to-mouth comments, followed by the quick turn-away snickers of the other players, and it dawned on him what a horrible mistake he'd made in subjecting his friend to this kind of test.

If Cecil had been the white CFO of a Fortune 500 company, he could have shot 140 and everyone would have joked and had a good time with it. But the standard for a middle-class black man at Hickory Hills was much tougher and crueler, and it gnawed at Charlie's gut every time he played after that. He and Cecil had talked on the phone only a few times over the last two years, occasionally exchanging emails, as their friendship dissipated. His estrangement from Cecil saddened Charlie whenever he thought about his old friend.

"No, Mal, I don't think I'll be coming back to the club again." Charlie took a sip of his beer. "In fact, I may be going away for a while, couple of years if things work out." He told Berman of his plan to be transferred to China and of conversations he'd had with Lucien Mackey. Charlie knew that Malcolm was closely involved with the project and knew as much about it as anyone outside the San Francisco office and Lucien Mackey.

"That's a tough one, Charlie. It technically belongs to San Francisco, which has half its people in Beijing already. Plus, it's not the kind of post a partner is often considered for." Charlie knew that Malcolm was referring to the fact that most of the partners, although highly educated and experienced engineers, generally arrived on the partners' floor through their business and political acumen, not their engineering talents. The real ability to manage the complex projects of a company like Dietrich Delahunt & Mackey lay with a small cadre of experienced engineers who'd spent their entire careers in the field, building mammoth structures around the globe, working for a fraction of a partner's income. They were the kind of engineers that Charlie Burden had once set out to become, before he became a rainmaker and had to come inside.

"I could build that dam, Malcolm."

"Lucien will know what's best, Charlie. Trust his judgment."

The sun was suddenly blocked out and Charlie looked up to see Ellen standing at the edge of their table, equipment bag on her shoulder, smiling down at them.

"Hello, Malcolm," Ellen said, before turning to her husband. "Shall we go, Charlie? Wouldn't want you to get too comfortable here. You may want to become a member again and spoil all my fun."

CHAPTER 5

THE STEERING OF NATTY'S HONDA FELT A LITTLE WOBBLY AS SHE turned onto Heaven's Gate, which, after a short, winding climb through Angel Hollow, would lead to Redemption Mountain Road. Another mile through alternating dark woods and sunlit green meadows would bring them up to the DeWitt farm. The 1980 Accord, at one time red, had faded to a dull maroon. She hoped the problem was just a tire that needed air. Even with Gus Lowe's garage giving her a break, she couldn't afford any repairs right now.

Natty loved to come back to the farm to see her mother, Grandpa Bud, Alice, and Uncle Pete. She loved the smells and the colors and sounds of the farm and the coolness of the air on Redemption Mountain. Even the pungent aromas of the pigpens and the chicken house brought back nostalgic flashes, and the greens of the trees and the cornstalks and the fallow pastures always appeared deeper and richer and greener than anywhere else. On the farm, food tasted better, the water colder and purer, and the air smelled fresher. Natty enjoyed walking barefoot in the fields, feeling the hot soft earth between her toes. She'd sit on the warm flat rocks in the stream with her legs numbed up to the knee by the ice-cold water that ran down from farther up the mountain.

But the farm was also the source of Natty's greatest sadness, and she couldn't walk through the house or the barn or the fields or sit on the porch for very long without thinking of Annie. Twenty-three years later she could still hear her voice, and feel her small hands and her downy cheeks, and see her running across the dirt yard with her arms upraised, the sign for Natty to hold her.

The melancholy of old memories was supplanted by the unbridled joy the children experienced at the farm, and Natty enjoyed sharing their excitement as they explored the world of her childhood. After the obligatory hugs and a suitable interval of fawning by their grandmother and great-grandparents, Pie would always beg for his release to run off with Uncle Pete to drive the old tractor around the farm. Cat, after a hand-in-hand walking tour with Great-grandmother Alice to see the newest piglets, would invariably sneak off to the warm floor of the sunroom, surrounded by the tattered yellowing picture books from Sarah's library. She could sit for hours, cross-legged, reading the stories out loud to herself, just as her mother had done with the same books many years earlier.

Natty was always struck by how run down the farm seemed. The gray clapboards of the house needed painting, the roof was worn and patched in a dozen places, and the long boards of the porch sagged noticeably. Sarah still kept her flower beds around the house, but they weren't as full or as neatly edged as they once were. The farm, like its occupants, was looking tired.

As Natty pulled into the yard in front of the house, Grandpa DeWitt and Alice were getting out of their chairs on the porch to greet them. While the children were hugging their great-grandparents and Uncle Pete, Natty's mother drifted quietly through the screen door and stood unnoticed on the porch, arms folded in front of her, a serene smile on her face as she awaited her turn. This was her manner—never impatient, never demonstrative or in any way calling attention to herself.

Sarah DeWitt was several inches taller than her daughter and had only recently started to put some middle-aged pounds on her thin frame. She was fifty-three but looked older, the weathered skin of her face and arms showing the effects of more than twenty years of farm life. Her hair was prematurely white, the color of thick smoke. It hung down her back, reaching almost to her waist. Today it hung loose, and with her faded cotton dress and well-worn sandals, she gave the appearance, as she often did, of a Native American.

After the children had run off, Sarah DeWitt turned her attention to her daughter. She pulled Natty close for a long hug, then carefully examined her face, looking for a telltale sign. Natty knew what she was doing. It had become their routine since the night Buck had beaten her.

"So, he's been leaving you alone, then." Sarah had a soft, unhurried way of speaking, a mannerism inherited by her daughter.

"*Yes,* Mama." Natty was irritated. "You don't always have to do this. Buck ain't like that anymore; he's fine."

"Of course he is. And he's given up drinking, and he spends all of his free time now with his children."

"He's getting better, Mama. He's trying, anyway. He'll be fine when the new power plant opens. He's made good friends with the head man from the construction company—a big company from New York—and he's promised Buck a job. And those are good jobs, too."

"Yes, I'm sure Buck will be very much needed at the new power plant," Sarah said.

They'd reached the point they always reached very quickly, when Sarah made her usual inferences about Buck, and Natty had to resist throwing her mother's lifestyle back at her. But Natty knew it would just make things worse. She didn't want to argue with her mother, and, she had to admit, it wasn't fair. Her mother never hurt anyone with her addictions.

They strolled slowly toward the barn, her mother bringing her daughter up to date on the insignificant details that make up the news on a small farm. They sat down on an old bench by the barn, where they could watch the pigs cool themselves in the wet mud.

"You look thin, Natty. Are you still doing all that running?"

"Every day, unless the weather won't let me. It's the best thing I do for myself, Mama. And I feel fine, I feel great."

"And your nursing job, how are all your patients?"

"I ain't a nurse, Mama. I'm a home health aide."

"*Aren't* a nurse, Natty. You don't always have to sound like a hillbilly."

"I know, Mama. I *aren't* a nurse." Her mother ignored the wisecrack. "Anyway, I haven't lost any this week, but I got a few headed for the wrong side of the grass pretty quick. They keep giving me more."

"No, I don't think we'll be running out of old people in McDowell

County anytime soon," Sarah replied pensively. "And you'll be working at the school again this fall?"

"In the mornings, for a few hours. Still gives me time to make my rounds, and I'll be able to see Cat once in a while. Make sure she's doing okay."

"That'll be good for her. And Pie, he's ready to go back to school?"

"He's going into seventh grade, about where he's supposed to be." Natty reflected for a moment on her remarkable son. "He still has problems with arithmetic. Numbers confuse him some, but it sure as hell confused me, too. You know that. But damn if he ain't the most entertaining little boy. He makes me laugh like we got no troubles in the world."

"You've done a good job with that boy, Natty. A great job, all by yourself."

Natty ignored her mother's subtle jab. Sarah hadn't liked Buck as a child, liked him less as the husband of her daughter, and now despised him as the father of her grandchildren. It had been several years since Buck had been to the farm and years since Sarah had been to Oakes Hollow. "Not just me, Mama. Mostly Mabel Willard at the school. Thank God for that woman. She's been teaching Pie since kindergarten, putting in extra time all these years."

"And with all your work, you'll still be having your football team again?"

"Hell, Mama, that's about the only fun I have in life, that and my running. And it's soccer, not football." Natty had to admit that her enthusiasm for coaching was waning. She was tired of being undermanned and outgunned against the all-boy teams from Bluefield, Princeton, and Welch. Even with Emma Lowe, her team always lost more games than they won. She wasn't sure if they would even be competitive this season, having lost a couple of capable players, but she had to run the team one last year, for Emma's sake, anyway.

Sarah's attention had drifted away, as it often did after a few minutes of conversation. She would appear deep in thought as she gazed off at nothing. Natty was used to her departures. She sat by her mother's side, looking over the old farm, content to let Sarah have *her own time,* as Natty called it when she was young.

She shielded her eyes and looked up toward the cornfield, the green stalks only three feet high. By September they'd be seven feet tall, with fat, heavy ears. She scanned the field to see if she could detect where Pete had hidden this year's weed patch. The pot was for their own use, Sarah told her, Pete having learned his lesson some years earlier. But Natty knew that Pete grew a lot of marijuana, and she had a suspicion that, while he may not be selling it, he could probably be persuaded to barter a bag now and then.

It had been more than a dozen years since Natty last smoked, with Buck in the backseat of his father's Chevy Blazer, a week before she learned she was pregnant with Pie. But Natty didn't begrudge her mother or Uncle Pete the small pleasures they took from the drug. They led an isolated existence on a dirt farm in the mountains, and the need for some relief was understandable. Not long after Natty, Pie, and Cat said their goodbyes and drove off down Mountain Road, Sarah and Pete would sit in their rocking chairs on the porch, their pipes and a small bowl of weed on the plastic table between them, Sarah with a glass of wine and a book, and Pete watching her, and watching the sun set over the hazy gray mountains to the west as the heavy night air swept in over the farm.

Natty knew that it was too late in life for Sarah to *just say no*. Drugs and the search for spiritual and psychological independence had been a part of Sarah's life too long for her to become somebody else's notion of a middle-aged grandmother. Her life had been uprooted, and, like a lot of other young people, she'd lost her way and a lot of her spirit during the 1960s. It was more coincidence than anything else that she'd finally found what she'd long been seeking on a tired little farm on Redemption Mountain.

In the afternoon, while the children played in the stream with Pete and Sarah, Natty took a quick run up to the cemetery to see Annie and her father. It was only about a mile, and afterward she'd race downhill all the way to the stream and plunge in, running shoes and all.

The DeWitt farm was about halfway up Redemption Mountain Road. A little farther up, the road split. The right fork continued to climb up the south side of the mountain, eventually running out at a rocky prom-ontory. The left fork continued along the gently sloped north side for another half mile, until it came to the small cemetery.

Natty dropped to her knees between two gravestones and began to pull up the weeds that had escaped the attention of Grandma Alice, who regularly made the hike up to spend a few minutes with her two oldest boys and her granddaughter. *There's a lot of heartache in these mountains,* Alice was prone to lament, and nowhere was it more evident than at the cemetery on Redemption Mountain.

Her weeding done, Natty said a short prayer for her father and sister before the tears came, splattering on the cool, smooth marble. She wondered if her sadness over Annie's death would ever leave her. A good sweaty run in the heat would take care of today. She thought about Cat sitting in the stream and wanted to get down to her, to hold her and splash around in the cold water and make her laugh.

As Natty started back down, a white pickup sped up the road. Running into anyone on the mountain was rare. No one lived beyond the DeWitt farm, and there was something official-looking about the truck that made her curious.

She looked up the road, where the truck had disappeared. A short run up the hill would give her a vantage point from which she could see long stretches of the road as it weaved its way up the mountain. Adopting an innocent jogger's pace, Natty made her way up to investigate. As the south side of the mountain came into view, she was surprised to see two white pickup trucks, one parked at the side of the road, the other farther up the mountain. She was even more surprised to see several men who obviously were not on the mountain to enjoy the scenery. Two stood by the first white pickup, talking and occasionally pointing out some spot higher up the mountain. Another peered through an instrument mounted on a tripod. Next to him, an assistant stood with a black walkie-talkie and a clipboard. All of the men wore hard hats, blue jeans, and construction boots.

When they saw Natty approaching, one of the workers nodded at her. His partner stopped talking and turned to watch as she jogged toward them. Natty slowed to a walk, pretending to catch her breath.

"Hey, how you boys doin' today? Hot enough for ya?" Natty got no reply beyond a half smile from the man who held a walkie-talkie. "Don't see too many people up here, let alone on a Sunday, and working to boot." Still no response. As Natty came even with the men, she stopped and wiped her forehead with the bottom of her shirt, exposing her thin waist. Behind the men, Natty saw the white pickup truck, a late-model

Dodge with an extended cab. On the side of the door, a company logo was painted in dark green. It read, SOUTHERN STATES GEOLOGICAL SURVEYS, and, under it, HUNTINGTON, WEST VIRGINIA.

She didn't recognize the men, and it was a good bet they weren't from McDowell County. It was clear that they weren't going to volunteer any information. "So," Natty said, as she looked around. "What are you all doin' up here?"

The man in charge avoided her eyes. After an awkward few seconds, the other man came to his aid. "We're just doing a little surveying, ma'am. Couple of days of readings, and we'll be done."

"It's for the road project." The supervisor had a deep, authoritative voice. "There's some federal money available for rebuilding mountain roads, and this one may qualify." He took off his hard hat and headed for the door of the truck. It was obvious that the conversation was over.

Natty felt like she'd been dismissed, and her anger started to grow. "Well, sure, that makes sense. A new road." She talked louder as the men walked away from her. "Could sure use a new road up here, what with all the traffic runnin' up and down Redemption Mountain. Like a damn freeway up here." Both men climbed into the truck now, and she raised her voice further. "What we really need up here is a couple of stoplights and maybe a McDonald's." Her sarcasm was lost in the roar of the big truck as it left Natty standing in a cloud of hot dust. She watched it drive up the road. "*Road project*—what a bunch of bullshit," Natty said to herself as the truck pulled away. She turned and began her run down the mountain, curious to see if Bud and Pete knew what was going on.

NATTY HELPED ALICE set the table and put out dinner. The children came in wet from their dip in the stream, followed by Sarah and Pete, who'd changed out of their wet clothing. Bud was the last to be seated.

While she was cutting Cat's chicken, Natty brought up the strange events she'd witnessed that afternoon. "Came across a whole bunch of men working at a surveying job up on the south road. I ran over to see what they were up to, but they were tighter than a new jar of pickles. Gave me some phony story about building a road." Bud and Pete stopped eating and stared at her with grim looks. It was apparent that they knew something.

"So, what's going on?" Natty asked softly.

Sarah, too, was curious. "Petey, Bud, do you know something?" Bud was picking at his food, clearly reluctant to comment.

After a few moments, Pete spoke. "Th-they was up there a c-couple o' w-weeks ago. Seen one o' the trucks go by th-this morning." Pete had stuttered all his life, and it pained him when he had to speak to more than one person.

Suddenly, Bud's deep voice filled the small dining room. "They're comin' for the coal."

Sarah reacted immediately. "Coal? What coal, Bud? There's no coal up here." Sarah didn't want to hear about coal. Coal meant nothing but heartache to her.

Bud DeWitt waited for silence. For seventy-two years he'd lived on the mountain, fifty-three of those years with his wife, Alice. He'd buried his parents, two brothers, a sister, two sons, and a granddaughter on the mountain, and he planned to be buried there, too. When Bud DeWitt talked about Redemption Mountain, it was time for everyone else to just listen.

Bud put down his fork, readying himself to tell the family what they had a right to know. "There is coal up here. A lot of coal. Big seam, about twelve foot thick, through most of the mountain, about halfway up. The mineral rights to Redemption Mountain was owned for years by a little company from down in Tazewell County, Ferris Mining. They ran a couple dog holes a few miles south of here and a deep shaft, as I recall, somewheres over near Jolo. Never much of a company, always non-union, lot of safety problems and such. They went bankrupt about the mid-sixties, but it got tied up in the courts, and I reckon the coal business lost track of Redemption Mountain."

Bud paused to take a drink of his ice water. "Then, at the end of the seventies, early eighties, you know, the coal business was going bust, and they was closing the deep mines. Most of the coal taken was from the surface mines in Logan and Mingo Counties, not much from McDowell. I figured Redemption Mountain was safe. But . . ." He stopped and looked out the window with a grimace.

Something serious was going on that Natty couldn't quite figure out. "But *what*, Grandpa? Why is this a problem now?"

Bud looked across the table at her. "About two and a half years ago, I'm looking at the *Welch Daily* and I glance at the legal notices. I see the name Ferris Mining in there, so naturally it grabs my attention. I read all that small print and learn that all the assets of the Ferris Mining Company was purchased by Ackerly Coal."

The name sent a shiver of recognition through Natty as she recalled that day, two years ago, when the helicopters came. The day the Canadian man gave her the OntAmex jacket. The night that Buck beat her.

"Now, that bothered me some, Ackerly getting the mineral rights," Bud continued, pulling Natty back to the present. "Ackerly's a big company, does a lot of work in them big mountaintop mines in Logan and Mingo."

Natty could see a scowl on her mother's face as she tried to understand how a seam of coal on Redemption Mountain could possibly affect their farm.

"I didn't think any more about it 'til I read about that circus down in Red Bone, and the fact that it was clear as day, they'd *already* made the deal with Ackerly to supply the coal. That smelled fishy to me, 'cause there's a number of companies in the southern counties already mining the low-sulfur soft coal they need for their power plant. But, okay, Ackerly's a big company, and maybe this OntAmex, which is a lot bigger than anything we ever been involved with, maybe that's how they like to do business."

Sarah calmed down and started to eat her dinner. "Well, Bud, just because this Ackerly company's got a contract to supply coal for the new power plant doesn't mean they'll open a mine on Redemption Mountain."

"Sarah, there's a little more to it," Bud continued. "About a month after the picnic, they had some hearings about a number of permits the company would need from the county and the town of Red Bone. Them permits was what that whole picnic show was about, and it worked like a charm, with nary an objection to anything the company wanted to do. I guess it's understandable, when you're holding all the cards and offering all them jobs and tax dollars and whatnot. But I'm reading the story in the paper about the permits, and there's somebody from the governor's office, trying to grab all the credit for bringing the power plant here, who says, 'And we're also pleased to announce that OntAmex Energy has agreed that all of the coal burned in the new plant will have to come from McDowell County.'"

Bud started to talk faster. "Now, for a second, don't think about *where* the coal is going to come from, just think about *whose deal it is.* This ain't something that the county commissioners negotiated. Those fellas mean well, but this is *way* out of their league. You can bet this was a deal made in Charleston, right at the beginning of this whole thing. And you can bet there was some serious negotiating going on, 'cause Ackerly Coal, and especially the OntAmex Energy Company, ain't about to let the poorest county in about the poorest state in the union tell them where to get their coal from."

Sarah was getting impatient with Bud's explanation. "So, what are you saying, that—"

Bud cut her off softly. "I'm saying that the negotiating went something like, Okay, Mr. Governor, we'll guarantee that the coal comes from McDowell County *and* guarantee a couple of hundred, good-paying mining jobs to local residents, but you guys have to guarantee that Ackerly Coal will get a surface-mining permit for the piece of land known as Redemption Mountain, 'cause there's plenty of coal up there and we need to be able to get at it quick and cheap. That's why surveying crews are running all over this mountain."

Bud paused to take a drink of water before continuing. "Sometime before the end of the year, they're going to come up here and take down all the trees and start blasting the top off this mountain, pushing it into the valleys, filling in all the hollows and covering the streams, and, sure enough, cover this farm under about a hundred feet of rock and sand." Bud's voice was soft with helplessness now. "There's enough coal up here to run that plant for years, good low-sulfur coal, the kind they got to have for their power plant. And it'll mean a lot of good jobs, and politicians and the union and every out-of-work miner in McDowell County will support the project."

"But, Bud," Sarah protested, "there's a ban against new mountaintop-removal permits. I remember signing a petition last year for Save the Mountains, remember?"

Her father-in-law looked at her irritably. "Sarah, you ain't been listening! A deal's been made, I'm telling you. They'll find a way around that injunction, probably get another judge to suspend it temporarily, just long enough to get Ackerly a permit for Redemption Mountain. They'll make a deal with the environmental groups, 'cause nobody really cares about what happens down here. Ain't nobody living on Redemption Mountain 'cept some no-account hillbilly family running a dusty little pig farm."

Natty was skeptical. "Grandpa, I don't know that it's going to be that easy to get a surface-mine permit for Redemption Mountain."

Bud pushed his plate away without having eaten much. "Natty, you're too young to know it, but this is the way it's always been. It's the history of West Virginia. The big companies come here, they make a deal in Charleston, and they take the coal, the timber, and the gas, and they get rich. And the people get poorer and the land gets tore up, and the water gets fouled, and it's okay, 'cause there ain't hardly anybody left in the coal counties, and, besides, they're all just old and poor and uneducated and don't matter to no one!" When he finished, he was almost shouting. "Way it's always been," he said, getting up from the table, letting his napkin fall to the floor. He went out through the kitchen to get back to work.

Alice DeWitt watched her husband leave, a pained expression on her face. She rarely spoke, so she immediately had everyone's attention. "Some men come up here a month ago and wanted to buy the farm," she said. "Bud told me they offered him a hundred thousand dollars cash."

"Wow, that seems like a lot for this place," Natty said. "What did Bud say?"

"He told them the farm weren't for sale at any price, which the men couldn't seem to understand. But Bud said he weren't going to discuss it. So we give 'em some lemonade and corn bread out on the porch there and sent them on their way. They wasn't too happy about it, I suspect, from the way they moped off. They was lawyers from Charleston—good-looking men with nice suits."

With the children finally in the car, having said their goodbyes, Natty started to back the Honda onto Mountain Road. Normally she wouldn't have thought of looking out for other cars on the road, but something made her stop, and not an instant too soon. The white Dodge pickups, going much too fast on the narrow road, raced by. The side windows of the trucks were tinted black, but through the windshield of the second truck she glimpsed three men in white hard hats. As she watched the trucks roar down the mountain road, Natty suddenly realized that everything Bud said was true. The hard hats were going to destroy Redemption Mountain and everything on it.

DRIVING UP THE gravel road into Oakes Hollow, Natty could tell that something was going on. It wasn't unusual to see the residents of Oakes Hollow shooting the breeze and drinking beer, especially on a hot summer evening, but there were too many.

Natty didn't see Buck anywhere. *Had something happened to him?* He'd been gone for three days, working for a crew that ran an illegal timber operation up in Monroe County. Every so often, when he needed some cash, Buck would go off for a few days and cut trees for the timber pirates. It was dangerous work, but he'd get paid two hundred dollars for a twelve-hour day, all the beer he could drink afterward, and a tent to sleep in. Buck was strong and he knew what he was doing, but Natty worried about him getting hurt or arrested, and now she feared that something must have happened.

Her panic subsided when she saw Buck's truck parked just beyond Roy Hogan's. On the deck outside their trailer, Buck lay on his back, unmoving, one foot on the top step, his other leg hanging down almost to the gravel. One hand clutched a can of beer. He was wearing denim overalls and a long-sleeved white T-shirt, both filthy with dirt and tree sap.

The parking area around the trailers was crowded, so Natty pulled the Honda off to the right of the driveway and walked the few yards up to join the group. "Hey, Buck! How'd it go?" Buck didn't move. She helped herself to a beer out of the cooler and asked, "So, what's going on here, somebody die or something?"

Sally lifted Cat up for a hug and lowered her back to the ground. "As a matter of fact, Nat, somebody did die. That guy Hugo Paxton—you know, the power-plant boss?"

Natty knew Paxton well enough from the Roadhouse, but she wasn't friendly with him, and she didn't like the way the fat man always found a way to rub against her. "'Course I know who he is." She took a swig of beer, relieved that it wasn't somebody in the family or a local person. "What happened to him?"

Roy Hogan took up the story. "Last night, Hugo has a big T-bone at the Roadhouse, then goes into Fat Cats, all fired up and ready for action. He gets himself a lap dance from that big girl, Doreen. You know, the one with the huge melons?"

"I'll have to take your word for that, Roy," Natty responded.

"So, Paxton's shuckin' and jivin' and really getting into it, and he's got a fistful of twenties ready to fly, when, *boom,* he hits the floor like he fell out of a damn airplane. Dead as a mackerel. Heart attack, it looked like. Ransom jumped down there and pounded his chest and blew some air into him for a while, but he's so fat, nothing's going to work on him."

"You should have had Sally do the mouth-to-mouth part," Natty said, with a wink to her sister-in-law. "He sure was hot for Sal."

Buck sat up slowly and tossed his empty beer can toward a box next to the stairs. He hadn't shaved in several days, and his black goatee was a little longer than usual. At the front and top of his head, his hair shot up like short porcupine quills. At the sides, it was longer and slicked straight back. Black wraparound sunglasses covered his eyes. As always, whenever Buck did anything, he commanded attention.

"I'm glad you all think this is so damn funny," he said, "after all the time I spent with that fat asshole. Drinking with him. Introducing him to my buddies. Making him feel like maybe he wasn't a complete fucking dork, just so's he'll put in the good word for me at the power plant." Buck stood up and pulled his T-shirt off over his muscular chest and shoulders. Tossing it down on the deck, he slowly, achingly, shuffled toward the door of the trailer. "Now they'll send some new asshole down here, and he don't know me from Jack-shit-outta-luck, and I get fucked again." The metal screen door slammed behind him.

Sally broke the silence that followed. "How's your mama, Nat?"

Natty immediately thought about the Redemption Mountain problem but decided to leave it alone for now. This wouldn't be the most sympathetic audience to enlist in a crusade against a mountaintop-removal mining project. Maybe the whole thing would just go away. She didn't need any more friction in her relationship with Buck.

"Mama's fine, Sal," Natty answered. "We had a real nice visit. It was beautiful up on Redemption Mountain, really beautiful."

CHAPTER 6

The July heat shimmered across the yard in waves. It hadn't rained in weeks, and a dusty haze hung in the air. Not the best day to be working on the stumps, Charlie Burden concluded. He sat down to rest on the edge of the hole he'd excavated around the remains of a large maple. At one time the project was to be Ellen's tennis court, but as their involvement with the country club became more extensive, her desire for a tennis court at home waned. Now it was just a good physical workout that Charlie could return to with no set timetable.

He wiped the sweat from his face with his balled-up T-shirt and looked down the hill toward the house. It was a comfortable house, a wonderful home. From a practical standpoint, it was too big now for only Ellen and him but not nearly as large as the one Ellen had her eye on.

She came out the back door, a cordless phone in one hand, and in the other a tall glass of ice water. She made her way up the grassy slope. "It's Scottie. He's in his car somewhere." Ellen smiled at Charlie as she handed him the phone and the glass.

"Thanks. Anything important?" he asked, gesturing to the phone.

"Something about business—you know Scottie." Ellen sat on a nearby stump to eavesdrop while Charlie spoke to their son.

"Hi, Scott, how are you?"

"I'm driving up to Nahant to look at some investment property on the water. You may want to get into this; I'll let you know." Scott was speaking quickly, as always. Charlie could picture his son speeding up Route 128 in the Porsche Carrera, the top down, his laptop open on the passenger seat. "Dad, real quick. What's Duncan up to, do you know? Lots of buzz yesterday. OntAmex in another big tender. Word is it's CES."

Charlie disliked it when his son treated him like another one of his many sources. Scott had squeezed him before for information about OntAmex, which under Duncan McCord's stewardship had been a very active and aggressive force in the world of global acquisitions. Hundreds of millions of dollars could be made on the knowledge of OntAmex's intentions. And Scott, Charlie continually had to remind himself, was not just some hack stockbroker looking for a hot tip. He was a stock analyst for a huge mutual fund manager, a frontline player in international investments.

Charlie couldn't confirm that OntAmex was going after Continental Electric Systems, but it was probably true. He recalled Duncan talking about CES two years ago. And now it fit the profile for an OntAmex takeover like a glove. Charlie changed the subject.

"Yes, Scott, I'm fine. How are you? Your mother wants to know when you're getting married." Ellen flashed Charlie a quick smile.

"Sorry, Dad, but I've got a call holding I have to take. Listen, just tell me if it's CES, okay? Can you do that?"

Charlie could see that his son was beyond making small talk on this call. "No, Scott, I can't confirm that. I haven't talked to Duncan in over a month."

"Okay, Dad. That's all right." Scott was unable to hide the irritation in his voice. They'd been over this ground before. "Say bye to Mom for me. I'll let you know about this Nahant property. We may want to get you out of pharmaceuticals for a while and into this."

"Okay, let me know what you want to do. I'll see you." Charlie and his son clicked off at the same time.

If Scott wanted to sell some stocks and buy real estate, it was fine with Charlie. His son had complete control of Charlie's investment portfolio. In only a few years, Scott had transformed Charlie's investments from a conservative collection of venerable blue chips and bonds into a diversified portfolio with a value of nearly $4 million. In the last year alone, Scott had increased Charlie's holdings by 25 percent.

The increased value of his investments seemed obscene to Charlie. To be able to make that much money without benefit of any constructive labor or even a creative idea worried him. *Should it be that easy? Is there a payback coming down the road?* And, most troubling to him, *Is somebody else paying the tab so I can live on easy street?* The economics at work in the creation of his wealth puzzled Charlie. He couldn't help thinking about his old friend Cecil, who he knew was smarter than he was, had about as much education, but had always struggled financially. *Was it just that Cecil was black, and fat, and unlucky? Or was it only because Charlie had gotten a hockey scholarship to Michigan and happened to play on the same line as Duncan McCord? If not, couldn't he very easily be Cecil's neighbor in North Haven? Maybe that wouldn't be so bad.*

"Scott just called to say hi and that he loves his mother very much," Charlie joked, as he put the phone down. Ellen smiled but stayed seated. Something was on her mind.

"Charlie, we need to talk." Ellen sounded forceful but not confrontational.

Over the years, Charlie had come to hate hearing those words. It always meant that Ellen was serious about something and wanted Charlie to know it before the conversation started. "Actually, there are two things I want to talk about. First is the house. Martha's pressing me about Dowling Farms. Said there's some new interest, and she wants us to get it, of course."

"I'm sure she does," Charlie answered, trying to sound more matter-of-fact than sarcastic.

"And if we're going to move, we need to list our house very soon. It's already the middle of summer. Martha thinks it would sell quickly if we priced it properly."

Priced it properly. Thanks very much, Martha. A smile flickered across Charlie's face. *Typical real estate agent. A quick commission beats a big commission every time.*

"What's the second thing you wanted to talk about?" Charlie asked, wondering if there was a more personal issue on Ellen's agenda.

"It's nothing, a minor thing." Ellen paused before going on. "Jennifer needs a new car. I want to surprise her when she comes out on Labor Day weekend."

So these were Ellen's pressing issues—buying a house and buying a car. Charlie was both relieved and disappointed that his wife didn't have any weightier concerns on her mind. "Jen doesn't *need* a new car," Charlie said. "Her Camry is fine; it's only eight years old. Those things last forever." *Plus, in less than a year she'll be graduating from one of the finest MBA programs in the world and marrying a dentist. For two people in their twenties, their income will be in the stratosphere, so let them buy their own damn cars.* "But if you have your heart set on spoiling your children long after the job's been so well done, by all means go ahead. But don't get too exotic, okay? What did you have in mind?"

Ellen smiled at Charlie's pretense of giving in reluctantly on the car before taking up the more important issue of the house. "Oh, I think a Saab would be fine. She'd like that. Charlie, let's talk about the house. It's something that I really want *us* to—" She was interrupted by the shrill buzzing of the cordless phone on the ground next to Charlie.

"Saved by the bell." Charlie gave Ellen a mischievous smile.

Lucien Mackey's baritone voice was louder than most men's. "Listen, Charlie, OntAmex is coming to town tonight. Jack Torkelson called me this morning. They'll be in tomorrow and there are some important issues we need to address. They're making a play for Continental, and we've also got some problems in West Virginia. They seem to be related. Torkelson was a little vague, but he's bringing in the whole crew plus some lawyers from West Virginia. It's a different bunch now that your friend Duncan and Red Landon are above all this."

"So it's true. They're going after Continental. Scott called me a few minutes ago, looking for confirmation."

"Tough to keep one that big under wraps. Official word will be out in London in a few hours. Doesn't affect us much, but Torkelson's got some issues we need to prepare for."

"That's fine, Lucien; I'll be in early."

"And I think I may have some good news for you, Charlie, about that change you're looking to make. Getting into the field again. And OntAmex will approve, too. We can talk about it tomorrow."

Charlie was elated and excited, but at the same time he was puzzled by Lucien's remarks. *What would OntAmex have to do with China?* It wasn't an OntAmex project. Going to the Far East would mean that Charlie would be leaving the OntAmex account. Is that what they were approving? Charlie didn't get along well with Jack Torkelson, OntAmex's director of U.S. operations, or with his staff, and he was embarrassed that Torkelson had called Lucien directly to set up a meeting with Dietrich Delahunt & Mackey. But this wasn't the first time that Torkelson had gone around him, sending a message that he didn't approve of Duncan McCord's handpicked OntAmex account manager. Even so, Lucien and Torkelson knew that, of the three of them, only Charlie had the number to Duncan's personal cellphone and his private email address.

"Now, Charlie, I'm afraid I've also got some bad news, but it's part of our situation. You know Hugo Paxton, our lead engineer down in Red Bone."

"Sure, I know Hugo. Spent a lot of time with him going over the project. He's a little strange, but a good—"

Lucien interrupted. "Paxton died last night, Charlie. Massive heart attack. In a strip bar down there. They tried to revive him, but he never even made it to the hospital."

"*Oh, God*, Lucien, I can't believe that. He was a young man, just in his forties."

"He was a liability, Charlie. A good builder but a time bomb ready to explode, and we both know it. But it is a shame, such a damn waste. His deputy—that young fellow Summers—is coming up tonight. There's a problem with the project, potentially a pretty expensive one, but Summers will fill us in."

Charlie remembered Terry Summers. He'd interviewed him several years earlier when Summers first joined the firm. He was a capable young engineer from Southern California—prep school, undergraduate at UCLA, a master's from Caltech—but somewhat cocky and arrogant. "I know Summers. Very sharp."

"Still a little green. Let's see what he has to say tomorrow." Lucien signed off.

Charlie thought about Hugo Paxton. He was divorced and had spent much of his career in Asia. In fact, he only took the West Virginia project so he could get back to China. It dawned on Charlie that Paxton's untimely demise could be fortuitous. That's what Lucien's good news referred to.

Ellen jarred him out of his thoughts. "Charlie, the house—it's important to me. You know we can afford it." She was pressing hard.

Charlie knew he couldn't avoid this discussion any longer. "Ellen, the timing isn't right. Some changes are happening at the company."

"Involving you?" Ellen leaned forward, sensing that something serious was about to surface.

"Yes, it involves me. Because I've requested a change." Charlie frowned, knowing that the hard part was coming. "I need to get away for a while, away from New York. I need to be an engineer again. I want to *build* something, Ellen. That's important to me. I'm tired of the politics and the meetings and the financial bullshit. It's strangling me. I need to build something to be proud of. It's what being an engineer is all about." He looked directly at his wife. "I also need a change personally. We need a change. We need to figure out what our life-after-kids is going to be."

Ellen saw her opening. "I know that, Charlie. That's what the house is all about. A change. Something different for us, now that the children are almost on their own."

"That's not what I'm talking about. I'm not talking about raising our standard of living another notch to impress the Hickory Hills crowd—"

"Oh, Charlie, that's not fair," she interrupted. Ellen shook her head irritably. "So, what does all this mean? What do you want to do?"

"I've asked to be transferred to China, to work on the second dam project. And, Ellen, I want *us* to go. Both of us, together. Sell the house and spend a couple of years over there. Asia—a different world. It'll be good for us."

She looked at him blankly for a few seconds, trying to digest his words. "*China,*" Ellen said, looking away.

"Lucien just gave his approval," Charlie added.

"China," she repeated quietly. She looked out toward the house and spoke in a calm, level voice. "Charlie, have you lost your mind? Sell the house and move to China, like we're in the goddamn Peace Corps or something? You want me to move to China, so you can play in the mud with your bulldozers and—"

"I'll go without you, Ellen. I love you and I want you to come, but this is important to me. I'm suffocating in this job." After a pause, he decided it was time get it all out. "And you know things aren't right with us."

Ellen stared into Charlie's eyes for a moment, then looked away. After a long pause, she spoke softly. "I'm sorry you found out about that, Charlie. It was . . . an aberration, something I needed to . . . Well, I don't expect you to understand. But it didn't mean anything. It's in the past."

Ellen rose, brushed off her skirt, and took a few steps down the hill before turning back to face her husband. "Charlie, *you* go to China. Do what you have to do, build what you have to build. We'll be okay. I'll still be here when you get back. I'll fly over a few times a year. We can meet in Tokyo or Singapore. But, Charlie, I can't go to China. I'm just . . . I'm just too *busy* to go to China." She continued down the hill.

"Ellen, what color is it?"

"What?"

"The Saab. What color is it?"

She smiled up at her husband. "It's white, Charlie, a convertible with a black top and a tan leather interior."

"Jen will love it."

"Yes, she will," Ellen replied.

As CHARLIE TURNED south onto Park Avenue, what was for so long the Pan American Building loomed over the street several blocks ahead and made him think about going to China. He'd have to get shots and talk to the guys in the San Francisco office. If everything worked out, he'd be able to hand off his projects and be ready in as little as eight weeks. It was a much simpler undertaking without Ellen.

The sixth floor was already humming with activity when Charlie got off the elevator. Several strange faces were in reception, and a waiter from a catering company pushed a cart with three coffee urns and a large platter of bagels and muffins covered tightly with plastic wrap. The door to the main conference room was open. Charlie looked in and saw Jack Torkelson and his right-hand man, Larry Tuthill, the director of Ont-Amex's U.S. power-generation facilities, along with four or five other OntAmex managers.

In his office, Charlie put his briefcase on the glass coffee table, hung up his jacket, and quickly checked his email. He only had a few minutes before his meeting with Lucien. A soft rap on his open door made Charlie look up. Warren Brand, a partner and member of the executive committee, came in, a disarming smile on his face.

A consummate office politician, Brand was the youngest partner in the firm and undeniably the most ambitious. He liked to speak in low tones that made every conversation seem of vital importance. "Charlie, I think congratulations are in order. Getting back out into the field. That's courageous, my friend!"

So the word was out; Lucien must've already tested the waters with some members of the executive committee. Still, it came as a surprise that Brand was signaling approval of Charlie's transfer to China. "Thanks, Warren. The word is already out?"

"Not officially 'til after the exec meets, but a few people know. Charlie, listen, this may seem a bit opportunistic, but I wanted to be the first to talk to you about the *tickets*." Brand moved even closer and talked more softly, as he usually did when he closed in on his real objective.

"Tickets? What tickets?" Charlie was genuinely baffled.

"*The* tickets, Charlie." Brand almost whispered. "Your New York Giants tickets. I'll pay you for them, of course—whatever's fair—you know that. I'm not looking for a gift here. But you probably won't be using them this season."

Charlie had to stifle a laugh. *Typical Brand, like a vulture, after his Giants tickets.* He hadn't given any thought to the upcoming season. The season tickets were a gift from Ellen's father after a few years in federal prison, when he'd finally accepted the fact that he'd be an old man before he ever saw another Giants game.

"I'll have to let you know, Warren, but thanks for reminding me." Charlie ushered Brand toward the door, so he could get to his meeting with Lucien Mackey. He knew right away to whom he'd be giving his tickets, and it wouldn't be Warren Brand. Plus, he'd still be around for a few games if he didn't leave for China until late September. It would be fun to get out to the Meadowlands for a couple of games before then.

Charlie put on his jacket and started down the hall to Lucien's corner office. Meetings with the managing partner were always illuminating, and Charlie had a feeling that this one would be the start of a new chapter in his career.

CHAPTER 7

FINALLY, IT RAINED. A HOT SUMMER RAIN THAT FORCED NATTY TO roll up the windows almost all the way. With no air-conditioning, it was hot and muggy in the small car. And Natty was tired. She'd already seen five clients and covered a lot of miles. She was glad the day was over and she wouldn't be doing any more sponge baths or wrapping any more varicose legs. A cold shower and a beer on the porch would be heaven. But she needed to make one more stop.

Natty had been thinking about Birdie Merkely since the previous week, when Birdie called and told Natty not to come by, that some of the church ladies were taking her out for lunch. Something about the call didn't sit right with Natty. Birdie sounded maybe a little too chipper about it all.

For the past year and a half, Natty had taken care of Birdie as she recovered from a broken hip, but Birdie hadn't been doing well. Her arthritis was worse, and her hip had not fully healed. She was in a constant state of discomfort. She'd also become more withdrawn—a distinct change from the cheerful personality that had led to her lifelong nickname.

At the turnoff to the dirt road that led several miles up to Birdie's cabin, Natty pulled into the small gas station and market. She parked next to the single pump, the needle of her gauge resting menacingly on empty. As the rain eased, Natty reached into the backseat for her knitted handbag. Only sixteen dollars left to buy gas and groceries for Birdie. *Damn, where did the money go?* She'd buy Birdie's food first and save a little for gas, just to get her up to the cabin, where Birdie would reimburse her.

Inside the store, Natty took a basket and walked through the cramped aisles, picking out the items that she knew Birdie needed: Ritz crackers, grape jelly, a half dozen eggs, milk, cranberry juice, ginger ale, Spam, Bumble Bee tuna (which Natty would have to open for her and leave in the refrigerator), sliced turkey, and a loaf of dark bread. She'd leave out the soup, Oreo cookies, ice cream, and sliced ham. The lettuce was too expensive, anyway. The total came to $15.11. Natty gave the clerk sixteen dollars and told him to put the change toward her gasoline. "The whole eighty-nine cents?" he asked.

On her way out, Natty noticed a small gray-haired woman whom she recognized as a friend of Birdie's and a member of her church. "Hello there, Mrs. Petrie."

The woman looked up, straining her memory to identify the thin girl with the friendly voice who knew her name.

Natty came to her aid. "I'm going up to see Birdie. I look in on Birdie."

Mrs. Petrie smiled with recognition. "Oh, yes, that's right, you're Birdie's nurse. We met once up at her house."

"That's right. Listen, Mrs. Petrie, have you seen Birdie recently? Did you take her out to lunch last week?"

"Oh no, no dear, not for lunch. But I did see Birdie Friday. She called in the morning and wanted to get her hair done"—Mrs. Petrie shook her head—"which was a queer thing for sure, as I can't ever remember Birdie having anything done to her hair before."

"So, you didn't have lunch with her?"

"Lordy, no, just picked her up and took her down to that little beauty parlor in Gary, did my errands, and brought her back up the hill later on. Didn't even invite me in for tea or nothin'."

With that, Mrs. Petrie turned to go. Natty watched her for a second and then started out of the store. The sound of the old woman's voice stopped her. "Honey, you be careful of that dip in the road 'bout half-ways up, where the water runs through the gully. With quick storms like this, the water can come running down real sudden like through there."

"Thank you. I'll watch for it," Natty answered. Mrs. Petrie probably worried about flash floods more than Natty did, simply because she was older and had more experience with the havoc that could result when millions of gallons of water, gathered quickly in a storm by the wide arms of the mountains, were sent ripping down narrow streambeds into the valleys.

It was still raining while Natty pumped gas into her empty tank. Her blue baseball cap with the red Spider-Man logo kept the rain out of her face, but after a few seconds she was pretty well soaked. The pump clinked off almost as soon as she'd started: $0.89, right to the penny. Not much more than a couple ounces. Enough, she figured, to get her up the mountain and back down.

Ledger Hollow was one of the many isolated pockets of poverty hidden away in McDowell County. Most of the inhabitants of the ramshackle huts and cabins lived well below the poverty line. A few years earlier, Natty had two other clients in the hollow, so she was familiar with the area.

A woman stood in the doorway of one of the cabins, leaning against the frame, an infant at her breast. She was about Natty's age and eyed her dispassionately. Natty had seen the blank look of despair before, the glassy stare that said she was too tired, too spent, too beaten down by life to care anymore. Natty smiled and raised her hand in a small wave to the woman, who nodded almost imperceptibly, moving only her eyes as the stranger in the faded red car drove off.

The home that Birdie Merkely had lived in for the past thirty-seven years sat in a small clearing about fifty yards up a deeply rutted dirt driveway. Natty got out of the car with the bag of groceries and knew something wasn't right. The front door was shut, a rarity in the summer. The mountain behind the rear of the house blocked out the late-afternoon sun, but no lights were on. There was no sign of life anywhere.

Out of habit, Natty had taken her small suitcase-like equipment bag from the car. She pulled the strap over her shoulder and readied herself for what she hoped she wouldn't find inside. Natty closed her eyes and whispered to herself, *"Oh, Birdie, please don't do this."* She went up on the porch and opened the front door.

The small house was cool and dark. The front parlor and dining room were neat and spotless, as always. The kitchen was cleaner than Natty had ever seen it. Usually, she had to spend the first few minutes at Birdie's washing up several days' worth of dishes and silverware. Today the sink was empty, and the countertop and even the floor shined from a recent scrubbing.

There was a slightly acrid smell in the house, noticeable even as a steady breeze wafted through the screened windows. Natty could make out the sound of soft music. She could see down the hallway to Birdie's bedroom, but the door was closed, which was also odd. That was where she knew she would find Birdie. Natty noticed the old rotary phone on the hall table, and wondered if she should just call the sheriff's office first. . . . *No, look pretty stupid if Birdie is just off visiting for a few days.*

But she wasn't off visiting. Birdie Merkely was lying faceup in the middle of the bed, her quilt pulled up to her waist. There was an unmistakable odor of death in the room, but not yet overpowering. Moving closer, Natty touched the old woman's forehead, then her cheek. She felt briefly for Birdie's pulse, knowing it wouldn't be there.

Birdie was dressed in her favorite blue silk dress. Her gray hair had recently been set in tight curls, and her face carefully made up with red lipstick, a faint smear of rouge on her soft, wrinkled cheeks, and even mascara. She wore a simple strand of yellowing pearls and scalloped gold earrings. The makeup and jewelry made her look much younger than seventy-six and revealed a woman Natty had never known, a woman who had once enjoyed life, before loneliness and constant pain defined her existence.

Under Birdie's clasped hands, in the fingers gnarled by years of crippling arthritis, Natty could see the serrated edges and yellowing back of an old photograph. She gently pulled it out to see a young couple seated on a park bench. Behind the bench was an iron railing, and in the distance was a stretch of sandy beach and then the blue-green ocean. A young Birdie Merkely leaned seductively against the young man seated next to her, her bright eyes focused on his face. He was a skinny boy wearing a military uniform, his billed cap pushed back jauntily, a khaki tie loose at his neck.

They both had a look of spontaneous laughter, as if they were responding to a funny comment by someone, maybe the photographer. In the bottom border of the picture, *Pensacola, Fla. 1946* was written in faded blue ink. Natty recognized the young man as Everett Merkely from pictures on the living room wall.

On the table next to the bed, Natty saw a familiar-looking plastic prescription bottle. She knew without reading the label that it was Birdie's Darvocet, a sixty-day supply, more than usually prescribed, because of her remote location. Next to the bottle was an empty wineglass with a trace of dried residue at the bottom. Natty walked over to the old Victrola, which was playing the Mozart Clarinet Concerto that Birdie loved. Natty turned it off.

In the hall she called the sheriff's department and told the dispatcher what she'd found. "Do you know which officer will be coming up?" Natty asked.

After a short pause the dispatcher replied. "That would be Officer Lester, Wayne Lester, ma'am."

"Great. Thanks." Natty couldn't hide her disappointment. The one deputy sheriff she didn't want to deal with. She'd known Lester since high school, where he was an obnoxious, overweight pervert who liked to cruise the halls, feeling girls' backs and announcing a "bra check." For a short time he'd focused his attentions on Natty, assuming that, due to her undeveloped appearance and lack of boyfriends, she'd be more receptive than the other girls. He didn't take rejection by the *flat-chested little hillbilly* too well.

Lester's disdain for Natty intensified after her marriage to Buck. His long-standing hatred for Buck was rooted in the unmerciful beating that Buck had administered to the bigger boy one summer afternoon when they were in their early teens. It was one of many fights that Buck soon forgot about. But Lester carried the painful memory of being embarrassed in front of a large gang of cheering kids, as Buck's superior boxing skills, strength, and innate instinct for cruelty turned Lester into a bloody, staggering hulk.

For years the memory and the desire for revenge smoldered, until one night Lester and another deputy got the call to respond to a domestic disturbance in Oakes Hollow. It was the day of the big announcement about the new power plant in Red Bone. The day the helicopters came. It wasn't clear from the call who was beating whom, but Wayne Lester knew who it would be as he opened the trunk of his patrol car to get his heavy lead-filled riot stick.

Drunk and out of control, Buck could be counted on to resist arrest, especially with a little provocation from Lester. The darkness provided sufficient cover for Lester to administer some solid shots to Buck's rib cage and a few to his calves and kneecaps, but it wasn't until they got

Buck to the jail's underground garage that Lester went to work with a vengeance. Buck ended up with several broken ribs, a collapsed lung, a broken nose and jaw, and a fractured tibia. He was in the hospital two weeks longer than Natty was.

When Natty turned on the lamp in the darkening parlor, her attention was drawn to several framed photographs that decorated the sparsely furnished room. There was a pastel-tinted wedding picture of Birdie and Everett, looking young and scared. The largest picture on the wall was a grainy black-and-white photograph of a group of coal miners. Behind the men, a sign identified the mine as U.S. STEEL NUMBER 9. In the foreground of the picture, *November 1954, Everett, 2nd row, #4* was written in white marker.

Natty knew all about Everett Merkely, even though he had died in 1985, five years after retiring from thirty-three years in the mines. Everett was Birdie's singular interest in life while he was alive and her number-one topic of conversation afterward. Her husband had come out of the mines with emphysema and black lung. His last years with Birdie were not pleasant, as he slowly suffocated in his own fluids.

Natty thought about the photo that Birdie had chosen to hold as she died and tried to recall the few pictures she had of Buck and her together. None revealed anything like the love and pure joy experienced by the couple in Pensacola. She went back into Birdie's bedroom and sat in a tall straight-backed wooden chair, awaiting Wayne Lester. Natty put her head back, folded her arms in front of her chest, and gave in to the exhaustion of a long day.

A booming voice startled her out of half sleep. "Well, if it ain't Natty *De*-nit-*Witt*, sleeping on the job!"

She looked up to see the hulking figure of Deputy Sheriff Wayne Lester filling the doorway of the bedroom. Six-four and closing in on three hundred pounds, Lester was an intimidating figure. Hooked onto his shirt pocket was a pair of aviator sunglasses. A pencil-thin black mustache adorned his pockmarked face. He wiggled a toothpick between his crooked teeth as he alternately eyed Natty and the figure on the bed.

Natty resisted the urge to come back with a *Lester the Molester* crack and decided to be civil so she could get out of the house and back home. "Hey, Wayne, how you been?"

"I'm fine, Nat, just fine." He was clearly encouraged by Natty's tone. "I see you running down the road real early sometimes, when I'm going through Red Bone headed up to Eve's for breakfast. You lookin' good these days, Nat, *real* good. Lookin' like a real woman now."

Maybe it was always a mistake to be civil to a slug like Lester. Natty smiled. "Thanks for noticing, Wayne."

Lester turned and walked toward the bed. "So what have we got here, then? *Bye Bye Birdie,* like the movie, right?" He chuckled as he leaned over for a closer look. "What do you think happened here, Nat?"

What happened here? God, what do you think happened here, Lester? Natty just wanted to go home. She didn't want to talk about Birdie, but she knew she'd be able to leave quicker if she helped him do his job.

"What *happened* here, Lester," Natty snapped a little too brusquely before catching herself, "is that Birdie got tired of always feeling the pain from her arthritis, tired of limping and hurting on her bad hip and using a walker." Natty's voice became softer as she looked at her friend on the bed. "And she got tired of being alone, having nobody to do things for, nobody to share things with, no one to love. And no one to love her." Natty paused for a moment. "So she went out and got her hair done, came home and gave her house a good cleaning, made herself up pretty as she could, put on her best dress, turned on her favorite music, lay down on the bed with her nice soft quilt, and had a glass of wine and a bottle of Darvocet pills."

Lester bent over to look at the label on the pill bottle. "She don't smell too bad, though. Not like that big nigger we found last summer, dead in his shed a couple weeks. Stunk so bad they had to burn that shed—"

"Lester, don't use that kind of talk around me. I mean it. Now, can I go? I need to get home."

"Well, not so fast there, Nat. Why don't you sit on the sofa for a bit, while I do my investigation? Then I'll come out and you can give me your statement." Lester put his fleshy palm to Natty's back and gently pushed her toward the doorway, taking his hand away with a subtle sideways rub.

After a few minutes, Lester came out of the bedroom and wandered into the kitchen. Natty saw him take off his equipment belt and lay it over the back of a chair. "Looks like the old bird left some groceries here on the table before she kicked off," Lester called out to Natty.

"I bought that stuff, Lester, for Birdie, and she owes me fifteen dollars. You think if we found her purse, I could see if she had some money and—"

Coming back into the parlor, Lester cut her off. "No can do, Nat. Uh-uh," he said, shaking his head. "Cannot remove *any* property, especially monetary funds, from the scene."

"Aw, cut the shit, Lester, I need the money for gas. I spent my last dollar on them groceries, and I ain't got even a quarter on me."

"That's okay, Nat, maybe I'll give you some money for gas later on." Lester took off his beaked cap and dropped it on one of the rocking chairs. He put a spiral notepad and his pocket tape recorder on the table as he sat down on the couch right next to Natty.

She started to stand up, but Lester shot his right arm around her and pulled her back down. "Now, hold on there, Nat. Don't be getting jumpy. I'm just going to take your statement." He edged a little closer and turned so that his left leg now blocked her escape.

Natty realized the predicament she was in, alone in an isolated cabin with a man like Wayne Lester. "Lester, you can get my statement at the kitchen table. Why're you doing this?" she pleaded, once again trying to get off the couch.

The policeman tightened his grip with his right arm and slid his left hand up Natty's thigh. Her white poplin pants were still damp from the rain. "You ought to take off these wet clothes, Nat, and let 'em dry. We got more than an hour before the M.E. gets up here." He pulled Natty closer. Her left hand tried to push his hand away, with no effect.

Lester leaned in toward Natty's face and did his best to affect a soft, intimate tone. "And I know you could use a little lovin', Nat, stuck with that shit-heel wife-beating husband of yours."

"Lester, stop this right now!" Natty yelled.

He nuzzled her neck as Natty turned away. "How is old *Bucko* these days? I hear he's back to visitin' that big gal up in Northfork again. Just can't stay away from her, I guess. You hear that, Nat?"

Natty stopped struggling. Lester had given her the means to escape. "Lester, you take this *any* further than it's already gone, then I'm going to have to go home and tell my husband everything that's happened here. And what do you think Buck Oakes will do after I tell him Wayne Lester tried to rape his wife?" She could feel a slight relaxing of his grip on her shoulder.

"Aw, fuck you, Natty." Lester got off the couch. "I ain't afraid of Buck." But Lester didn't sound convincing as he gathered up his notebook and tape recorder. "Plus, he's still on probation. Get in big trouble, assaultin' a law enforcement officer," he added. "But I guess I made a mistake here. Just takin' a shot, Nat, you know, hoping that . . . Well, you can take off now."

"Okay, Lester, that's good. You made a little misjudgment is all," Natty offered, as she straightened out her clothes.

The deputy looked relieved. "Thanks, Nat. Got a little carried away for a minute. You're lookin' real good these days, Nat, so I was just hoping, you know."

Natty smiled, trying to ease the large man's embarrassment. "Thanks, Lester. But I *am* a married woman." She was relieved the episode was over. Buck didn't need any trouble with Wayne Lester. And she didn't need any trouble with him, either, as he served on the county's youth sports coaches board, which supervised the soccer coaches.

Natty walked past Lester into the bedroom and said goodbye to her friend Birdie. She squeezed Birdie's hand, then picked up the Pensacola picture and stuffed it into her pocket. She wanted a remembrance of Birdie, and her friend's last image of life on earth seemed as fitting as anything else.

In the hallway, she stopped to pick up her equipment bag. "Now I got to go, Lester. Take care of Birdie for me." She left the grocery bag where it was on the counter and went out the front door. He followed her onto the porch.

"So, we're okay, Nat, right? You ain't going to say nothin' about . . . You ain't saying nothing to Buck?"

Natty turned her head to reply as she walked to her car. "We're okay, Lester. Take care of Birdie. I'll see you." She put her case in the backseat. But there was something else hanging over her now, something she couldn't leave without knowing. She stood with her hands on the top of the open door and looked back at Lester. "Wayne, what you said in there, about that woman in Northfork. You just bringing up old news, or you knowin' something?"

The deputy gazed off into the distance, a new toothpick bobbing between his teeth. "Well, Nat, I can't personally vouch for anything, but, you know, cops hear lots of stuff; some true, some ain't." He looked back at Natty. "So, maybe there's nothin' to it at all."

Natty gave Lester a brief nod of understanding. She turned the Honda around in the tall weeds in front of the house and drove past the white police cruiser, feeling as alone as she had in a long time.

She ran out of gas a mile from Oakes Hollow. Natty sighed, then had to laugh at what was such a fitting end to the day. She pulled off her white nursing shoes and knee-high nylons, tossed them into the backseat, stuffed her purse under the front seat, and sprinted home barefoot, finally allowing the tears to flow freely for her friend Birdie Merkely.

JUST AFTER MIDNIGHT, a dark-blue Crown Victoria with a spotlight mounted on the driver's side door made the sharp turn onto Redemption Mountain Road. A half mile from the DeWitt farm, the big car pulled off the road into the well-hidden driveway of a cabin that had long ago been destroyed by fire. The driver turned off the ignition and looked at his watch.

"We wait," he said quietly to his passenger.

"Tell me again why we gotta do this tonight, with a full moon?" the passenger asked.

"Gotta be able to see what we're looking for. And I want to do this quick. We find what we're looking for, then get out with nobody knowin' we were here."

At one-thirty, the men left the car and walked up Redemption Mountain Road toward the DeWitt farm. They were dressed entirely in black and had smeared their faces and hands with black camouflage cream. The driver wore a black lightweight nylon jacket, zipped to cover his shoulder holster and .45 automatic. Both men carried small bamboo rakes.

They split up as they entered the cornfield. The passenger went quickly to the end of the field and searched in a back-and-forth pattern as he made his way back toward the driver, who did the same from the other end of the field. They would meet somewhere around the middle. Each moved methodically between the towering cornstalks, dragging the small rakes behind them to obliterate their tracks. If they found nothing, evidence of their tracks wouldn't matter. If their search was successful, it would be imperative that they left no trace.

Near the center of the field, the driver heard a soft *pssst* a few yards away. He reached inside his jacket for the .45 and pushed through the corn. His partner was squatting amid a distinctly different-looking section of the field, which was covered with dozens of shorter, weedier-looking plants. He looked up with a wide grin shining through his black-smeared face, as he broke off a branch of a marijuana plant to take with them. "Bingo," he whispered.

CHAPTER 8

T HE DOOR TO LUCIEN MACKEY'S CORNER OFFICE WAS OPEN, BUT Charlie Burden knocked as he walked in. The senior partner was hunched over a large conference table that dominated one end of the massive office. "We fucked this up pretty good, Charlie," he said, peering at a set of blueprints. He frowned. This was going to be a bad day for someone at Dietrich Delahunt & Mackey.

Moving closer to the table, Charlie recognized the layout of the OntAmex plant in West Virginia. "What's the problem down there?"

"The goddamn pond is in the wrong spot. Can you believe that? After all this time? We've been building this thing for over two years, with Paxton and a battalion of contractors, surveyors, and engineers crawling all over it, and nobody notices that the cooling pond is situated on a hundred feet of solid bedrock that a fucking nuclear bomb couldn't blast through!" Lucien took a deep breath to control his anger. He tossed down his pencil and offered Charlie his hand. "Good morning, Charlie. Thanks for coming in early."

Mackey gestured toward the black leather couch. "Sit down. We need to talk, and we don't have a lot of time." Charlie sank uncomfortably into the center of the couch, as Mackey took one of the chairs. "Terry Summers will be along in a few minutes, and we need to come to an agreement before he gets here."

Charlie had known his boss long enough to know when he was having trouble getting to the point. "Lucien, what do you want me to do? We always agree on what you want."

Lucien smiled. "Charlie, about this China thing . . . You're a valuable asset here. You've brought in a lot of business with OntAmex, a *hell* of a lot of business, and we want to accommodate you. Hopefully we'll be able to." Lucien took a sip of green tea. "But right now we've got a problem in West Virginia. And with OntAmex. This pond thing is a very expensive problem for them, even though they okayed all the plans. Torkelson's on the warpath. So what we need to—"

Suddenly it all came to Charlie as if a brilliant spotlight had been snapped on. *Wow, how dense can you be? Lucien's call. Paxton's death. Torkelson and Tuthill in town. Terry Summers. Even Brand going after his Giants tickets. Lucien wanted him to go to West Virginia, not China! He wasn't going to be working on one of the engineering marvels of the millennium. They wanted him to babysit a half-built coal burner in the backwoods of Appalachia.*

"You want me to take over the West Virginia project, is that it, Lucien?" Charlie interrupted.

"That's it, Charlie. OntAmex wants a senior-level person down there to straighten this mess out." Without looking at Charlie, Lucien continued. "And Torkelson wants that person to be you. It was just a coincidence that you happened to mention getting out into the field, so it's good timing. This would be good for you, Charlie."

Charlie rolled his eyes. "Lucien, come on. It's West Virginia. The plant's half built. I need to create something new."

"A year, Charlie, maybe less." There was a pleading quality in Lucien's voice. "You go down there, help Tuthill with the local politics, fix the pond problem, and get the turbines in place. They're scheduled to arrive in the spring. Then we'll let Summers mop up and we'll see about China."

"Just fix the pond problem and get the turbines in," Charlie said, thinking out loud.

Lucien hesitated. "There's one other issue that Torkelson will brief you on, something they're really concerned about, because they think it could have some impact on this takeover of Continental."

Charlie's radar lit up at the mention of Continental. Mergers that went bad were expensive, litigious, career-ending occurrences. Once you made the announcement, billions of dollars were at stake—the kind of money that made individuals, companies, politicians, and regulators do curious things. If whatever was happening in West Virginia could have an impact on the takeover of CES, it was a lot more serious than a site plan with a cooling pond in the wrong place.

"Okay, Lucien, let me have it. I want the straight dope before I listen to Torkelson's version."

Lucien got up and closed the door. "Fair enough, Charlie. Here's where we stand. Torkelson's ass is hanging out a mile here; Tuthill's, too. They've been in charge of the West Virginia project from the beginning. They've done nothing illegal, mind you, but they got a little too *inside* on this deal, did a little too much conniving, simply because it's their nature, I think. They can't just do things straight up, like McCord and Red Landon used to. Anyway, almost three years ago, Torkelson made a deal with Ackerly Coal, which is owned by CES, to supply all the coal for the new plant. At the same time, they're negotiating with the governor's economic-development people about the taxes and acquiring land adjacent to the property and all that business, holding out that billion-dollar carrot your friend Duncan loves to beat small towns over the head with." Lucien paused for another sip of tea.

"Then, someone in the governor's office came up with a condition that all the fuel for the plant should come from mines in McDowell County, a real depressed area. But the Ackerly guys tell Torkelson that isn't a problem at all. In fact, it presents a good opportunity to lower OntAmex's fuel costs for quite some time. Seems that Ackerly owns the rights to a huge seam of good coal down there, enough to supply the plant for fifteen years. And it's only about ten, twelve miles or so from the plant. An easy trucking operation. Eliminates the need and the expense of putting in a new railroad spur."

"What's Ackerly's problem with the mine?" prompted Charlie, anxious to get to the heart of the matter.

"The problem is that the coal isn't down in a mine; it's halfway up a mountain. And the best way to get the coal out, the most economical way, which of course is what Ackerly and OntAmex are both acutely interested in, is through a surface-mining operation."

"So they need some permits."

"More than just permits." Lucien frowned as he thought about the situation he was about to describe. "Charlie, are you familiar with term *mountaintop-removal mining*?"

"Sure. It's a surface-mining technique. But I thought it had been outlawed in most places."

"You're right. A federal judge handed down an injunction barring the EPA from issuing any permits in West Virginia, where, as you might expect, it was doing the most damage." Lucien hesitated, reluctant to put his company and himself at odds with an important client. "It's an insidious practice, Charlie. It's an environmental crime that for years was rationalized in the name of jobs and local economics. The mining companies would say, in effect, if you want us to continue mining operations here, and you want the jobs and the tax revenue, then you have to let us destroy your mountain and fill in your valleys and streambeds. And, down there, the mining industry and the EPA and the Corps of Engineers have been embedded with one another for so long, it's hard to tell who's regulating who. The environmental requirements placed on strip miners simply say that, after you've exhausted a surface mine, you're required to return the land to its approximate original contour—"

Charlie interrupted Lucien. "But in Montana and Wyoming, they were basically digging a big shallow hole. When you fill it, the contour of the land is just reshaped a bit."

"Right, but in Appalachia it's not that easy," Lucien continued. "Because of the way the seams run in Kentucky and in the big Pocahontas Coal Field in West Virginia and Kentucky." Lucien ran his hand in an up-and-down pattern to demonstrate. "There's a lot of coal up in some of the mountains, usually right around the midpoint of the elevation. Back in the seventies, the coal companies said, since we've got all this huge land-moving equipment, like those monstrous draglines, let's do surface mines, like we did out west. But the whole thing is a ruse, Charlie, it's semantics. These mountain sites can't possibly be returned to their original contour, so the variance basically says, do your best and return the land to a condition that's *in harmony with the natural habitat*." Lucien grimaced. It didn't surprise Charlie that his boss had strong feelings about the subject. Lucien was a consummate environmentalist.

"So they go up in the mountains and they blast away, on a huge scale.

Charlie, there are mountaintop sites down there where they used more explosives than both sides used in the Civil War. Two hundred, three hundred feet or more of overburden, covering an area as large as ten square miles. And they push everything—trees, vegetation, animal habitats—down into the valleys, covering the streams and the meadows with rock and sand and mineral deposits to expose the coal seam."

A knock at the door curtailed Lucien's tirade. He took a deep breath and smiled at Charlie. "That would be Summers."

Lucien opened the door and welcomed Terry Summers. The young engineer wore a chic light-gray summer suit with a black shirt and a dark gray tie. He had a wide, classically handsome face, with dimpled cheeks and brilliant white teeth, which he revealed often with a practiced smile that he flashed on and off as a kind of visual emphasis to his words.

Lucien gestured toward the couch. "You remember Charlie Burden, of course."

Summers turned and took Charlie's outstretched hand. "How are you, Charlie? Congratulations. It's great, you'll be taking over in West Virginia."

So Summers had already been told. Charlie wondered if Summers's comment was another subtle show of arrogance. *Or did he actually think that the West Virginia post would be a promotion? No, he'd have figured out that Charlie had been chosen as Jack Torkelson's sacrificial lamb in case the situation in West Virginia led to the blowup of the Continental merger. And he'd have figured out with whom he would align himself in order to come out of West Virginia in an advantageous position.*

"Hello, Terry. Nice to see you again." Charlie smiled as Summers sat down.

Lucien continued the discussion. "Of course, not everyone agrees with my position on mountaintop removal," he said, an obvious invitation for Summers to join in.

Summers unbuttoned his jacket and sat back. "If you took a poll today of McDowell County, you'd have a tough time finding anyone who would oppose a surface-mining permit. The county needs the three hundred good mining jobs and millions of dollars of tax revenue. It would be crazy to take all that away from those people just to save an otherwise worthless mountain."

"And *that*, Charlie," said Lucien, "is our official position on the matter. We support our client OntAmex Energy, and the Ackerly Coal Company, in their efforts to get a surface-mining permit in West Virginia." Lucien added, "No matter how distasteful that prospect is to some of us." Lucien looked drained. He'd obviously had a contentious meeting with Torkelson and Tuthill the night before.

It occurred to Charlie that he hadn't officially accepted the job in Red Bone. That's what Lucien had wanted to settle before Summers arrived, but he'd gotten sidetracked. Lucien would be in a fix if Charlie turned the job down, which, as a partner, he could very well do. But he could never refuse his boss, his great friend, though Lucien must be agonizing over his decision.

Charlie turned to Summers. "Terry, first of all, give me our options on the pond. Then we'll talk about surface mining before we meet with Torkelson and Tuthill." It was clear Charlie was taking charge of the Red Bone project. Lucien turned his eyes toward him, and Charlie flashed him a quick wink across the room.

"There've been a number of scenarios discussed—" Summers sounded as if he was ready to occupy the floor for a while.

Charlie interrupted him. "Just give me the top two."

"Okay, well, there's fast and cheap, and slow and expensive. Fast and cheap, we relocate the pond to some open acreage on the site, just inside the northern border of the property. We'd have to make the pond a little deeper and build a levee along the road for about a hundred or so yards, but it would be easy excavation and the levee would be cheap to build. That's what Paxton planned to recommend."

"So what's the problem with fast and cheap?" Charlie knew there had to be a catch, or the problem wouldn't have reached New York.

"The problem is the unknown," Summers continued, "in the form of the town planning board. To move the pond, we have to get a variance to the site plan from the planning board at their next meeting, which isn't until September. Before this we haven't needed them. The project was settled in Charleston between OntAmex and the governor's people. That's the way they like to work, at a high level. OntAmex doesn't like to screw around and, you know, when you're ready to spend a billion dollars in a state as poor as West Virginia, you can sidestep a lot of the local crap."

Terry Summers got up to pour himself a cup of coffee. "So, the problem is, now we go before the board for the first time and we don't know if they've got some beef with the whole project, like maybe one of our cowboy iron workers ran over one of their dogs or something. We go in there with our Charleston lawyers and tell them that we need to move our pond, and these hillbillies look at each other, laugh, and say, 'Hell, no!' Then they get up and high-five each other, drop the gavel, and go fishing. It could happen."

"And then we've got a real problem." Charlie knew enough about rural politics to realize that Summers's scenario wasn't far-fetched.

"Then we have option two," Summers continued. "Slow and expensive. We stick with the site plan and blast through the bedrock." Charlie knew what was coming and almost didn't want to hear the gory details. "All work on the plant stops for four months minimum, all the subs leave, and we have to reschedule all the work until the springtime. We blast away the rock and move it to who-knows-where. We postpone delivery of the turbines, which is going to cost a fortune, and when it's all done, we've come to the biggest problem—"

Charlie finished his sentence. "The structural integrity of the plant that's already been built after all that blasting so close to the main building. We'd be lucky if we didn't have to tear down the whole thing and start over." Charlie did a rough estimate of the cost of *slow and expensive*. It was a minimum of a hundred million dollars.

"Okay, then," Charlie said quietly, "our only option is to make sure we get the variance, and then we take them fishing. Now tell me how Torkelson's planning to get the other variance, for the mountaintop-removal permit."

Summers squirmed a little before answering. "As I understand it, they've got a superior court judge who's going to lift the injunction temporarily, on some technicality that will allow the EPA to issue the variance. It's all being handled out of Charleston and Washington. The EPA has already told their West Virginia people what's going on. The governor's office is handling the environmentalists and the DEP. The state's going to cancel a big road project up in the northern part of the state that the environmentalists have been fighting for several years. It'll be a major victory for them, plus a couple of big developers get it stuck up the ass, which the tree huggers always love. So, the judge lifts the injunction, the EPA issues the variance, and *bam*"—Summers clapped his hands for emphasis—"a few weeks later the court issues a statement saying the technicality has been cleared up, the injunction is back in force, and the environmentalists are satisfied. It's all about this one mountain."

Charlie envisioned all the hushed conversations that must have taken place in unofficial venues in Washington and Charleston to put this deal together. OntAmex would've put all their lobbyists, lawyers, and politicians on it. But there would be no paper trail. A lot of cash would have been spread around, plus some tickets and junkets for the bureaucrats; contributions—both hard and soft money—to the politicians and their phony foundations and PACs and to both parties. That's how OntAmex worked. They would have taken care of everything at a high level. That meant the problem must be on the ground, locally, in Red Bone.

Summers spread his arms wide in summation. "Charlie, the low-sulfur coal at Redemption Mountain will make the Red Bone plant the cleanest and most efficient coal-fired generator in the world, and it will bring economic prosperity to the families of McDowell County." He flashed a high-wattage smile. "And what OntAmex wants, OntAmex gets."

TEN MINUTES LATER, Charlie, Summers, and a young lawyer from DD&M's legal department were seated at the boardroom table for the meeting with OntAmex. Jack Torkelson took a chair at one end of the table, separate from the rest of the OntAmex team lined up across from Charlie and Terry Summers. Larry Tuthill was in charge of the meeting. He began by introducing two men from OntAmex's legal department and three lawyers from Kerns & Yarbrough, "the most prestigious law firm in Charleston." Charlie wondered how much Kerns & Yarbrough was soaking OntAmex for. Fifty thousand a month, anyway, plus expenses. In the legal business, there was nothing quite like having a deep-pocketed utility for a client.

Vernon Yarbrough was broad, tanned, and distinguished-looking, with silver hair, a large silver pinky ring, and a gold Rolex. "Hara you, Mister Bur-dan. Anything you need in West Virginia, you just call us, and we'll git it done." Charlie wondered if sometimes Southerners didn't pack on a little extra accent when they came to New York. Charlie glanced over at Jack Torkelson, who hadn't said a word so far.

Charlie wondered why Torkelson was in the room at all. He and the other OntAmex people were meeting later with some financial writers about the merger, but why was he bothering with this pond issue or Redemption Mountain? It was out of character for him. Normally he'd let Tuthill handle operational matters like these.

Jack Torkelson was in his early sixties, completely bald, with a neatly trimmed gray beard and wire-rimmed glasses. A Harvard grad, Justice Department lawyer, and a former counsel to the Federal Energy Regulatory Commission, Torkelson was Duncan McCord's handpicked architect of OntAmex's strategy for managing the deregulation of the utility industries. This was Jack Torkelson's mandate. The method of coal mining used by an insignificant vendor in West Virginia was not. He must have real concerns that it could interfere with the CES merger. If that were in fact the case, Torkelson's career with OntAmex would be over. The merger was friendly—at the premium OntAmex was offering, possibly too friendly—because Duncan McCord didn't have the time or the energy to waste on a hostile takeover. It was supposed to be a slam dunk. If Torkelson screwed it up, he'd be gone.

When Charlie refocused his attention on the meeting, the lawyers were droning on about a liability clause in the master contract. Enough was enough. Charlie raised his hand and interrupted. "We'll go before the planning board in September and get a variance to build the pond on the north end of the property and on schedule. Now let's move on. I've got some packing to do."

Across the table, Larry Tuthill grinned and slapped the table. "Goddamn straight, Charlie! That's the attitude we need here. You go on down there, you and Vern, and take care of this. Do what you have to do, but get it done." He glanced sideways at the Charleston lawyers, who nodded their enthusiastic agreement.

"And we've got this to help you prepare." Tuthill slid a manila folder across the table. "It's the bios and some other info on the planning-board members. We had a private investigator do some homework. Some interesting stuff on these boys in there."

Charlie slid the folder into his notebook. Typical Torkelson and Tuthill. Hire a private investigator. Find some dirt to use. Nothing was ever simple with OntAmex anymore. It was more fun when he worked directly with Duncan and his right-hand man, Red Landon, the big, affable Canadian who never took himself as seriously as his replacement did.

"I'll read it when I get down there." Charlie didn't want to get into a discussion about the personal lives of the Red Bone planning board.

Before Tuthill could continue, Jack Torkelson spoke his first words of the meeting. He spoke softly to force the attention of his audience. "Charlie, it's good that you're taking over the project. Now, about the Redemption Mountain issue, I'm sure Lucien has given you his synopsis of the situation, but I'm afraid Lucien doesn't understand rural West Virginia. There's nothing nefarious or underhanded about this project. Everyone agrees that the judge's injunction against variances for mountaintop mining was misguided and unfair—to the industry, the miners, and their families, to the people of West Virginia." Torkelson was ably pleading his case. "You'll find hardly a soul down there in opposition."

Charlie knew that *someone* had to be against the project, but he'd let Torkelson make his case. Sooner or later he'd get to the real problem. Torkelson looked at his watch. He reached down for his briefcase and stood up as he resumed speaking. "The Redemption Mountain coal will make Red Bone the most efficient non-nuclear generating plant in the world. There's a lot riding on this, too much to let one old hillbilly farmer screw it up. You get down there, Burden, spend some money if you have to, but make sure this thing goes our way." Torkelson turned and walked out the door.

One old hillbilly farmer. Charlie almost laughed. *Some old hillbilly farmer in West Virginia had Torkelson by the nuts. It was going to be hard not to root for the farmer.*

Tuthill dismissed all the lawyers, except the three from Charleston. He reached into his briefcase and brought out another thin manila folder and slid it across the table. "The farmer," he said with a grin.

Charlie saw the name *DeWitt* written on the tab of the folder. He added it to his notebook. Some private investigator was having a pretty good year on OntAmex, too.

"So, the farm is in the way? The mountain can't be mined without taking the farm?" Charlie wanted to fully understand the situation.

Tuthill snickered. "Charlie, when Ackerly starts blasting the top off that mountain, it's going to be like the siege of fucking Khe Sanh on that farm."

Charlie looked over at Yarbrough. "What does the farmer say? I assume we've made him an offer."

"Yes, sir." One of the Charleston lawyers joined the discussion. "Mr. Yarbrough and I went up to see him, beginning of summer. Offered him a hundred thousand, which was just our opening number, you understand, but a good price for that kind of property—which isn't really worth anything."

"Turned us down cold," Yarbrough added. "Wouldn't discuss selling. We went back up a few weeks later and increased the offer, but still no interest." Yarbrough leaned back in his chair. "This farmer DeWitt's a hard-boiled character. A real hillbilly. Probably hasn't been out of the state more than a couple times in the last sixty years. Born on that farm and poor as a church mouse. Doesn't know what money can buy."

"What's the actual number? How high are we willing to go?" asked Charlie.

Before Yarbrough could answer, Larry Tuthill slapped the table lightly with the palm of his hand for emphasis. "One million," he said. "You guys can go to a million for the farm, but we need a deal by the end of October. Our judge is going to vacate the injunction against mountaintop variances in mid-November. But he wants to see that we own that farm before he does anything. We've got to get our variance and blasting permits and be in operation by December, and we're not going to get dick if that farmer isn't long gone from Redemption Mountain."

"Well that's a shit pot full of money," said Yarbrough, "but, thing is, I don't think we're going to need anywhere near a million to make a deal with that farmer."

"Why is that?" Charlie asked.

"Let's just say we got a secret weapon our investigator is working on down there, which may make this whole thing easier than a two-inch putt. That's all I can say about it right now."

Charlie was content to let Yarbrough's plan drop without further discussion. The whole issue of evicting the farmer made Charlie uncomfortable. He accepted a lot of what Summers had said about the project. It would undoubtedly be a boon to the economy and make the Red Bone plant a fabulous asset for his client. Yet he couldn't shake the nagging feeling that he was lining up on the wrong side of this issue. *The rich get richer and the poor get thrown off their farms.*

"All right," said Charlie, "after I get settled down there, Mr. Yarbrough and I will go up and visit this farmer and find out what he needs." Charlie wanted to move on the merger problem. "Now somebody tell me how this whole thing is going to affect the Continental deal."

Tuthill looked at Yarbrough, who gave him an almost imperceptible nod. Tuthill rose to his feet. "I think we'll leave the room to Charlie and Vernon now, boys." Then he faced Charlie. "Vernon will explain it to you, Charlie; you don't need us for this." He reached a hand across the table. "I'll see you in West Virginia in a few weeks. Glad to have you down there."

It was obvious that Yarbrough didn't want any witnesses to what he was about to say. He waited until the conference room door was shut, then got up and came around to Charlie's side of the table.

"It's the Public Utilities Commission, right, Vernon? Is that what Torkelson's worried about?"

"That's it, Charlie. Except it isn't so much the PUC as it is the settlement process they have to go through to approve the merger. The head of the PUC is a good boy, friend of mine, member of my club. Couple of weeks ago, Larry gives me a heads-up on CES and tells me to bounce the Redemption Mountain initiative off my PUC guy, see if there's any worms in the oatmeal there. Well, he'd already got wind of the Redemption Mountain variance—these regulators are all wired in together—but he tells me the commission's all for it. He thinks the injunction against mountaintop mining is bullshit. And he knows low-sulfur coal is their salvation, their *only* salvation. Ain't any Indian casinos or Jap carmakers moving in down there anytime soon, so he's all for it—even if it is Ackerly, which he isn't too fond of, but, shit, everyone hates the coal companies."

"Then what's his problem with the merger?"

"The settlement hearings'll be scheduled for spring. Going to sail through. They'll go ahead and rubber-stamp all the PR bullshit, all the usual crap about the merger being good for customers and increasing competition and being just peachy for the environment and all that boiler-plate stuff. But, as you know, the public, anyone—a business, another regulatory body, the man in the fucking moon—can file a complaint with the commission about any picayune aspect of the merger, and it would have to be officially investigated and discussed in public session. So, if someone files an objection based on, say, some improprieties between the two companies with regard to the variance for a mountaintop-removal permit, the commission will have to launch a thorough investigation."

They were finally getting to the heart of the matter. "What are they going to find there, Vernon? What's got our friend Torkelson so worried?"

"Most likely nothing comes out of such an investigation, but . . . you know, you talk to the wrong person, at a weak moment somebody says something, and you never know what kind of story might come bubbling up to the surface."

Before he spoke again, Yarbrough's demeanor changed. He stared coldly back at Charlie and the smile disappeared from his face and his voice, along with most of his accent.

"Now, Mr. Burden, you make a clear mental note to yourself right here that I am using the word *hypothetically*, as in, hypothetically, if the investigation were to show that someone connected to OntAmex were to have possibly bribed a high court judge in the course of these events, then the PUC of West Virginia, and probably a whole bunch of other states, would have a big problem with the merger between OntAmex and Continental Electric Systems. All of which is not very pleasant for our client, not to mention the shit storm of judicial activity that would no doubt ensue."

The lawyer held up his hand as Charlie started to speak. "I have no knowledge that this is the case, but it has been relayed to me by knowledgeable sources that, *hypothetically*, this kind of accusation could possibly come out of a PUC investigation. So, Mr. Burden, our job down there, yours and mine, is to make sure that no one files anything regarding Redemption Mountain with the Public Utilities Commission or any other regulatory body in the state of West Virginia. What that means, Mr. Burden, is that we create as little fuss and muss as possible in displacing that disagreeable old pig farmer from that decrepit mountain, 'cause he, my friend, is our only loose end down there." Yarbrough rose out of his chair.

"Vernon—" Charlie wanted more information.

Yarbrough gathered up his notes and smiled broadly at Charlie. "Mr. Bur-dan, you make sure you bring your clubs down, and we'll have you up to my club one weekend real soon. Send the chopper down and have you on the first tee before you can finish your cold drink." The lawyer nodded to signal the end of the conversation, picked up his briefcase, and left the boardroom.

Charlie sat at the conference table, reviewing what he'd just heard. It would be bad for everyone if the PUC launched a formal investigation of Redemption Mountain and a crooked judge came to light. Especially bad for Torkelson and Tuthill, who would lose their jobs and could end up in jail. But in the long run it would be almost as bad for his friend Duncan. His company's name would be dragged through the mud, and a huge, expensive merger would go down the drain. The stock price would be battered, and Duncan's image would be forever tarnished with the board of directors and the financial community. His spectacular career in the utility industry would be over. Yes, Charlie would do all in his power to prevent that. Torkelson knew what he was doing when he brought Charlie into the fold by letting him in on their dirty little secret. And now everyone's fate, as Yarbrough said, lay in the hands of a pig farmer on Redemption Mountain, West Virginia.

Torkelson had dragged Charlie into a no-win situation. If Torkelson went down over Redemption Mountain, the vortex would swallow everyone involved, including Charlie. If Torkelson was successful, his power within the company would be guaranteed. Not even Charlie's close friendship with McCord would save him.

Charlie went back to his office to make the call he'd been dreading all morning. Ellen was on her way to Vermont with Linda Marchetti, headed for Mount Snow for three days at the golf school, then up to the house at Sugarbush. He'd have to leave for West Virginia before she returned on Sunday night. He reached her on her cellphone in Linda's car, just outside Brattleboro.

"*West Virginia?*" She was incredulous. "That's, like, down next to Mississippi, right? *You agreed to go down there?*" Ellen was more upset than Charlie had anticipated. He'd underestimated how much of his company's corporate culture she'd assimilated, and she knew that, unlike a posting to China, West Virginia wasn't a positive career move for a partner of the firm. There was something afoot, and it didn't bode well for her husband, or for her own ambitions.

Charlie had no answers for her. She was right, and he couldn't explain why he had to go. He didn't want to bring Lucien into the discussion. It was too complex to get into over the phone. He told her not to worry, and Ellen told him to call her next week. Then she clicked off abruptly.

Charlie Burden sat at his desk and wondered if Ellen and he were still in love or if they'd just been through so much, so many years together, that they pretended to be. Charlie needed to get away for a while, to postpone the decisions they'd be forced to make—decisions he wasn't ready for. Maybe Lucien was right. Maybe West Virginia would be good for him.

He looked at the picture on the wall next to his desk. It was a collage of family photos. It had been a Father's Day present from Ellen and the kids. It was outdated, but for years it had hung next to Charlie's desk in several different offices. He enjoyed the nostalgia that engulfed him when he looked at the pictures of the children when they were small: Scottie holding up an old brown baseball, wearing a glove that was far too large; Jennifer, at four, sitting on the grass, holding a puppy, their first dog, Mr. Pips; a picture of Charlie and Ellen in front of their house in Connecticut. They looked like they'd been doing yard work. Charlie wore a dirty shirt and work gloves and had an arm around Ellen, pulling her close, their faces cheek-to-cheek. His hair was a little darker then, hers a shade lighter. Charlie stared at the picture. It was so long ago that it seemed like a former life to him now. He couldn't remember the last time he and Ellen had looked so happy together.

CHAPTER 9

THE CONSTRUCTION SITE WAS DESERTED. THERE WAS SUPPOSED to be a full-time watchman on duty, but Charlie didn't see any sign of life as he peered through the twelve-foot-high chain-link fence. *Late on a Friday afternoon. Should have expected it.*

The massive shell of the main building dominated the landscape, rising five stories behind a flat-roofed administrative building. Behind it were a dozen trailers and a few of the small shacks that pop up unnoticed at large construction projects. Beyond the stacks of pipes, beams, and cinder blocks, Charlie saw a huge yellow-and-green earthmover. Piles of dirt, sand, and stone were spread throughout the vast site.

Charlie gazed around the interior, resigned to the fact that he wouldn't be getting onto the grounds tonight. He slumped against the fence, hot and tired from the ten-hour drive from New York. He could feel rivulets of sweat running down the middle of his back to gather at the waistline of his tan Dockers. Behind him, the steel-blue Lexus sat with the engine running, the driver's door open, the air conditioner's compressor and the cooling-system fan racing madly to adjust to the heat.

As he took in the complexity of the project, Charlie was consumed by a sinking feeling of inadequacy. *Was it all a colossal mistake? Maybe he did belong behind a desk, on the phone, having lunch at the Four Seasons. Maybe he'd been away from it all too long.* And now here he was, in the middle of nowhere, and he couldn't even get through the gate at his own project.

When Charlie turned around, a boy was sitting on a bike next to his car. Charlie smiled. "Hey, how ya doing, buddy?" he said.

The bike was a beat-up banana-seat model, with no fenders and plenty of rust. The boy wore a dirty white T-shirt, long brown shorts with big utility pockets, black high-top sneakers, and white athletic socks that were now light brown from a covering of road dust. On his head he wore a dark-blue cap turned backward, like kids everywhere. His skin was fair, with a good coating of summer freckles. As he rocked slowly forward and back on his bike, observing the tall stranger, the boy could have been just an average ten- or eleven-year-old, Charlie guessed, except for the mongoloid features of his head and face and his short, thick legs and arms. Charlie flashed back to his own brief but intense research effort into the affliction of Down syndrome, some twelve years earlier.

The boy looked at Charlie through squinting eyes, the tip of his tongue protruding through tightly pursed lips. It was a hard face to read. "Can you speak, son?"

The boy's face relaxed, his eyes widening with some amusement. "'Course I can thpeak. You think I'm thum *dummy*?" His voice had a hint of hoarseness.

"Well, no. I wasn't sure, that's all."

"You locked out?" the boy asked.

"I guess I am. You ever see a man inside the fence, a security guard?"

"Thumtime. He go out in hith truck a lot. You want to get inthide?"

"You can get in? You've been inside before?"

"Lotth of time. Want me to take you?"

Charlie got into his car and turned off the ignition. He closed the door of the Lexus and locked it with the remote. The car beeped twice.

"Nobody take your car here," the boy said, as he laid his bicycle down.

Charlie knew the boy was right, but he felt uneasy about leaving the car unlocked with his luggage and computers inside. "I know. It's just a habit, I guess. I'm from New York."

"New York Yankees."

"That's right. You play baseball?"

The boy started down the path alongside the fence. "No. No bathball. Can't throw. Can't catch. I am thoccer player. My mama ith the coach."

"Well, that's good. Soccer's a great game."

"My daddy wath a football player. A great football player. He played football in college."

Charlie could see that it meant a lot to the boy. "Wow, that's great. What college did he play for?"

The boy stopped abruptly and squinted his eyes in thought so he could get it right. "Played football for Wetht Virginia Univerthity." He continued along the path until they came to a deep gully. At its bottom, a thick growth of bushes and vines concealed a gap of about two feet between the bottom of the fence and the ground. Pulling up the fence, the boy gave Charlie ample room to slither underneath. Once on the other side, Charlie stood up and brushed the dirt off his pants and shirt. He felt like a kid again, having an adventure, like when Cecil and he would sneak into the Yale Bowl or the New Haven Coliseum to watch a game. It had been a long time since Charlie Burden had crawled under a fence to get into anything. He made a mental note to notify security about the breach.

Outside the fence, the boy stood with his hands in his pockets, watching. Charlie thought he'd play a little game with his new friend. He turned without a word and started to walk away. After about ten yards, he stopped and turned back to the boy. "Well, aren't you coming?"

The boy's face scrunched up with a huge smile as he dropped to his belly, scrambled under the fence, and ran to catch up to Charlie. It felt good to have a companion, even this strange boy with his easygoing self-confidence. Charlie realized that the boy was the first person he'd met in West Virginia. "Hey, buddy, you know what? We haven't been introduced." Charlie held out his hand. "I'm Charlie Burden."

The happy look of inner laughter came over the boy's face again. He took Charlie's large hand in his short, chubby fingers as best he could. "Hello, Charlie. I am the Pie Man."

Charlie looked down at him curiously. *"The Pie Man,"* he repeated slowly. "That's your name, the Pie Man?"

The boy nodded his head affirmatively. "Yeth, I am the Pie Man," he said proudly.

Charlie smiled. *This is definitely not Westchester County.* "Well, I'm very happy to meet you, Pie Man. Now, let's have a look around."

Charlie could only imagine the number of OSHA violations he was committing by walking through an open construction site after hours with a child, neither of them wearing a hard hat. He'd have to keep a close eye on the boy.

They ventured into the cavernous main building. It was cool and dark on the ground floor. A steel stairway led to the second level, where there was more available light from the numerous openings in the walls. Charlie showed the boy the huge cavities that would be filled by the three giant turbines arriving by train in a few months. They walked inside the massive boilers that would burn the pulverized coal and turn purified water into steam. Charlie thought about the amount of coal that the boilers would consume and the Redemption Mountain problem, which, he knew, was the primary reason he was in West Virginia.

Charlie pointed out the three exhaust portals that would lead to the scrubber assembly and tried to explain how they cleaned the smoke produced by the burning coal. The boy was mesmerized by Charlie's endless knowledge and seemed elated at the attention the man was paying to him.

They clambered noisily down the stairway and back out into the sunlight. Around the outside of the plant, the ground was rough with muddy trenches left by the heavy machinery. Charlie had forgotten how much standing water was indigenous to large construction sites. He would need a pair of high rubber boots.

Charlie walked to the original site of the cooling pond. He could see several places where the hard brown rock pushed through the sandy soil like the back of a whale lurking just beneath the surface. *Anyone could see that this was going to be a horrible place to build a pond. What the hell were the site architects thinking about?* Charlie chalked it up to arrogance, a quality available in great supply in the mega-project engineers who considered themselves *masters of the universe* and wouldn't worry too much about an insignificant detail like the location of a cooling pond.

He turned north, in the direction of the alternative pond location at the far end of the site. It was about a ten-minute walk up to the spot that would need the planning board's approval. He'd skip it for today. Charlie wanted to get into Bluefield to find the company condo.

He started back toward the administration building, the boy by his side. "Tell me, Pie Man, when you sneak in here at night when the guard isn't around, what do you do?"

The boy pursed his lips tightly. Charlie laughed, understanding that the boy thought he might be in trouble. "You can tell me," Charlie cajoled. "It'll be our secret."

With that, the boy stopped and pointed toward the collection of bull-dozers and dump trucks. Charlie followed his gesture. *Of course! What kid could resist monster toys like those?*

He smiled at the boy. "I don't blame you, Pie Man. That's what I'd be doing if I was a kid around here." He pushed the boy's cap down. "But I've got a feeling the security guard may be paying closer attention in the future. C'mon, let's see if we can get into the administration building."

When they got close, Charlie noticed that the main gate was open and that the boy's bicycle was lying in the weeds. In the paved parking area sat a black Chevy Suburban with the unmistakable OntAmex Energy logo.

"It looks like our security guard has finally turned up," said Charlie. The boy slowed down noticeably, and Charlie saw him glance between the truck, the gate, and his bike, as if measuring the distance to his escape route.

"It's all right, Pie Man. You're with me." But the boy lingered behind, preferring to stay within sight of the open gate and his bike.

"I wait out here, Charlie. I wait here."

"Okay, I'm just going to see if he's inside," Charlie answered, as he walked toward the main door. Then he heard a deep voice from around the end of the building.

"Hey, you, *kid*! What the fuck are you doin' on my property? Get over here!"

The boy sidled nervously away from the voice, looking around the side of the building as if trying to spot Charlie.

"Hey, kid, you deaf or wha—" The security guard stopped abruptly when Charlie came into view. The guard was tall and powerful-looking, with a full gray mustache and the look of an ex-military man or state trooper. He wore a dark-blue shirt with ONTAMEX SECURITY on the right breast and the name HICKS emblazoned on the left pocket.

"The kid's with me; he's okay," said Charlie.

"Yeah, and who the hell are you, and why are you and Charlie Brown here trespassing on my property?"

Charlie offered his hand. "Hi, I'm Charlie Burden. I'm the—"

"How'd you assholes get in here?" Hicks continued, ignoring Char-lie's hand.

Charlie felt his patience drain away. He could sense the boy's nervousness as he tried to edge away from the two men. *The kid didn't deserve to be frightened over this.* Charlie gritted his teeth. "All right, Hicks, that's enough! If you want to keep your job beyond the next thirty seconds, you'll shut up and listen."

The security guard's face softened as it came to him: the expensive car with New York plates, the name *Burden* . . . the new guy! Hugo Paxton's replacement.

"I'm Charlie Burden, and I'm in charge of this site. You may be getting paid by OntAmex, but you now work for me, and your first day on the job isn't going well. If you were doing your job, you'd know how we got in. So when I come to work on Monday morning, you'd better be able to show me, and you'd better have it taken care of."

Charlie moved away from the now-docile Hicks toward the boy, who stood wide-eyed at how his new friend had spoken to the guard. Charlie put his hand on the back of the boy's neck and started walking him toward the gate.

"Hey, Mr. Burden, I'm sorry. I didn't know it was you. All I saw was that kid there, and . . ." Hicks's tone showed real concern over the prospect of losing his overpaid job.

Charlie turned back. "Mr. Hicks, this is my good friend the Pie Man, and anytime he wants to come on the grounds to see me, he's welcome. Okay?"

"Yessir, Mr. Burden. I'll see you on Monday morning, and we'll start fresh."

Charlie didn't bother to answer. He was tired and hot, the sun was getting lower, and he still needed to get to Bluefield. A cold shower and eight hours of sleep was what he needed.

The boy picked up his bicycle and stood with his legs straddling the front wheel as he straightened the loose handlebars.

"Should have your daddy put a wrench on that and tighten it up, Pie Man," Charlie said, as he unlocked the Lexus. The boy didn't respond. He seemed a little subdued. When he looked up at Charlie, he squinted with one eye closed and turned his head at an angle to avoid looking directly into the sun over Charlie's shoulder.

"Charlie, am I really your good friend, like you tell that man?"

Charlie grinned at the expression on the boy's face. He stepped forward and turned the boy's cap around so the bill shielded his eyes from the sun.

"Pie Man, you're the best friend I have in West Virginia."

The boy looked away, as if he was embarrassed. Then he turned back to Charlie as he jumped onto his bicycle seat. He had on his scrunched-up happy face, with the smile so tight it closed his eyes and pushed the little pink tip of his tongue out even farther. He rode his bike a few yards down the entry road, then circled around slowly and came back toward Charlie.

"Thank you for thowing me where the turbines will go."

"You're welcome, Pie Man. Thanks for showing me how to sneak in."

As the boy started to ride off, Charlie called after him. "Hey, Pie Man." The boy stopped and turned back to Charlie. "How old are you?"

The boy held up ten fingers. "I am twelve," he said, concentrating on his fingers. Charlie had to laugh at the expression on the boy's face as he pedaled off toward the logging road that ran through the woods to South County Road. Twice he turned back to see if Charlie was still watching, and he waved. He still had the strange, happy look on his face. Charlie tried to recall the last time he spoke to a twelve-year-old. *Had it really been that long?* It was fun being with a child again. And there was something about this boy with Down syndrome that was very likable. Charlie wondered if he'd see him again.

ON THE WAY out to the OntAmex site, Charlie had passed through the center of Red Bone—an old-time Main Street with a few side streets and a half dozen or so old dark-stone buildings of three and four stories. He remembered a place called Barney's, which looked like a general store with a restaurant on one side. It was in a four-story building on a corner at the center of town. He'd stop there on the way back to get directions to Bluefield and a cup of coffee to go.

Charlie drove leisurely east on South County Road toward Old Red Bone, taking in the sights. He went past a boarded-up motel with a heavy growth of weeds pushing through long-neglected cracks in the parking area. Several other abandoned buildings could've once been small manufacturing companies or warehouses. A two-story red-brick building with hundreds of small windows, mostly broken, had probably been a school at one time. There was very little along the road that seemed to be function-ing. Nothing new had been built on South County Road for many years.

From a long way off, Charlie could see the old buildings of Red Bone etched against the mountain by the light of the sun setting in the west behind him. He drove up the long, steep hill to Main Street, pulled around the corner, and stopped in front of Barney's General Store. The lights were out on the store side on the left, but he could see a woman sweeping the floor in the restaurant. Probably closing up and too late for coffee. But Charlie still needed directions.

The restaurant could have served as a set for a fifties movie. Wooden booths with individual jukeboxes ran along the front windows. The counter snaked out and back in the typical space-saving U-shaped pat-tern. Overhead, large ceiling fans turned slowly, and fluorescent lights kept the restaurant bright as day.

The woman looked up from sweeping as Charlie entered. She looked to be in her late fifties, with short gray hair and a fleshy face. She had a tired, end-of-the-day look about her.

"Let me guess," she said, leaning on her broom. "White-water guy, down here for the rafting on the New River. You missed your exit, got lost, and now you need directions up to Fayette County, right?" She smiled at Charlie, enjoying her game.

"You got part of it right. I do need directions. I'm looking for the best way to get to Bluefield." Charlie took a few steps into the restaurant. It reminded him of the New Haven diners of his youth.

"Was that all you wanted when you come in here, directions?" she asked. "Or were you looking to eat? 'Cause I can't turn on the grill again, but I got some cold stuff, if you're hungry."

"No, that's okay. I was looking for a cup of coffee to go, but that's all right."

The woman leaned her broom against one of the booths and went behind the counter. "You sit down a minute, then, and I'll make you cof-fee." Charlie protested, but she waved him to a stool. While the coffee brewed, she told him how to get to Bluefield. When he asked about the condo development, she drew a little map for him. "You must be a power-plant guy. A lot of them live over there in Bluefield."

"That's right. I'm here to work on the OntAmex project."

"Well, then, welcome to West Virginia. I'm Eve Brewster," she said, holding out her hand. "This town really needed that project. Been good for my business, I'll tell you."

Charlie shook her hand over the countertop. "I'm Charlie Burden, Eve, and I'm very happy to meet you. But, I do wish you hadn't made coffee just for me."

Eve Brewster looked at him with a wry smile. "So, you're the new *big mule* from New York."

Charlie laughed. "The big what?"

"The big mule. The boss. It's an old coal-mining expression."

"Word travels fast."

"Your man Summers—young guy with the white sports car? He was in tossing your name around the other day. Said you were on your way down."

"I'm surprised anyone would care," said Charlie.

"The big mule at the power plant is pretty important stuff around here. You're kind of a celebrity. Like poor Mr. Paxton was, rest his soul."

"You knew Hugo?"

"He was about my best customer. Man could eat cheese omelets like he just got out of a Japanese prison camp. Good tipper, too." Eve poured coffee into a tall Styrofoam cup. "He'd stop in on his way out some evenings, and buy his beer or liquor. And cigarettes." Eve Brewster let out a hearty laugh. "*Goddamn* if it don't sound like I killed that man single-handed."

Charlie laughed. "It must've been the omelets."

Eve looked out the window as a car pulled around the corner. Charlie glanced over his shoulder long enough to see a red Honda. "Mr. Burden, you feel free to sit there and enjoy your coffee. I'm going to have to open the store for my sister-in-law here," Eve said, as she moved toward the front door.

"No, that's okay. I'll be going." Charlie stood up and reached for his wallet. But Eve had gone out of the restaurant as the bell over the front door tinkled, and a new voice filled the vestibule.

"Hey, Evey. Can you open the store for a minute, please? I'm runnin' late, and I got to bring the boys their medicine."

"Yes, Natty. I know, it's Friday, and you're in a hurry, like always." The lights went on in the store. "Everything okay in the hollow? Hey, I'm sorry about your friend Birdie."

"Thanks, Eve. It was a shame, but, even so, you and I should go like Birdie Merkely did when our time comes."

Charlie had nothing smaller than a twenty, but he couldn't leave without paying for the coffee. And he wanted to say goodbye to Eve and thank her. He sipped his coffee and wandered over to the bulletin board just inside the door of the restaurant. It held a few business cards, several ads, and some notices of upcoming church events.

One caught Charlie's eye. It was headlined NEW YORK TRIP and described a bus trip to New York in November to *see the sights* and *Les Misérables*. The trip included two nights at the Milford Plaza. The total cost was $321, which seemed pretty reasonable. Anyone interested should call Ada Lowe at the Baptist Church Social Club.

"Gimme a pint of Jack, carton of Marlboros, and a six-pack of Bud tall boys." Charlie couldn't help overhearing Eve's sister-in-law. She had a slow, gentle voice with a hint of a Southern accent. "And a can of Red Man for Woody."

"Damn, still chawin' at his age. Surprised that man can still spit," Eve replied.

"Not a pretty sight. Gets a lot of it on him, but he enjoys his chew, and he ain't got much else to enjoy these days." Natty glanced out the front window and remembered that there was another car parked next to hers—an expensive car that surely didn't belong to anyone in Red Bone. "Eve, you got a customer over there?"

Eve told her sister-in-law about the handsome new boss of the power plant. With a twinkle in her eye, she offered to take her over and introduce her. Natty absentmindedly felt for the faded green bandanna that she'd used to tie back her hair.

"No, I can't now, I've got to get across the street and take care of the boys," she said.

Charlie could hear Eve ringing up her sister-in-law's purchase. He was about to wander over to the store, when he noticed one more item on the bulletin board. A handwritten three-by-five card read: *Alva Paine's apartment for rent. Clean, furnished, spacious, porch with spectacular view of sunsets. 4th flr. Barney's Bldg., no elevator. Utilities included. Cable and phone extra. See Eve.*

"Damn, Eve, thirty-two bucks for cigarettes! Every time I come in here they cost more," Natty said. She counted her money out onto the counter while Eve bagged her purchase.

"Generics are cheaper," Eve replied.

"You know Mr. Jacks; got to be Marlboros." Natty curled one arm around the bag and started toward the vestibule. "Anyway, I'm stealing these pork rinds here," she said, flashing a wide grin. Eve shrugged resignedly. As Natty turned her head back toward the front door, she almost ran into Charlie Burden.

"Oh, excuse me," she said, looking up at the tall stranger. She immediately recognized Duncan McCord's handsome friend. For two years, she'd held the picture in her mind of the two sophisticated men at the OntAmex picnic and then her embarrassing and exhilarating moment with McCord. She looked as if she wanted to say something else, but she couldn't speak.

"Save a lot of money if you just quit." Charlie tried to sound friendly, but his comment sounded like a lecture.

"Thanks a lot. That's a great idea," Natty said, as she moved around him. He'd only gotten a quick glimpse of the woman's face, partially hidden by a shock of sandy-blond hair, but he was surprised by her angelic beauty and blue eyes. For some reason, he hadn't expected Eve Brewster's sister-in-law to be attractive. He wished he hadn't made the comment about the cigarettes. He tried to amend the situation before she got to the front door.

"Sorry," he said to her back. "I know it's not easy. I used to smoke. I quit when I turned forty."

Natty stopped at the door and readjusted her package. "Yeah, well, I quit when I was in high school. About the time I got pregnant, the first time. So I guess we both quit a long time ago." Her voice was slow with a soft, easy drawl, but her irritation was clear. She went out the door and crossed the street.

Charlie watched her through the front window of the store as she entered a large dark-stone three-story building. Above the wide entryway was a black sign, its lettering almost completely faded away, which read: POCAHONTAS HOTEL.

So, I guess we both quit a long time ago. Nice dig. "I think I insulted your sister-in-law," he said to Eve, with a sheepish look.

"She'll get over it," Eve replied with a laugh. "Nothing bothers that girl for too long."

"Does anybody buy anything but booze and cigarettes in here?" Charlie joked.

Eve laughed again. "Nat takes care of a couple old colored gentlemen, got a room cross the way. Friday afternoon, she stops in for their *medicine,* she calls it, before going up." Eve looked out the window. "Nice men. Old coal miners. The two been together for years and years. Ain't got much time left, so Nat does what she can. Ends up paying some outta her own pocket, which she can't afford to do, but she won't say nothin', won't ask . . ." Eve's voice trailed off as she turned back to Charlie.

"Here, I didn't pay you for the coffee yet. That was very nice of—"

Eve cut him off as he pulled out his wallet. "No need for that. It's my treat, Mr. Burden. Besides, I already put the restaurant cash away." Charlie protested, but Eve waved him off.

"I'll be back in tomorrow to look for some waterproof boots. Then I'll pay you for the coffee, too," said Charlie.

"I'll just overcharge you for the boots, like we do to everybody from New York," Eve said with a wink. "Good night, Mr. Burden."

"Good night, Eve. Thank you."

INSIDE THE FRONT door of the former Pocahontas Hotel, Natty Oakes slumped against the door frame and peeked through a once-frosted window back across the street. She watched as Eve turned off the lights in the store. Natty closed her eyes and grimaced as she replayed her embarrassing encounter. *Damn! What was she thinking about? Copping an attitude with the new power-plant boss! The only person around who could give Buck a decent job finally. Maybe even save their marriage. He was just trying to be friendly. And that crack about getting pregnant—jeez, what a dope!* She shrugged resignedly and started up the stairs to the third floor.

Today, she'd probably have a little glass of Jack Daniel's with the boys before she left.

EVE BREWSTER'S DIRECTIONS to Bluefield and the condo development were easy to follow. Fifty-five minutes after leaving Red Bone, Charlie found the turnoff to what was unmistakably the entrance to an upscale community. It felt suddenly familiar. He could've been in New York or Connecticut or New Jersey, where similar cookie-cutter buildings had been punched in the seventies to house the young professionals not yet ready to give up the carefree life for a heavy mortgage in the suburbs. The look and feel of the place surprised Charlie after his afternoon in Red Bone.

When he found his building, Charlie pulled in next to a new white Corvette convertible with California plates, which he knew would belong to Terry Summers. From the trunk of the Lexus, he took out a tennis duffel bag that held most of his casual clothes and his shaving kit, then locked up the car. A few units down, a group of men and women, all in their early thirties, relaxed on a second-floor deck, drinking red wine.

Inside, Charlie dropped his bag on the leather couch in the living room and tossed his keys on the credenza in the hall. Along one wall of the living room was an expansive entertainment center with a wide-screen television. The place was sumptuous and comfortable. Somewhere outside, an air-conditioning unit hummed. He went into the kitchen and pressed the red blinking button on the answering machine. There was a message from Terry Summers, telling him he'd stop by at nine on Saturday morning and drive Charlie in to take a look at the plant.

Charlie took a slow tour of the apartment, but he had known what he was going to do, even before he came through the front door. He didn't want to be in West Virginia, but if he had to be here, he wanted to experience the real McDowell County, to experience Red Bone.

He'd already gotten a taste of it—the boy at the construction site, Eve Brewster, and even her harried sister-in-law, the little woman with the blue eyes. It was a different world, which was what he needed for a while, and it felt good. In the phone book in the kitchen, he found the listing for Eve Brewster. Her address was the same as Barney's General Store, on

Main Street in Red Bone. She must have an apartment in the building. Charlie looked at his watch, hoping that ten-fifteen wasn't too late to call.

After several rings she answered. "Hello, this is Eve."

"Eve, this is Charlie Burden. I met you earlier tonight. I came into the—"

Eve Brewster chuckled as she cut him off. "Yes, Mr. Burden, I remember. It wasn't that long ago. Are you all right? You didn't drive off the mountain, did you?"

"No, I'm fine. I hope I didn't wake you up."

"No, it's okay, Mr. Burden. I had to get up to answer the phone, anyway."

Charlie smiled at the old joke. "Listen, Eve, that apartment you have up on the bulletin board. Is it still available?"

"What?" Eve sounded genuinely baffled.

"The apartment. The one on the fourth floor. It's advertised on the board."

"Oh, *God*, Mr. Burden. That apartment's not for you. This is an old building. Plus it's up on the fourth floor, and there's no elevator."

"That doesn't matter. Is it still available?"

"*Available?* Hell, that place'll be available 'til the building falls down. Ain't but a handful of people in all of Red Bone could make it up them stairs without an oxygen bottle."

"Could I take a look at it? Tomorrow morning?"

"What happened to that place in Bluefield?"

"It's fine. It's just not what I'm looking for."

"Well, Mr. Burden, you can sure look at it if you want to."

"Tomorrow morning?"

"I'll be here. I'm always here. Good night, Mr. Burden."

CHAPTER 10

Buck oakes's twelve-year-old pickup always had a distinctive sound as it accelerated up the steep stone-covered road to Oakes Hollow. The engine would whine as Buck spun the tires through the well-worn ruts, sending stones flying off into the woods like machine-gun fire. Buck tended to drive too fast, even when he hadn't been drinking.

The sound had become both a comforting and frightening signal to Natty. At first she would be relieved that he'd finally come home, then apprehensive about his condition. After he parked his truck, she'd listen for the telltale signs—how hard he slammed the truck's door, the sound of his boots on the deck—to determine how drunk he might be and if he'd reached that critical stage at which it was best for Natty to hunker down under the blanket and feign deep sleep.

Tonight, Natty had woken up several times to find Buck's side of the bed empty. It was almost morning when the sound of the truck accelerating up the hill, the beam of the headlights bouncing madly up and down on the window screen, awakened her once again. *Damn you, Buck! Why are you doing this to us again?*

Natty pulled up the sheet, debating, as she had so many times before, whether to say anything when her husband entered the room. Usually, silence ruled. She waited with her eyes open, thinking about what Deputy Sheriff Wayne Lester had said up at Birdie Merkely's cabin about the woman in Northfork, an old high school girlfriend of Buck's. The woman that Buck had gone to live with for six months, right after Cat was born.

She could hear Buck rooting around in the refrigerator, and then in the bathroom, taking a long pee, splashing water on his face, and finally shoving open the squeaky sliding door. He pulled his T-shirt over his head and sat heavily on the bed to take his boots off.

"So, where you been, Buck?" The sound of her own voice startled her, but her husband showed no reaction, tossing his second boot loudly to the floor. Buck stood and unzipped his blue jeans. He staggered slightly, reaching out for the corner of the dresser to steady himself. Natty could smell the mixture of sweat, liquor, and perfume coming off him. Suddenly a rush of anger enveloped her, and she sat up in the middle of the bed.

"Buck, where the *fuck* have you been all night?" she demanded loudly. "Tell me. I deserve an answer."

Her husband had turned back toward the bed with one knee on the mattress as Natty sat up. In the darkness, she couldn't see his large left hand as it snapped out and slashed across her face. The sting of Buck's high school ring caught the corner of Natty's mouth, causing her to see stars.

"Don't give me any of that shit, Natty." Buck's voice had a cruel edge. "It's Friday night. I been out. Pourin' cement all day for forty fuckin' dollars, I deserve some time away from this dump." Buck rolled heavily onto his back as Natty got up from the bed. Tears ran down her cheeks to mix with the blood from her upper lip.

"Goddamn you, Buck, you prick. You swore you'd never do that again." Natty made her way around the bed, stumbling on one of Buck's boots. "I try so hard, Buck. I try so damn hard," she said angrily as she fled the bedroom.

At first light, Natty went back into the bedroom and got her running shoes and shorts. She couldn't wait to feel the cool air of the dawn and lose herself in a long, hard run. Later, she'd take the kids and Amos into town for some of Eve's blueberry pancakes, then maybe to the mall in Bluefield. Anywhere to get away from the hollow for the day. She longed for the refuge of Redemption Mountain. But not this day. Not with a new red welt on her cheek and a cut on her lip. Natty couldn't go home today. Her mother might finally persuade her to stay.

EVE SMILED AS she saw the blue Lexus pull up in front of the store. "*Damn,* he really is serious," Eve said to herself.

The restaurant had a different feel in the morning, filled with people who'd known each other for years. Charlie could feel all their eyes on him as he walked in.

"Morning, Mr. Burden," Eve said, as she came over with a mug in one hand and a pot of steaming coffee in the other.

"Good morning, Eve."

"Still interested in the apartment, or did you come to your senses yet?" she asked quietly.

Charlie laughed. "I'd like to see it. And I want to look at some boots, too."

"Well, the store don't open 'til nine, so why don't you have some breakfast first? Fourth floor, there's two apartments. Mr. Hankinson's on the right; the empty one's to the left. Door'll be open. If you want the place, we'll find a key somewhere, though I don't think Alva Paine ever locked the door in thirty-one years up there."

Charlie's eyebrows went up. "Thirty-one years he lived there?"

"Long time," she said. "He was a wonderful man, Mr. Paine. Hank's closest friend for a long, long time. Ain't been the same since Alva died. Hank won't admit it, but he's been real lonely this past year." She handed Charlie a menu. "Anyway, you go take a look at it if you want to, and no hard feelings if you decide not to take it, okay?"

"It's a deal." Charlie ordered the pancakes, then left a message on Terry Summers's machine, telling him to meet him in front of Barney's General Store at ten o'clock.

The hike up the four flights didn't bother Charlie, although he had to concede that you wouldn't want to be making too many unnecessary trips. At the top of the stairs to the right, the door held a small plastic sign that read: DR. P. J. HANKINSON. Under it was the word PRINCIPAL.

The apartment on the left opened into a wide living area dominated by three large windows that provided a spectacular view of West Virginia beyond. Toward the back of the apartment was a small dining area and a kitchenette. Big enough, thought Charlie, for cooking for one.

Through the kitchen, another door led out to a large covered porch, which ran the entire width of the building. The porch yielded another stunning view, westward. The sunsets beyond the seemingly endless stretch of mountains would indeed be spectacular. Looking straight down South County Road, the porch also offered a bird's-eye view of an athletic field at the bottom of the hill.

At the other end of the porch was a door from the adjoining apartment. Halfway between sat a small square table and two identical high-backed wooden chairs. The table held a wooden cribbage board, from which nearly all the surface paint had been worn. Next to it, a wooden cigar box held several well-used decks of cards and a black notebook.

Charlie slid out the notebook. It was an appointment book for the year 1979. For the first three quarters of the book, every page was covered with columns of minute numbers and dollar signs. At the top of each page were the names *Alva* and *Hank*. Under each name was a list of plus and minus amounts, followed by a horizontal line and what looked like a running total of the cumulative score. Charlie thumbed to the last page of entries. The last entry showed *Hank +$1,192.*

Through the living room was the bedroom, another oversize room with a high ceiling. Like the rest of the apartment, it was furnished with a mismatched variety of pieces, but it was clean and spacious. Charlie knew right away he'd take the apartment. It had beautiful views and a lot of personality. He was about to go down to find Eve when he heard something coming from a door in the bedroom.

Charlie opened the door to find a large bathroom, brilliantly lit by a round skylight in the roof. In the center of the white-tiled floor sat an antique tub with brass fittings and ornate claw feet. Sitting in the tub, staring at him in wide-eyed surprise, was an elderly man with shoulder-length snow-white hair, a classic white handlebar mustache, and a matching goatee that reached the middle of his chest.

In an instant, the old man's look of fright was replaced with an angry glare. He lifted a long, bony arm out of the bathwater and gestured a sarcastic welcome to Charlie. "Barge right in on an old man's bath, why don'tcha? Don't knock. Don't announce yourself. Just come right on in."

Charlie was taken by surprise. "Er, no. I'm sorry, I . . ." he stammered.

"So you're the one Eve called me about this morning. Says you're thinking about renting Alva's place. From New York, the hot shit new boss of that silly power station." He reached over the side of the tub and brought up a glass jelly jar half filled with a brown liquid. He spit a generous addition into the jar. Charlie winced involuntarily.

"Ain't got a problem with chawin' tobacco, do ya? Better get used to it down here, boy. West Virginia's number-one state in the country for chawin' tobacco." After a pause, he added a little more softly, "Back when we had enough people livin' around here to qualify for such things." He returned the jar to the floor. "Can't light up down in the mines, is why."

"You were a coal miner?" Charlie took the opportunity to enter the conversation.

"Sure, I was a coal miner. For one goddamn month," the old man nearly shouted. "Worst job ever was. Seventeen years old, and I cried like a baby every day, crawlin' around in the dark, waiting to get buried alive or blown to little pieces. Hitchhiked off to Huntington and worked my way through Marshall University just to stay out of them damn holes. So, you writin' my goddamn biography or lookin' for an apartment?"

He suddenly rose out of the bathwater and climbed slowly out of the tub, dripping water across the tiled floor. His skin had a reddish hue, with many brown liver spots, and hung in loose folds where the flesh was losing the battle with gravity. He had narrow shoulders and a pear-shaped body, which was once probably around Charlie's height but had lost a few inches to a hunched back. He covered himself with an old terry-cloth robe that hung on a rack on the opposite side of the bathroom.

Charlie offered his hand. "Charlie Burden," he said.

The old man hesitated, as if he were sizing Charlie up, before finally taking his hand. "Pullman Hankinson," he offered grudgingly. "But all anyone ever calls me now is Hank." More to himself than to Charlie, he added in a low voice, "Alva Paine used to call me *Doctor* Hankinson, but, well, that was a different . . ." His voice trailed off.

Hankinson shuffled over to the door to his apartment. With his hand on the knob, he turned back toward Charlie. "So, you going to take the place or ain't ya? Got to let Eve know if it's okay, if you're okay with me, 'cause now I'll have to share the goddamn bathroom again."

"I'd like to take it. If it's okay with you."

The old man sniffed and nodded. "Eve can use the rent money, for sure. No, I don't mind." He took his hand off the doorknob and pointed a bony finger at Charlie for emphasis. "But don't you let her go jackin' up the price 'cause you're from New York. Next thing, she'll be lookin' to dicker with my rent."

"No, I'll bargain hard with her," Charlie replied sincerely.

As Hankinson opened his door, Charlie stopped him. "Hey, Hank? How long have you lived here?"

Hankinson tilted his head back, as if the answer might be written on the ceiling. "Twenty-one years I been here. Six months after my wife died, I moved in. Twenty-one years," he said, as if it were the first time he'd thought about it. He closed the door behind him, then opened it again. "Hey, Burden!" he called out.

"Yeah, Hank," Charlie answered softly, still standing in the doorway.

"You play cribbage?"

"I play."

"Maybe we'll have a game, then. Play for a little something, just to keep it interesting."

"That'd be good, Hank. We'll play some cribbage."

The old man nodded his head affirmatively as he closed the door once more.

CHARLIE FOUND EVE Brewster behind the counter of the store. She was hanging up the phone as Charlie entered. She smiled and looked up, indicating that she'd been talking to Mr. Hankinson. "Forgot to tell you about sharing the bathroom."

"That's all right," Charlie replied. "He's quite a character, isn't he?"

"Hank? He can be a pain in the ass, but he's about the smartest man in McDowell County. Anything you need to know about history or anything else around here, Hank will know it. Taught school at Red Bone High for forty-four years. Even after he was the principal, he kept teaching. Still goes in and teaches a history lesson now and then, though they can't pay him, 'cause he's retired." She turned her eyes back down to Charlie. "So'd Hank scare you off, or you going to move in with us, Mr. Burden?"

"No, he's fine. I like Hank. We're going to play some cribbage together. But I told him I'd bargain hard on the rent, so you wouldn't be raising his."

Eve laughed. "Up until about three years ago, Mr. Paine was paying two hundred sixty dollars a month, which was the deal he and my late husband Barney made a long time ago. Told him I had to get more, so we settled on two seventy-five. That's what Hank pays. Think you can afford that?"

Charlie pursed his lips, pretending to struggle with the figure. He was shocked at the ridiculously low rent. He paid his landscaper in Mama-roneck more than $275 a month. "It's worth more than that, Eve," Charlie answered.

"I guess. But old schoolteachers around here," she glanced upward again, "they don't get the greatest pension. So, we all try to get by with what we need. You understand, Mr. Burden?"

"Yes, Eve. I think I do."

Over Eve's protestations, Charlie wrote out a check, paying a year's rent in advance. "If I leave before then, just keep the balance, and don't tell Hank." Charlie had his bags in his car, and they agreed he'd move in that day. He said that if Alva Paine didn't need a key, neither did he.

When they'd concluded their business, Charlie browsed through the store, slowly making his way to the shoe section. A shelf in the rear was crammed with a dust-covered selection of black leather boots with steel toes. Some looked as if they'd been there for years. Above them were the knee-high rubber boots Charlie was looking for. He sat on a low stool to try on a pair in his size.

As he pulled on one of the boots, Charlie realized someone was standing directly in front of him. He recognized the black high-top sneakers and the baggy shorts. The boy was wearing the same outfit he'd had on the previous day.

Charlie looked up to see the scrunched up look of laughter on the face of his new pal. The boy's eyes were narrowed to slits by the tightness of his round cheeks. The point of his tongue protruded from the tiny mouth. His short, stocky arms hung straight down as he leaned forward toward Charlie in an expression of surprise. He was obviously overjoyed to see his new friend. "Hello, Charlie. I am the Pie Man!" He held up his open palm for a high-five.

"You sure are," Charlie laughed, as he slapped his palm firmly against the boy's small hand. "How are you, pal? What are you doing here?"

"We have breakfast. Me and Mama and Cat and Grandpa Amos. Very delicious pancakes." Charlie noticed a maple-syrup stain on the boy's shirt. Suddenly the boy turned and darted back around the corner of the shoe aisle. He called out excitedly, "Mama, Mama, my friend Charlie is here!"

Charlie pulled on the second boot and looked up to see a small girl with long blond hair peeking around the corner. She stared at him with intense curiosity. As she pulled her head back, Charlie heard footsteps coming toward him.

"Mama, my friend Charlie is over here."

Charlie readied himself to do some explaining as to how Pie and he had met. Then he heard a voice from the next aisle that sounded familiar. "Whoever he is, Pie, you can't be bothering him." With a look of excitement on his face, the boy reappeared around the end of the aisle, his chubby fingers wrapped firmly around the slight wrist of Eve Brewster's sister-in-law. Charlie rose to his feet, concealing his surprise at seeing the petite woman with the blue eyes from the night before. She was not what he had been expecting.

"Oh, *God,* it's *you,*" Natty blurted, with an expression of embarrassment that Charlie didn't understand. Maybe it was her outfit. She was wearing baggy jeans, loosely tucked into a pair of well-worn construction boots, a man's white dress shirt, and a blue baseball cap with a red Spider-Man figure on the front.

"I'm sorry," she continued. "I didn't mean it like that. Pie's been talking about his new friend all morning, and I . . . I was just surprised that it's you. From last night, I mean."

Charlie studied her face as she talked. She had a thin, straight nose, a sharply defined but delicate chin, and a wide, sensual mouth. But there was something different about her this morning. Her eyes were still a stunning ice blue, but they looked a little glazed, as if maybe she'd been crying. And there was a small cut at the corner of her mouth. *Had that been there yesterday?*

When she stopped speaking, there was a moment of silence between them. Then she seemed to relax. "I'm Pie's mother. Natty Oakes," she said. With Pie between them, it was awkward to offer her hand, so she didn't.

"It's a pleasure to meet you, Mrs. Oakes. I'm Charlie Burden."

"So, are you?" Natty asked quickly.

"Am I what?" Charlie was puzzled.

"A burden."

"Well, I hope not," Charlie replied to the old joke.

"Sorry. Probably heard that one before, huh?" Natty rolled her eyes at her own embarrassment.

"Been a while." Charlie smiled as he watched Pie, beaming with pride, intent on catching every word of the conversation between his mother and his new friend.

"I met Pie at the power-plant site yesterday," Charlie said, pushing the back of the boy's cap over his forehead. "He showed me around."

"That's right, you're the new boss—"

"I'm the big mule," Charlie added, at which Pie bent over in spasms of laughter. Natty and Charlie laughed, too, at the boy's reaction. Pie finally pointed to Charlie and said, "The big mule!" and they all went into another round of convulsions. Eve Brewster's appearance at the end of the aisle helped them all gain some composure.

"What the hell's goin' on back here?" Eve tried to suppress a giggle as she watched the three of them wind down from their laughing fit.

"Oh, it's nothing, Eve," Natty answered. "Pie said something funny, that's all. Come on, Pie Man, we got to get going. Amos is waitin' in the car."

Charlie sat back down on the stool. He couldn't remember when he'd had such a good laugh. It was the boy's fault, of course. *Damn, that kid is contagious.*

On the wooden boardwalk in front of the store, Natty saw Sally Oakes's orange Camaro pull around the corner and take the spot between Natty's Accord and a gleaming white Corvette convertible. Pie and Cat ran over to take a closer look at the sports car.

Sally had to maneuver carefully between the children and the open door of Natty's car. In the front seat, Amos Ritter sat sideways with his feet on the ground, his hands on his thighs, unmoving, except for an occasional slow turn of his head and blinking eyes. He was happy to be away from his stool on Oakes Hollow for a while.

Across Main Street, Emma Lowe was walking hand in hand with her grandmother Ada. Natty waved, and they started across the street toward Barney's. Emma broke off to say hi to Pie and to look at the fancy car, while Ada stopped at Natty's car, leaning in close to speak to Amos.

Sally bounded up onto the boardwalk, wearing her trademark tight shorts and a revealing halter top. She was smoking a thin brown cigarette and working over a large wad of gum.

Eve came out of the store. "I see you met our Mr. Burden, Nat," she said, smiling at Natty.

Natty shook her head in disgust. "Damn, Eve. I talked to that man twice now and made an asshole out of myself both times."

"Seemed like he was enjoying himself," Eve replied.

"That was Pie. He got us laughing, you know, and—"

Sally perked up at the reference to a man. "Who's this? What man you all talkin' about?"

Eve supplied the details. "The new power-plant boss. Down here from New York. His name's Charlie Burden. Come in yesterday and our sister-in-law almost knocked him down as he left the store last night. All she could come up with for conversation was to tell him that she got herself pregnant in high school."

Natty scowled. "Wasn't like that, Eve—"

"So, what's he look like?" asked Sally, getting to the point.

"Aw, he's *ugly*," Natty offered quickly. "Not your type at all, Sal. Fatter than Hugo Paxton, and shorter, too."

"I'll bet," said Sally, eyeing the tall stranger who'd just come out the front door.

Before the women could say anything, the Pie Man had Charlie's attention. "Charlie," he called excitedly, as he pulled a dark-skinned girl up to them. "Thith ith my friend Emma. Emma's on my thoccer team. Emma's the betht thoccer player in the whole world." Charlie shook hands with the girl, who shrugged and smiled shyly.

Natty introduced Charlie to Ada Lowe. Then, to Sally's consternation, she brought him down to introduce him to Amos, seated in her car. Charlie squeezed the old man's hand firmly. As Natty started to introduce him to Sally, Charlie turned back toward the store, where Terry Summers was striding aggressively out of the restaurant.

Summers stopped short when he saw Charlie and the collection of locals. With his sunglasses hooked on to the front of his white polo shirt, tan slacks, and brown Italian loafers, he was the picture of Southern California chic. As he took in the scene, he smiled broadly, revealing his perfect white teeth.

"There you go, Charlie." He held out his arms expansively, palms up, presenting the group before him. "Welcome to West Virginia." Natty bridled at Summers's comment, but Sally beat her to a response.

"What was that crack, Summers? What was that supposed to mean, *Welcome to West Virginia*?"

Summers tried to laugh it off. "Nothing, Sally. A little joke, that's all." He flashed his highest-wattage smile around the group.

Natty wouldn't let him off so easily. "Sal, I think Mr. Summers was trying to warn Mr. Burden about what a backward place he's come to, so he'll know not to expect too much out of us hillbillies."

Sally caught on right away. "Probably a good thing, too. With all these retards and crippled old people we got around here . . ."

"And cheap-lookin' women," said Natty, firing a mischievous eye at Sally, who made a quick face back at her before she took over.

"And *ignorant,* too. Why, Mr. Burden, you come to about the most backward place in America. Ain't that right, Summers?"

"Come on, Sal," Terry Summers pleaded. "I didn't mean—"

"It sure is that," Natty interrupted. "Why, you remember that movie *Deliverance*? That kid with the banjo—why, he'd o' been the damn superintendent of schools up here."

It was Sally's turn. "And the people here're *so* ugly—that guy the Elephant Man, he coulda moved to Red Bone and taken that bag off his head, and nobody woulda even noticed."

A quick wink from Eve told Charlie that the women were just having fun. He stood with his arms folded, enjoying the skewering that Summers was taking. He'd deal with the insensitivity of his remark later.

"'Course, you know what our state flower is, don't you, Mr. Burden?" said Natty. "It's the satellite dish."

Summers took it all in good humor, and Charlie used the opportunity to look more closely at Natty Oakes. When she smiled, she glowed, and in spite of her unflattering clothing, she had a slender, attractive frame and a disarmingly alluring way about her. And she was the Pie Man's mother, which also intrigued him.

Finally the two women ran out of material, and Terry Summers turned to greet his new boss. "Welcome to West Virginia, anyway," he said, glancing at Sally Oakes. She shot him a flirtatious look as she headed into Barney's. Charlie told him about taking the fourth-floor apartment. Summers squinted up toward the top floor. "Check out the fire escape," he advised. "I think the closest fire department's in Charleston. Good idea, though, moving into town. Get on good terms with the locals."

Charlie watched as Pie and his mother walked toward a heavy black woman who was climbing the steps. "Terry, speaking of the locals, it doesn't help anyone to make comments like that."

"Yeah, that just kind of slipped out," Summers said. "But it's true, Charlie. People are fucking weird down here." Charlie ignored the comment and told Terry to meet him out at the construction site after he took care of a few things. Summers lowered himself into the Corvette and rumbled off around the corner.

Charlie wanted to move his things up to the fourth-floor apartment and thought he'd ask Pie to help him. The boy would get a kick out of that, plus he'd give him a few dollars.

As Charlie approached the group, Natty and the black woman stopped talking so Natty could introduce them. The black woman was as wide as a door, with rolls of fat and huge arms that strained the short sleeves of her purple flowered dress. "Mabel, I want you to meet Mr. Burden. He's the new *big mule* out at the power plant." She flashed a quick smile at Charlie, then looked around quickly for Pie, relieved that he hadn't overheard her. "Mr. Burden, this is Mabel Willard. Mabel's the special-ed teacher at the elementary school, and she's the reason your friend the Pie Man is such a wiseass."

Mabel waved off Natty's comment and reached out to engulf Charlie's hand in a firm handshake. "Well, let me welcome you to West Virginia, Mr. Burden, and to our little town of Red Bone. That's a wonderful thing you all are doing out there, putting our boys to work and all. And that's so Christian of you fellows to leave your families and come down here." She tilted her head slightly. "You *do* have a wife, children, Mr. Burden, back there in New York City?" She fixed Charlie with a huge smile of brilliant white teeth, accented by several shining gold caps.

"Don't be asking Mr. Burden such personal questions," said Natty, but Mabel ignored her and continued to hold on to Charlie's hands.

Charlie smiled. "Mrs. Willard, it's a pleasure to meet you, and, yes, I have a wife and two children—one in college, and one now living on his own in Boston. And I actually live in Mamaroneck, but my office is in the city. And, please, call me Charlie."

Mabel released Charlie's hand, seemingly disappointed. "Well, that's fine. Very nice to meet you, Charlie," she added sincerely. Suddenly she became energized, pulling Natty with her as she moved past Charlie. "Now, where is that boy?" she bellowed. Then quietly to Natty, "Sammy got somethin' real important he got to ask you," she said.

A black boy loped up from the street and touched knuckles with Pie. "'Sup, Pie Man? Hey, Em." He was a little taller than Emma Lowe, with a lean, muscular build.

"Sammy, get on over here. Miz Natty ain't got all day to wait on you," Mabel thundered.

Natty smiled as the boy came up to them. "Damn, Sammy, you've grown a foot this summer, just like Emma."

"Now, Sammy, you go ahead and ask Miz Natty what you wanted to," instructed Mabel.

He fidgeted, his hands thrust deep into the pockets of his denim overalls. "Miz Natty, I was wonderin' if I could, uh, play on your team this year, you know, get back to playing soccer."

Natty was clearly taken by surprise. "Soccer? You're not going to play football this year?"

"No, ma'am," he said, as he looked toward Mabel.

"But, Sammy, you're one of the best football players in the county. You haven't played soccer for, what, three years?"

"I can still play," Sammy said. "And I'm supposed to tell you Zack wants to play soccer on your team, too."

Natty was speechless. Sammy's twin brother, Zachary, was the football team's star quarterback. The two Willard boys had played on Natty's soccer team when they were younger. Both were wonderful athletes, and Natty knew that what they lacked in polished soccer skill, they would make up for with blazing foot speed and competitive drive. Zachary was an extremely gifted athlete, who hated to lose at anything. Natty knew that, even after several years away from competitive soccer, the brothers would quickly become two of the best players in the league. This was like a gift from heaven.

Natty looked to Mabel for an explanation. "What's up?"

Mabel folded her arms. "The boys ain't playing for that coach Lester this year, is all."

Wayne Lester. Of course. He had been named coach of the football team the previous season. Natty knew firsthand that he'd always been pretty much of a bigot, but it must be worse than she thought for him to lose the Willard boys, his two best players.

"Of course you can play, and Zachary, too. I'm thrilled to have you, but you boys are going to have to brush up on your soccer skills. First practice is in a few weeks, and we got a game right away. So, come on, we'll walk down to the library and get you a couple of balls to take home and kick around." Natty looked at Mabel for consent.

"You kids go on ahead," said Mabel. "Natty, why don't you take Mr. Burden down there and show him that poor roof on your library? Maybe his big company might be able to plug up that hole for you. Cat can stay here with me." Natty looked at Charlie, but before she could say anything, Pie grabbed Charlie's hand and started pulling him toward the corner.

"C'mon, Charlie. I will show you our thoccer field."

Natty protested, "No, Pie, I'm sure Mr. Burden is too busy to—"

Charlie cut in. "No, it's okay. I'll take a look at your roof." Then he added, "And I'd love to see where my little pal plays soccer." If Charlie had been watching Natty's face, he would have seen a look of puzzlement at this stranger's affection for her son.

Emma and Sammy ran ahead, and Pie soon dropped Charlie's hand to try to catch up. Natty and Charlie crossed the street and walked down the sidewalk.

"So, what's this, punishment for you?" Natty asked. "Getting sent down here? New York City to Red Bone, West Virginia—that's got to be serious. Get caught diddlin' the boss's wife or something?"

Charlie laughed. "No, no. I volunteered, sort of. The company needed someone here, and OntAmex, our client, they wanted me. It's an important project, and—"

"I was just making a joke. I didn't mean to insult you or anything."

"I know," Charlie assured her. "Anyway, I'm not going to be here that long, maybe nine months. Then I'm going to China, to work on a big hydroelectric project."

"Wow, that sounds exciting. China. Jeez, I'm hoping to go to *Myrtle Beach* someday." They didn't speak again until they approached the small building at the end of the soccer field.

"This is the library? This little building here?" Charlie asked.

"Well, it's supposed to be a children's library, but a lot of the books got ruined by the water leaking in. Had to throw 'em away. I packed up the rest in some boxes and moved them to a dry spot. But you can't have kids sitting around in a wet, leaky building, reading books, so it's closed now. I don't know what we'll do with it. Probably nothing. Just wait for it to fall down." Then she added softly, "Like everything else around here."

She reached up over the metal door frame for the key. "Kids used to come in and read here or take the books home for a while. Then the damn roof started leaking and, well, you can see what a mess it is." Natty pushed open the door and flipped on the lights. A small puddle of water remained in the main room, but Charlie could tell from the watermarks at the base of the walls that the water had once covered the entire floor. The dropped ceiling had several panels missing, and most of the other panels were stained brown from rainwater.

"If we could just get the roof fixed, then we could get some new furniture, and some more books, and be back in business," Natty said hopefully. "I was going to get a computer so the kids could—well, that ain't going to happen." Natty went into an adjacent room crowded with maintenance supplies, a portable blackboard, and several wicker baskets full of athletics equipment. Hanging on a wall was a mesh-net bag of white soccer balls. She took it down and brought out two balls.

Charlie found an old wooden flagpole and used it to push up several ceiling panels to get a better look at the roof. Standing on the back of a long green plastic-covered couch, he pulled himself up into the rafters. Natty came back into the room and heard him climbing around in the roof trusses. She went outside and threw the balls down to the kids on the soccer field. When she returned, Charlie was coming down from the ceiling.

"Mr. Burden, you didn't have to do that. The roof ain't your problem." She watched while Charlie used some paper towels to wipe off his hands.

He had strong, muscular arms and a hard-looking chest under his T-shirt, a lot like Buck.

Charlie finished cleaning his hands and threw the paper towels in a cardboard box on the floor. "You need to rebuild the whole roof structure. The trusses are rotting, and the whole thing is sagging. Foot of snow up there in the winter and it'll cave in."

"Damn," she said dejectedly. "That sounds expensive."

"Well, it's more than a patch job." They went around to the back of the building and down a long flight of crumbling cement stairs to the soccer field. Emma and Sammy were playing keep-away from Pie, who ran around like a madman as they dribbled and kicked the ball back and forth. Pie had a big *happy face* on, and every few seconds he would check to see if Charlie was still watching him.

The field was overgrown with weeds, dandelions, and large patches of crabgrass. In front of the goal was a large indentation that was certain to be a foot-deep pond after a rainstorm. Across the field, Charlie could see several more depressions and some ruts made by water runoff. In Mamaroneck, the parents wouldn't have used the field for a parking lot.

Going back up the hill, Emma took off at a quick sprint, pursued closely by Sammy. Pie ran after them for a few yards but soon gave up the chase, his short legs no match for the hill or the other children. He fell into a labored hike a few yards in front of the adults.

Halfway up the hill, Charlie called out, "Say, Pie Man, how'd you like to make ten bucks and help me move my stuff up to the fourth floor?"

Natty looked at him with surprise. "You're moving in here? Alva Paine's apartment on the fourth floor?"

"I looked at it this morning. It's fine, and a lot closer to the project than Bluefield. The price is right, too." When Natty didn't answer, he asked, "Is there something wrong?"

"No, no. I'm just surprised, is all. That's good. That's good for Hank. He needs someone up there. I'm glad you're moving in here, Mr. Burden."

"You know Hank?" Charlie asked.

Natty smiled at him. "Damn, you still don't know where you are, do you, Mr. Burden? *Everybody knows everybody* in Red Bone." She looked up toward the fourth-floor porch. "Mr. Hankinson was my history teacher, two years in high school, before I got—before I left. He was the principal for a long time, too. Tried his best with me, but I guess I was beyond hope," she said with a laugh.

"Why did you—"

Natty cut him off. "Pie would be more than happy to help you move your stuff, and don't even think about giving him any money. That right, Pie Man?"

Continuing to trudge up the sidewalk, the boy pulled his pockets inside out, showing that he was penniless.

"Yeth, Mama," he called over his shoulder. "I help Charlie."

Charlie and Natty laughed. They could see that the boy was chuckling over his little joke. A few yards from the top of the hill, Natty winced when she heard the unmistakable sound of Buck's truck whining to make it up the hill behind her. She didn't turn to look. She didn't want to see Buck. Most of all, she didn't want this moment with the kind, considerate man from New York to end. And she certainly didn't want a scene with Buck, not with this outsider present. *Maybe he'll just drive by without stopping.*

The white pickup came to a rough stop a few yards farther up the hill, the front right tire jumping over the short stone curbing. Charlie was startled at first, but he could see from Natty's reaction that it was some-one she knew. Buck fixed Charlie briefly with a cold eye before turning to Natty and leaning over toward the open passenger window.

"C'mon, Nat. We need to talk. Get in." It was the apologetic voice that Buck could summon up when he needed it, but he was never able to mask the look in his eyes that said there was trouble rumbling just beneath the surface. Natty knew the look and didn't want to provoke any trouble. She stood still for a second, looking down at the ground, then walked toward the truck. She turned back to her son.

"Pie, you go help Mr. Burden move his things. I'll get you at Eve's later." She got into the truck and stared straight ahead as Buck roared away from the curb faster than he had to. Charlie watched the boy stare after the truck as it accelerated noisily away. The Pie Man didn't say any-thing. He just trudged more quickly up the hill, staying a little ways in front of Charlie.

AFTER A LONG afternoon touring the construction site with Terry Sum-mers, Charlie declined his invitation to dinner with some of the construction workers at a place called Moody's Roadhouse and returned to the apartment in Old Red Bone. The store and the restaurant were closed, and Main Street was deserted. Charlie suddenly felt quite alone as he hiked up the four flights of stairs.

On the kitchen table, wrapped in aluminum, was a large turkey pot pie still warm from the oven, with a note from Eve Brewster that read, *Welcome to West Virginia*, and, in parentheses, *P.S. This is Hank's favorite*. In the refrigerator was a homemade apple pie from Mabel Willard. Charlie rapped on the back door to his neighbor's apartment and invited Mr. Hankinson over for dinner and some cribbage.

After devouring a good portion of the turkey pie, the two men went out on the porch and took their chairs at the card table. Hank went over the stakes as Charlie admired the orange sunset, which cast a warm, comforting glow across the table. "We play for twenty dollars a game, plus a dollar a point, five for the high hand, double for a skunk." He looked up quickly to see if Charlie had any objections. The stakes seemed a little steep to Charlie, until he remembered the scorebook with the thousands of games and the running total.

Charlie won the first game and lost the next three. On a piece of scratch paper, Hank totaled up the damage. "That's fifty-eight dollars, my friend," said Hank, sounding pleased with himself. "Pay up."

The demand took Charlie by surprise. "What about the book?" he said.

"Oh, no," said Hank gruffly. "Last time I did that, the guy stiffed me for eleven hundred bucks." He stared at Charlie unflinchingly.

Charlie reached for his wallet. "Well, okay," he said, bewildered. "I guess we can do it like this." He thumbed out three twenties, then he looked up and saw Hank grinning through his white mustache.

"Gotcha there, Burden," the old man said, slapping the table loudly. He reached for the scorebook. "We'll put it on account and see how things go. May have to lower the stakes, if you're as lousy a player as you showed today."

"Don't worry about me, Hank," Charlie said, relieved that they wouldn't be playing for cash. He watched Hank write in the book that he and Alva Paine had shared for twenty-one years. Charlie thought he saw Hank sigh when he looked at the last page and wrote Charlie's name in place of Alva's at the top of the column. "You two played a lot of games, huh, Hank?"

"Lot of games," Hank said softly.

THAT NIGHT, CHARLIE called Ellen at the house in Warren, Vermont. Ellen and Linda Marchetti were making dinner for some people from the tennis tournament. Charlie could hear loud voices and sporadic laughter in the background. "Darling, how's everything in Virginia?" Ellen asked grandly, as if for the benefit of her guests. As always, she sounded full of life and in command.

"West Virginia. Red Bone, West Virginia," he corrected. He told her about the drive down, the apartment, and shopping for boots. "They have a Barney's here," he said.

"Oh, that's wonderful. You'll have somewhere to shop, then." She and Linda were playing in the finals of the tennis tournament the next morning, then driving down to Manchester for some outlet shopping and staying over at the Equinox. "You'll be up for Columbus Day weekend, darling? The foliage is going to be fabulous this year. And I've made the reservations in Aspen for Christmas." Ellen enjoyed playing for the crowd. Charlie visualized her waving a wineglass like an orchestra conductor's baton, head tilted back to air out her words.

"That's fine, Ellen. Shouldn't be a problem," said Charlie. He wished her luck in the tournament, and Ellen said something in reply that Charlie didn't catch but brought a laugh from her dinner guests. Then she clicked off.

CHAPTER 11

EIGHTEEN THOUSAND FEET OVER CENTRAL PENNSYLVANIA, A silver-and-black Gulfstream V flashed across the evening sky, heading for Toronto's Lester Pearson International Airport. Alone in the luxuriously appointed cabin, Jack Torkelson sat in one of the four beige leather captain's chairs. To his right was a communications console with two telephones and a fax machine. Torkelson sipped a mineral water and studied the rows of figures on the computer while he waited for the conference call to begin.

After a weekend at home in Georgetown, Torkelson was headed for his biweekly meeting with upper management, before heading back to the Washington office on Wednesday. Torkelson disliked having to spend time at the Toronto headquarters. He found dealing with the bright-eyed, simple-minded Canadians tedious at best and the time he spent north of the border an inefficient use of his time. He needed to be in Washington, the vortex of the global energy industry, not in the OntAmex boardroom, facing the overachieving Duncan McCord and his chief lieutenant, the roughneck Red Landon.

The phone buzzed softly, and Torkelson waited for the others to come on the line. Larry Tuthill joined first, from his hotel in Chicago, then Vernon Yarbrough, the lawyer, from his home in Charleston, and finally, from his apartment in Bluefield, West Virginia, Terry Summers of Dietrich Delahunt & Mackey. After the obligatory salutations, Torkelson got down to business. "So, Mr. Yarbrough, how did your meeting go with the judge?"

"Couldn't have been better. He'll make his ruling in November, and we'll have our variance for Redemption Mountain within a week. All according to plan—as long as Ackerly Coal has a deed for that pig farm. But, if DeWitt hasn't sold out by mid-November, the whole thing is off. The judge isn't going to make this an open-ended deal."

Larry Tuthill broke in. "Now tell Jack the good news, Vernon."

"What news?" Torkelson asked quickly.

The others could hear the tinkle of ice in Vernon Yarbrough's cocktail glass before he spoke. "Well, Jack, seems that we've got ourselves some leverage now. Should make that old pig farmer a little more receptive with regards to the magnanimous nature of our offer."

"What leverage?" Torkelson asked quietly, trying to hide his impatience. He held Southerners in about the same regard as he did Canadians, and Southern lawyers, with their sham degrees from country-club law schools like Vanderbilt and Duke, were barely tolerable.

The lawyer had a smile in his voice. "Now, Jack, what would you say if I told you that we've established firsthand that our favorite pig farmer, or more likely his grown son—Petey, they call him—has about half an acre of commercial grade, SWAT-team-ready, early-news-quality cannabis plants growing smack in the middle of his cornfield?"

Larry Tuthill laughed. He enjoyed Yarbrough's facility with words.

The lawyer continued. "*And* that son Petey, during his early adulthood, did a yearlong stretch at one of our fine penal institutions for a previous felony, which would be child's play compared to the time he'd face for a second offense of this magnitude—*if,* that is, someone were to bring the illicit herb garden to the attention of our county and state law-enforcement agencies."

Jack Torkelson couldn't suppress a wide smile. Finally they had the advantage over that unreasonable pig farmer who didn't care about money. This was better than money. This was family. "They're growing pot? In the cornfield?" He was genuinely amused.

"Yessir, and a nice healthy crop it is, too," Yarbrough responded. "Getting plenty of good sunshine up on that mountain."

"All right, that's good. But we don't use it unless we have to," said Torkelson.

"My thoughts exactly," replied Yarbrough. "Our judge is going to want to see that the farmer got a nice payday, so he can feel good about the whole thing. But now we got a mulligan to use if we need it."

"Good," said Torkelson. "Now, what about our cooling-pond problem?"

"We've got a date before the town planning board the third week in September," said Yarbrough. "We'll put together a first-rate presentation, plus we'll have representation from the governor's office, couple of state senators, and probably some county politicians, too."

"Don't worry, Jack, we'll get that done," added Larry Tuthill.

"Don't screw it up," Torkelson responded calmly. "Then take care of the pig farmer. Larry, keep me informed. Good night, gentlemen."

LATE IN THE afternoon, walking from the generator building to his office, Charlie glanced toward the main gate and saw a familiar figure riding his bike in circles just outside the gate. The boy didn't see Charlie, or maybe he didn't recognize him in his white hard hat until he neared the fence and called out to him, "Hey, Pie Man, get over here!"

The boy wheeled the bike around and pedaled to the open gate. "Hello, Charlie!" he said. "I am the Pie Man!" He held his hand up in the air for a high-five.

Charlie took the boy to the administration building and introduced him to the people working at the computers in the engineering room. The boy was amazed at the complex images dancing across the large-screen monitors. A young engineer lifted him up on a stool and showed him how to manipulate the mouse, moving trees and shrubs around the screen. Charlie watched as the boy's face scrunched up with glee or went slack with awe. As a new image came up on the screen, he pointed at the monitor and looked at Charlie with obvious pride. "Turbines," he said.

Charlie laughed as he looked at the screen. "Right you are, Pie Man, that's where the turbines are going."

The technician patted the boy's back. "Kid, you're a born engineer."

"Pie Man is an *engineer*," he said proudly, sliding off the stool. "I will be an engineer, like Charlie."

Charlie glanced at his watch. "Hey, I've got an idea, Pie. C'mon, let's go outside." On their way out, Charlie ducked into a storage room and came out with a brand-new white hard hat, which, after adjusting the fitting band, he placed ceremoniously on Pie's head. The boy's face couldn't have lit up brighter as he and Charlie walked through the site, headed toward the mammoth yellow and green vehicles. They finally stopped next to a huge yellow bulldozer. "Well, c'mon, Pie. Let's go!" said Charlie, scrambling up the ladder to the driver's compartment.

There was plenty of room for them on the wide seat, which was one reason Charlie had selected it. Another was the incredible noise it made when Charlie hit the starter button. Charlie laughed as he watched the expression of fear and excitement on the boy's face when the engine belched to life, puffs of black smoke exploding from the tall exhaust pipes.

"Hang on, Pie," he yelled, as he squeezed the handgrips and pulled on the levers that sent the heavy treads into action. The boy pressed in close against Charlie and squeezed the bar in front of him. They left the equipment yard and headed toward a large open area at the northern end of the site.

Charlie noticed a white pickup moving quickly toward them on Cold Springs Road. The truck slowed as it came abreast of them, then came to a complete stop in the middle of the road. As they drew even with the truck, Charlie recognized the cold stare from the angry-looking driver. Pie stared at the truck, his happy face gone. After a few seconds, the driver turned away and the white truck accelerated out of view.

Back at the equipment yard, Charlie turned off the engine. The sudden cessation of the noise and the vibration engulfed them in stillness. The boy took off his hard hat and looked at Charlie. "That was my papa in the truck."

"Is he going to be mad at you for being here?"

"No, Papa won't be mad. He won't be anything."

Charlie let it go. He liked the boy, but he didn't want to push his way into a family problem. Better to stay out of it. They sat quietly for a few moments before Charlie noticed tears in the boy's eyes.

"C'mon, Pie Man. What's that for?" Charlie asked.

The boy stared at his shoes. Finally he looked up and wiped his nose with the back of his hand. He glanced around at all the trucks and tractors that he'd played on so many times, alone at night after sneaking under the fence, then turned to Charlie. "Charlie, thith wath the betht day of my whole life."

Charlie ran his fingers through the boy's hair, then placed the hard hat back on his head, knocking it down tight with a rap of the knuckles, making the boy laugh. "C'mon, let's go get a soda."

DRIVING BACK INTO Old Red Bone as the falling sun cast its warm, comforting glow over the red-stone buildings, Charlie had an idea. On his cellphone, he called Hank and invited him over for dinner. Then he called Eve in the restaurant and asked her to pick up a box of spaghetti, some meat sauce, grated cheese, a loaf of bread, and a bottle of red wine before she closed.

"Sounds like a hot date." Eve was curious.

Charlie laughed. "No, just Hank, and I feel like spaghetti. That's all. Hey, Eve, why don't you come up, too?"

"No, you'd probably make me do the cooking, but, thanks for asking, Charlie. I'll leave the food on the stairway."

An hour later, Charlie and Hank sat out on the porch, drinking a glass of wine and enjoying the view of the setting sun while the spaghetti sauce simmered. A few minutes passed in silence. Then Hank asked, "Everything okay down at your power plant?"

"Oh, sure. Everything's fine, Hank," Charlie said, before deciding to broach the subject of the cooling pond. Hank might have some insight into how the members of the planning board would react. "We do have one problem coming up, though, that we're going to have to bring before the planning board. We're going to have to move the cooling pond to another area of the site because of the underlying rock strata."

"That's a problem?" Hank inquired.

"It's a significant change to the site plan, and the planning board has to okay it."

"Planning board, huh?"

"You know those fellows?" Charlie remembered the thin manila folder with the information about the board members that Larry Tuthill had passed to him at their meeting in New York. The file was still tucked away, unread, in Charlie's briefcase.

"I know 'em," said Hank. "Miserable pricks, all three of 'em." He rose out of his chair and went to the porch railing to spit a large gob of tobacco juice over the side. "Be lucky to get out of that meeting with your balls still in your pants. Disagreeable old hillbillies, and dumb as rocks, too."

"Really?" Charlie was alarmed at Hank's assessment. "This is an important variance and could be potentially a very expensive problem. If we can't move the pond, the project could shut down for months."

Hank shook his head. "Well, good luck with that bunch."

As they sat eating their spaghetti dinner at Charlie's small kitchen table, Charlie's thoughts returned to the Pie Man. "Hank, there's a kid I met out at the project the first day I got here, a kid with Down syndrome—"

"The Pie Man," said Hank, a wide smile coming across his face.

"That's him. The Pie Man. You know him?"

"Burden, let me tell you something," said Hank, shoveling another forkful of spaghetti into his mouth. "That kid's going to be governor of this state someday. An amazing kid."

"He sure is," Charlie agreed.

"O' course, to my mind, he won't be the first retarded governor we ever had, not by a long shot."

Charlie laughed. "He came by the site today. I took him for a ride on one of the big machines. He had a good time." He paused, then added, "So did I." After a few quiet moments, Charlie said, "I met his mother, too, last weekend, down in the store."

"Natty Oakes," said Hank.

"She's got a funny sense of humor. Nice woman, seems like."

"Nice, hell. Woman's a damn saint. Works like a dog, too, takin' care of the old people all over McDowell County. Home nurse kind of job. Takes care of two old miners across the street, she don't even get paid for anymore."

"How's that?"

"Woody and Mr. Jacks. You've seen them probably, down in the restaurant. Eve don't charge 'em even half price."

"Pie says she works a lot," said Charlie.

"All the time. Works in the elementary school, too," Hank replied. "She's a runner, like you."

Charlie was surprised. "Is that right?"

"Comes up the hill every morning, rain or shine. I'm surprised you

ain't seen her. Ain't a bad-lookin' woman, either." Charlie didn't comment. "When she cleans herself up and does something with her hair,"
Hank continued, "and don't dress like some Raggedy Ann doll. Little too
skinny, though."

"She's got pretty eyes, anyway," said Charlie, trying to avoid the subject.

"Beautiful eyes," said Hank.

Charlie refilled their glasses with wine. "What about her husband,
Pie's father? We saw him today, and he and the boy didn't even wave."

Hank pushed his plate away and took his time wiping his mouth,
mustache, and beard with his napkin. "He's a bum. Drunk most of the
time. He's bad news, Buck Oakes. Stay away from him."

"The kid said he was a football star in college."

Hank shifted around in his chair so he could see the last vestiges of
the orange sun drop behind the mountains. "Buck played some football,
all right," Hank said, taking a sip of wine and pausing to recall some far-
off memories.

"Source of all his problems, football. Buck Oakes was about the most
famous football player there ever was at Red Bone High. Set all kinds of
records as a running back. Played linebacker, too. I was still principal at
the high school then.

"He was fast and strong—and cocky. Handsome devil, too, with
black curly hair and a smile like a damn movie star. The girls were crazy
about him.

"Football was also his daddy's sport. Big Frank Oakes, one of those
blowhard Notre Dame fans, made it known to everyone that Buck was
going to get a full scholarship to play for the Fighting Irish. Talked it up
so big that everyone around here believed it, including the kid. It was
Notre Dame for him, and then the pros.

"Then, toward the end of his junior year, Buck had a real unfortunate
thing happen to him. He had one of those rare games that becomes a
legend, you know? A game so big that it distorts reality. It was against a
team from up in Wyoming County, kind of a weak team as I recall, but it
didn't matter. Buck scored six touchdowns, couple of 'em on kickoff
returns, and ran for about three hundred yards. Had a few interceptions
on defense. Well, it was a big deal in the sports pages all over the state.

Charleston sent TV crews down here. Buck even got his picture in that little column in *Sports Illustrated*, I forget what it's called."

"'Faces in the Crowd,'" said Charlie.

"That's it. But the game was a fluke. It happens sometimes. He was never as good as that game. Anyway, his last couple of games, college scouts were all over Red Bone, and Buck did okay. Had a couple of decent games and got a lot of interest from the recruiters. Started getting letters from all over the country. He'd bring 'em into school and toss 'em around and talk about Notre Dame being the only team good enough to get him and all that cocky rubbish.

"So Buck spends the summer before his senior year drinking and partying and he puts on some weight and slows down a little. Scouts stop coming around about halfway through the season, 'cause they seen enough, and Big Frank goes into a panic 'cause there's nothing from Notre Dame and nothing from Penn State, which would have been their second choice. In fact, there's hardly any interest at all from the big-time schools. No Ohio State or Michigan. Big Frank calls up Notre Dame, and they tell him they never heard of his son.

"Finally, Big Frank, who had some political connections 'cause of his county job, and the football coach at the high school, they get together at the last minute and get to somebody at WVU, and Buck gets a one-year scholarship, renewable if he makes the team.

"So Buck goes up to Morgantown, still cocky as ever, thinkin' he should really be at Notre Dame or Penn State and everything's going to be that much easier at a place like WVU, 'cause it's a couple of pegs down from where he belongs."

From his experience with college athletics, Charlie could guess what was coming. "And Buck found out it was tougher than he thought, right?"

"As I heard it, first week on the practice field, Buck got run over like he ain't never got run over before. Welcome to big-time football. Those boys were all bigger and faster, lifting weights all summer long, while Buck was lifting sixteen-ounce Budweisers. Buck took a beating—physically and psychologically—he ain't never recovered from. Come back down here and been a fuckup ever since. Permanent chip on his shoulder. Still telling some story about getting injured at practice and the university screwing him. Pure bullshit," Hank said. "Been nothing but trouble for a lot of people ever since."

Hank rose to his feet in the dark kitchen. "Thanks for the spaghetti, Burden. Too late for cribbage now. I've got some reading to do." He went to the rear door, limping slightly on his stiff legs. With his hand on the screen, he turned back to Charlie. When he spoke, there was sadness in his voice.

"Buck Oakes never wanted a kid. He didn't want to be married, but he got Natty pregnant, and Big Frank was disgusted with him so he made him marry her. And he *sure* didn't want the kid he got, so Buck's just pretty much ignored him his whole life."

Hank stood in the doorway, silhouetted by the light-gray evening sky. "You know, Buck Oakes's 'bout the luckiest man in McDowell County, and he . . . he don't know a thing about it. Damn ignorance," Hank growled. "Good night, Burden."

"'Night, Hank." After cleaning up the dishes, Charlie went over to the rolltop desk and opened one of his stuffed briefcases. Hank's ominous opinion of the planning board bothered him. He searched through the folders for the one in Larry Tuthill's nearly illegible handwriting: *Planning Board*. The file was in the middle of the briefcase, next to another thin folder marked *DeWitt*. It was the background information on the farmer. Charlie placed both folders on the desk.

He opened the *Planning Board* folder and stared incredulously at the first document, an eight-by-ten copy of a black-and-white photograph, an enlargement of a newspaper clipping. Charlie looked at the caption at the bottom for confirmation: *The Red Bone planning board convened its quarterly meeting last week at the high school.*

Charlie stared at the three men seated at what looked like a school cafeteria table, each with a nameplate in front of him. He stared at the picture for a few more moments, then shook his head slowly and smiled. Holding the picture up to the light, he began to laugh as he focused on the center figure, with the familiar white handlebar mustache and long goatee. The sign in front of Hank read, PULLMAN J. HANKINSON, and, under his name, CHAIRMAN. Charlie looked at the caption again: . . . *seated are Burt Fitch, P. J. Hankinson, and Bobby Hagerman.*

"Miserable pricks, all three of 'em," Charlie said out loud, still chuck-ling. *Welcome to West Virginia, Burden,* he thought. He picked up the folder marked *DeWitt.* Curious, he opened it to find another grainy enlargement.

It was a newspaper photo of three people: an older woman, a man in the middle, who was obviously the farmer, Bud DeWitt, and, next to him, a tall, gangly younger man. The caption beneath the picture read, *Alice, Bud, and Petey DeWitt of Redemption Mountain, enjoying the McDowell County Fair.* All three wore taciturn expressions. Bud DeWitt had the hard, weathered look of a man who'd engaged in physical labor his whole life. He wore what appeared to be a brand-new baseball cap with a PETERBILT logo on the front.

The second sheet in the folder appeared to be a graduation picture. This was a professionally done glossy color print of a stunningly beauti-ful young woman. She had light blue eyes and a relaxed, natural smile that showed perfect white teeth. Long blond hair, parted in the middle, and the heavy eye makeup and pink lip gloss had the unmistakable look of the sixties. The back of the picture read, *Sarah Carlson DeWitt, b. 1946, Waukesha, WI, wife of Thomas DeWitt (deceased, 1977), high school graduation picture, 1964.*

Charlie turned the picture over again and stared at the face. It seemed so familiar. He shook his head and tossed the picture back into the file and went to bed.

CHAPTER 12

IT WAS NEARLY 6:30 P.M. WHEN NATTY FINALLY PULLED UP IN FRONT of the Olander Legal Clinic in Welch. Through the large storefront windows, she could see the lawyer pacing, his hands in his pockets. He had reluctantly agreed to stay until 6:00 p.m., the soonest she could get into Welch.

Ted Olander greeted Natty with an impatient smile and ushered her into his cramped office. He was in his midforties, slightly overweight, and well dressed in a charcoal suit with suspenders. He glanced at his watch as he took his chair behind the desk and pulled a yellow legal pad in front of him. "Now, Miss . . . Mrs. Oakes? What can I do for you?"

"It's Mrs., and I need some legal advice about coal mining."

"Coal mining," the lawyer said, dropping his pencil on the pad. He'd made a quick assumption, watching her get out of the car, that her concern would be of a domestic nature.

"Yes, sir. Coal mining, specifically mountaintop-removal mining on Redemption Mountain." She told him about her grandparents' farm, the recent activity of the surveyors, and about Bud's suspicions regarding the OntAmex deal with Ackerly Coal. She described the offer to buy the farm for considerably more than it was worth. At this, Olander showed a flicker of interest and made a quick notation. "So, Mr. Olander, what can we do to stop this? And what would it cost?"

Olander was speechless for several seconds. Finally, a thin smile crept across his face. "I'm sorry, Mrs. Oakes. I don't mean to make light of your situation, but let me give you some advice." Olander leaned forward, his elbows on the desk. "Ackerly Coal is a huge company, one of the largest coal producers in the world. It's owned by Continental Electric Systems, which is probably fifty times bigger than Ackerly. And OntAmex—which, incidentally, is in the process of buying up Continental—is probably a hundred times bigger than Continental. It's one of the biggest energy companies in the world." He paused to let his words sink in.

"Mrs. Oakes, if these companies want to mine coal on Redemption Mountain, there's nothing you or your grandpa or anyone else can do to stop them, because OntAmex and Ackerly will have the county, state, and federal government in their pocket. And the OntAmex plant in Red Bone is a real bonanza for the state and McDowell County. It's a billion-dollar plant, with millions of dollars in tax revenue and spin-off economic activity. The state lobbied real hard to get OntAmex to build here instead of over in Kentucky or in Virginia, so you can just bet that the OntAmex Company got everything they wanted."

Olander looked at his watch and proceeded to wrap things up. "Now, in answer to your question about cost, you'd need one of the big Charleston firms—New York or Washington would be better, but one of the Charleston outfits could do it. The cost would probably be in the area of five million over the two, three, four years it would go on, somewhere in that ballpark." He waited a few moments, then stood, indicating that he needed to leave. As he put on his jacket, he added, "In the end, Mrs. Oakes, you'd lose. You could win all the legal battles, but eventually they'll carve up Redemption Mountain and take their coal." He glanced at his watch again, then at Natty. "Way it's always been here."

Natty sat for a few seconds, then replied to the lawyer, "So what you're saying is that we got a real good case here." She grinned as she got up from her chair. Olander smiled with relief when he saw she was making a joke. He walked her toward the front door and spoke in a quiet voice, as if he didn't want to be overheard.

"Mrs. Oakes, the thing you have to realize is that these utility and coal guys—they're a tough bunch. They're not like regular businesspeople. They're cutthroats in fine suits. They've been fighting the unions and the regulators and each other for so long, they're used to it. Hell, they enjoy it. It's what they do—hire big law firms, buy politicians and judges, run over people, and mostly they get their own way. You don't want to go up against a company like Ackerly or OntAmex. Tell your grandpa to sell. Get a good price and sell, 'cause in the end, those boys aren't going to play fair."

When she was gone, Ted Olander locked the front door and returned to his office. He'd done his best for the woman from Red Bone, given her some damn fine legal advice—*gratis*. Now maybe he could score a few points for himself. He thumbed through the large Rolodex on his desk and pulled out the card for Kerns & Yarbrough. He didn't expect to reach anyone in the office at 7:00 P.M., but he wanted to leave a voice mail to see what kind of interest it might generate. "I've received an inquiry from the granddaughter of a farmer on Redemption Mountain in McDowell County, concerning a possible surface mine by Ackerly Coal. Call me in the morning at . . ."

Driving as fast as she dared, the front end of her car shaking noticeably, Natty headed south out of Welch on Route 103. She would take the new road around the power plant. It bothered her that she'd be the one getting home late, because Buck had been good all week, working at the temporary cement job and coming home early without stopping off anywhere. She knew it wouldn't last—they'd been through these make-up periods before—but she needed to make it last as long as possible. They had such little good time together.

Thinking about Buck reminded her of the previous Saturday, the day that had started out so enjoyably in Eve's store, laughing to tears over that silly joke with Pie and Charlie Burden, who was so nice to her son. Then the walk down to the soccer field with Emma and Sammy and Pie—so proud of his new friend. She and Charlie chatting like two teenagers, and him taking an interest in her library. Then the irresponsible, exhilarating, erotic episode in Buck's truck—which filled her with a level of guilt she hadn't felt for a long time.

She was still livid with Buck, but she had no choice but to get in his truck. Buck had sped away from the curb. In the truck's side-view mirror, Natty stole a peek at Pie and Charlie, watching from the sidewalk. Buck drove for a mile before he spoke. He tried to sound contrite, but it was a hard role for him to play. Natty knew he felt bad about hitting her, but he was never very good at apologizing.

"Nat, I'm sorry about smackin' you last night. I wasn't thinking. You know I'd never want to hurt you. I was drunk, and I was pissed off about stuff, and, well, that ain't never gonna happen again." Natty was silent.

Buck had driven north on Mountain Road, then turned off on an old logging road that ran through dense forest. "So, who was that guy you and the kid was walking with? Huh? Never seen him before. Nat?" She didn't answer. "Nat, I *asked* you, who was that guy?"

Natty could feel his anger growing. "He's nobody, Buck. He's just the new power-plant guy. Took Hugo Paxton's place. He took a look at the library, see how bad the roof is, that's all."

"The guy from New York? The construction guy?" Buck shot a glance over at her. "That's good, Nat—you gettin' friendly with that guy. That's *real* good."

They rode for several minutes before Natty spoke again. "Buck, that was the last time. You can't hit me no more, ever."

"Nat, I swear—"

Natty cut him off. "And you can't see that woman in Northfork. You got to choose. If you go again, don't you ever come back to me. I mean it, Buck."

"Aw, Nat, that's done with. It's over. That gal was just an itch I had to scratch. She don't mean nothin' to me."

Natty drew in a quick breath to combat the sick feeling that engulfed her with the confirmation of Buck's latest infidelity. She had known it was true the moment Wayne Lester said it, but it felt different, like a kick in the stomach, coming from Buck's own lips. Tears filled her eyes. *What else was there to say? What the hell was she even doing here, trying to make her marriage work? Did she really love Buck, or was she just another ignorant hillbilly with nowhere else to go?* She blinked and leaned toward the open window to let the breeze dry her tears.

"Remember this place, Nat?" Buck had made a sharp turn off the logging road, and they bumped down a narrow dirt road.

She looked up. "I remember, Buck." They would come down this road to where it ended in a small clearing, surrounded by thick trees, where no one would ever see them. This was where Natty learned about sex. Where she learned to bear the pain and the embarrassment and to pretend it was good. And, later, to enjoy it without reservation and take pride in her ability to satisfy Buck. They'd come to their spot two or three times a week the summer following Natty's junior year.

In the beginning, they'd come after going to the movies or a dance or a party. Later on, as Buck began to lose interest in hanging around with Natty's friends, he would pick her up and they'd come straight to the woods. Most times, he'd had a good deal to drink before he picked her up, and gradually their time spent in the front seat got shorter and shorter. Toward the end, Buck would turn off the truck and they'd crawl over the seat and get right to it. It wasn't how she wanted it, but she treasured every moment with Buck, and if sex was all they had, that's what she would take. It ended in September, when she went back to school for her senior year and found out she was two months' pregnant. The thought of coming back never came up after that.

The clearing was still there at the end of the road, but the trees and the bushes now left barely enough room to squeeze by in the wide pickup. Buck turned off the engine and pulled on the brake. Natty gazed through the windshield at the light-green canopy that enveloped them like a bubble. She felt cool and dark and protected. Through the open window, she could smell the earthy aroma of the woods, and it filled her with nostalgia for that brief season, thirteen years ago, when she had Buck so completely to herself. And now they were in the truck, in the woods, alone again.

She shouldn't be here, not today, not with Buck, after what he did. Why was she letting this happen? She knew where he was going when he turned down the logging road. She gazed out the window and let her mind drift back to the morning, and thought about Charlie Burden. *They were alone in the library after Charlie had looked at the roof. The kids had gone back up the hill and the door was locked. They were only a yard apart in the dimly lit room.*

Buck adjusted the bench seat back as far as it would go, then slid over next to Natty. She felt his arm around her shoulders, pulling her closer. He tossed her Spider-Man cap onto the dashboard and reached up with both hands to take the elastic out of her ponytail, letting her hair partially cover her face. He ran his fingers over her face as he brought his mouth to her cheek and whispered, "Nat, I ain't been much of a husband lately. I'm gonna make it up to you."

She closed her eyes and leaned back. Buck's left hand was on her thigh, rubbing gently up and down from her knee. *She felt a stirring inside and took a deep breath. She moved forward and reached both hands under Charlie's T-shirt, feeling his ribs and the muscles on his chest and shoulders, as he pulled his shirt over his head. He caressed her neck, then held her face gently with both hands. He kissed her forehead lightly and then, slowly, her left cheek. Very softly, he said her name, then pulled her chin up and kissed her fully on the mouth.*

Natty turned to Buck and opened her mouth to his, their tongues pressing warmly against each other. She put her hand on top of Buck's and pulled it over to her crotch as she slid down in the seat, stretching out her legs. Buck pulled her to him as she spread her legs. With her right hand, she unhooked her belt and the button of her blue jeans. *She kissed Charlie wetly on the mouth and pushed him down on the couch. She ran her hands over his chest as she worked her way down to the zipper of his khaki shorts. His eyes were closed, and his mouth opened as Natty pulled off his shorts. She straddled his hips with her knees and straightened up as she pulled her still-buttoned shirt up over her head. Charlie's hands clasped her small waist and moved up her rib cage to the front of her bra, releasing her breasts.*

Natty felt herself being lifted and spun, her left shoulder glancing hard off the steering wheel. She opened her eyes to see Buck, his blue jeans rolled down to his knees, working at pulling down his shorts. He put both hands under her small buttocks and pulled her up toward him. The contrition was gone from his voice. "This is what you like, Nat, huh," he groaned. "This is what keeps you coming back," he whispered, as he pushed himself deep inside her.

Natty reached over her head with both hands and held on to the frame of the door. She closed her eyes. "Yeah, Buck," she finally managed to say, "that's what I like." She bit her lower lip and hid her tears.

ON THE RIDE back to Red Bone, Buck prattled on about some new scheme that he was cooking up with Roy Hogan. Natty had heard it all before—the enthusiasm for a half-baked idea that would soon turn to nothing—and remained quiet. She was preoccupied with what had just happened and was trying to rationalize her guilt. It wasn't about the sex. Lord knows, she was feeling randy enough to deserve a good lay from her husband, even if she was pissed at him. No, it was about fantasizing about another man when she was with Buck. That had never happened to her before, and it was a strange, uncomfortable feeling. *Here she was, fantasizing about a man who most likely didn't even remember her name. In a short time he'd be gone, and he sure as shit wouldn't remember much about the time he spent in Red Bone, West Virginia. But Buck would still be here. He'd always be here. And so would she.*

Buck slid to a stop in front of Barney's General Store. Natty tucked the ends of her white shirt into her blue jeans and tried to brush back her unruly hair with her fingers. "So, Nat, we're okay," said Buck, "right? I'll see you at home later on?" Natty shut the door of the truck and gave her husband a thin smile.

"Sure, Buck," she said, "we're great." She turned and walked up to the front of the store, hearing the familiar sound of Buck's truck speeding away.

From the vestibule, she could see Cat in the restaurant, seated on a counter stool with an ice cream cone, swinging her legs while she watched Pie and Charlie Burden in a nearby booth. They were playing some kind of game, and she could hear the glee in her son's voice and see the genuine affection Charlie had for Pie.

"Oooh, Charlie almotht get a touchdown." Pie was on his knees on the bench, squirming about excitedly. Natty moved into the doorway, content to watch for a few moments. They were flicking a packet of sugar back and forth across the table. Pie must have scored. He leaped up, shouting, "Touchdown, Michigan!" Charlie laughed and was giving him a high-five when he saw Natty in the doorway. He smiled and said something to Pie, who wheeled around excitedly.

"Mama, Charlie and me play sugar-bag football. Mama, come thee."

Cat jumped off her stool and ran over to her mother. Natty stayed where she was. She didn't want to go into the restaurant. She suddenly felt exhausted and didn't want to get into a conversation with Charlie Burden—not right then.

"Come on, Pie, we need to get going. We've already imposed on Mr. Burden enough," she said.

Charlie stayed seated in the booth as he watched Natty in the doorway. If she wanted to keep her distance, he would respect that. As Pie walked over to her, Charlie noticed how different she looked from the first two times he'd seen her. The baseball cap was gone and her hair was down, falling unevenly to her shoulders. The man's white shirt was now tucked into her blue jeans, the belt pulled tight at her small waist. As she gazed back at Charlie with a tired smile, hands in her pockets, the effect was dramatic. Without any effort or awareness, she could have been a model, posing for a leisure-clothing ad in *Vanity Fair*.

As the children went out through the doorway, Natty lingered for a moment, still looking at Charlie. Finally, she straightened up and mouthed a silent *thank-you*. Charlie nodded and watched her walk out toward the store.

NATTY ALMOST DROVE past the turnoff from Cold Springs Road. It was cool and dark on the smooth new road that ran along the boundary of the OntAmex site. Far up on the hills, the trees reflected the deep orange glow of the setting sun. Natty had to turn on her headlights to follow the road, which had no guardrails or painted lines to navigate by.

Trying to make good time, Natty leaned forward and kept a firm grip on the shimmying steering wheel. As the Accord rounded a bend, the shimmy in the front end suddenly stopped, and Natty felt the steering wheel go slack. The car bucked, listed forward, then screeched along the pavement, out of control. Sparks flew up around the right fender before the car slid to a stop, a few feet from a drainage ditch. Afraid the car might catch fire, Natty quickly turned off the ignition, gathered up her purse and client files, and yanked her equipment bag from the backseat. She put her things down on the road, then went back to inspect.

CHARLIE BURDEN WAS about halfway through his second lap around the power plant. He ran another two hundred yards before he heard a car door slam on the road ahead.

"Damn piece of shit car. Fucking cars!"

When Charlie rounded the bend, the air smelled of burned metal and rubber. The old Honda was parked on the shoulder of the road, listing awkwardly to the right. Charlie stopped.

"Hello. Is anyone there?" He walked toward the car and saw a head pop up in front of the hood. He didn't recognize Natty until she spoke.

"That you, Mr. Burden?"

"Oh, hello, Mrs. Oakes. I heard someone, uh, yelling, but I didn't recognize your voice."

"Sorry—nice mouth, huh?" She laughed. "I didn't know anyone was around."

"What happened to your car? Smells like something's burning," Charlie said, as he walked around to the front of the car.

"Think maybe I got a flat tire."

Charlie leaned out over the drainage ditch and saw that the right front wheel had broken off at the axle and was lodged under the frame of the car. Metal shards were visible at the end of the axle, and brake fluid was leaking into the sand. Charlie couldn't help letting out a laugh when he saw the extent of the damage. Natty Oakes, he was beginning to understand, had a most amusing gift for understatement.

"What's so funny? It's a flat tire, right?" she asked, smiling.

"No, it's a lot worse than that," Charlie answered. "The whole wheel came off."

"Aw, man, that doesn't sound good. Shit. I don't need this right now." A troubled look came over her face, as she realized she would have another bill she couldn't afford.

Charlie wished he hadn't laughed. "You're going to need a tow truck. Is there a garage you can call? We can use the phone in the office," he said, gesturing toward the power plant. Natty stood in the road, looking at her car, shaking her head in disgust.

"Damn. I got a lot of clients to see tomorrow. Friday's a busy day for me." She started toward her things lying in the road. "I can call Gus Lowe. He's got a tow truck. If I can use your phone, I'll call home and get a ride."

Charlie took Natty's equipment bag and slung it over his shoulder while she gathered up her files, and they started off up the road toward the main gate.

"Car's only got two hundred fifty thousand miles on it," Natty said, with a quick glance back at the Honda. "You'd think you'd get at least three hundred before the damn wheels started falling off."

Charlie smiled. He enjoyed Natty's sense of humor. Eve Brewster was right—nothing bothered her sister-in-law for too long.

"If you're stuck, you can use my car for a few days," Charlie offered, looking down at her. He could use Hugo Paxton's Navigator, which was still parked at the condo in Bluefield. "The company has an extra truck," he added.

The offer didn't seem to register right away. "Huh? I'm sorry. What did you say?"

"I said you could take my car for a few days, if you need to," Charlie replied.

Natty looked at him curiously. "You'd let me use your car? Why would you do that? You hardly even know me."

Charlie laughed. "Hey, don't you know, everybody knows everybody in Red Bone?"

Natty smiled at Charlie's imitation of her. "Thanks, anyway, but I couldn't do that. I'll find another car somewhere," she said.

Charlie let it pass. "Pie came by the plant this afternoon," he said. "He comes by every day, late in the afternoon."

"That's all he talks about now. I heard all about the ride you gave him on the tractor."

"Bulldozer," Charlie corrected.

"If he's being a pest, I'll tell him to stop," Natty said earnestly.

Charlie smiled. "No, he's not a pest. Everyone in the office loves it when he comes in. He's funny. He's a great kid. He really is." Charlie wanted to tell her how much he looked forward to the Pie Man's visits now that he'd gotten to know the boy so well. He wanted to tell her about the vacuum in his life since his own kids left home, but he knew that would sound strange.

They walked a ways down the dark road before Charlie brought up a subject that he'd been thinking about since he first met Pie. "I was wondering how Pie got that name, the Pie Man. Once you get used to it, it seems really natural, but—"

"Still, a pretty stupid name for a kid, I know. It ain't really much of a story," she said.

"If I'm being too nosy, just . . ."

Natty thought for a moment before responding. "Truth is, Mr. Burden, you're all Pie talks about these days. You're about the only adult man that's ever given that boy the time of day, including his father. 'Course it's your business."

"I was curious."

"First, it probably helps to know that his real name is Boyd," Natty said with a chuckle. "How's that for a handle? Makes *Pie Man* sound pretty smooth, don't it?" They both laughed.

"Well, one day when Pie was almost five, I asked Buck to read to him from a big nursery-rhyme book that Pie loved. It was a mistake. Buck was in a shitty mood, but he surprised me and said okay. It was the first time he ever put Pie on his lap and tried to read to him, 'cause Buck, he don't read too well for one thing, and, second, he never paid much attention to Pie from the beginning, 'cause . . . Well, that's another story.

"Anyway, Buck opens the book to Simple Simon, which Pie knows by heart, 'cause we read it so many times. And Buck starts reading, 'Simple Simon met a Pie Man,' and he stops and points to the picture, and he says to Pie, 'That's you, kid, the simpleton, Simple Simon, the retard,' and he keeps saying it, even though Pie don't know what the hell he means. I tell Buck to quit it, and he starts yellin' at me, and I'm yellin' at him, and all of a sudden, Pie jabs his finger at the picture and yells, 'No, I am the Pie Man, I am the *Pie Man*,' 'til Buck and I shut up. Then Buck pushes him off his lap onto the floor. He stomps out, and Pie just sits there with that stubborn look on his face—I'm sure you've seen it."

Natty took a deep breath. She'd never told the real story to anyone. She'd always told the sugar-coated version—that Pie really liked the picture in the book and started saying, "I am the Pie Man, I am the Pie Man." Now she'd told the truth to this near-stranger. Damn, why hadn't she just given Charlie Burden the *storybook* version?

Charlie was waiting for her to continue. "I picked him up and put him on my lap, and he looks at me and says again, 'I am the Pie Man.' It was strange, because it was like the first time he'd made some kind of decision . . . the first time he'd shown that he was really thinking about something, you know? It's a weird name and everything, but it was *his* decision, and it was the first sort of intelligent thing he ever said, after the usual baby-talk stuff. So I said to him, 'Yes, you are the Pie Man,' and that's what he's called himself ever since. That's all *anyone* around here calls him, even in school. I don't think he even *remembers* the name Boyd." They rounded a bend and could see a light shining on the administration building. In another few minutes, they'd be at the front gate.

"Pretty pathetic story, huh, Mr. Burden? Welcome to West Virginia, right?"

"No," Charlie answered. "It isn't at all," he said, trying to sound understanding.

"Listen, Mr. Burden, don't think too poorly about my husband. I probably shouldn't have told you that story, but you've been real special to Pie, and . . ." Natty gazed up at the hills as she arranged the words in her mind. "This is a hard place to live. I mean, I love it here, and I could never live anywhere else. But *there's a lot of heartache in these mountains.* That's what my grandma Alice always says, and it's true. And I think it's harder for a man. It's not an easy place to make a living, with the coal mining mostly gone. That takes a lot out of a man. . . ." Her voice faded. "Getting trapped here and not being able to support a family."

They walked in silence for a few moments, then it was time to change the subject. "Hey, I'm sorry to spoil your run," said Natty. "It's a nice night for a run, too."

"That's okay. I already did a lap around the plant. I usually run in the morning, but I had an early meeting."

"That's when I run," said Natty.

"That's what Hank said."

"I go through Old Red Bone about six-thirty and see Hank out on your back porch most days, having his tea. Sometime I'll show you my course. It's about five and a half miles through the woods, on a trail along the south side of Red Bone Mountain."

"I'd like that," said Charlie. "How about Monday?"

"Um, Monday?" She hesitated. Natty knew she'd made a mistake, and now she was stuck. She hadn't meant to invite Charlie Burden to go running. *What was she thinking?*

"I'll watch for you from the porch around six-thirty, and I'll meet you in front of the store. Don't worry, I won't hold you up too much," Charlie added with a laugh.

Natty couldn't find a polite way out. "Sure, we could do that. I'll look for you on Monday."

Once they were inside the gate, Natty conceded that it made more sense to let Charlie drive her home than for her to call for a ride. She was mesmerized by all the lights and gauges on the Lexus's dashboard, the soft leather seats, and the feeling of quiet luxury in the car. She'd never ridden in a car so new or so expensive.

Charlie drove slowly on the dark, narrow access road through the woods and out to South County Road. When they approached the intersection, Natty said, "Take a right here, and go about a half mile—"

Charlie suddenly stopped the car in the middle of the road and pulled on the emergency brake. He left the engine running, opened the driver's door, and got out and instructed Natty to get out, too.

"What are you going to do now, kill me?" she asked.

Charlie laughed. "No. I'm going to finish my run, and you're going to take my car until you get yours fixed," he said, stuffing his wallet and keys into a Velcro fanny pack.

"No, c'mon, I can't do this," Natty protested.

"You need a car tomorrow; I don't," Charlie replied.

"But I can't drive this. Please, Mr. Burden, I don't—"

"It's just like a Honda. Put it in gear and go. Don't worry about it. I'll see you Monday." He loped off at an easy gait and disappeared into the dark.

Natty glanced at her watch. It was past nine o'clock. She walked around the car, got into the driver's seat, and shut the door. It took her a few seconds to figure out how to use the electric seat adjustment so she could reach the pedals. She pulled the steering wheel down to a comfortable position, then played with the accelerator to get a feeling for the smooth, powerful engine. As she looked over the gauges and the luxurious interior, she bit her lower lip. How the hell was she going to explain this one to Buck? she wondered, as she shifted into drive and headed west toward Oakes Hollow.

CHAPTER 13

OVER THE WEEKEND A LATE-SUMMER HEAT WAVE HAD SETTLED over the mountains like a blanket. The air conditioners in the administration building hummed at full power at nine o'clock in the morning. Charlie would spend a couple of hours reading and answering his emails, as he usually did on Monday mornings. He opened a message from Ellen. Her realtor had called to tell her that the owner of the Dowling Farms house had lowered the price and that there was some new interest, so they would need to make a decision soon. Ellen added that Jennifer would be home from Evanston the last week of the month and would head back to school on Labor Day weekend, so she hoped Charlie could get back to Mamaroneck for a few days.

Charlie knew that Ellen would be pushing hard to close the deal when he went home. He skipped over a dozen messages from the New York office that he knew would involve inquiries about the projects that he'd been working on before leaving for West Virginia. Then he opened a message entitled *Redemption Mountain,* from Larry Tuthill.

It said that Vernon Yarbrough and Kevin Mulrooney from Ackerly Coal would arrive by helicopter on Thursday morning to accompany C. Burden to a meeting with B. DeWitt to reach an agreement on the purchase of the Redemption Mountain farm. It was followed with the notation, *This is a highest-priority meeting.* Charlie replied to all that he would be available to attend the meeting.

After a few more emails, his mind drifted back to earlier that morning and his exhilarating run along the side of Red Bone Mountain with Natty Oakes. It was an experience he couldn't wait to repeat.

Charlie had been stretching in front of the store as Natty rounded the corner. "Morning, Mr. Burden," she said, without slowing down. Charlie noticed that she didn't seem to be breathing overly hard from the run uphill.

"Good morning, Mrs. Oakes," Charlie replied, as he fell in beside her. He found the pace a little quick for five miles.

"How's your car?" asked Charlie.

"I got rid of it." Natty had a mischievous twinkle in her eyes. "I don't need it anymore. Got a new Lexus," she added, smiling at Charlie. "It'll be ready tomorrow. Is that okay?" *The car would be ready, but how she'd handle the $580 bill at Gus Lowe's garage was another story.*

"That's fine," said Charlie, as Natty veered right and headed for a field of high weeds and scrub bushes.

"Come on. I'll show you what heaven is like for a runner," she said, turning her head back toward Charlie. He followed her up a narrow dirt path across the small field, over a set of railroad tracks, and into the woods. They ran single file for a hundred yards until suddenly the tree line ended, revealing a spectacular view of the rugged southern slope of Red Bone Mountain.

The view was breathtaking, as was the sheer drop-off just a few yards from the trail's edge. Natty looked back to catch Charlie's reaction. "Great, isn't it?" she called back, partially to alleviate his anxiety.

"It's beautiful," he answered.

"The trail's fine, but you have to watch your step in a few places. Just follow me."

"I'm right behind you," replied Charlie, a little nervously. But the trail quickly leveled out, alternating between peaceful glides through dark woods and thrilling jaunts along the edge of rocky precipices. He was awestruck at every turn, stunned that such a manageable course could be found along the side of a mountain, taking them right up to the edge of such a remote and breathtaking landscape.

Charlie also took the opportunity to study Natty Oakes. He wondered if she owned any clothing of her own. She wore a pair of oversize khaki work shorts that hung down to her knees and a navy-blue man's golf shirt that hung down past her thighs.

Yet beneath the camouflage of the ill-fitting clothing, Natty Oakes moved with the economy and grace of a thoroughbred. Whether going uphill or down, her slender legs maintained a long, powerful stride. Charlie could discern the broad shoulders, straight back, and narrow hips of a natural athlete beneath the large shirt and baggy shorts.

At the midpoint of the trail, Natty glanced up at the large boulder jutting out a hundred feet above them. They ran past the entrance to the steep goat path that went up to her special place. It would have been a wonderful morning to lie on the rock for a few minutes, but she wouldn't be visiting her spot today, not with this man she hardly knew.

A mile past the boulder, they reentered thick woods. Natty led them through a stand of tall pines, where their footfalls seemed to echo in the stillness of the forest and the sound of their rhythmic breathing was amplified. Just as Charlie's lungs were screaming for a rest, Natty slowed her pace to a walk, then stopped in the middle of the path. Charlie came up beside her, breathing heavily, and started to speak. She quickly put a finger to her lips and pointed down the path with her other hand.

Charlie stood with his hands on his hips, breathing deeply, and spotted the deer—a good-size buck—not twenty yards away. It walked slowly but confidently out of the trees and across the path, immediately followed by a doe and then three fawns. They moved through the trees like smoke, with hardly a sound, and in a few moments they were gone from sight. Natty started walking down the trail again.

"See a lot of deer around here this time of year," she said. "Then, in the fall, my husband and his brothers come up here and bow-hunt 'em."

"Your husband likes to hunt?" asked Charlie.

"*Lives* to hunt is more like it. Been doing it his whole life." Natty turned to Charlie. His face was flushed, with sweat dripping down his forehead. She smiled at him. "You okay, Mr. Burden?"

"I'm fine," he answered, thankful that they were still walking. "We almost done?"

Natty laughed. "Well, I am, but you still got the hardest part ahead of you, running back up to Old Red Bone." She walked to the edge of the path and stopped. "This is where I get off." She pointed down a hill that was covered with rugged outcroppings, a few thin stands of birch trees, and thick, short bushes. "This is the top of Oakes Hollow. I live down there." Charlie came over to her side of the trail and looked downhill. He could see the top of a house about a hundred yards away and, farther down, two smaller houses and two trailers.

"Keep going down the trail a little ways, and you'll come to a dirt road. Go right, and it'll take you down to South County Road. Then you got a nice run ahead of you, back up to Main Street." She glanced at her small watch. "I got to go," she said, as she stepped off the trail onto a narrow path hidden by overgrown bushes. Charlie watched her disappear, then reappear briefly a little ways down the hill.

"Hey," he called out. "Thank you. Thanks for showing me your trail. It's beautiful." She smiled back at him and waved. "Will you be running tomorrow?" Charlie asked.

Natty smiled at him. "I run every day," she said, then dropped out of sight as the path went behind a large rock formation.

AFTER SEVERAL HOURS on the computer, Charlie was interrupted by a rap on his open office door. He looked up to see one of the young subcontractors who'd been working in the main computer room. "Some guy wants to see you. Old guy, says his name's Nickerson, or Hankerson, or something."

"Hankinson," Charlie corrected him. "Send him in." Charlie and Hank had played cribbage several times since Hank had duped him about the planning board, but Charlie hadn't let on that he knew Hank was on the board. He was waiting for the right occasion.

Hank wore a brown suit and a white dress shirt that had long ago turned a pale yellow from years of starching. His white hair was pulled back, tied in a short ponytail. Under his arm, he carried an ancient-looking accordion file, tied shut with black string.

"Morning, Hank," Charlie said, looking up from his computer.

"Burden," Hank answered, looking around the tiny office. He put the file down on the edge of the desk and sat facing Charlie.

"So, what are you up to today, Hank?" Charlie asked.

"Working," stated Hank flatly.

"Working? On what?"

"We need to take a look at what plans you got to move that cooling pond of yours."

"Cooling pond?" Charlie tried his best to look puzzled. "Oh, yeah, moving the cooling pond. It's not a problem anymore. We decided to go ahead and keep the pond where it is." Charlie leaned back in his chair, his hands clasped behind his head. "After you told me about those guys on the planning board, we did some research, and, *boy*, were you right. Miserable pricks, and that's about the nicest thing anyone had to say." Charlie did his best to put a disgusted scowl on his face. "We asked around all over town, and everyone said the same thing: '*Forget about it,* those boys on the planning board are just too *stupid* and too *ignorant* to know what you're talking about. Plus, they're too belligerent and mean and disagreeable to reason with, and they're all pretty damn ugly to boot.' That's what they said. So we're just going to leave the pond where it is." When he was done, Charlie folded his arms and stared across the desk at his neighbor.

After a ten-second staring contest, Hank's mustache moved, showing a smile growing under the thick whiskers. He reached out and slapped the desk with an open palm. "Ha! You got me, Burden," Hank said with a loud laugh. "When'd you find out?"

"Company gave me a file on the planning board. Got your picture in it."

Hankinson nodded as he mused over the fact that OntAmex had gone to the trouble of assembling information on the planning board. At least Charlie was good enough to tell him. "Let's go take a look at your cooling pond," said Hank, rising out of his chair.

Charlie deliberated for a moment about the efficacy of meeting informally like this with the chairman of the planning board. He knew Yarbrough would have a problem with it. *What if Hank was looking for a payoff?* Charlie decided to trust his friend. He had a feeling that Hank was doing him a personal favor by coming to talk to him about the pond.

They took the Navigator out to the original site of the cooling pond, roughly in the middle of the development. They walked over the hard rock, laid bare in several wide expanses where the loose soil had eroded away. Charlie pointed out the proximity of the original pond site to the main building, fifty yards away. He explained how the shock of blasting

would weaken the subfoundation of the main plant. Hank gave a knowing nod.

"You boys really fucked up here, didn't you?"

"We sure did, Hank," Charlie answered, wondering if he should be
admitting that to the planning-board chairman.

"Okay, let's go see where you want to move it to." They drove up to the
north end of the property, just inside the fence along Cold Springs Road.
Charlie reached into the backseat, brought up a scrolled blueprint of the
revised pond design, and gave it to Hank. The old man studied it carefully
as they drove around the perimeter of the proposed new location.

When Charlie stopped, Hank continued to study the blueprint, occasionally squinting at some detail, then looking up to study the topography
of the land. After ten minutes, he rolled up the plan and got out of
the Navigator. He walked directly north toward the boundary fence and
stopped where the land sloped down to Cold Springs Road. Then he walked
along the edge of the hill parallel to the fence for a hundred yards and
stood still for a few moments, visualizing the future pond.

Finally, he turned and walked slowly back to where Charlie waited for
him. Hank sat down on the sandy ground and gestured to a spot in front
of him. "C'mon, Burden, let's make a deal," he said.

Charlie sat and crossed his legs Indian style. "What'd you have in
mind, Hank?"

Hank put the plans on the ground next to him. "Now, everything's up
to standard for water impoundments—the pumping and release systems,
and the levees; your boys can read the regs as good as we can. But you're
going to have to make a couple of changes you probably ain't going to
like too much." Hank reached into his pocket and pulled out his tobacco
pouch. Charlie put his hands on the dusty ground behind him and
leaned back on his arms. He was apprehensive about what was coming. If
Hank was looking for a bribe, now was the time.

"What kind of a change, Hank?" Hank put a plug of chewing tobacco
in his mouth and took off his jacket. The midday sun beat down on them,
and Hank was sweating through his white shirt. He held his arm out and
pointed.

"Around this northern half of the pond, where the land goes down
away from the mountain, you're going to have to build that containment

dike two feet higher than you got it laid out. And you'll have to reinforce it with steel."

"Two feet higher? Reinforced with steel? That's way beyond the code, Hank. You said yourself, everything met the regulations." Charlie was perplexed more than disappointed. He did a quick calculation and estimated the cost of Hank's requirements. "You know, Hank, that would cost us about a hundred thousand, maybe a hundred fifty," Charlie said, looking around at the site.

Hank turned his head and spit a gob of tobacco juice in the sand. "Tough shit," he said. "Your client can afford to build a safe pond."

"Wouldn't a pond built to code be safe enough?" Charlie asked.

"Safe enough for the state and for the county. Safe enough for the board, too, legally, 'cause I can't *make* you go beyond the code." Almost to himself, he added, "Not safe enough, though, for families living along Cold Springs Road years from now, when you and I are long gone and other people got responsibility for—" He stopped and turned to Charlie with a pained look on his face. "The levee needs to be higher, and it needs to be reinforced. It's something *I* need you to do."

Charlie was relieved that Hank wasn't looking for a payoff. He'd known him only a short time, and while he'd concluded that Hank was a man of integrity, you couldn't be sure until the moment of truth. It had now come and gone, and Hank obviously had concerns about the project that were on a much higher plane. "What's it all about, Hank? There's more to this than code requirements, right?"

Hank gazed around at the surrounding hills with a faraway look in his eyes, as he resurrected the painful memories from twenty-eight years earlier. After a few moments, he nodded his head slowly, as if telling himself that it would be all right to share these memories with Charlie. "It was a lousy day," he started in a low voice. "Raining and drizzling for three days straight. February twenty-sixth, 1972. It was a Saturday."

Hank paused to gather his thoughts. "I was a schoolteacher and assistant principal at the time. Well, about noon, I get a call from a good friend of mine, a deputy sheriff here. Tells me that a dam let go up in Logan County—a coal-waste dam the mining companies build to make water impoundments to clean their coal. A hundred years they been doing it like that, in spite of all the problems they cause.

"Anyway, he tells me it looks like there could be some damage and maybe some injuries, and he was heading up to provide assistance. Reason he called me was he knows I got a cousin up there in a little coal camp town called Lundale, couple miles down the creek from the dam. Cousin was married to a miner, and they had a little girl." Hank sighed. "So he picked me up out at the house and we drove on up there. Up to Buffalo Creek."

For the next twenty minutes, Charlie didn't utter a sound as Hank told him the story of the Buffalo Creek disaster, the worst dam failure in West Virginia history. After a week of snow and rain, a series of three coal-waste dams breached, sending 130 million gallons of water crashing down the narrow valley of Buffalo Creek in southeastern Logan County. When the twenty-foot-high wall of black water and coal-waste sludge had finished its eighteen-mile path of destruction, five towns had been totally obliterated and nine others severely damaged. Four thousand people were left homeless. Seven hundred homes were destroyed, along with fifty house trailers, thirty businesses, and nine hundred automobiles and trucks. After weeks of searching through the rubble and debris, the death toll ended at a hundred twenty-five, including seven whose bodies were never recovered.

"We drove up as far as we could before the road disappeared, below Amherstdale, and then we started walking. The state police were there, and you could see they were pretty shaken. Told us we wouldn't believe how bad it was." Hank paused and shook his head slowly, as if he were fighting off the horror of the memories.

"We came to a railroad trestle across the creek, and on the other side of it was this huge pile of rubble—must have been thirty feet high, covering forty or fifty yards of the creek bed—all packed in so tight you couldn't pull a board out of there. Looked like a pile of matchsticks, with a bunch of toy cars thrown in. But they weren't toys. It was what was left of most of the houses and buildings from all the towns for the next eight miles, up to where the dam broke in Saunders.

"We kept walking, and pretty soon there was nothing—houses gone, road and the topsoil washed away; even the railroad tracks were gone. People were wandering around with that dazed look on their faces— mothers calling out for their babies, children looking for their parents. . . .

It was horrible, Charlie. Worst day I ever had to live through." Tears rolled down Hank's face.

"Anyway, we get up to Lundale, and there's nothing left. Ground is scraped down to the gravel. Wouldn't have known there was once a town there, if you didn't know the hollows and the shape of the hillsides. Total devastation all the way up to the dam." Hank turned to spit tobacco juice in the sand. "Cousin's house was gone. They found her body the next day and her little girl about a week later. Her husband was early shift down in one of the mines when it all happened. Later on, he gets his settlement check . . . pathetic little retribution payment—about twenty-eight hundred dollars, as I recall—and he turns into a drunk and moves away. Never heard from him again." Then Hank added softly, "Can't blame him, though.

"Next day, the National Guard moves in, takes over, and shuts everything off. No volunteers, no media, no nothing allowed into the valley. Damn governor's in bed with the coal companies, and they're scrambling to cover their asses, calling it an *act of God*, just another natural disaster, *too much rain*, they said. And they don't want people snooping around and taking pictures of the dam or the destruction they caused—or the bodies of kids lying in the mud." Hank's voice was bitter.

"They knew the dams weren't safe. State inspectors had been up there and cited them a year earlier for not having any emergency spillway. But they never did anything—nobody did—and the state didn't give a shit. They all just let it happen. The *motherfuckers!*" Hank slammed an open hand against the ground, sending up a cloud of dust. "They knew the night before that the dams might collapse, but they didn't warn *anyone!*"

Hank shook his head in frustration and wiped his eyes with his shirtsleeve. "Lot of 'em were kids, Charlie. Forty-three of the dead were under the age of fifteen. Had all these little bodies piled up in the cafeteria down at the middle school. Whole families wiped out. Jesus."

The anger was back in his voice and in his dark eyes when he continued. "A hundred and twenty-five good people died at Buffalo Creek, Charlie. Wasn't any act of God. God had nothing to do with it. Was an act of *man!* And corporate greed, and arrogance from a hundred years of taking and taking and keeping the people poor and dependent and powerless . . ." Hank stopped to take a deep breath and calm himself down before continuing in a softer tone. "Three of the bodies they found were babies that no one could identify. Think about that, Burden. Three kids with no name, no identity."

Hank pulled out a handkerchief and blew his nose quietly. "You know what gets me the worst, Burden?" The old man looked at Charlie with sad, imploring eyes. "No one from the company, or from the state, or the federal government—no one ever said they were sorry for what happened. No one apologized to the survivors of Buffalo Creek for their years and years of nightmares or apologized to the relatives for their lifetime of heartache. And surely no one ever apologized to the people of West Virginia for making us look like . . . like backward, hillbilly fools livin' in flimsy shacks where we shouldn't be, like the flood was the fault of the people living there. Goddammit."

Listening to Hank relate the story of Buffalo Creek, Charlie felt as close to the old man as he'd gotten to anyone in many years. It clearly wasn't a story that his friend enjoyed telling or one that he told very often. Charlie also had a newfound appreciation for his neighbor's strength of character and his sensitivity to the plight of his fellow West Virginians. *What was it Natty Oakes said her grandmother always said? . . . There's a lot of heartache in these mountains.* Hank would surely agree with that, thought Charlie. He chastised himself for even considering that Hank might've been looking for a payoff.

"So, Burden, when it comes to water impoundments, I go beyond the code. Make it as safe as I can. 'Cause I can't bring back any of those kids from Buffalo Creek, but maybe I can help save . . . Well, you know what I'm saying. Maybe it's just a symbolic gesture, but that's the way it is, and right now I got the gavel, so that's the deal." Hank started to get to his feet. Charlie bounced up quickly and extended a hand to help pull the old man erect.

Hank spoke first. "We got a deal, Burden?"

Charlie smiled at his friend and offered his hand. "Yes, Hank, we've got a deal. We'll build a safe pond, for now and for years to come. What about the other two board members?" Charlie asked. "Will they be okay with this?"

"Oh, them? Miserable pricks, both of 'em." Hank laughed. "But they'll be okay. They'll listen to me. What about your client? What are they going to say?"

"OntAmex? They're mostly miserable pricks, too. They'll approve it on my recommendation, though. Actually, Hank, they'll be thrilled with the deal. A hundred thousand is a cheap price to pay to keep the project on schedule."

"Should've asked for more, then," Hank said jokingly.

"Well, Hank," Charlie said, as if he were thinking aloud, "maybe you'll get a little more. I've got an idea I need to work on. We'll talk about it before the planning-board meeting."

They drove back to the administration building and parked next to Hank's beat-up old Chrysler. Hank refused Charlie's invitation to buy him lunch out at the Roadhouse, but they agreed to meet that evening for some cribbage and a shot or two of some local moonshine one of Hank's former students had brought over. Charlie watched Hank drive out through the gate, the rumbling exhaust of the Chrysler belching white smoke as it accelerated toward the access road. The big car rode low on shocks and springs that had given up long ago. In a few days, Hank could be driving a brand-new car, any make he wanted, Charlie mused, if he were at all interested in such things. One call to Vernon Yarbrough, and the next day Charlie would have a gym bag full of cash for the planning-board chairman. Of that, he had no doubt.

But Pullman Hankinson didn't care about cars or living high. He cared about people, his neighbors, and his town, and certainly about West Virginia. And he cared most fervently about the injustice of poor people dying because they were poor enough not to matter. Charlie felt a rush of pride in having Hank for a friend. It was a rare episode he'd experienced out in the field, a demonstration of selflessness and emotional exposure that didn't seem to exist anymore in Charlie's world. *Maybe that's what he had been searching for these past few years. Personal nobility.* A hazy cloud of dust hung in the air in the Chrysler's wake. Charlie smiled and whispered out loud, "You're my hero, Hank."

THE NEXT MORNING, Charlie was on the porch when he saw his blue Lexus coming up South County Road. Natty flashed the headlights and waved. She was standing in the middle of Main Street, ready to go, by the time Charlie got downstairs. "Keys are over the visor," Natty said, as they started out at a slow jog. "Thanks for the car. It was a big help."

"You're welcome," said Charlie. It was then that he noticed Natty's appearance had changed. The long baggy shorts were replaced with lightweight red running shorts. On top, she wore a black T-shirt that fit snugly across her back and shoulders and hung loose at the waist. The shirt was short enough to occasionally reveal her small waist. In place of the customary Spider-Man cap, her hair was pulled back in a dark-green bandanna. Charlie smiled as he watched Natty's narrow hips and thin legs churn confidently in front of him. He wondered if she knew how good she looked in normal clothing.

When they exited the woods and hit the mountain trail, Natty picked up the pace and was soon twenty yards ahead. Charlie made no effort to catch up, as it seemed obvious that Natty wasn't interested in chatting. She was probably a little uncomfortable, as was he, with the idea of running together two days in a row, as if they were establishing a routine.

They ran through the dark woods above Oakes Hollow and down the logging road without slowing their pace a step. When Charlie finally crossed the wooden footbridge to South County Road, Natty was fifty yards ahead of him, and his lungs and thighs were burning. A half mile from Old Red Bone, Charlie saw Natty stop running. She turned around to look for him and then began to walk slowly to allow him to catch up.

By the time Charlie reached her, they were abreast of the soccer field, now thick with late-summer weeds, the bare-earth patches cracked from dryness. Natty had stopped to assess the work ahead of her in getting the field ready for their first practice in less than two weeks.

"God what a mess," she said. "Have to get it mowed down pretty soon. Got our first practice the Saturday after next."

"How's your team going to be this season?" asked Charlie, wiping the sweat from his brow.

Natty looked out over the field. "We'll be fine, if we can find enough players." They resumed their walk up the hill. "We got the Pie Man, of course." She laughed. "And a few other decent players who should be back. Plus Sammy Willard and his brother, Zack. They'll be terrific play- ers, once they practice a little. Got a good goalie—girl named Brenda Giles. And, of course, we got Emma. You met her in front of Eve's place."

"Pie says she's a pretty good player."

"Emma Lowe's the best thirteen-year-old girl soccer player in the country," Natty said matter-of-factly.

"Whoa, that's a pretty big statement," said Charlie. He'd been around kids' sports long enough to have heard the exaggerated praise of individual players by parents and coaches. Invariably, the praise fell somewhat short of reality.

"I know. You'll just have to come watch a game and make up your own mind. We could use a few fans, and Pie would love it if you came."

"Of course I will. Be a lot of fun." Natty nodded, nervous at the thought of the new power-plant boss attending one of their ragtag soccer games. "Probably miss the first game, though," said Charlie. "I have to go back up to New York for a while."

"Business?" Natty asked, happy to change the subject.

"No, not really. My daughter's coming in from Illinois, and I want to see her before she goes back to Northwestern. Also, my wife's going to force me to make a decision on a house she wants to buy."

"Don't sound like you're crazy about the idea," Natty said, looking up to see if she could read anything from Charlie's face.

After a pause, he replied, "No, I'm not." He sounded as if he was thinking out loud. "But she really wants it, and she deserves it, too. I don't know. It just seems so wasteful to me. The house is too big, and it's over a million bucks."

Natty swallowed hard, trying to hide her shock. *What was it he just said? Over a million bucks.* "That's a lot of money, all right. Must be a pretty nice house," Natty said, recovering enough to sound polite. *What kind of world did this man live in? "Forced to make a decision" about buying a million-dollar house. What was he even doing here in Red Bone, this beautiful, sensitive, super-successful man, walking up South County Road with a plain-looking, no-account hillbilly girl?*

"Oh, it's a beautiful house, but it's also Westchester County, one of the most expensive real estate markets in the country. Million bucks doesn't buy as much house as it used to."

"Yeah, must be tough trying to get by up there," Natty said, playing along. *God, they were like two people from different planets. This was one daydream that would never make any sense.*

When they got back to Main Street, Natty got her purse out of Charlie's car and walked to Gus Lowe's garage to pick up her Accord. The new rocker panel was black, the color it would stay. She wrote out a check for $80, which, she told Gus, was all she had until payday, when she might be able to give him another $100. She'd try to clear it up as quickly as she could, but they both knew that Gus's bill would soon be lost in the growing pile of debt in the Oakes household.

She drove home, feeling sick to her stomach, thinking about the money she owed Gus and how he hadn't uttered a word of protest. The Accord felt old and noisy compared to Charlie's Lexus, which Natty had just been getting used to.

CHAPTER 14

THE *WHUMP WHUMP* OF THE HELICOPTER BLADES ANNOUNCED THE arrival of the lawyers from Charleston. Charlie glanced at his watch. It was 10:00 A.M., right on schedule. The gleaming black helicopter with the silver lightning bolts roared in over the trees from the northwest, pulled up over the middle of the site, and feathered gently down onto the landing pad adjacent to the parking lot. As Charlie stood to pull his sport jacket from the rack in the corner, he was surprised to see Terry Summers in the doorway. "Ready, boss? Looks like it's showtime." Summers flashed Charlie one of his trademark smiles.

"Hey, Terry," Charlie answered. "You going up to see the farmer with us?"

"Wouldn't miss it for the world. I know the way there, so it'll be easier if I drive."

Vernon Yarbrough came across the parking lot like a candidate for the U.S. Senate, his arm outstretched, his big hand searching for Charlie's, as if he were greeting a lifelong friend. "Mr. Bur-*dan*. How the hell are *you*, sir? Goddamn, you're looking *fine*, just *fine*. Our mountain air must agree with you." The silver-haired lawyer gave Charlie the two-handed shake, his left hand at Charlie's right elbow.

Kevin Mulrooney from Ackerly Coal stepped forward and was introduced. Charlie remembered meeting him a couple of years earlier, when they were all down for the original announcement of the Red Bone plant. Mulrooney was red-faced and sweating from the heat. A scowl on his face said that he didn't want to be there. Technically, Ackerly Coal was to be the purchaser of the farm, although it had now become an imperative for OntAmex due to the CES merger.

Charlie tossed Summers the keys to the Navigator. Yarbrough took the front seat. Charlie sat behind him with Mulrooney. "Take us about forty minutes to get there," Summers announced.

"That's fine, just fine," Yarbrough answered, looking at his gold Rolex. "Put us at the farm about eleven o'clock." He turned to address the passengers in the backseat. "Talked to Farmer DeWitt last night. Told him we were coming up today to give him some real good news. 'Course, he protested. Said he wasn't selling, but I told him I was bringin' some pretty important folks and wasn't taking no for an answer. So DeWitt says, 'If y'all are coming up, may as well come around lunchtime.'" Yarbrough laughed as he shot a knowing glance at Mulrooney. He was in a pretty good mood, Charlie thought, considering DeWitt's stubborn insistence on keeping his land.

"What we're doing here today, gentlemen," Yarbrough continued, "is giving Farmer DeWitt one last chance to make a good deal and save his ass." He turned back around to face front. "'Cause next time I have to come up here, that pig farmer ain't going to be inviting us to lunch. You can bet your ass on that." Yarbrough, Summers, and Mulrooney joined in a short, knowing laugh. Charlie got the feeling he was missing something. They drove along in welcome silence for twenty minutes.

"Hear any more noise from the granddaughter?" asked Mulrooney.

Yarbrough turned again toward the back. "No, nothing more from her. And I don't think we will. She took her shot, and that's probably the end of it."

"What happened?" asked Charlie.

"It seems the farmer's granddaughter went to see a lawyer in Welch, asking questions about mountaintop-removal mining. Looks like the family figured out a few things. Think we got it pretty well contained, though. We got the lawyer on our side now, case she tries to stir things up." Yarbrough faced front. "We're okay. Just got to wrap up this farm business sooner rather than later—like today. Then we don't have to worry." He glanced at his watch again. "Five hundred thousand. That's our number. Five hundred thousand, or we move on to Plan B," he added.

"What's Plan B?" asked Charlie. In the front seat, Yarbrough shifted his weight a little uncomfortably.

"Let's just say we got some other avenues to take with this boy. Some legal remedies we can pursue." He let it drop for a few moments, then added, "But five hundred grand's a huge number for that place, so ... we'll be okay."

Clearly he didn't want to go into any of the details of what Plan B might be, so Charlie let it go. Mention of the money, though, reminded him of the meeting in New York and Larry Tuthill's million-dollar figure. It was a strange offer. Charlie understood that Tuthill and Torkelson were in a bind over the CES merger because *someone*—according to Yarbrough—may have bribed a superior court judge to set aside a court ruling against mountaintop-removal variances. And now they needed to purchase the farm quickly and quietly. It was the reason Charlie was in West Virginia—to help OntAmex and, in doing so, protect his friend Duncan McCord. But the money and the source didn't fit. Maybe Tuthill was panicking, envisioning his career going down the toilet in a messy PUC hearing over the CES merger. Charlie's nagging doubts about the whole Redemption Mountain deal made him reluctant to get further involved. He hoped that Yarbrough could close the deal with DeWitt today.

"Here we are," announced Summers, as he made a sharp turn onto Heaven's Gate. An old wooden sign with an arrow pointed them in the direction of Angel Hollow, and they started a winding climb, the road barely wide enough for the big Navigator to ride without scraping the tree limbs on either side.

Gradually, the thick woods gave way to thin stands of birches and maples and rolling meadows sprinkled with white and yellow flowers. Large boulders and flat rock pushed up through the ground. Soon they came to another sharp turn. Summers cut the wheel to the left, then accelerated up a steep incline onto Redemption Mountain Road. After a long gentle curve, the road straightened and the trees fell away on the left side of the road, revealing how high they'd come.

A minute later he announced their arrival. "This is it," Summers said, as he pulled the Navigator into the front yard of the DeWitt farm. He parked in the shade of a huge oak tree, and the four men exited the vehicle in a noisy succession of slamming doors. Acorns crackled under their feet as they stretched their legs and put on their suit jackets.

There was no one in sight, but a picnic table was set up in front of the house, covered with a yellow plastic tablecloth, a large glass pitcher of ice water, and a stack of brown plastic cups. Charlie was reminded of the tired old farms on the back roads of Vermont. The patches in the roof of the house, the sagging porch, and the ominous lean of the walls of the barn told a familiar story.

"Hello, in the house. Mr. Dewitt," Yarbrough called out loudly. There was no answer. Summers leaned inside the Navigator and pushed on the horn for several seconds. The rude sound pierced the quiet. Charlie flashed Summers a look of disapproval, which he returned in the form of a wide, amused smile.

At that moment, the front door swung open and an elderly woman backed through, carrying a tray covered with a red-checked cloth. Carefully, she made her way down the short flight of steps, placed the tray in the middle of the table, and stood up stiffly. "Bud'll be down in a minute," she said, looking toward the cornfield. "I'll bring out the coffee."

"Fellows, this is our hostess for today," said Yarbrough grandly, "Mrs. Agnes DeWitt." The men said hello and took turns shaking hands with and introducing themselves to the woman, who said nothing. She hesitated for a moment, as if she had something to say, then turned and went slowly up the steps and into the house.

Mulrooney stepped forward, pulled back the cloth covering the tray, and helped himself to a chicken salad sandwich. "Imagine living way the fuck up here," he said, as he stuffed half a sandwich into his mouth. "Have to go nuts after a while, wouldn'tcha think?"

Before anyone could offer an opinion, a green tractor came into view, churning up a cloud of dust. Bud DeWitt parked the tractor next to the barn and walked over to a wooden bucket and washed his hands and face. He dried himself with a small white towel as he walked toward the picnic table.

Charlie recognized him from the picture in the folder. Medium height, a weathered face creased by years of squinting into the sun, and a thin, wiry build. Except for his stiff-jointed gait, he looked younger than seventy-two. DeWitt was wearing the same Peterbilt hat that he wore in the picture. "Mr. Yarbrough," he said as he got closer.

"Nice to see you again, sir," replied Yarbrough. "We appreciate your lettin' us come up here, and I think we're prepared to close this deal today. And we do appreciate this fine lunch that your lovely wife has put out for us."

Bud DeWitt sat down at the picnic table and reached for a sandwich. "Got only a half hour," said DeWitt, as he poured himself some ice water. "Better get started."

Yarbrough introduced Mulrooney, the head of Ackerly Coal, and then Mr. Charlie Burden, down from New York, the head of the power-plant construction project. Charlie reached across the table and shook hands with DeWitt. The farmer had a naturally strong grip and clear gray eyes. As they shook hands, he studied Charlie's face, as if trying to discern what part he might play in the negotiations. Summers sat at the end of the picnic table. Mulrooney remained standing, rather than risk trying to squeeze onto the bench, from which he might not be able to extricate himself.

"Looks like you got yourself a bumper crop of corn coming in," Yarbrough said, as he gazed up the hill to the field of corn. "Bet that's some real sweet-tasting corn up there."

DeWitt poured himself another glass of ice water. "Hogs like it," he replied. He looked up to see Charlie smiling. The farmer gave him a quick wink.

Yarbrough reached for a napkin and wiped his mouth, signaling that he was ready to get down to business. "Now, Mr. DeWitt, you know why we're here. Last time we came up, we offered you a hundred thousand dollars for your farm, a more-than-fair price, as you well know."

The farmer stared back at Yarbrough, knowing it wasn't his turn to speak.

"But, today, sir, and today only, I am authorized to extend to you one more offer. And I'm sure you'll agree that it is pretty astounding. What would you say if I told you that the amount I'm authorized to offer you today is two hundred fifty thousand—that's a quarter of a million dollars, for this little farm." Yarbrough leaned back from the table with a triumphant smile on his face. "What would you say to that, sir?"

Bud DeWitt stared at the ground and drummed his fingers on the table. It appeared that he was mulling over the offer, so Yarbrough tried to speed the process along. "But I have to remind you that an offer of this magnitude can stay on the table for today only. After that, we—"

"I understand, Mr. Yarbrough," said DeWitt, holding up his hand to interrupt the lawyer. "You don't have to play that game, 'cause it don't matter. Like I told you on the phone, the farm ain't for sale, for any price."

Yarbrough stared at the farmer for a moment, then slapped his palm down on the picnic table. "Goddammit, man, that's a lot of money! Do you know what you could do with that kind of money?"

DeWitt didn't flinch at the outburst. "It ain't the money, Mr. Yarbrough," he said in a slow, strong voice. "I know you gentlemen will never understand it, but this has been my home for seventy-two years. I was born on this mountain. I grew up here. Raised my family here. My parents and grandparents are buried up there," he gestured up the mountain, "along with my two oldest boys. My granddaughter, too. This is the only home I ever known. It ain't for sale. Now, fellas, I got to get back to work."

It was Mulrooney's turn to explode. "Just what the fuck is wrong with you, DeWitt? You're going to turn down a quarter of a million bucks so you can go on living in this shit-hole pigsty? I don't get it. I don't get this game you're playing. What's your price? Stop fucking around with us!" Mulrooney's face was beet red, and spit flew with every word.

Charlie scrambled to his feet. "Mulrooney, knock it off! What's the matter with you?" Charlie moved quickly to get the large man away from the farmer.

"Kevin, sit in the truck for a while and let me handle this," said Yarbrough.

Mulrooney glared. He wasn't done. Suddenly he wheeled around, shaking Yarbrough's hand off his arm, and approached the farmer. "Listen good, you fucking hillbilly. We're going to take this farm one way or the other. There's coal up here, and we're going to get it. Like we always do. Don't you know who you're dealing with here?" Finally he got in the car.

DeWitt was walking back toward his tractor. "Mr. DeWitt," Charlie called out to him. "I'm sorry. I apologize for the rudeness of my colleague."

DeWitt held up his hand and shook his head. "Wasn't rudeness, Mr. Burden. It was a history lesson."

Yarbrough strode toward Charlie, holding his index finger up to the farmer. "Just hold one second, sir. I've got one more thing I need to discuss." Then he murmured to Charlie, "Burden, I'm going to take a walk with our friend and up the ante to five hundred grand—see if I can close this deal. Why don't you go in the house and work on the old lady a little. See if you can get her on board at that number, okay?"

Before Charlie could respond, Yarbrough swung an arm around the farmer's shoulders and ushered him slowly up the road. Charlie had no intention of *working on the old lady.* Yarbrough and Mulrooney would have to get it done without his help. But he needed something to do. Charlie picked up the tray of uneaten sandwiches and carried it into the house.

The front door opened into a narrow hallway. To the left was a small dining room. Diagonally across from it was a doorway that led to the kitchen, where Charlie assumed he would find Mrs. DeWitt. As he entered the dining room to bring the tray into the kitchen, Charlie noticed that the walls of the room were covered with photographs.

What drew Charlie's attention were the sepia-toned formal portraits of what must have been DeWitt's ancestors, taken at a time when everyone dressed like the Astors in the photographer's studio. There were several prints of stern-faced couples—the men with mustaches and bowler hats, the women in uncomfortable-looking woolen dresses—in ornate metal frames. As he moved closer to the kitchen, the photos were more recent and the formal poses disappeared along with the fancy frames. Charlie examined a photo of DeWitt and his wife on the front porch with three boys standing in front of them. The last two pictures were color photographs of handsome young men in military uniforms. Charlie glanced back at the teenagers in the family photo to confirm that the soldiers were the boys in the picture.

"Can I take that from you, Mr. Burden?"

Charlie almost dropped the tray at the sound of the woman's voice. "Oh, jeez," he stammered, then laughed when he saw who it was.

"I'm sorry, Mr. Burden," she said with a thin smile. "I didn't mean to scare you."

"No, that's okay. I was just bringing in the tray, when I noticed the pictures. I hope you don't mind."

She looked at the photos thoughtfully before answering. "No, it's fine. They're nice pictures, aren't they?"

"Yes they are," said Charlie. "Are these your sons here, Mrs. DeWitt?"

"Please, call me Alice," the woman replied.

"What? I'm sorry."

"It's Alice. My name is Alice."

"But I thought Mr. Yarbrough said your name was Agnes."

"Well, he's pretty much of a horse's ass, isn't he?" said Mrs. DeWitt, with a twinkle in her eye.

Surprised, Charlie let out a hearty laugh and nodded his head. "He sure is, Alice. He sure is."

Alice DeWitt looked at the two photos of the men in uniform and the smile left her face. She reached out a hand and made a subtle adjustment to one of the frames. "Yes, these are my boys, Mr. Burden. This is Tommy, my oldest. And that's Earl," she said, touching the next picture. "Earl was a Marine. He was killed in Vietnam." She looked back at the other picture. "Tommy went to Vietnam, too. But he came home. Then he died in a coal mine, up north. He was twenty-eight." Alice took the tray from Charlie's hands.

"God, that's got to be hard to take," Charlie said. "Losing two sons."

She gazed at the pictures with vacant eyes and a thin smile that said she'd long ago come to terms with the loss of her boys. She started toward the kitchen. "There's a lot of heartache in these mountains, Mr. Burden," she said, and went through the doorway.

As Charlie turned toward the other wall of pictures, it hit him at once. The old woman's words were ringing in his ears: *There's a lot of heartache in these mountains.* *That's what my grandma Alice always says.* And there she was, in a small color snapshot when she was a child—probably ten or eleven—but unmistakably her, skinny as a rail, the same bony shoulders and thin neck, and the delicate face with the ice-blue eyes and the full, soft mouth. Her blond hair was much lighter and cropped short like a boy's. But Charlie recognized Natty immediately.

Standing next to her in the picture was the woman from the DeWitt file that Tuthill had given him in New York—Sarah Carlson DeWitt. Natty's mother looked much older than the picture in the file. Charlie quickly scanned the other pictures on the wall, trying to sort through the implications of Natty and the Pie Man being so intimately connected to the Redemption Mountain issue. Yes, there he was, in several pictures— Pie with his grandparents; with his sister, Cat, up on the green tractor.

A group of more-recent photos included another picture of Natty with her mother; this one must have been taken within the year. Natty had her arm around her mother, pulling her close and making her laugh. Charlie couldn't help staring at the young woman in the picture. His heart beat faster as he leaned in close. Natty was wearing her ever-present faded blue jeans and a loose-fitting blue sweater. Her hair hung like a dried mop, down to her shoulders. *Only Natty could care so little about her appearance and still look so great,* thought Charlie. It was the face of innocence, so unconcerned with herself, so unaware of how attractive she was. His concentration was broken by a sound in the kitchen.

Charlie left the dining room quietly and went out the front door. Summers leaned against the Navigator, talking to Mulrooney, who smoked a cigarette in the backseat. Yarbrough and DeWitt were nowhere in sight. Rather than join the men at the truck, Charlie wandered across the road to better enjoy the view.

Then a movement at the back of the house caught his eye, and Charlie strolled in that direction. As he came around the corner of the house, he found Sarah DeWitt, a bundle of weeds in each hand. She smiled politely and looked at him with the same sparkling blue eyes he'd seen in her high school picture—Natty's eyes—but she didn't speak. Charlie offered his hand, though she still clung to the weeds. "Hello, Sarah," he said. "I'm Charlie Burden."

She turned away and dropped the weeds into a small wicker basket, then wiped her hands on the side of her gray smock. She offered her hand. "You know my name," she said quietly.

"I've met your daughter, Natty," Charlie replied, not wanting to tell her that he also knew her name from a private investigator's file. "And Pie and Cat, too," he added. Sarah smiled at the mention of her grandchildren and nodded as she digested what he'd said. She had a dreamy, introspective quality about her, as if she were having difficulty focusing.

"You must be one of the coal men," she said.

"Actually, no, I'm here to build the—" Charlie was cut off by the Navigator's horn, repeated three times in quick succession. Yarbrough must have returned, anxious to get going. "To build the power plant," he continued. "Up in Red Bone."

Sarah smiled. "Looks like your friends are ready to go, Mr. Burden." She thrust her hands into her pockets.

"Sounds like it," said Charlie. "It was nice meeting you, Sarah," he offered, but she just nodded in response.

Charlie had nearly rounded the corner of the house when she spoke again. "Mr. Burden?" she called out.

"Yes, Mrs. Dewitt?"

"Are you going to take our farm?"

"Well, I think that . . ." The words were right on the tip of his tongue, the pat answer about how it would be good for everyone, how it was inevitable, and the best thing the DeWitts could do was to take the money and stop fighting a losing battle. But something made him stop. He stared at the ground, unable to speak. Charlie didn't want to give the answer, because it wasn't *his* answer. It was the answer the rich gave to the poor. The answer the corporations spun to the media. It was the answer that he'd grown so sick of over the last few years.

He looked up past Sarah at the green meadows behind the farm. He listened to the music of the birds and the rustle of the trees in the breeze. *God! No wonder DeWitt doesn't want to leave this place. Seventy-two years. His entire life.* The horn blared again, and Charlie thought about the people he was with: Yarbrough and Mulrooney, scheming, filled with greed, rude and vulgar; Summers, following in their footsteps. Then he looked at Sarah DeWitt as she watched him struggle with her simple question. He thought about Bud and Alice and Sarah, such likable, genuine people—like Eve Brewster and Hank—people he respected and enjoyed being with. And then he thought about Natty, the woman he couldn't get out of his mind. The woman he realized he was rapidly falling in love with. This was her home, too. *How did he get on the opposite side of these people? The kind of people he'd been searching for—unconcerned with status and ego and the accumulation of wealth. And here he was, as always, on the side of the big money trying to get bigger by taking this little farm away from the only people on earth who could truly appreciate its beauty and its legacy.*

"Mr. Burden, are you okay?" Sarah DeWitt took a step closer.

Charlie nodded as he reached some internal decision. "Sarah, I don't know if you're going to lose your farm or not." He saw the Navigator pull up to the edge of the road, clearly waiting for him. "But I'm going to do whatever I can to prevent it. I don't know if I can stop it, but I'll try." He took a step toward Sarah and offered his hand. "But this has to be our secret, okay?"

"I understand," she said, as they shook hands once more. Then she added, "Thank you, Mr. Burden."

Charlie walked slowly back to the Navigator and climbed in next to Mulrooney. Yarbrough twisted around to look at him. "So, any luck with the old lady?"

Charlie shook his head. "No, she's just like her husband. No interest in selling. And her name's Alice."

"Huh?"

"DeWitt's wife. Her name is Alice, not Agnes," Charlie said a little louder.

Yarbrough turned forward. "Whatever. We gave 'em a chance. Can't say we didn't make 'em a fair offer. Seven-fifty, I went to with the farmer. Seven hundred and fifty thousand bucks that boy turned down." Yarbrough laughed and shook his head in disbelief. "I'll be back, Mr. DeWitt," Yarbrough said, more to himself than to the other passengers. "I'll be back real soon."

CHAPTER 15

THE FIRST SOCCER PRACTICE OF THE SEASON WAS AN EVENT THAT Natty anticipated with mixed emotions. She was anxious to see the kids again and looked forward to the excitement of the games and to the additional time she got to spend with Pie. But soccer had become the dividing line between summer and fall, and there was a sadness attached to the passing of another season. The sun would remain hot for another month even as the air became cooler, but it wasn't summer anymore after soccer started.

Walking down the cracked cement steps from the library, the large mesh bag of soccer balls over her shoulder, Natty watched Pie carrying shovelsful of dirt from a pile in back of the goal to fill in the holes in the field. Next week, the kids would go back to school, and Natty would return to her second job as a teacher's aide for three hours each morning. She wasn't looking forward to rescheduling many of her home nursing clients to the afternoon and early evening, but the $120 a week was important, especially now that she had another good-size bill for her car.

Natty dropped the bag of balls on the grass and set up the blackboard in front of the bleachers. Most of the kids wouldn't show up until around 9:15 for the 9:00 A.M. practice. That's the way it had always been, and there wasn't much Natty could do about it. She absentmindedly took another look up the hill toward Old Red Bone, to the back porch on the fourth floor of the Barney's building, as she had several times already that morning.

She had to squint into the sun, but she could see that the porch was unoccupied. Of course, she didn't expect to see him there. Charlie had told her he was going back to New York for at least a week. Natty knew he was still gone because Pie came home every day with a long face and told her, *Charlie gone away. Gone to New York. My friend Charlie go home.*

On her morning runs, she had waved at Hank a couple of times but resisted the impulse to ask about Charlie. Toward the end of the week, although there was no reason to think he might be back and out in front of the store waiting for her, Natty would take a deep breath to still her beating heart and swallow hard to clear her throat in nervous anticipation as she came to the top of the hill and rounded the corner. Her anxiety was nothing personal, she told herself. She got a little nervous because Charlie Burden was an important man, and she would use their friendship to try to get Buck a job at the power plant. *That was all there was to it.*

Of course, maybe now there was another opportunity for Buck beyond the power plant, as she recalled the spreading rumors that Ackerly Coal would be opening a big surface mine on Redemption Mountain to feed the new power plant, and the union would be supplying two hundred miners, with McDowell County men getting first crack at the jobs. *So it was true, and the word was out.*

Buck, his brothers, and just about everyone else in town were excited about the good news. And she and her family would be a small, powerless minority in the fight to save Redemption Mountain. Except . . . how did her mother put it when she called a few days ago? *I met your Mr. Burden today,* Sarah had said. *I asked him straightaway if we were going to lose the farm. He seemed to think about it for a long time, and then he said, "I'm going to do everything I can to prevent it." Now, why would he say that, Natty? Does he have any say in this? Have you talked to him about us?*

Natty went back over the few brief conversations she'd had with Charlie. *He had to be on the other side of this fight for their farm. He was working for OntAmex, wasn't he? Why would he tell her mother that he "would try to prevent it"? It didn't make any sense.*

Car doors slamming behind her brought Natty back to the present. A group of five boys from the trailer park were the first to arrive. Natty turned around in time to wave to Gladys Steele, as she pulled away in her old station wagon. She'd dropped off her twin boys, Gilbert and Hardy, two overweight redheads; Jason Bailey; Matt Hatfield, who, next to Emma Lowe, was the team's best all-around player; and Billy Staten, an uncoordinated, timid black boy, who didn't seem to enjoy the game but returned year after year and did his best.

Natty noticed Emma Lowe and Brenda Giles, the team's goalie, running down the hill. Then a pickup pulled up, and Jimmy Hopson and George Jarrell, two mainstays of the team, jumped out. Neither was a gifted athlete, but they'd become technically solid players, and their outgoing personalities made them the team's leaders. Jimmy took a look around the field and saw the Steele brothers. "I see the fat-boy twins are back. Hey, Gilbert," he yelled, "have another doughnut!"

Gilbert looked over at Jimmy with a big smile and stuck his middle finger in the air. "Suck my dick, Hopson," he called back.

"Gotta find it first," yelled George, as he and Jimmy ran onto the field. Natty shook her head. *This could be a long season.* She glanced at her watch. Almost nine-twenty and still no sign of the Willard boys. She blew her whistle, and just as she was about to start her annual *board talk*, reviewing the responsibilities of each position on the field, a heavyset woman and a thin boy with a blond crew cut came over to her. The boy was wearing a light-blue shirt with black pinstripes and a black collar—a real soccer jersey, not the cheap T-shirts worn by the Bones—dark-blue nylon shorts, and white stockings over his shin guards.

Natty put her chalk down. The woman's name was Helen, with a long, unpronounceable last name. She and her husband were from Poland and had moved to Red Bone several years ago. "Mrs. Oakes," she said. "I like to see you again. I am Helen, do you remember?" She had a heavy European accent.

"Yes, sure I do, Helen, how are you? And who is this handsome young man?" Natty asked, smiling at the boy.

"This is Pawel." She spelled his name. "But here he is just Paul. He is the son of my sister, who comes to live vid us. He could play football on your team if you can. Okay? He play much football in Poland. Okay?"

Natty laughed. "Of course Paul can play, if he's under fourteen. How old is he?" she asked, looking at the boy.

"Yes, yes, he is only turteen," she said. "But Paul speak not much English. Okay he can play?"

After years of coaching kids' soccer, Natty knew a player when she saw one. Pawel was thin, but his neck and arms were well muscled. His cleats, she noticed, had also seen many a game. Natty led her newest recruit to the bleachers. "This is Paul," she announced. "He has just arrived from Poland."

After an interlude in which the team stared at Paul and he stared nervously back, Pie jumped down from the bench and hopped over in front of the new boy. "Hello!" he said, holding up his hand for a high-five. "I am the Pie Man." Paul peered down at the strange little boy, smiled, and did a gentle high-five. Pie grabbed the boy's wrist and led him up to a seat next to his. Natty glanced at Emma Lowe in the back row and gave her a wink. *Now, if the Willard boys ever show up, we might actually have a pretty decent team.*

As if on cue, Sammy and Zack Willard sauntered toward the field. Natty could see that there was an attitude problem. She blew her whistle. "Pay attention," she said loudly. "I don't want anybody on the field who doesn't know the rules and doesn't know their position." Ignoring the Willard brothers as they took seats in the back row, Natty reviewed all the rules. Then she painstakingly described the responsibilities of each position on the field and assigned each player their primary and secondary positions. When she got to Paul and the Willard brothers, Natty assigned Paul and Sammy to the midfield and made Zack the sweeper.

Zack glared. "Aw, Miz Natty, what kind a booshit is that? I's a *scorer*, not a damn sweeper."

"Well, Zack, we don't need any more scorers. What we need is a damn sweeper, so that's where you're going to play. Okay," she concluded with a hand clap, "let's play some soccer."

As the team ran onto the field, Natty watched the Willard brothers dawdling in the back row. "Sammy, Zack, c'mere," she said. The boys sidled up slowly. Natty grabbed the necks of their T-shirts and pulled the boys in close. "Don't you boys ever, ever, disrespect this team again by showing up late! You want to play soccer, come and play soccer, but you get here on time. You ever show up late again, you're off the team." The boys mumbled a soft *yes, ma'am*, and stared at their sneakers.

"Okay, then," Natty said, releasing her grip. She stepped back and smiled. "Your grandmaw's the finest woman ever lived. I don't want to disappoint her by chuckin' either one of you off the team. So don't make me."

Natty called for a full-field scrimmage, six against six. Pie would be a sub for whoever got tired and needed a break. As soon as the game started, Natty realized that she had been right about Paul. He was a skilled player, who could dribble the ball as if it were glued to his foot and had a powerful kick and tremendous speed. It was apparent that he was accustomed to a much higher level of competition. Natty noticed that Emma, who rarely showed any emotion on the field, was smiling as she watched Paul play; Natty also saw how all the other players improved under his direction.

Both teams played with an intensity and skill level that Natty had never before seen at practice. The Willard brothers brought speed, power, and desire. Paul could kick the ball a mile. Emma was Emma, and she wasn't really trying to score. When Gilbert Steele went to his knees at midfield and threw up what must have been a very large breakfast, Natty blew the whistle to end the game. The players were beat, but there was a palpable excitement on the field, as many of them dared to believe that, finally, they might be on a good team.

Natty looked over at Zack, who approached Paul and threw his arm around the new boy's shoulders. "Man, you is a soccer player," Zack told him. Paul smiled and nodded his head, although he couldn't understand the compliment. Zack laughed and ran his hand roughly through Paul's bristly crew cut. "Das okay, we be teachin' you all da words you gotta know," he said, flashing a smile at Natty, who shuddered at the thought. She reminded the team about Wednesday night's practice and their game next Saturday.

Packing the balls back into the mesh bag, Natty noticed Pie sitting quietly on the bench. She felt badly that he hadn't played. "Hey, Pie Man," she called over to him. "I'm sorry, I should've put you in the game. I forgot. . . ."

"Thath okay, Mama," he said, getting up from the bench. "I don't mind. I wath tired, anyway." He had a sad look on his face.

"So why the long face?"

Pie kicked at the dirt. "Mama, when will Charlie come back? Did Charlie go away forever?"

Natty put her hand on the back of his neck and pulled him toward her. "No, Pie," she said. "Charlie's coming back in a few days."

Pie looked up the hill toward Old Red Bone. "I mith Charlie, Mama. Charlie ith my good friend."

Natty tucked the blackboard and easel under her arm. "I know, Pie. Charlie *is* a good friend."

THERE WERE TWO young horses grazing in the tall grass of the corral. Charlie had to laugh at the pains Ellen and her realtor had taken to set the stage. Sitting at a wrought-iron table in the back garden, Charlie could see that the pool had been reopened. After two hours in the hot sun at Hickory Hills for the cocktail party honoring the outgoing president of the club, Charlie wished he had brought his bathing suit.

The new house would undoubtedly help Ellen's campaign for the presidency of the country club, although Charlie couldn't pinpoint exactly why. Maybe it was just that successful people liked to associate with successful people, and this house and this address reeked of success.

Charlie fished his cellphone from his jacket to check his messages. On a Sunday afternoon, he didn't expect anything urgent, but you could never be sure. There was a message from Larry Tuthill, calling to discuss *strategy and logistics* for the presentation to the Red Bone planning board. This was one conference call Charlie was looking forward to. The only other message was from Carlos Marché, inviting Charlie to attend the Yankees game with him and Lucien on Monday night. The Red Sox were in town.

Tuthill's message reminded Charlie of Red Bone. After ten days back in New York, he'd been able to put West Virginia—even Natty—out of his mind. This infatuation was just the sort of thing that happened when you moved alone to a new place, he told himself. *She's a nice person, and Pie's mother. But that's all it was.*

Ellen came onto the patio, a bottle of champagne in one hand and, in the other, two long-stemmed red champagne flutes. Stopping abruptly, with an evil smile, she kicked off her high heels, sending one flying into a thick island of multicolored impatiens. She'd taken off her jacket, revealing a very sexy sleeveless blouse. Charlie felt a visceral stirring as she placed the champagne on the table and leaned over to plant a long, warm kiss on his mouth. She sat down across from him while Charlie poured the champagne.

"So how did I do today?" he asked. "Okay?"

Ellen laughed. "The perfect trophy husband."

They touched glasses. "To the next president of Hickory Hills Country Club," said Charlie, raising his glass. "Do you think you'll get it?"

Ellen smiled wryly. "Of course I will." They sat watching the horses in the corral feed contentedly on the untended grass. It occurred to Charlie that, with Jennifer around most of the week, he and Ellen hadn't had many opportunities to be alone.

Of course, this had been well planned by Ellen and her realtor—the horses, the pool, the champagne in the refrigerator. The scene had been set, and Charlie knew what was coming. He'd decided to make Ellen's job easier. He'd thought about things a lot over the past month, and he wanted this to be a special day for her. She shouldn't have to beg. Putting his wineglass on the table, Charlie stood up, walked to the edge of the patio, and scanned the grounds for a few moments. He walked back to the table and smiled down at Ellen. "Well, this is quite a house we're buying here, isn't it?"

Ellen blinked with surprise, then smiled broadly. "Thank you, Charlie," she said, getting up and going to him. Charlie kissed her and held her close. He whispered into her ear, "I seem to remember the master bedroom having a nice thick carpet."

"Yes—no, wait," she said excitedly. "I have to make some calls first," she said, reaching for her handbag. She flashed Charlie an embarrassed smile as she pulled the phone from her bag. "Just a few minutes, darling." She walked quickly across the patio, squinting at the small phone as she squeezed out the tiny beeps with her thumb.

Charlie poured himself another glass of champagne, wandered down to the pool, and sat in a lounge chair. Closing his eyes, he was back on his porch in Red Bone, looking out at the mountains and down the hill toward the soccer field. He saw the bouncing dot coming toward him at a good pace—running, not jogging—wearing the blue Spider-Man hat and the oversize shorts. Natty looked up and waved and smiled the smile that made his heart skip. Charlie opened his eyes and stood up quickly to dismiss the vision. He drained his champagne and started back toward the house to find his wife.

CHAPTER 16

THE BLACK BELL 430 ROSE OFF THE TARMAC OF THE YEAGER AIR-
port, did a quick spin in the air as it gained altitude, and roared
south out of Charleston for McDowell County. Charlie settled into the
window seat and watched greater Charleston recede, giving way to the
rolling green forest. Occasionally, the green carpet would reveal brown,
gray, and black scars, like open sores on the verdant landscape. They
reminded Charlie of pictures he'd seen of Army and Marine bases carved
out of the jungles of Vietnam.

The pilot's voice came over the speaker. "About an hour twenty now
down to Red Bone, Mr. Burden. Put down six o'clock." The timing was
fine, thought Charlie. He'd pick up his car at the construction site, get
back to the apartment in time to get some dinner at Eve's, then stop in
and see Hank. Maybe even get in a game of cribbage on the porch.

Charlie was looking forward to returning to the mountains and seeing
the Pie Man again. He'd missed the boy, more than he would've thought.
He reached down to touch the white plastic bag holding the Yankees hat
and program that Charlie had purchased at the game he'd attended with
Lucien and Carlos.

From the liquor cabinet just behind the bulkhead, Charlie poured
himself a Canadian Club, then settled back into his seat to think about
the problem that had been nagging him since leaving New York: *What
was he going to do about Natty Oakes? He couldn't avoid her, not in a
place as small as Red Bone, not with his relationship with Pie. No, he'd
just have to deal with it, as a man who'd always been faithful to his wife*

*and wasn't about to get involved with another woman. He'd treat her like
any other acquaintance. Nothing more, nothing less. That was how adults
handled situations like this.*

But it wasn't going to be easy. He knew when he saw her picture in the
DeWitt farmhouse that he had serious feelings for her, and she hadn't
been out of his thoughts since. *And the Redemption Mountain issue complicated things. Why the fuck did he ever tell Sarah DeWitt he'd try to save
their farm? He should stay out of it, and let Yarbrough and Mulrooney do
their thing. The DeWitts were going to lose their farm, and OntAmex
would cut his balls off if he did anything to prevent it. This whole thing—
his infatuation with Natty Oakes and switching sides on the Redemption
Mountain issue—was nothing but trouble for him, personally and professionally. The best thing he could do was go back to New York right now and
tell Lucien he wanted out, that he wasn't the man for the job in West Virginia.*

Charlie finished his drink and approached the cockpit. He sat down
in the unoccupied copilot's seat, and, after a few moments of watching
the scenery, he had an idea. He leaned closer to the pilot to be heard.
"Listen, down south of here a ways there's a place called Redemption
Mountain. It's about twelve, fifteen miles from Red—"

"I know where Redemption Mountain is, sir," the pilot interrupted.
"Flew down there a couple of years ago."

Charlie was surprised. "Two years ago? Do you remember who you
took down there?"

"Sure," the pilot answered without hesitation. "Mr. Torkelson, Larry
Tuthill, and that lawyer from Charleston, Yarbrough—had to stop in
Charleston to pick him up. Second time, 'bout six months later, was those
three, plus the big guy from the coal company, the Irish guy . . ."

"Mulrooney," Charlie prompted.

"That's him. He was a load. Haven't been back there since."

Charlie's curiosity was piqued. He glanced at his watch. "We're a little
early. Would you mind taking a ride down there? Just a quick flyover,
that's all."

"Sure, no problem," said the pilot, as he threw the powerful helicopter
into a hard bank to the southwest. From the air, Charlie could see that
Redemption Mountain was much larger than he'd perceived on their

drive up to the DeWitt farm. He tried to imagine a thick seam of coal running through the middle of the mountain and envisioned the massive job it would take to uncover it by removing the top third of the mountain. They flew in low over the farm. It looked even more remote and more idyllic than it did from the ground.

The farm disappeared behind them as the helicopter heaved over a craggy peak to reveal the long, rocky south face of the mountain. The pilot pointed out where he'd landed on his earlier trips and asked Charlie if he wanted to traverse the south slope. But Charlie had seen enough. "Let's head back up to Red Bone," he told the pilot.

IT WAS BARELY 7:00 P.M. when Charlie approached Old Red Bone. The stone buildings on Main Street, bathed in light from the falling sun, had the surreal quality of an old oil painting. It was a stark change from the never-ending traffic of Westchester County and the cacophony of Manhattan.

Approaching the soccer field at the bottom of the hill, Charlie pulled quietly to the side of the road and stopped. He sat and watched Pie Man as he played an imaginary game with himself, running and kicking a well-scuffed soccer ball. Finally, about ten yards in front of the goal, he rolled a slow pass toward the middle of the field, circled the ball quickly, and attempted to blast it into the goal. But his left foot slipped, and he only brushed the top of the ball, which rolled lazily toward the goal, as the boy sat watching. When the ball crossed the goal line, he scrambled awkwardly to his feet, his arms raised in celebration.

As he spun around, the boy noticed Charlie's car parked at the side of the road. He dropped his arms to his sides and mouthed, *Charlie.*

Charlie climbed out of the car, holding the white plastic bag. He walked onto the field and held his arms out wide. "C'mon, Pie Man, get over here!"

"Charlie!" the boy yelled. "Charlie ith back," he said, as he broke into a sprint. When he reached Charlie, he stopped abruptly. His face was contorted with glee, but he wasn't sure what to do next. Charlie reached under Pie's arms, lifted him high overhead, and spun him around as he squealed with delight. Then he hugged him and spun him around again, before depositing him on his feet.

Up the hill, next to the library, Natty stood next to her red Honda. She watched Pie race across the field to Charlie. She saw him lift her son and spin him around. As she watched Charlie hug her little boy Natty couldn't prevent the tears that ran down her cheeks as Pie enjoyed the kind of moment that for so long he had been cheated of.

Charlie sat down on the grass. "C'mon, Pie Man, tell me what you've been up to."

Pie fell to the grass, bubbling over with news about his soccer team. Then his eyes went wide when he saw the bag with the New York Yankees logo. "Thith ith for me, Charlie?" He pointed at the logo. "New York Yankees," he said excitedly.

Charlie laughed. The boy would've been thrilled with just the bag. "C'mon, Pie, open it up," he prodded.

Pie reached inside the bag and pulled out the hat. He stared at it for a few moments, then ran his fingers over the embroidered insignia. "Oh, Charlie, thith ith a real hat like the New York Yankees batheball players wear."

"C'mon, try it on," Charlie said, taking the hat from him. He adjusted the band to fit Pie and pulled it onto his head.

Immediately, Pie jumped up. "I have to thow Mama," he said.

"Wait, Pie, there's something else in here."

Pie pulled out the thick program, and his eyes again grew large as saucers. "Oh, Charlie, I love thith book," he said. Then he ran up the hill. "I have to thow Mama my New York Yankees hat," he yelled back at Charlie.

About ten yards away, the boy stopped running as abruptly as he'd started. He turned around and walked back toward Charlie. "Thank you, Charlie. Thank you for my Yankee hat and for my Yankee book," he said.

Charlie pressed his hand against Pie's and held on to it for a moment. "Pie Man, thanks for being my best friend in West Virginia."

The boy stood still for a moment, thinking over what Charlie had just said. Finally he asked, "Charlie?"

"Yeah, Pie Man?"

"Charlie, can I have the Yankees bag?"

Charlie laughed and poked Pie in the stomach. "Of course you can." The boy grabbed the bag and Charlie watched him run off across the field. Up the hill next to the library, he noticed Natty looking down at them and felt the now-familiar pang of longing whenever he was near her.

NATTY HAD WATCHED Pie run back to Charlie for the white bag. Then he stopped again and spoke to Charlie. And suddenly Charlie was unmistakably looking up at her, leaning a little to his right to see beyond Pie. Her tears had stopped, and she wanted to rub her eyes and wipe her cheeks, but she didn't want to give anything away. She smiled and gave him a brief wave.

Natty wondered if Charlie Burden even remembered her name. He'd only addressed her as *Mrs. Oakes,* and though he'd loaned her his car and they'd gone running together, he'd never said anything of a personal nature. He was always courteous and usually talked about the Pie Man. *What was she thinking? She was just another backwoods nobody to him. If it wasn't for Pie, they wouldn't have said word one to each other.* But now Pie was clambering up the cement steps to the library, and Charlie stood on the field, looking up at her—*or maybe he was just watching Pie run up the steps.*

WHEN CHARLIE DIALED in to join the conference call, Larry Tuthill was already on the line in Los Angeles. "Hi, Larry, how's everything?" asked Charlie.

"Great, Charlie. Everything's moving ahead on schedule. Couple of more rolling blackouts out here, the feds'll be begging us to build more plants, and the EPA will be working for *us.* And these Enron guys are un-fucking-believable. Deregulation is beautiful, Charlie. Nothing gets results like pulling the plug for a while. These tree huggers out here are against everything in the utility business, but you turn off their air conditioners and their cappuccino machines for twenty minutes and they're ready to build a nuclear plant in the neighborhood schoolyard. It's like heroin, Charlie; America is addicted to electricity."

"You're right, Larry, and you guys do a terrific job of pushing it," Charlie said, trying not to sound sarcastic. A few seconds later they were joined by Vernon Yarbrough and a public-relations man from Charleston.

"All right," Larry said to start the meeting. "Next week, we're sched-uled to go before the planning board. As you know, this is a critical issue, and we need it to go smoothly and in our favor. This is one of those thorny issues where we're stuck dealing with the locals and can't rely on our people in Charleston or Washington to take care of it for us. Usually we can avoid this kind of crap, but sometimes you just have to pucker up and kiss some local asses to get the job done."

Yarbrough jumped in to describe the presentation that he and the PR firm had assembled to show the severe economic impact if the plan wasn't approved. "Plus, we got a bunch of good people comin' down from the governor's office to do a little intimidating for us if we need it, a real show of force," continued Yarbrough, "so I think we'll be in good shape."

"Sounds good, Vernon," replied Tuthill. "Charlie, what do you think?" Charlie glanced at the notes he'd made on the yellow legal pad on his desk. Then he leaned back in his chair and paused, to get the moment right.

"We got a problem," he said.

"What? What do you mean?" asked Yarbrough.

"I had a little talk with the planning-board president—"

"You had a meeting with Harkinson, on your own, without counsel?" Yarbrough was clearly perturbed. "You shouldn't have done that, Bur-den, you should have waited for—"

"*Hankinson,*" Charlie interrupted. "His name is Hankinson, and he lives in my building. I ran into him one day and mentioned the pond problem; next thing you know, he shows up out at the site and wants to take a look at the thing."

"So, what's his problem, Charlie?" asked Tuthill.

"He wants a couple of things that are going to raise the cost of the plan a little."

"Like what?" snapped Yarbrough.

"He wants us to raise the height of the retaining levee by two feet and to reinforce it with steel framing. He's got a personal thing about these water impoundments. He wants the pond safe," said Charlie, "and it's not negotiable."

"What's this going to cost us?" asked Tuthill.

"About a hundred, hundred-fifty thousand at the most."

Tuthill snorted. "That's nothing. What's the problem?"

"What else does he want, Burden?" Yarbrough asked. Charlie noticed that the lawyer seemed to have less of a Southern accent when he was vexed.

"Hankinson told me that the other two planning-board members, along with a few of the townspeople, have been griping that OntAmex hasn't done much for the town so far. And they kind of have a point. Most of the contractors have brought in skilled labor from outside, and those guys spend their money over in Bluefield and Welch. They've hired a lot fewer locals than originally promised."

"What's his point?" asked an irritated Yarbrough.

"Hankinson says they aren't going to approve *anything* for OntAmex."

"So, how do we get to these boys?" asked Tuthill.

Charlie took a sip of coffee, to let Tuthill suffer for a moment, before answering. "Hankinson feels that we need to find a local project to put some money into that'll make the townspeople feel good and get them off the backs of the planning board. Then they'll vote with the company and approve the plan."

"Shit, that's just a minor PR problem, right, Greg?" asked Yarbrough.

Greg, the PR man, came to life. "Sure, Vern. With a little time on the ground, we'll be able to find a cause that we can cost-effectively address—"

"Excuse me, Greg," Charlie interrupted, "but I think I have a solution that may kill two birds with one stone."

"Let's hear it, Charlie," said Tuthill.

"It has to do with DeWitt's granddaughter—the woman who went to see the lawyer in Welch?"

"What about her?" asked Yarbrough.

"She's got a project that would be perfect for us," Charlie said. "Seems she's tried to open a children's library in a small building next to the athletics fields. But the roof leaks badly. And she could use some kids' books to replace the ones ruined by water. It would make a nice high-visibility project, and the woman—Natty Oakes—is a real pistol, as you know. She'd most likely lead the lynch mob against us, especially with her interest in Redemption Mountain. If we could neutralize her by taking care of her pet project, it could quiet her down."

"I like that, Charlie," replied Tuthill. "What do you think, Vern?"

"Could work, if Burden can pull it off," Yarbrough answered cautiously. "You sure you can get her to pull in her horns if we take care of this library?"

"I think fixing up her library will make her back off," said Charlie.

"Good. That's it, then," announced Tuthill. "You orchestrate it, Charlie. Talk to the girl and to the planning-board guy. Spread a little cash around if you need to. Vernon, you'll go through your presentation, and then when the shit starts flying, Charlie and the DeWitt girl—"

"Oakes," said Charlie.

"Huh?"

"Her married name is Oakes."

"Right. You and the girl put on a show about the library. Everybody's happy and we move on. That about right?" asked Tuthill.

"That's it," said Charlie.

"Great. Thanks, everybody," said Tuthill. "I won't be able to get down there for the meeting, so, Charlie, you and Vern will speak for OntAmex. Vern, call me right after the meeting."

"Will do, Larry; so long. Charlie, I'll see you week after next," added Yarbrough.

Charlie clicked the hold button on his phone and covered the speaker with his hand. Then he gently pressed the hold button once more. He could hear the hollow sound of an open phone line, then Larry Tuthill's voice again. "Oh, I almost forgot. Charlie, you still there?" Tuthill asked. Charlie remained silent. "Vern, you there?"

After a few seconds, Yarbrough's voice came on again. "I'm here, Larry."

"We're alone. When you gonna move on the farmer?"

"Based on what Burden said, I'm thinking that we should wait until right after the planning-board meeting. Don't need any repercussions affecting the pond thing."

"I think you're right," said Tuthill.

"We'll go up the week after the planning-board meeting. Need a little more time to find a local boy to put on the team. The sheriff down there's a real straight arrow, but I got a line on another fellow—a deputy named Wayne Lester—supposed to be willing to play ball."

"Everything else all set?" asked Tuthill.

"Like the invasion of Normandy. The staties are all set, and the DEA, and our judge. We'll have warrants to search, inside and out. That hillbilly pig-fucker'll be wishing he grabbed that seven-fifty was on the table last time I had to go crawling around that dump, eatin' his shit. I'll give you a call when it's going down."

Tuthill and Yarbrough clicked off. Charlie sat, unmoving. He replayed the conversation in his mind. What the hell was Yarbrough planning? To have DeWitt arrested? For what? This was obviously the Plan B that Yarbrough had let slip, and it didn't sound good for Bud DeWitt.

But what, if anything, could he or should he do about it? If he sabotaged OntAmex's effort to acquire the farm and was exposed, his career would be over. And OntAmex would probably sue for breach of contract and bankrupt him with legal fees. Ellen's dream home would again be taken away from her. Even if Charlie could live with the consequences, it wouldn't be fair to her. *No, he'd have to go slowly on this and see how it played out.* He quietly hung up the phone.

THE SWEAT POURED off his forehead, running down to his already soaked T-shirt. Charlie looked at his watch—five minutes to go, and he was still a good mile from the climb to Main Street. When a horn blared behind him, he leaped to the shoulder of the road. Natty's Honda accelerated past him, then stopped about fifteen yards up the road. She got out of the car and smiled at him. "Need a ride, sailor? Don't look like you're going to make it back to town."

Thankful for a reason to stop running, Charlie slowed to a walk. "This part of West Virginia hospitality?"

"No, not for everyone," Natty said, squinting into the setting sun, "just guys with nice legs. Hey, thanks for getting Pie that baseball hat. He wore it to bed the last two nights."

"I knew he'd like it," said Charlie.

"And he hasn't put that magazine down. I think he's memorizing it." Natty's face lit up with her trademark smile. "How about I buy you a cold beer at the store when you finally make it up there?"

Charlie laughed. "It's a deal," he said, starting to run again.

As the Honda passed him, he noticed the exhaust pipe swaying back and forth, suspended on a twisted coat hanger. Ten minutes later he made it to Eve's. Natty was seated on the bench in front of the store. Next to her was a small plastic bowl filled with ice and a sixteen-ounce can of Budweiser stuck in the middle. "Hot night for running," she said, offering the beer to Charlie.

He sat down across from her, pressing the ice-cold can to his forehead. He saw Eve peering at them through the large window. He waved, but she only nodded before disappearing into the store. He wondered if Eve had a problem with him having a beer with her sister-in-law. *Maybe she thinks there's something going on between us.* Charlie took a long, satisfying drink. "Thanks," he said, gesturing with the can.

Natty finished the beer she'd been drinking and tossed the can into a cardboard box next to her bench. He noticed her equipment bag near the steps down to the street. Next to it was a small brown grocery bag from the store, in which he could see the top of a Jack Daniel's bottle and a carton of Marlboros. It was Friday night, and she must be on her way over to the two retired miners she took care of.

"Been meaning to ask you something, Mr. Burden." Natty's voice had a more serious tone than usual.

"Sure," Charlie said.

"I been tryin' to figure out . . . um, when you went up to Redemption Mountain and you talked to my mother, how'd you know who she was? I never said anything about being a DeWitt."

Charlie recalled the picture of Natty in her baggy sweater and the wild hair with the shock hanging down across her forehead—the face that he couldn't erase from his mind. As he looked at her now, it dawned on him that he had never seen her wearing any makeup. Not on her eyes, or her lips—nothing. Then something else occurred to him. She never wore any jewelry. No earrings, necklaces, bracelets. He checked her hands quickly—no rings of any kind, just a small white-faced watch with a brown leather strap.

"'Course, you don't have to tell me if you don't want to," Natty said.

Charlie smiled at her. "No, I'm sorry. I saw your picture on the dining room wall."

Natty smiled. "I forgot about them," she said. They sat quietly for a few moments. Then Natty spoke again. "How are you going to save our farm, Mr. Burden? Like you told my mother."

It was a question Charlie didn't want to hear. He squeezed his beer can flat and tossed it into the box.

"I don't want to make you uncomfortable, Mr. Burden, but this is important," she pressed him. "All your friends are trying their damnedest to take that farm, but you tell my mother that you're on *our* side?"

She deserved an honest answer, he knew, not some corporate spin. "Natty, I'm not sure I *can* save your farm," he answered. "There are a great many powerful people who will stop at nothing to take it."

NATTY WATCHED AND listened as he labored over his answer, but all she could think about was how, for the very first time, he had called her *Natty*. He said it so naturally, as if they'd been friends for years. He really did know her name.

"I told your mother I would do what I could, and I will, to a certain point. But this is serious business to a lot of people and several companies. Trying to save Redemption Mountain could mean the end of my career, so I have to be careful." He reached down and loosened the laces of his running shoes. "I'll do what I can, but your grandfather is most likely going to lose his farm."

The cold fear of reality replaced the giddiness Natty felt from hearing her name on Charlie Burden's lips. She nodded. "That's fair enough." She looked at her watch. "Got to take care of my boys," she said, standing up. Natty slung her case over her shoulder and picked up the grocery bag. "Want to come over and meet a couple of old coal miners?" she asked.

Charlie looked over at the old building across the street. He hesitated, then said, "I'd like to meet them sometime, but not tonight."

"That's okay. I understand. Some other time. They'd get a kick out of meeting the big mule."

They both smiled. Then Charlie took a step toward her. "Natty, this has to be our secret, about Redemption Mountain, you understand that."

"I know," she said. "I can see the fix you're in. You're the only friend we got in this thing."

"You're right about that," he said, moving toward the door.

"Hey, Charlie."

"Yeah?"

"Thank you. Thanks for everything." She turned and headed for the Pocahontas Hotel.

INSIDE THE BARNEY's building, in the pitch-black basement, Eve Brewster stood on an old wooden packing crate, looking out the open basement window directly under the boardwalk. When she was certain that Natty was safely across the street at the Pocahontas Hotel, she quietly closed and locked the small window.

CHAPTER 17

CHARLIE LAY STILL IN THE DARKNESS OF THE BIG BEDROOM, TRY-ing to figure out where he was, as he often had to do when he woke up in the apartment. Then he heard the toilet flush in the adjoining bathroom and Hank, standing at the sink, hacking up his morning ritual. Sharing a bathroom was a drawback, but Charlie could live with it.

After fifteen minutes of tossing and turning, Charlie abandoned his attempt to go back to sleep. He thought about Ellen and the house in Mamaroneck, which was now on the market. In some ways he was more uneasy about the sale of the old house than he was about the purchase of the new one. He had an empty feeling as he thought about losing another part of the life he desperately wanted to hold on to. They had spent so many years and created an album of family memories in the old house, and now it was all being wiped away too quickly.

He thought about the power plant, and the pond problem, and Redemption Mountain, trying to figure out some way to make it right for everyone—which didn't seem possible—or to extricate himself from the situation while doing the least amount of damage. Then, inevitably, *she* came into his thoughts. He smiled to himself when he thought about Natty standing next to her car the previous day. *Need a ride, sailor? Don't look like you're going to make it back to town.* Natty made him laugh. *She could be a real ballbuster when she wanted to.*

Charlie got out of bed and went through the small kitchen and out onto the porch, eager to see the morning view of the mountains. Then he heard her footsteps. Faintly, almost imperceptibly at first if one wasn't attuned to the sound, then more clearly as she approached the bottom of the hill. Charlie retreated into the apartment behind the screen door. He didn't want Natty to look up and see him—so obviously waiting for her—and get the wrong idea. He heard Hank's door clap shut and the gentle creak of the porch floorboards under his neighbor's slippers.

"Morning, Natty," he heard Hank call down.

"How you doin', Hank? Be expecting you at the soccer game later on. Playin' Welch, so we could use some fans."

"Wouldn't miss it, Natty. Going to win some games this year?"

"Gonna try." Charlie could hear the smile in her voice.

"Then I'll see you later on," said Hank. Charlie had forgotten about the soccer game. Maybe he'd take a walk down the hill and watch a little of the game, for Pie's sake.

FROM HIS STOOL at the counter in Eve's Restaurant, Charlie saw Hank shuffle past the window. He walked with a cane, which he probably needed to make it down and back up the steep hill from the soccer field. Charlie had folded up *The Charleston Gazette* and was pulling out some bills to pay for his breakfast just as Eve Brewster came out from the kitchen.

"Goin' down to watch Natty's team play, Mr. Burden?" she asked, as she headed out of the restaurant.

"Sure, have to watch my buddy the Pie Man—"

But Eve breezed past him. It wasn't like her to be so brusque or to call him *Mr. Burden*. Again he wondered if perhaps she was suspicious of his friendship with her sister-in-law. He made a mental note to talk with Eve. He liked her too much to have her angry over a misperception.

As Charlie left the restaurant, three boys in blue soccer uniforms came out of the store, carrying bottles of Gatorade. They wore dark-blue shorts with the Umbro logo and light-blue stockings over their shin guards. Even in Westchester County, their uniforms would have been considered sharp.

The boys had the kind of swagger that identified them as confident, experienced players. Charlie followed behind as they made their way down the hill to the field. He was ten yards back but close enough to overhear their conversation. "So their best player's some girl. We gonna kick some butt today, right, Gabe?"

The boy named Gabe replied over his shoulder, "Dicky, you better shut up 'bout playin' *some girl*, 'cause you ain't never played against Emma Lowe before." He turned around and walked backward as he spoke to his teammate. "You're playin' defense, Dicky, so you better not let Emma *touch* the ball, 'cause, if she does, you ain't gonna see it again. Emma Lowe's the best player *you'll* ever play against, girl *or* boy." The boys broke into a trot to join their team warming up on the field, leaving Charlie more intrigued about watching Emma Lowe play.

Charlie took a seat next to Hank on the last row of the bleachers. Eve Brewster was already seated with Ada Lowe, Mabel Willard, and several other women Charlie didn't know. From the look of the players warming up and the number of supporters on their side of the field, the blue team was formidable. Charlie chuckled as he picked out Pie, still wearing his Yankees cap.

Charlie was impressed with the powerful shots of the two black kids, one of whom he recognized as Sammy Willard. The other boy must be Sammy's brother, Zack. A blond boy also had a competent way with the ball, and Charlie wondered if that was the boy named Paul that Pie had told him about. Then he looked for Emma Lowe, but the only girl he saw on the field was a large black girl wearing the dark shirt and gloves of a goaltender. He turned to Hank. "Where's that girl Emma, who's supposed to be so good?"

Hank looked over the field for a second, then pointed to their right. Charlie turned to see the girl spread-eagled on the ground, her arms stretched out over her head. She remained like that as Charlie watched her, until Natty blew her whistle to summon her team to the sideline.

A few cars pulled up to park on the shoulder of the road just up from the bleachers. Charlie saw Natty's sister-in-law, Sally, get out of an old orange Camaro, accompanied by a rugged-looking man of about forty. Charlie wondered if Natty's husband would be joining them. He looked around for the white pickup but saw nothing.

"Charlie! Charlie!" The Pie Man's excited voice brought Charlie's attention back to the field.

Charlie waved. "Hey, Pie Man," he called back. "Have a good game."

Natty turned and saw Charlie. Then she quickly turned back and busied herself with her clipboard.

"Morning, Mrs. Oakes!" A voice bellowed from somewhere on the field.

Natty winced when she heard the voice of the commissioner of the soccer league, Kyle Loftus, with whom she'd had several run-ins the previous season. The owner of the Loftus Insurance Agency was a large man who moved purposefully, cellphone glued to his ear, ensuring that no one missed his entrance.

As much as she disliked this pompous man, Natty knew she had to try to stay on his good side so he wouldn't cause her any trouble. She knew he had it in for her and would love to suspend her from the league, if he got the chance. Loftus and several other coaches agreed that the league would be better off without this feisty little woman coach and her *girls* playing in a boys' league. "Field's still pretty substandard, Mrs. Oakes. Worst in the league," said Loftus, making a show of kicking a rock toward the sideline.

"Been a real dry summer, Mr. Lof—" Natty stopped, as Loftus held up his palm to her and shifted his attention back to his phone conversation. She turned around and sent her team onto the field.

The Welch team had the ball to start, and after the initial touch, their left forward lofted the ball downfield and gave chase. Charlie watched the action for a few seconds, but he couldn't help looking over at Natty. She was on the sideline, closer to the Bones' end of the field. She'd taken off her blue sweater, and from the back, in her red Bones T-shirt, she could have been one of the players. When she turned to an older couple sitting along the sideline, Charlie saw the white flash of her smile and felt the pang in his gut that he hadn't felt since high school.

Charlie heard two car doors close behind the bleachers. Two women walked around the bleachers toward the field. One of them, who looked to be in her midtwenties, was tall, with an athletic build and short curly brown hair. She wore a powder-blue warm-up suit and white Nike sneakers. Her companion was a little older, with black hair, and was dressed as if she were going to the office. She cradled a leather notebook in her left hand.

Charlie eyed the women with curiosity, because even he could tell they weren't from Red Bone. There was something too professional, too major league about their demeanor, to mistake them for locals. The women made their way through the few spectators on the first two rows, the well-dressed woman in charge, leading the way with a practiced, polite smile. As they reached the seats directly in front of Charlie and Hank, the older woman caught their eye and said, "Good morning, gentlemen." As the younger woman turned to sit, Charlie read the white lettering embroidered on her warm-up jacket: UNIVERSITY OF NORTH CAROLINA SOCCER.

Emma Lowe stood in the middle of the field with her arms crossed, watching her team struggle to clear the ball. College scouts here to watch a thirteen-year-old, thought Charlie, *from the perennial number-one powerhouse team in women's soccer?* Charlie wanted to warn Emma to look alive and get busy. The well-dressed woman scanned the field for a minute, then turned around to Charlie. "Excuse me. Is that Emma Lowe?" She pointed toward midfield.

"Yes," Charlie answered. "That's her." She nodded and turned back to her companion, who rolled her eyes with disinterest. Charlie leaned forward and tapped the dark-haired woman on the shoulder. "Are you ladies here to, uh, scout Emma?"

"We don't call it scouting when they're this young, but we're looking at a few kids up in Beckley, and the coaches there keep telling us we need to come down here and see Emma Lowe play."

They all turned their attention back to the field, where the Welch team was getting ready to take their third corner kick of the game. Natty's team had been panicking under the pressure of their more experienced opponents, giving up the ball on bad passes and booting it out of bounds to regroup. They hadn't been able to get the ball across midfield, and only some aggressive goaltending by Brenda Giles had prevented Welch from scoring.

Finally one of the Welch forwards made a mistake, trying to juke around Matt Hatfield. He gave up the ball and was headed in the wrong direction as Matt started up the field with some room to run. He passed the ball to Paul in the middle of the field, who sliced smartly through two defenders and looked for Emma. When the Bones began to advance upfield, Emma started to trot backward. Paul waited until a blue midfielder was almost upon him, then he pulled the trigger, lofting a long, high ball down the field to land well beyond the blue fullbacks.

Emma's acceleration was explosive as she streaked past the surprised fullbacks, circling slightly to the right to put herself on a better angle to the goal. The ball took one long bounce on the rock-hard ground; Emma leaped into the air to control the ball before it bounced a second time. With her right leg stretched out straight in front of her, she took the ball three feet from the ground and tipped it over the head of a quickly closing defender.

Charlie literally gasped when he saw Emma's midair move. "Oh, *man!*" he blurted. "Did you see that?" Hank smiled, but the women in front of them sat unmoving, their eyes riveted to the action on the field.

A moment before the blue sweeper reached her, Emma took two quick, measured steps toward the ball, then one powerful stride with her right leg. With her knees bent low and her head down, she fired her left foot through the slowly rolling ball with a sharp crack. The defenders hadn't expected a quick shot from twenty-five yards out and were taken by surprise. The ball left her foot like a bullet, alive with vicious, hooking spin, on a low, rising path to the far post. The goalie, who had started to come out toward the action, watched as the ball rocketed past him and buried itself high in the net. He shrugged helplessly.

The Bones whooped it up on the field and shared high-fives while the scouts stared out at the field in rapt concentration. The attitude of the woman in the warm-up suit had changed dramatically.

The Bones had regained their confidence and were executing the passing triangles that Natty drilled them on at practice. They now played aggressively, as a team, while their opponents played tentatively and started to bunch up.

After a few minutes of dominating the play, the Bones scored again, on a corner kick. Emma took it with her right foot from the left corner, sending a screaming hook toward the far post of the goal. As the ball came through the goalie's box, Paul took it out of the air with a vicious sidewinder kick that put the ball into the back of the net.

Charlie again leaped to his feet, and Natty couldn't help smiling at his enthusiasm. It was nice to have a man along their sideline who wasn't too old or too reticent to let out a cheer for her team.

After several near-misses and great saves by the Welch goalie, Sammy Willard sent a long crossing pass into the middle of the penalty area.

Emma soared through the air, two feet above several defenders, and headed the ball into the back of the net, past the unsuspecting goalie. The North Carolina women finally stood to cheer. This is what they wanted to see. Emma's foot speed and powerful shots had become evident to the scouts early in the game, but they'd been reserving judgment until they saw if Emma could play in the air, a major part of the game at the college level. As they stood clapping, Charlie leaned between the two scouts. "So, what do think?" he asked. "Think she'll play for your team someday?"

The women from North Carolina looked at each other and smiled. Then the younger woman in the warm-up suit turned back to Charlie and said, "She could play for our varsity right now."

After the third goal, Natty put Pie in the game for Hardy Steele. He ran onto the field, turning several times to make sure Charlie was watching. It was readily apparent that Pie would never be much of a soccer player, but it was also clear that no one enjoyed his time on the field more. On the few occasions when Pie came across the ball with some room to run, he would put his head down in concentration and dribble the ball upfield as fast as he could, before running straight into a defender. But his delight at being a part of the action was contagious, and his brief solo dashes with the ball became a crowd favorite, on both sides of the field.

A few minutes before halftime, Emma put on a show, dribbling and spinning through three Welch defenders, the ball seemingly glued to her feet as she broke into the penalty area. From eight yards out, she could easily have blasted the ball into the net on either side of the goalie, frozen in his tracks on the goal line, but she surprised everyone by continuing to dribble toward the right end of the goal. The goalie lunged out as Emma calmly sent a firm, accurate pass across the length of the open goal to Paul, standing all alone three yards from the goal post.

But instead of just slamming the ball into the net, Paul turned and sent a slow rolling pass to Gilbert Steele, eight yards away. Panting from his run up the field, Gilbert's eyes went wide with excitement as the first goal he'd ever scored in a game went skidding into the net. The chubby forward raced off to high-five all of his teammates as Natty walked onto the field to give him a hug. Walking back up the field, Emma looked over at Paul, pointed her index finger at him, and winked.

The scout with the notebook sat with her eyes glued on Emma. "She's incredible," she said, without turning away from the field. "Five years from now, she's a national champion."

At halftime, Charlie talked Hank into taking a walk uphill to the children's library, where Charlie explained his plan for the hearing before the planning board. "We've made the changes to the pond design that you wanted, Hank," said Charlie.

"That's good, Burden," said Hank. "I already told the other fellas what was happening. You'll get your permit."

"I got something else for Thursday's meeting." Charlie laid out his plan to have OntAmex fund the repairs to Natty's children's library. He would have Natty testify about how little the town had gotten out of the construction project and offer up the library project in exchange for the board's cooperation. He told Hank how he had already gotten tacit approval for the repairs. Now it was just a matter of putting on the show.

"I'd like to have a couple of other townspeople go up before Natty. If they said a few negative things about the project and opposed the plan to move the pond, it would set the stage nicely," Charlie explained.

"They won't be hard to find," said Hank, spitting a gob of tobacco juice over the cement wall. He looked over at the library building with its sagging roof. "This is a good thing you're doing, Burden," said Hank. "But it ain't necessary. You're getting your permit 'cause I said you were getting it. So, tell me." Hank studied Charlie's face. "Is this about the library, or is this about the Oakes woman?"

Charlie smiled at Hank's directness. "It's a little of both, I guess. It's a good project for OntAmex, *and* . . ." He paused to search for the right words. "I do like Natty—and Pie, too. I'd like to help her out with this, the library. It's something she's worked hard for, and she needs help. That's all."

"That ain't all, and you know it," Hank said irritably. "You're a big boy, Charlie, and you can take care of yourself. But you got to be careful in this area, 'cause Buck Oakes ain't somebody to fool with. He's a violent man, and he's mean-tempered."

"Like you said, Hank, I can take care of myself," said Charlie.

Hank shook his head with irritation. "Burden, it ain't *you* I'm worried about."

Charlie looked down at the soccer field, where Natty sat on the grass surrounded by her team. "Okay, Hank. I understand. Don't worry. Nothing's going to happen there."

IN THE SECOND half, the Bones continued to dominate the game. The final score was 8–0, the largest margin by which any of Natty's teams had ever won a game. At the end of the game, the two scouts from North Carolina hurried down to introduce themselves to Natty. They thrust their business cards into her hand and asked if they could meet Emma. Natty put her arm around her shy star. "Emma, these women are from the University of North Carolina, and they came to watch you play today." Emma could only manage a tight, nervous smile and a shrug. She could do anything on the field but was consumed by her shyness off it.

The older woman tried to put her at ease. "Emma, you're a wonderful soccer player. The best I've ever seen at your age." Emma blinked, as Natty smiled with pride. "Someday," the scout continued, "we hope you'll think about coming to the University of North Carolina to play soccer. Just keep us in mind, okay?"

Natty was excited for her star player. This would be Emma's ticket out of McDowell County. She wasn't going to be trapped here in the mountains. "Ain't that great, Em?" Natty enthused. "The University of North Carolina!" Emma smiled and whispered to Natty. Natty laughed. "Emma wants to know if you know Mia Hamm."

The scouts both laughed. "No," the woman answered. "Mia was gone before we got there." She shook Emma's hand. "But I hope I'm there when Emma Lowe arrives."

CHAPTER 18

THE MORNING AIR WAS FINALLY STARTING TO FEEL LIKE LATE September. Natty went back inside the trailer to get a jacket to put over Amos Ritter's shoulders. She wouldn't have to bother putting an ice cube in his coffee anymore. He'd be looking forward to the hot metal cup to warm his brittle fingers. But he would still be there every morning, on his stool until the snow fell.

Natty loped off down the hill and headed up toward Old Red Bone at a comfortable pace. As she came abreast of the soccer field, a wave of elation came over Natty at the thought of last Saturday's game. It couldn't have gone much better. *And didn't Emma put on a show, in front of the women from the University of North Carolina, to boot!* Natty was still thinking about Emma when she reached the top of the hill and was startled to see Charlie Burden standing in the street in his running shorts. "Morning, Mr. Burden," Natty managed. "Thought maybe you'd given up on running in the morning."

Charlie fell in beside her, thankful for the easy pace. "No, I still go once in a while, but mostly after work," he said. "Not much to do around here in the evening."

"You're right about that," said Natty.

"Do you mind?" asked Charlie. "Me running with you?"

Natty laughed. "'Course I don't mind. Is that why you stopped coming out in the morning, 'cause you thought I minded?"

"No, I just thought it would be . . . well, I didn't think it was a good idea to be running together every day."

Natty thought about pressing for more of an answer, but she decided to let it go.

"But there is something I need to talk to you about," said Charlie. "Before this Thursday's planning-board meeting."

Natty was surprised. "Planning board?"

"I think we can get OntAmex to fix the roof of your library." Charlie explained his plan. All Natty had to do was go up last and offer her library roof as a worthwhile community-service project. He and Hank would do the rest.

"That's all I gotta do?" Natty sounded skeptical.

"That's it," said Charlie. "It'll be easy."

"Yeah, easy," said Natty sarcastically, as she ran on ahead. The path narrowed and they ran in single file for several minutes, enjoying the scenery. They passed through a glade of birch trees, then back out to where the mountain rose up steeply on their right. It disappeared precipitously on the left side of the path, dropping off hundreds of feet down to boulder-strewn chasms below. Charlie looked up to see that Natty had slowed to a walk, about ten yards in front of him.

"C'mon. I want to show you something," said Natty. She left the trail, scrambling up a narrow goat path that climbed through the pine trees. Charlie followed, trying to keep up with her as she sure-footedly navigated the winding passageway. In some places, the trail was so steep he had to hold on to some exposed roots to pull himself up. Then the path ended, and Charlie found himself standing amid a small grotto of fir trees.

"Boo!" Natty suddenly appeared from behind a tree, making him jump. She laughed and started off through the trees toward the light. "C'mon," Natty said. "This way."

Charlie followed her to the edge of the trees, where she stopped. "Okay, now close your eyes and don't open them 'til I tell you to."

"I'm all yours," said Charlie, smiling as he made a show of closing his eyes tightly. Natty reached out and took hold of his right wrist, conscious of the fact that this was the first time they'd touched, and led him onto the surface of a gently sloping boulder. Charlie could feel the change in the light and a gentle breeze on his face.

Natty instructed Charlie to sit down on the slope of the smooth rock and to continue to edge his way farther out until she told him to stop.

"You ain't afraid of heights are you, Mr. Burden?" she teased as he came to the edge of the boulder. "Okay," Natty said, sitting next to him with her legs over the edge. "You can open your eyes."

Charlie's stomach rode up as if he were on a roller coaster. He was literally hanging off the edge of the earth, surrounded on three sides by open space. Only a few feet of rock were between him and a fall of what seemed like thousands of feet. *"Oh, God,"* he said breathlessly.

Natty couldn't help laughing at his reaction. She'd sat on this same spot so many times since she was a teenager that she'd forgotten how precarious a newcomer might find it. "Relax, Mr. Burden, you're fine," Natty assured him. "Just don't lean too far out," she added, with a mischievous laugh. Charlie sat up, his palms pressed firmly against the rock on either side of his hips. Natty watched him with a broad smile.

After a few moments, he began to relax and was able to appreciate the spot. It was more than simply the view. It was the feeling of being suspended in midair, with nothing above or below to confine or limit—as close to flying as one might get while still in contact with the earth. Charlie nodded to show that he was all right. He edged down the rock to where Natty was and inched his legs over the side as she had done. "This is a pretty incredible spot," Charlie said, peeking tentatively over the edge.

"Been coming here since I was twelve," said Natty. "My girlfriends and I would come up here to smoke cigarettes and talk about, you know, girl talk. Then sometimes we'd bring our beer up here—lucky no one ever fell off—and our pot, when we were in high school."

"Ever do anything legal when you were a kid?" Charlie asked.

Natty laughed. "Those girls are all gone now—they all left, like most of the young people. Funny how even the poorest hillbilly kids can find a way to go to college if they got a mind to—or they just move on, to Ohio or Pittsburgh or down to Charlotte. Anywhere to get out of the coalfields."

"But some people stay," said Charlie, watching her closely.

Natty shrugged. "Some people get *trapped*." Turning back to the view, she added, "And then they grow to love the mountains so much, they never want to leave."

"So you've been coming up here alone all these years, since you were in high school?" Charlie asked.

Natty smiled. "You're the first person I been up here with since I told my girlfriends I was pregnant, beginning of my senior year."

"I'm honored," said Charlie.

"You should be." Natty pulled her feet up onto the rock and sat with her arms around her bent knees. Charlie gratefully followed her, crawling backward like a crab to a spot a few feet farther up the boulder. "Now I come up here 'bout once a week to have my quiet time and work on my daydreams."

"What kind of daydreams?"

Natty laughed. "Aw, you know. The typical hillbilly-girl dreams. Kind you have when you're alone a lot in the mountains."

"Tell me," Charlie encouraged.

She stretched out her left leg and bounced her knee up and down on the rock. "Well, I can't tell you about the big one, the one every little girl in the mountains has." She laughed and flashed a mischievous smile. "But I got others." Charlie waited.

"They're mostly about my husband," she said. "Ain't nothing too exciting. Main one is that we're living in this cute white house with a nice lawn and some bushes in the front. It's in a nice neighborhood—like the ones I sometimes drive through over in Bluefield, with lots of friendly people and kids playing—and in my dream I know all our neighbors, and Pie and Cat got lots of friends. And I'm standing in the front doorway, and Buck and Pie and Cat are coming up the front walk and holding hands, with Buck in the middle. . . ." Natty's voice trailed off.

"Don't sound like much of a daydream, does it?" Natty asked. "Thing you got to realize is that I ain't once, in twelve years, ever seen my husband hold hands with either of his kids. It just ain't something Buck would do. He don't pay much attention to 'em."

Charlie recalled the angry-looking man in the white pickup who'd stared at him and Pie up on the bulldozer.

Natty interrupted his thoughts. "How about this daydream? Buck and I are sitting in a real fancy restaurant in a big city someplace, having a bottle of wine. Then Buck pulls this little box from his pocket and gives it to me. I open it, and it's this beautiful diamond ring, 'cause we never bothered to get a ring when we got married. And Buck says"—Natty looked up at Charlie and fluttered her eyelids playfully—"'I *love* you,

Nat.'" Natty leaned back on the rock. "Stupid, too, 'cause I don't even care about rings."

When she leaned back, Charlie noticed the curve of her breasts under the jersey, pulled tight by her broad shoulders. As she lay on the rocks with her thin, smooth legs, still shiny with a light coating of perspiration, Charlie thought she looked like an extremely sexy woman and a little girl at the same time. He had an urge to reach over and pull her to him. He took a deep breath and was relieved when Natty spoke again.

"Reason it's a fantasy, 'case you're trying to figure it out, is that Buck ain't once—since we been married—told me he loves me. Oh, he let it slip out a couple a times when we were goin' at it in the back of his daddy's Blazer, when I was in high school. 'Course, he was usually drunk, and it was right before he—well, you know." She smiled at Charlie. "Got carried away by the moment." Natty sat up and braced her arms behind her. "But never after I told him I was pregnant." She continued in a low voice, almost to herself. "Ain't a big deal, but a woman'd like to hear it once in a while."

Charlie didn't know what to say. He hadn't expected Natty to share such intimacies, but he was glad she had and didn't want her to feel embarrassed. "So why did you marry him?" he asked, instantly regretting how insulting it sounded.

Natty wasn't insulted. "*Why? God!* 'Cause I'd been in love with Buck ever since I was in the fourth grade. All I ever dreamed about for most of my life was marrying Buck Oakes." She gazed up at the clouds overhead. "'Cause that was the best day of my whole life, is why." Natty turned toward Charlie, and, with the sun on her face, he noticed for the first time an unmistakable thin white scar over her left eyebrow. Then he saw an even fainter scar just over her lip, also barely visible.

"I adored Buck all through school, and he never even knew I was alive." Natty dropped her head slightly, shading her face with the brim of her cap, as if she knew the sunlight exposed her. "I was two years behind him, and he had plenty of girlfriends. I'd write his name all over my book covers and watch him in the hallways and the cafeteria. Then I'd go to all the football games and pretend that I was his girlfriend. I'd make believe that we were going to meet up after the game and that, whenever he looked up into the stands, he was trying to find me." Her voice fell away. "Wasn't as pathetic as it sounds," she said. "I was just a kid in love."

Charlie laughed, transfixed by her soft, wide mouth. "What happened? How did you finally get together?" Charlie asked, not wanting Natty to quit talking.

"What happened was the *luckiest* day of my life, is what happened. Day before Thanksgiving, my junior year, my girlfriend and I are out late, driving around drinking beer, and we end up out at the Roadhouse. Couldn't go inside 'cause we were only seventeen, but we used to hang out in the parking lot. Anyway, across the street from the bar, there's a little store that's also the bus station. So, about eleven o'clock I walk over to get some cigarettes, and my heart practically comes to a stop, 'cause there's Buck Oakes, sitting in the bus station waiting room.

"Buck was in his first year up at WVU on a football scholarship, but there he was, sitting all by himself with this big suitcase and a duffel bag, looking like a pile of last week's dog shit, with this sad, scared look in his eyes." Natty smiled briefly and rubbed her eyes with the sleeve of her jersey.

"I could tell something was up, 'cause of all them bags, and the look on Buck's face said he wasn't just home from Morgantown for the holiday. Normally, I'd've swallowed my tongue and run out of there, but that night I was feelin' a foot taller from the beer and all, and Buck's sitting there looking . . . real ordinary, you know. So I walk up to him and I says, 'Hey, Buck'—first words I ever said to him—'Remember me, from school? I'm Natty DeWitt.' And Buck looks up and squints at me with those bloodshot eyes, and the first words Buck ever says to me, he says, 'Oh, yeah, little Miss No-tits.'" Charlie and Natty both laughed. "Anyway, Buck and I get talkin', and he tells me that they threw him off the football team 'cause he hurt his knee and couldn't play." Natty sighed. "God, he seemed so much different from when he left. So much of the fun had been sucked out of him.

"And the reason he's just sitting there is because he's afraid to call his daddy to come pick him up. So I says to Buck, 'Well, I got some beer in the car if you want to drive around a little, and then *I* can take you home,' and Buck perks up and says, 'Sure, we could do that,' 'cause I'm sure that driving around, drinking beer with little Miss No-tits still sounded a hell of a lot better than waiting for an ass whuppin' from his old man." Charlie laughed.

"I run back over to the Roadhouse and tell my girlfriend that I got to take her car and the beer, and she's going to have to find a ride home from somebody, 'cause this is like the biggest break I ever got in life." Natty laughed. "And I don't even have a license. *Hell*, I never even drove a car before. But I pick up Buck, and my heart's beatin' like a damn drum. I'm nervous and grinding the gears, driving down the middle of the road with the headlights off, 'cause I don't know where the switch is. But I'm acting real cool, you know, and Buck's laughing and drinking beer and yelling about how I'm the worst driver he's ever seen."

The smile faded from Natty's face as she picked absentmindedly at one of her running shoes. "Anyway, we end up at this spot way back in the woods, and then one thing led to another . . ." Natty's voice trailed off.

"Then we're in the backseat, and the moment came, you know, to shit or get off the pot, so to speak, and I didn't even hesitate. I was scared to death, 'cause I never done anything like that before. Hell, I never even *kissed* a boy before that night. But I went ahead, 'cause I knew if I didn't I'd never see Buck Oakes again."

Natty was speaking again in a soft voice, almost to herself. "I'm glad I did. Everything worked out fine." After a long pause, she turned back toward Charlie. "Buck was right, his daddy was rip-shit about football. He stayed pissed at Buck for a long time. I always figured that had a lot to do with why Buck, uh . . . that he made Buck . . . Well, it don't matter now." Natty smiled at Charlie. "Everything worked out fine. Got married. Had Pie and Cat—wouldn't trade them for anything. So . . . yeah, worked out good." She glanced at her watch. "I got to get going," she said, quickly getting to her feet.

Charlie did the same. She was right. It was getting late and they'd sat for too long, although he could listen to Natty talk forever.

Back in the middle of the grotto formed by the tall pines, Natty stopped. "Look," she said, pointing up to the shafts of morning sunlight that penetrated the high branches. "It's just like a church, with the light coming through the stained-glass windows."

"Wow," said Charlie softly. "It's beautiful." When he looked back down, Natty was facing him, about ten feet away. Charlie could see she was anxious, twisting her fingers together in front of her. "What is it, *Mrs. Oakes*?" he added, trying to ease her tension.

She let out a sigh. "Charlie, there's something I need to know," she said quietly. "Something I need to get out of the way, 'cause I don't know much about this stuff . . . ain't met many men in my life, as you probably already figured out. But I need to ask you something personal, which I figure is all right, since I just told *you* all about the first time I ever got laid and a whole bunch of other intimate stuff." They both laughed.

"Sure," said Charlie, leaning against the trunk of a hickory tree.

Natty flashed an embarrassed smile. "Charlie . . . is there anything, um, happening here?" She waggled her index finger back and forth between them.

"You mean—"

Natty interrupted him. "Yeah," she said, "between us."

Charlie smiled. "Natty, come on. I'm old enough to be your father."

She eyed him warily. "Hell, around here, man your age could about be my *grandpa*, but that ain't what I asked you."

Charlie immediately regretted his shallow reply. It was obvious that Natty was serious, and deserved an honest answer. *But what should he tell her? Should he tell her that she was the most alluring woman he'd met in years? As well as the kindest, most unpretentious, and emotionally honest? Should he tell her that he'd never known a woman who could make him smile at the thought of her, even when she wasn't around?*

"I don't mean to embarrass you, Charlie," Natty said.

"No, no," said Charlie. "It isn't—"

"But, you've been real special to Pie. *God*, that boy loves you—"

Should he tell her that he loved her small delicate face, and her beautiful eyes, and her smile, and tell her how badly he wanted to put his palm against her cheek at that moment, and touch her soft lips?

"—and there ain't no man ever been as kind to me as you have, letting me have your car for that week, helping us with Redemption Mountain, and now getting the library fixed, and . . ." She shrugged. "Just talking to me like you do."

And how much he enjoys listening to her voice, and how his heart beats faster whenever he sees her—and that he longed to run his hands around her small waist?

"'Course, I never met anyone from New York before, so I'm thinking maybe it's all *professional courtesy,* 'cause probably that's why you're down here, to be nice to people and—"

Should he warn her that he was just two steps away from pulling her against him and never letting her go?

"But then, like that day you came back from New York, and I watched you down on the soccer field with Pie, giving him that nice hug. And I saw the way you looked up the hill at me; it seemed like, you know, maybe you were thinkin' about . . . and then that night we sat in front of the store and talked about Redemption Mountain." Natty's voice grew soft. "And you said my name."

Charlie smiled, trying to mask his own nervousness. "Natty, since that morning in the store . . ." He hesitated, to collect his thoughts, then started again. "Since that morning I first met you, I've been thinking about you every minute of every day."

"What?" she blurted.

Charlie laughed. "I said—"

"No, I'm sorry, Charlie," Natty said. "I heard you. I just . . . I guess I wasn't ready to hear you say *that*." Natty turned away from him. *"Damn, Charlie,"* she whispered, "nobody's *ever* said something like that to me." Natty folded her arms together in front of her and started moving around in small circles. Her shoulders were hunched up as if she were getting cold.

Charlie's heart was beating crazily. He hadn't said anything affectionate to a woman other than Ellen since he was in college. "Listen, Natty, I . . . I, uh . . . in twenty-six years of marriage I never even thought about another woman, until I met you." Natty turned slightly toward him, listening. "And now I hardly think about anything else," he added. Natty shut her eyes tightly as if she were in pain.

"Are you all right?" Charlie asked. She nodded, with her eyes still closed. "I love my wife, Nat," Charlie went on. "She's a wonderful woman. But we've had some problems the last few years, and I don't know how they're going to work out.

"We've changed a lot, Ellen and I. Since the kids grew up. You know, you invest so much of yourself in your children, then all of a sudden they're gone." Charlie paused. "Things changed for both of us. Your career changes. It's why I came down here—to get away from what my job had turned into. To get away from . . . a lot of things. And to do something constructive. I needed to build something, to be an engineer again." Charlie rocked on the balls of his feet. "I'm not sure what all that means, except that I'm not as certain about things as I used to be. I'm still married, though, and I've never done anything I couldn't talk to my wife about."

"*Oooh, Charlie,*" Natty groaned, bending over.

"Natty, what's the matter?" he asked, as she expelled a violent stream of orange-colored vomit, scoring a direct hit on one of Charlie's new Asics running shoes. He hopped back quickly, but the damage was done. Natty stayed bent over with her hands on her knees, spitting out the residue of her Special K and orange juice breakfast.

Charlie ignored the mess and leaned over to see Natty's face. "Natty, you okay? What happened?" He resisted the impulse to put his hand on her back and felt helpless as she remained bent over. After a few moments, she raised a hand to him, indicating that she was all right. She wiped her mouth with the bottom of her jersey, then slowly straightened up.

Natty looked at Charlie and smiled weakly. "So, I guess you won't be trying to kiss me this morning," she said. They both laughed.

"Oh, *shit*, Charlie," Natty said. "Look at your shoe. What a mess. I'm sorry, Charlie."

"It's okay, really. You sure you're all right?"

"I'm okay," she said. "C'mon, let's go," she added, motioning toward the path down to the running trail. "I'm going to be late for work."

After a few yards on the trail, Natty looked at her watch again and started a slow jog. She could feel Charlie's eyes on her back, and for the first time she felt self-conscious. Before, they'd just been friends, but now that had all changed. *Goddammit! What was wrong with her? Taking him up to the boulder and telling him all that stuff. How much more trouble did she need in life? Then, the first time a man says something nice to her, she pukes on his foot!* Natty shook her head in disgust and ran a little harder.

When the trail entered the woods, Natty slowed, then walked a few yards to catch her breath. She came to a stop and waited for Charlie, who had fallen behind. Natty thought about what Charlie had said up in the trees. She'd asked him a very personal question, and he'd given her an answer—a beautiful, honest answer that scared her to death, an answer that she would replay in her mind for the rest of her life. It wasn't fair to

Charlie to throw up on his shoe and run off without answering the same question. If she could.

Charlie slowed to a walk as he reached the edge of the woods and saw Natty waiting for him. "You okay?" Charlie asked. The sound of his voice was amplified by the acoustics of the woods.

"I'm fine," said Natty sheepishly, looking down at Charlie's fouled shoe. "Sorry about your sneaker." Charlie just smiled. After a moment of silence, Natty spoke again. "Got sick 'cause I got scared. Hearing you say the words—that was different from, you know, sitting on the rock thinking foolish *girl things*. All of a sudden it wasn't pretend anymore." She had a pained look on her face. "For as long as I can remember, the only man I ever thought about was Buck." Almost to herself, she added, "And Buck's the only man ever showed any interest in me. Then you come down here, and next thing you know, you're telling me that . . . you know, what you said up there."

"Ah, I was making all that up," Charlie said.

Natty smiled back at him. "Yeah, thanks," she said. After a few moments, Natty began again. "Listen, Charlie, I need to . . . I want you to understand what—"

"Natty, you don't need to explain anything," Charlie interrupted. "We can just leave it like it is for now, and—"

"No. It's important to me for you to understand this."

Charlie sat on the edge of an old stump that had been cut about two feet from the ground.

"Charlie, what I said up there, about marrying Buck and everything working out all right, that ain't exactly true. Actually, it's pretty much all bullshit. Fact is, it's been a pretty sorry twelve years, except for the kids. But living with Buck—that ain't been easy." Natty stared at her hands and debated how much Charlie Burden needed or even wanted to hear.

Should she tell him about the maddening silence, the surliness? Or how Buck ignored her and the kids most of the time? About the mean, drunken nights, and, the slaps, and the beating two years ago—the day the helicopters came—when she first saw Charlie Burden and Duncan McCord? Or about the time Buck moved in with the woman from Northfork right after Cat was born? Charlie would have a tough time understanding all that. That was between her and Buck.

So were the tears. Buck's tears, which nobody else ever saw. When he'd bury his head against her breast and let go of the anguish of one more failure, one more disappointment that had defined his adult life after so much unbridled success in his youth. Only Natty shared those moments with him. Charlie Burden didn't need to hear any of that stuff. She didn't want him to pity her or Buck.

Charlie watched as she seemed to struggle with a difficult thought. "I'm not ready to give up on Buck just yet," she said. "I been working at this for twelve years now, trying to make a home, make a marriage." She looked at Charlie with an embarrassed smile. "Trying to get Buck to love me, love his kids. Thing is, Buck's had one bad time after another. Mostly his own fault, but not all of it." Natty paused for a moment before adding, "I was part of it, too. Part of his bad breaks."

Charlie started to protest but decided to remain silent.

"The college-football thing, well, that was the start of it. Then he comes home and, next thing you know, he knocks up this dumb little hillbilly girl and finds himself getting married when he don't want to and, not too long after that, having a baby he don't want. Then, to top it off, it's a baby with a funny-lookin' head." Natty stared down at the ground and moved a rock around absentmindedly with her toe. "Buck was just twenty years old then. Still a kid himself. Wasn't fair to him. Wasn't the way it should've been."

Natty shook her head as she recalled the missteps in her husband's attempts to make a living in a terminally depressed economy. She told Charlie about the ill-fated hunting lodge; the worm farm that ended with thousands of dollars' worth of dead worms; Buck's brief, misguided career selling insurance for the Loftus Agency, before being fired by the insufferable Kyle Loftus; and then the expensive foray into long-haul trucking, which would continue to drain their finances many years into the future. She omitted the dozen or so short-term jobs, some that ended badly due to Buck's drinking or volatile personality.

"So, what I'm trying to say here, Charlie, is that I understand what you were saying up there about not knowing how things are going to work out." Then she added, more tentatively, "How your marriage is going to work out. 'Cause I don't know, either. But right now I can't give up on Buck, 'cause I've been loving him for too long, and I know there's still a chance for us to be a family, you know—like you and your wife had. I know Buck, and I know there's a good man in him, and a good father, if . . . if he can just get a break and get some of his self-respect back."

She started walking down the path. Charlie got up and fell in next to her. At the break in the bushes at the top of Oakes Hollow, they both stopped.

"Charlie," said Natty, "thanks for what you said up there. That felt real nice."

Charlie just nodded to her and smiled. It seemed like everything had already been said. He turned to start his run again and then stopped and looked back toward Natty. "Hey, does Buck have any experience cutting wood? Big trees, commercial work."

Natty nodded. "Sure, he has. He's done plenty of wood cutting. Most of it illegal, for the timber pirates, you know. But he's cut down plenty of big trees."

"Okay," said Charlie. "We just hired a contractor to cut the right of way through to the power-grid connection. Several miles through really rugged terrain. About a three- or four-month job. They're going to hire about thirty men next week. I'll give them Buck's name so he won't have to wait on line. It's good pay. I know, 'cause they're really screwing us on the contract," he added with a laugh. "Buck will have to join the union, though. But he'll get some benefits. I'll let you know what he has to do."

"Okay—*great*," said Natty excitedly, as Charlie turned and began to jog. Natty watched him go. "Thank you, Charlie," she said to herself. "Again."

CHAPTER 19

CHARLIE SPENT MOST OF THE DAY AT HIS DESK REVISING THE request for variance they would present to the planning board that evening. Late in the afternoon, the Pie Man burst through the door.

"Hello, Charlie," Pie said.

Charlie found it impossible not to laugh when Pie made his entrance. The boy was irrepressible, always capable of lifting Charlie's spirits regardless of the mood he was in. They exchanged high-fives.

"Hey, Pie Man," Charlie said. "What's going on?" He reached out and pushed the boy's Yankees cap down over his eyes.

"Charlie, we win another thoccer game yethterday!"

"That's great, Pie," said Charlie. "Score any goals?"

"Pie Man not thcore any goal, but Emma thcored four or five. Lot of goalth, I forget," the boy said, holding up a hand with his fingers spread out.

"I'm glad you came, Pie Man," said Charlie, getting up. "Got a surprise for you." Charlie showed Pie the computer on which he'd installed a math tutorial, as well as a few games. Over the screen, the words *The Pie Man* were printed on transparent tape. "C'mon, sit down," Charlie said, as he turned on the computer. "This is yours."

"Look, my name ith on the computer," the boy said reverently, running his fingertips across his name. He attacked the math program enthusiastically, rocking back and forth on his stool as he repeated to himself in a kind of low chant, "I will be an engineer, jutht like Charlie." After twenty minutes on the computer, Pie got bored and ran off again.

Pie's visit reminded Charlie that he would see Natty that night. He hadn't seen her since their eventful run. Thinking of Natty reminded him of Buck and the phone call he had to make. He thumbed through the Rolodex until he found the contractor who'd won the bid to cut through the forest. Charlie had met Pat Garvey several times in the course of the negotiation. He reached him on his cellphone in his truck. After some small talk, Charlie got to the point. "Pat, I need a favor."

"Sure, Charlie," said Garvey, ever mindful of future business the big mule could steer his way.

"I got an experienced tree cutter who could use a job," said Charlie.

"You know, Charlie, since we got the contract, woodcutters have been breaking down the door. I'm about filled up."

"You can always use one more, Pat," said Charlie. "It'd be a personal favor to me."

"For you, Charlie, I could probably put one more on—but he's got to be good, 'cause that's serious work. Real rugged terrain, and I don't want nobody getting killed. Who's your guy?"

"Name's Buck Oakes. Lives in Red Bone." There was no reply. Charlie could hear the sound of Garvey's truck motoring down the road. "Supposed to have some woodcutting experience. Strong guy, too."

Finally, Garvey's voice came back over the phone. "Yeah, Buck's cut some wood," he said, sounding less than enthusiastic. "Listen, Charlie—"

"Pat," Charlie interrupted. "I know Buck's got some problems. I'm trying to give him a break. If he causes any problems, fire him, no questions asked. I'll take care of the union."

"Okay, Charlie. We'll give it a try, but Buck's a hothead and a boozer. What's your connection with him, anyway?"

"He's my landlady's brother. Trying to do her a favor."

"Okay, Charlie." Garvey paused a few seconds before speaking again. "You know, Buck beat the shit out of his wife a couple years ago. Came home drunk as a skunk one night and beat the daylights out of her. She was in the hospital for a while."

Charlie had to take a deep breath. He thought he might drop the phone. *Why hadn't she said anything, in all that talk about Buck? Why was she still living with him?*

"Poor kid's face was black and blue for months."

Oh, Christ! Those scars over her eye and her mouth, and she sat there talking about how much she loves him. . . .

"Nice girl, too. Took care of my grandma few years back."

Charlie fought back his anger as he thought about Natty getting pummeled by the ignorant brute who'd glared at him from the white pickup. "Yeah, I heard about all that," Charlie lied softly.

"All right, Charlie," Garvey said, resigned. "I'll get in touch with Buck and give him the good news. Hope it works out, 'cause Buck's a good woodcutter. Be the best-paying job he's had in a long time, I'll guarantee you that."

"And, Pat, when you call him, don't mention anything about me. Okay?"

"Sure, if that's how you want it."

Charlie felt sick and angry. He decided to call it a day and go for a run to clear his head before the planning-board meeting.

THE RED BONE high school was a cavernous old building, constructed of huge blocks of red and brown stone and wide-plank flooring. It had been built in the 1920s, at a time when the population around Red Bone could generate three hundred high-school-age children to fill it. The gymnasium, where the planning-board meetings were held, was in the middle section of the building, accessible via a long, dimly lit hallway.

Charlie, Summers, Yarbrough, and his PR man strode noisily into the empty gym. They were a half hour early. Over dinner, the group had run through their presentation and now wanted to set up their exhibits. A representative from the governor's office, a state senator, and the director of the West Virginia Economic Development Commission would be joining them to testify in support of the petition.

At seven-fifty, the gym was still empty. Charlie wondered if their presentation would be made to a sea of empty chairs. Then, as if a bus had pulled up outside, the locals began to arrive in groups of three and four and five, and the gym filled. Charlie recognized a few of them: Mabel Willard and Ada Lowe, along with a couple who Charlie figured were Emma Lowe's parents. Eve came in with Sally and her family and sat in the middle of the gym, among a group of out-of-work miners.

As he watched the citizens file quietly and orderly into the rows of chairs in front of him, a sinking feeling came over Charlie. The gym looked as if it could be anywhere, but this group of people was definitely not from Westchester County. In Mamaroneck, a meeting such as this would quickly develop into a chat fest of smiling, handsomely dressed couples shaking hands and waving across the room.

The faces that Charlie saw showed little contentment. They were faces of concern, if not abject despair. Smiles were forced and short-lived, and the chatter was brief and subdued. This was serious business to these people. They were looking to the power plant for their economic salvation, the source of a family-saving job for a husband, a brother, a son, anyone who might bring home a paycheck. This wasn't a game to them. These people were genuinely concerned about the project and the jobs it could create—concerns brought about by the rumor so artfully crafted by Yarbrough that the project might shut down permanently if they weren't granted a variance. They didn't know the fix was in, as it always was with companies like OntAmex.

Charlie sat erect in his Joseph Abboud suit and looked at the lawyers and the politicians who'd joined them at the power table, all similarly dressed for intimidation, and he realized again that he was on the wrong side of the room. *He should be the one grilling these assholes and making them pay, not shills like poor Natty Oakes, who's got enough things to worry about without having to be a part of their parlor game.*

Charlie watched as Hank settled into a chair at the center of the table. Making a little extra noise, Charlie pushed his chair back and went over to Hank. As they shook hands, Charlie whispered, "Hank, I want you to pull me away from the table, like you've got something important to tell me. And keep talking."

Charlie made certain that his back shielded Hank from Yarbrough, whose eyes he could feel boring into him. When Charlie went back to his chair, Yarbrough leaned toward him. "What's going on?"

The loud bang of Hank's gavel on the aluminum table interrupted Charlie's response. "Tell you later," Charlie whispered. "I think we're still okay." Yarbrough scowled.

The gymnasium was nearly full. Then the door opened once more, and Natty and the Pie Man entered. They made their way up the center of the room and found seats on the aisle. As always now, Charlie's heart beat faster when he saw Natty. Again, Natty amazed him with her ability to be so inconspicuous and attract so little attention. Here she was, one of the most beautiful women Charlie had ever met, and she could walk into a room, looking so plain in her unflattering blue jeans and boots, with no makeup or jewelry, that hardly a man would take notice.

Hank began the meeting by reading the executive summary of the request for variance. Then he laid out the ground rules. "First, the Ont-Amex side, represented by Mr. Vernon Yarbrough from the law firm of Kerns and Yarbrough of Charleston and Mr. Charles Burden of the project's engineering company, will present their petition."

At the mention of Charlie's name, Pie leaned across his mother's lap, his face scrunched in excitement, and pointed the index fingers of both hands toward Charlie. Charlie had to look away quickly to avoid laughing.

"After that," Hank continued, "if anyone's got anything to say, for or against the plan, or you just want to have some fun beatin' the hell out of a big utility company, you can take your shot at the podium."

Then Hank turned the meeting over to Vernon Yarbrough. The silver-tongued litigator had announced his objectives at dinner earlier: to make friends with the audience; to extol the benefits of the project to the local economy; and then to scare the shit out of everyone by implying that the project may well be terminated if the variance was denied. He was a master of his craft.

When Yarbrough finished, Charlie began the technical portion of the presentation, admitting that the fault lay with the engineer who'd worked on the original site plan. The admission seemed to strike a sympathetic chord with the audience and the planning board.

Using a large board showing a diagram of the site, Charlie pointed out the main building, the administration building, and the front gate. Pointing to a spot to the left of the main gate, he noted, "Right about here is where I understand the local kids used to sneak under the fence, before I arrived." There was a smattering of knowing chuckles in the audience as Charlie took two strides up the aisle and grinned directly at the Pie Man, who shrank down in his seat, unsure if he was in trouble. The look on Charlie's face reassured him, and slowly a blushing happy face closed his eyes to slits. "Fortunately," Charlie continued, "one very nice young man from your town offered to show me where the hole was, so we were able to fix it."

Natty smiled down at her embarrassed son, afraid to look up, afraid to find that Charlie might be looking at her. She waited until he started talking again before she turned back toward the front of the room. She'd been nervous since the moment she entered the gym and saw Charlie sitting behind the table at the front of the room with all the other important men. Now, as she watched him occupy center stage, she felt as if she had a hole in her stomach. She replayed for the hundredth time the words he had said to her up in the grotto. And there he was, the same man, up in front of all these people, sounding so professional and so good at his job, in control of the room, and so confident. He wore an exquisitely tailored dark suit that looked perfect and natural on him—clearly an outsider, from a different world, like the other men at the front table. It made her feel foolish for what she had been thinking the past few days.

Charlie talked about blasting the rock formation at the original pond site. For the sake of the miners in the audience, he went into some detail, using technical terms like *seismic echoes, metal fatigue,* and *stress tolerances,* which the miners seemed to understand. He described the location and design of the new pond and the containment dike with its steel framework that would be several feet higher than the code required.

Then questions started to come from the audience. "Mr. Burden, we been hearin' a rumor about a big surface mine openin' up on Redemption Mountain to fuel your new power plant, and I 'as wonderin', sir, if you could say whether dat's true or it ain't, cause there's a lot o' idle miners here be interested in 'at."

Charlie stood still with his hands in his pockets and thought about how he should answer. He decided to evade it as best he could and let Yarbrough address it if he wanted to. Charlie took a few steps toward the audience.

"The contract for the coal to be used in the power plant was awarded to Ackerly Coal," said Charlie. "It's up to them how they meet the terms of that contract."

"Yessir, I un'erstan' 'at," the miner replied, coming to his feet again. "But what I'm askin' is if your company and the OntAmex company are involved in tryin' to get Ackerly a new mountaintop-removal permit to use on Redemption Mountain, 'cause word around the union is there ain't no way Ackerly goin' to get it by itself without you big boys pitchin' in."

Thankfully, Charlie heard Yarbrough's chair scrape against the wooden floor. The lawyer came around the table to take the stage again.

"Thank you, Charlie. Nice job," said Yarbrough, patting Charlie on the shoulder.

"This is a ticklish situation," Yarbrough began. "As a representative of Ackerly Coal, I can tell that there's a lot of interest in opening a new surface mine in McDowell County. A mine big enough to supply all of the coal for the new plant for the next twenty years. A mine big enough to create more than two hundred fifty new jobs for local men." A few grunts of agreement came back from the audience. Yarbrough nodded his head affirmatively, then continued, his voice growing louder. "Lot of interest, from Charleston to Washington, because what this county needs is a big new mine, to put everybody to work at good union wages." The audience seemed to lean together and murmur as one in reaction to this excellent news. Yarbrough paused for a few seconds in thought. "That's the best I can answer your question right now," he said, holding his palms up to the audience.

Charlie saw Hank staring at him with cold, hard eyes. This was the same smoldering anger Hank had displayed when recounting the story of Buffalo Creek. Hank, better than anyone in the room, could see through Yarbrough's bullshit and know that the big companies were at it again and that there was a lot more to the story than Yarbrough would ever divulge at a public meeting.

After a few self-serving comments by the politicians in support of the petition, Hank opened up the floor to more questions. The first to walk to the podium was a miner. "I'd just like to say that the only thing I'm any good at is pullin' coal out of the ground. But I ain't been able to do that for the past four years, so me and my wife and three little ones'd appreciate the board helping out any way you can." His voice trailed away. "It's about the only hope we got."

Charlie cringed. He didn't need such a sincere endorsement at this stage. Thankfully, one of Hank's shills was next, a science teacher at Red Bone High. He thought that the new pond would be too close to Cold

Springs Road and proposed a six-month delay so the board could study the plan further. Hank had coached him well. A six-month delay sounded like an easy compromise, but Charlie knew that it would be catastrophic to the project and that the lawyers would be gnashing their teeth over the proposal.

Then Mabel Willard lumbered up to the podium from the rear of the gym. Her thunderous voice, coupled with an undaunted attitude of righteous indignation, was exactly what they needed. "My problem with this whole show," roared Mabel, "is that this big-time company come to our town with all kind of promises and so far I ain't seen diddly-squat!" There was a murmur of support from the audience.

"Seems to me," she continued, "that I see an awful lot of out-of-state license plates drive out of that construction site every night and not too many Red Bone men put to work." Support from the crowd was growing, causing looks of consternation on the faces of the Charleston lawyers. She was perfect, thought Charlie.

Then it was Natty's turn. Charlie watched as she fidgeted nervously. "Anyone else have something to say?" asked Hank, looking at Natty. Reluctantly, she rose to her feet. At the podium, she pulled the microphone down, trying to get comfortable.

"My name's, uh, Natty Oakes," she said. "And I agree with everything Mabel said. There ain't been much to show for all the OntAmex promises." Natty glanced over at Hank, unsure of what she was supposed to propose.

Hank came to her aid. "Mrs. Oakes, I believe that you might have come here tonight to offer up a worthwhile community-improvement project that OntAmex might want to undertake in order to make a meaningful contribution to the town. Is that about right?"

Grateful that Hank had gotten right to the point, Natty leaned in to the microphone. "Yes, sir, that's what I'd like to do." She saw that Charlie had moved his chair out to the end of the table and was sitting back casually, his legs extended with his ankles crossed.

"What I was thinkin'," said Natty, sounding a little more relaxed, "was that we got this children's library next to the soccer field. I was going to someday get some computers in there for the kids, but the roof started leakin' and there was no money to patch it. All the books, they got ruined and . . ." Natty looked over at Hank, unsure what to say next.

Hank turned to the OntAmex table. "What Mrs. Oakes is proposing is that you might find some way to fix the roof of her kids' library there and get her some new books and a computer. That about right, Natty?"

"Yeah, Hank. That'd be great."

Hank turned back to the lawyers. "And we'd take that into consideration when we're ruminatin' over this request for a variance."

Yarbrough nodded. "Miz Oakes, I was wonderin' if you might have a ballpark figure in mind as to the cost of fixing your roof?"

God, what a showman, thought Charlie. *Pretending to care about the cost of fixing the roof!* The lawyers would be giddy that the request for variance would pass, and at a cost that was little more than tip money to OntAmex.

"No, sir, I wouldn't know about that," said Natty. "But Mr. Burden took a look at our roof one day," Natty smiled at Charlie, "and he's such a smart man, he'd probably have a guess at the cost."

"What do you think, Charlie?" asked Yarbrough, playing along. "This a viable project for our client?"

Charlie came to his feet slowly. "No," he said in the direction of the lawyers, before turning toward Natty, whose mouth dropped open in bewilderment. "I looked at the roof of the building, and it's a mess. But the building's got bigger problems. You could put a new roof on it, but it would still be unusable. The heating system is shot, and there's no air-conditioning, which you'd need for the computers. In addition, the walls have been weakened by the water, and the drainage problem goes all the way down to the soccer field. That would have to be fixed before you could make any improvements to the library. So, no, it doesn't make a lot of sense to fix the roof."

Natty stared at Charlie in disbelief. *How could he do this? Ask her to get up in front of everybody to propose the roof project, and then say no!*

Then Charlie smiled at her. "So, here's what we're going to do in place of Mrs. Oakes's proposal. We're going to demolish the present building, along with the parking lot and the stairs down to the field. We'll tear up the soccer field, the lower parking lot, and the old baseball field. Then we'll build a drainage system to channel the runoff to the stream on the other side of South County Road. We'll build a new building on the present site, with a library on the upper floor and shower rooms and athletics facilities on the ground floor. And we'll build a new soccer field, baseball field, and a new parking lot."

It was evident to Yarbrough that Charlie had given this some thought prior to this evening. He didn't understand what was going on, and what he didn't understand he kept quiet about. It was OntAmex's money and Charlie Burden's neck on the line, not his.

"Whole project should take a few months, if the winter isn't too bad," Charlie continued. "This is what the town needs," he said. He took a few steps toward Natty. "We want to do something that we can all be proud of for a long time and that you and your children will benefit from for years to come."

Yarbrough rose to his feet, eager to take some credit. "Charlie, I think this is a splendid project—" He was interrupted by Mabel Willard clapping her huge hands together. Seconds later, the entire gym was on its feet clapping, drowning out Yarbrough's words. The Pie Man was jumping up and down on his chair, clapping his hands over his head.

Charlie walked over to Hank and the other planning-board members, who were applauding. He shook hands with Hank, who pulled him closer and spoke into Charlie's ear. "Now you're fucked," he said, smiling at Charlie.

"You're right about that," Charlie replied with a laugh.

CHAPTER 20

P. J. HANKINSON WAS ALREADY SHUFFLING THE CARDS WHEN Charlie came out onto the porch. Charlie hadn't seen Hank since the planning-board meeting, which he thought was a little strange, but now here he was, ready for their Sunday-night game.

"Evening, Hank," Charlie said, taking his seat across the table.

"Burden," Hank responded gruffly, as he cut his card for the deal. Beyond the necessary announcements of card totals and point counts, they played the game in silence. Charlie knew something was up when Hank skunked him without any of the usual crowing and subtle barbs he enjoyed on the occasion of such a slaughter.

"Okay, Hank," said Charlie, picking up the deck of cards and placing it on his side of the table. "Let's have it." Hank pulled over the score book and recorded the financial result of their game. Posting the score meant that no more games would be played that evening. He stretched the rubber band around the book, placed it back in the cigar box, and looked at Charlie.

"Burden, I ain't sure I can trust you anymore."

"C'mon, Hank, what are you—" Hank held up a hand to hush him.

"Charlie, reason you're down here, with all them lawyers and politicians at your table, is to get a surface-mining variance for Redemption Mountain. It's the reason why you're building that power station here within easy trucking distance."

"Hank, you got this wrong," Charlie protested.

"Do I?" Hank asked. He pushed himself to his feet, walked over to the railing, and spit his tobacco juice over the side. "Soon as that miner got up at the meeting, it hit me like a bucket of ice water. Ain't no way an idle miner like him knows anything about anything, lest it comes from the union. And the union sure as hell don't know anything without Ackerly or OntAmex telling them what to know."

"Sure, Hank, there's an option that some people are working on to fuel the plant with coal from Redemption Mountain," said Charlie. "But it's just one option."

Hank spit over the side again and turned to glare at Charlie. "Option, *bullshit*. It's the only reason you and your pals are here. Without the coal from Redemption Mountain, that plant gets built over in Logan or Mingo County, or more likely in Kentucky or Virginia, but sure as hell not in Red Bone or anywhere else in McDowell County."

"Hank, you're speculating, and I don't know how much of your theory is real or not, but what's it got to do with me?"

Hank stood silently at the railing, pondering his answer. "Burden, you may not know or care much about mountaintop mining, but that's why you're down here, to help make that happen, that and getting a variance for your pond," he said softly. "It's why you're here, living in this old fire trap and making friends with an old man who happens to be on the planning board and . . ." Hank limped back to his chair and leaned over the table to focus his dark eyes on Charlie. "Tell me again, Burden, what's your interest in the Oakes woman? Nothing personal, you told me, right? So it's just coincidence that you've become so friendly with this little hillbilly girl and her little boy? The granddaughter of Bud DeWitt—who you're going to have to move off Redemption Mountain pretty quick here to get your surface mine started before the end of the year." Hank leaned back in his chair and took a breath. "Yeah, I know what's going on here, Burden."

Charlie forced himself to calm down before replying. He didn't want to get into an argument with his friend. "Hank, part of what you said is true. One of my jobs down here is to help OntAmex get a variance for a surface mine on Redemption Mountain. To do that, we need to buy the DeWitt farm. The pond is obviously my responsibility, too."

Hank sat, stone-faced.

"But, Hank, none of that has anything to do with me taking this apartment, or us being friends, and it's certainly got nothing to do with Natty Oakes. I met Pie the first day I was here, and Natty the next, and it wasn't until several weeks later that I found out she was a DeWitt." He looked Hank in the eye. "It's important to me that you believe that."

After a long pause, Hank put his hands on his knees and seemed to slump in his chair as his shoulders relaxed. "Okay, Burden. Okay," he said quietly. "I didn't really think you were that cunning. Had to know, though. 'Cause this whole thing with Redemption Mountain, it's like the damn history of West Virginia, and I hate it in my gut." He turned to look out at the mountains and spoke in a low voice, almost to himself. "Big companies been coming down here squeezing the blood out of these people for a hundred years, takin' their land and keepin' 'em poor and ignorant and dependent, all with the help of the damn government, 'cause the money and the power has always been with the coal companies. It'll never change. Way it's always been in West Virginia."

"Hank, c'mon, that's a little extreme. We made the DeWitts a fair offer for the farm."

"*Fair.* Burden, let me tell you something. There ain't *nothin'* fair about what the coal companies done to the people of West Virginia." Hank shook his head slowly.

Charlie leaned forward to argue his case. "Hank, even if you're against mountaintop removal because of the damage to the environment, you still have to admit it's going to put a lot of men to work. Isn't that good for McDowell County, Hank? Isn't that good for West Virginia?"

Hank stared back at Charlie through narrowed eyes. He rose out of his chair again, moved to the edge of the porch, and leaned against the supporting post. He gestured out toward the mountains. "Charlie, under all of this land, far as we can see from this porch, is the Pocahontas Coalfield, the richest seam of pure low-sulfur coal the world has ever known. Miners have been pulling it out of the ground in West Virginia for a hundred seventy years—to fuel the Industrial Revolution, fight two world wars, power the railroads and the steel mills of the Ohio Valley, and heat the homes and factories of the Northeast for most of this century."

Charlie could see that the veteran teacher in Hank was preparing a lesson, and he sat back in his chair to listen.

"D'you know that it was coal from central Appalachia that powered the U.S. Navy in World War One? Navy had to have the smokeless coal so the German U-boats couldn't see the plumes of the ships through their periscopes. That's when the Red Bone mine first opened, 1917, to supply the coal for the Navy."

Hank turned and spit tobacco juice over the side of the porch. "The railroads changed everything when they opened up the coalfield. Just as important, they brought in the thousands of workers needed by the coal-mining industry—all the *throwaway* people that the mines needed because it was so labor-intensive and dangerous. The railroad brought in the people who didn't have any other options, the poor Southern blacks and the Euro-peans right off the boat from Ellis Island—the Italians, Slavs, Irish, Hun-garians. They came by the thousands. Soon as they got off the train, they were in debt to the company—a debt they'd never get out of."

Hank shuffled back to his chair at the table and continued in a more somber voice. "In 1907, Charlie, there was an accident, up in Monongah, an explosion. Official count was three hundred sixty-two fatalities—worst mine disaster in U.S. history. But unofficial accounts at the time said the death toll was much higher, because of all the immigrants who couldn't speak English and had names too hard to write, so they'd send them down the hole without accounting for them." Hank shook his head. "That's the way it was. In the first two decades of the century, more than twenty thousand U.S. coal miners were killed. It didn't matter, 'cause they were replaceable, and it was the only way to get the coal out of the ground. There was a study done that showed that the life expectancy of a West Virginia coal miner during World War One was shorter than that of an infantryman on the battlefields of Europe.

"Even before the railroads came, the mining companies and the spec-ulators with their broad-form deeds—*the vilest legal instrument ever devised by man*—bought up all the land and the mineral rights. Farmers were forced off their land, and West Virginia became the property of the mining companies. Still today, most of the state is owned by out-of-state companies." Hank looked up at Charlie to make sure he was listening. "Companies like Ackerly, and Continental Electric, and OntAmex."

"But, Hank, a lot of people have made a very good living as miners—"

Hank slammed his hand down on the table, making the cribbage board jump. "Goddammit, Charlie! You ain't been listening to me at all.

A good living! What's a good living, Charlie? A hundred years of pulling coal out of the ground to help this country fight two great wars and power the most prosperous economy the world has ever known, and what do we have to show for it? Look around you, Charlie. You see any great wealth, see any *old money*, around this town? What's our legacy from the coal industry?"

Hank stared out at darkness, the silhouettes of the mountains barely visible against the night sky. "What we got is the second-poorest state in the union and about the highest child-poverty rate. We got a population that's dropping like a rock, 'cause there's no jobs, no future for the young people, and we got too many old people to take care of—too old and too poor to go anywhere else. We got fifty thousand retired miners with the black lung, suffocating in their own fluids, getting ready to die before their time, and the rest of 'em losing their retirements and their health insurance 'cause all the old coal companies've been picked clean of any assets and now gone bankrupt." Hank was getting louder. He leaned closer to Charlie over the table, and spit flew from his lips with every word.

"We got abandoned buildings and abandoned towns. And we got monuments—all over West Virginia we got monuments—to the men who gave up their lives to this heartless industry. And we got old coal mines and gob piles leaking acid waste, turning our streams orange, and polluting our water. We got abandoned mines caving in, swallowing people's homes, and we got companies still coming here to openly rape the land with their *mountaintop disasters,* to get what's left of the coal, 'cause *what the fuck*!" Hank slammed his palm down on the table again. "This is *West Virginia,* and that's the way it's always been down here, so it don't matter none!"

Hank paused for a few moments, then nodded his head in thought. "That's the worst of it, Charlie. Our legacy from the coal industry is that West Virginia's a joke to the rest of the country. Poor, ignorant hillbillies, too dumb to raise themselves out of poverty. So it don't matter what the big companies do down there, 'cause it's *just Appalachia* and them hillbillies don't care, so why should anyone? That's the worst of it, Charlie."

Hank leaned onto the table. "Let me ask you something, Burden. If you wanted to blow the top half off Redemption Mountain and push it all over the side—ten square miles of overburden—destroying the streams and wildlife habitat and hundreds of years of forest growth, but instead of West Virginia, Redemption Mountain was in California, or Oregon, or Vermont, or in the Catskills, how successful do you think you'd be? Could mining companies get away with that anywhere else but West Virginia or Kentucky?"

Charlie could only smile weakly, conceding Hank's point.

"You bet they couldn't, and they wouldn't even try. But this is *Appalachia*, so who gives a shit." Hank's voice grew weak and he turned away, as if he was now talking to himself. "People here are still poor and desperate, with no options. Like we just arrived from Ellis Island. So don't tell me how good coal mining is for the people or the state or McDowell County. Always been a deal with the devil, and the devil's been winning for a hundred years."

They sat quietly in the dark. Finally Hank stirred and rose stiffly from his chair. "Time for an old man to get to bed."

"Me, too," Charlie said, getting up. "Good night, Hank."

At his door, Hank stopped and looked back toward Charlie. "Burden, that's a good thing you're doing with the kids' library and the ball fields. Nobody's ever done something like that for this town before. Nobody's ever given this town anything."

"Thanks, Hank. I appreciate you saying that."

THE MOMENT HE reached the power plant, Charlie knew something was wrong. The main gate had been wheeled open, and several vehicles, including a white police car, were lined up on the road over the drainage ditch.

Charlie turned through the gate and noticed another car to his right. It was a dark-blue Crown Victoria with a spotlight mounted on the driver's door. Two men in sunglasses were inside.

Security Officer Hicks was standing outside the small guardhouse. Hicks was never on duty this early. As he drove past the line of vehicles, Charlie saw that the insignia on a black Suburban was for the U.S. Drug Enforcement Agency. In the parking lot outside the administration building, Charlie noticed Terry Summers's white Corvette. As Charlie got out of his car, he saw the OntAmex helicopter out in the middle of the field. *This is it, then, the infamous Plan B that Yarbrough has been holding in reserve.*

Just then the doors to the building burst open, and a collection of men streamed into the parking lot. Charlie recognized Yarbrough and Summers, but the rest were strangers. Two of the men wore vests with DEA in large white letters on the back; .45-caliber pistols were holstered at their sides.

A heavyset policeman with a toothpick in his mouth stood by his cruiser, as if awaiting further instructions. Four other men—two wearing business suits, and two in rugged-looking casual wear—climbed into a Land Cruiser. Vernon Yarbrough walked toward Charlie.

"Morning, Burden," said Yarbrough with a quick nod.

"What's up?" asked Charlie, motioning toward the motorcade.

"Going up to see our pig farmer one last time. Want to come?" he asked without enthusiasm.

It was obvious that Charlie wasn't intended to be part of this operation. "No, thanks," he answered. "Let me know how it turns out."

Yarbrough eyed Charlie warily. "Thought it best to keep this option under wraps."

Charlie watched the other men as they got into their vehicles. "Why all the firepower?" he asked.

Yarbrough glanced over at the entourage. "It appears that Farmer DeWitt's been growing some contraband that our law-enforcement friends may have a problem with. I'm going along 'cause I just might be able to help DeWitt get through this situation, but you never know what a man will do when he's up against the wall." Yarbrough turned and strode quickly away toward the Navigator. Terry Summers was at the door of the big vehicle, watching Charlie. Yarbrough spoke into a walkie-talkie as he climbed inside.

The caravan pulled out onto the access road in close formation. Charlie watched as the vehicles disappeared into the woods, sending up a cloud of dust, then he walked quickly to the door of the administration building.

"Fuck!" said Charlie. He moved quickly through the main room, passing by the big center table that was used for reviewing blueprints. Several empty doughnut boxes and numerous paper coffee cups littered the table.

"Goddamn motherfuckers!" he said, as he reached out and swept a box off the table. Back in his office, he dropped into his chair and yanked open the bottom drawer of his desk to find the small McDowell County phone book.

Stop and think for a minute. This was serious business now. He'd be putting his career and his company's future on the line, and there would be huge repercussions if it was discovered that he'd interfered with their raid on the DeWitt farm.

Charlie slumped back in his chair. *Could he even stop what had already been put in motion?* He looked at his watch—6:25 A.M. He thought about the DeWitts up on Redemption Mountain. Probably having breakfast, unaware that the power of the federal, state, and county government would be descending on them within the hour and their lives would never be the same.

Charlie thought of Sarah DeWitt and his promise to her. *I don't know if I can stop it, but I'll try,* he'd said to her. And he'd told Natty the same thing. Then, to his surprise, Cecil Thomas, his boyhood pal, flashed through his mind. Cecil, his best friend in the world for so long, whom he'd left behind when he was anointed *prince of the city* by Duncan McCord. Charlie shook his head. "Cecil, you prick," he whispered.

He tore open the phone book . . . *Dewire, Dewolfe . . . no DeWitt. Shit! Now what?* Charlie grabbed the phone and dialed information. No listing for *DeWitt.* Natty would have the number. He started to look up *Oakes. Damn, he couldn't call her at home. What if her husband answered? Plus, he couldn't leave a trail, and Yarbrough's investigators were certain to check phone records afterward, if Plan B went into the toilet.* Charlie looked at his watch. *She'd be out running now, anyway—on the mountainside if she'd started at her usual time.* Charlie grabbed his keys. He felt the outside of his jacket pocket to make sure his cellphone was there.

Hicks was on duty at the front gate. His presence meant that he had long been part of Yarbrough's team. Charlie climbed into the Lexus and drove slowly to the gatehouse and lowered his window. "Forgot my laptop. Gotta go back into town. See you later." He pulled slowly out onto the access road, making a mental note to fire Hicks the first opportunity he got.

Coming out of the woods to South County Road, Charlie stopped in the middle of the road. He shaded his eyes and looked as far up toward Red Bone as he could, trying to spot Natty. If she'd started later than usual, she might still be on this leg of her run. Seeing nothing, Charlie turned right and floored it. He glanced at the clock on the dash, calculating when Yarbrough's caravan would reach the farm. He had to find Natty within the next ten to fifteen minutes.

The road that led up past Oakes Hollow seemed steeper than it had when he'd run down it. He sped past a narrow stone-covered road on the left marked by a hand-painted sign. It read OAKES HOLLOW. The weather-beaten sign looked more like a warning than a greeting. In another minute, he was at the spot where the old logging road cut into the forest. He turned off the car, leaving the keys in the ignition, and started off at a trot toward the mountain trail.

THE BOULDER FELT cool and damp on Natty's bare legs as she sat on the edge, her feet dangling over the side. She glanced at her watch. Another few minutes, then she'd have to hustle. She didn't want to be late for school, but it was her first visit to the rock since she'd brought Charlie Burden up here. She closed her eyes and replayed Charlie's words.

Then she thought about Pat Garvey's phone call to hire Buck for the woodcutting project—the job that Charlie Burden had arranged. Finally, a call that wasn't bad news or a bill collector. As she stood up, she noticed a movement far down the trail—something out of place in a scene with no moving parts. She focused and saw that it was a person, too far off to identify, but someone was coming toward her, which was cause for concern.

Natty passed quickly through the grotto, climbed down the path back to the trail, and resumed her run. Whether there was someone on the trail ahead or not, she was going to be late for work if she didn't keep a good pace all the way to the top of Oakes Hollow. A few minutes later, the figure came into view and she saw that it was Charlie. She smiled with relief, then suddenly was alarmed. *Charlie Burden, in his work clothes.* As he drew nearer, Charlie pulled a cellphone from his pocket.

"Natty, call your grandfather," ordered Charlie, handing her the phone. She took it without comment. "They got something growing up there they shouldn't have?" he asked.

"Oh, shit!" Natty exclaimed.

"Tell him the Marines are on their way."

There didn't seem much point now in worrying about being late for work. The school would survive without her for a few minutes. Her mother answered the phone. "The police are on the way up. They know about the cornfield. You have about twenty minutes" was all that Natty said, before hanging up.

Charlie described Yarbrough's strike force, including the DEA agents and police. "There was also a cop from the sheriff's office. Big guy, overweight, with a thin mustache."

Natty nodded knowingly. "That'd be Wayne Lester, a deputy sheriff. Went to high school with him. He was an asshole then, and he's still an asshole."

They walked together in silence, but Natty could sense Charlie's curiosity. "Mama always told me that Petey grew it just for them—for him and Mama—and didn't sell any. But I *know* that ain't true. Petey grows way too much for just the two of them."

Natty recalled the first time she ever smelled it—the terrible summer after Annie died, when everyone was miserable. "I went walking down to the chicken house, peeked around the corner, and smelled this sweet smoke floatin' by. Sittin' there on the rocks next to the stream is my mama and Uncle Petey, both smokin' these corncob pipes, with a plastic bag full of weed on the rock between them. 'Course, I didn't know what it was at the time." She paused. "That was probably about the time they started sleeping together.

"Petey went away for a year when I was in sixth grade, for growing it. But now, instead of Petey going to jail, Bud and Alice are going to lose their farm." Natty glanced up at Charlie. "That don't seem fair, does it?"

Charlie thought about Hank's history lesson: *Nothin' fair about what the coal companies done to the people of West Virginia.* "No, it's not fair, Natty, but let's wait and see what happens," Charlie said, trying to sound optimistic.

They walked along, engrossed in their own thoughts, until they entered the dense woods at the end of the trail. As Natty's jumping-off point drew near, they slowed their pace.

"Buck got the call," Natty said, smiling up at Charlie. "About the timber job."

"That's good," said Charlie. He searched Natty's face.

"That was the best call we've had in twelve years." She reached a hand out and touched Charlie's arm. "Thanks for doing that, Charlie. Buck really needed that."

"I hope it works out for him," he said, sounding sincere.

She turned to face Charlie. "Should I call you later? If I find out what happened up there?"

Charlie took a step toward her, reached out, and gently moved the shock of hair that fell across her eyebrow. The tip of his index finger grazed the scar. "Why didn't you tell me about this?" he asked. "When you were telling me about Buck?"

Natty wanted to be mad, to be indignant at his question, but the look of concern on his face wouldn't let her. No man had ever shown her the kind of affection that Charlie Burden had shown with one little gesture, one little question.

"Ain't nothing to tell about," she whispered. "People make mistakes, is all."

"That's not a mistake," said Charlie angrily. "Natty, I'm sorry if you think this is none of my business, but . . ."

Natty turned toward the gap in the bushes. "But *what*, Charlie?"

He shrugged. "I'm worried about you, Natty. I'm worried about you and the kids."

Natty didn't want to talk about Buck and the beating he gave her, *ever*, with anybody, but she took in a deep breath and turned back to Charlie. "It was a hard day for Buck, that time he hit me. It was a queer day for everyone in Red Bone. All these strange, rich, beautiful people come flying in on helicopters, giving out free food and booze. Well, *shit*, wasn't all Buck's fault *that* day." Natty saw the quizzical look on Charlie's face. "That was when you and your friend Duncan McCord came to Red Bone."

"Natty, when was—"

"You and Mr. McCord came walking alongside the tent, past where Buck and all his boys were drinking themselves silly."

Charlie looked puzzled. "I vaguely remember coming down for the announcement, but . . ."

"'Course you don't remember it, Charlie. Why would you? Wasn't a big deal for you. Was nothing for *you*. But for *us* . . ." Natty recalled the memory of looking up and seeing Duncan McCord standing in front of her.

"Natty, I don't understand what the connection is with that day and Buck."

"Well, that's just *it*, Charlie," Natty said. "You don't understand how things are down here. This ain't Westchester County. Ain't no million-dollar houses down here. This is a hard place to live. Hard place for a man to make a living and have a family. I told you that once." She paused to calm herself.

"Buck sees men like you and Duncan McCord come down here for a couple hours, looking so successful, flying around in shiny black helicopters—well, 'course he's going to be envious, feel like more of a failure than he already is." Natty glanced back toward Oakes Hollow. "Just wasn't fair to Buck that day, Charlie," she said softly. "Wasn't fair to him."

Charlie watched her, thinking about the irony of Buck's envy. *Should he tell her how much he ached to trade places with Buck? To be her husband and care for her, protect her, and make love to her, and be a father to Pie and Cat.*

"Ain't an easy place for a woman, either, Charlie, to try to answer your original question." She took a couple of steps closer. "Especially a woman with kids, and one with special needs, to boot. Ain't a lot of prospects for a woman down here, so you don't tend to pack up and head for the door every time there's a little *excitement* in your marriage. Got enough welfare families without me takin' Pie and Cat off to live in some dirt-floor shanty with no heat and nothin' to look forward to 'cept a jar of corn liquor and that glassy fix your eyes get when you quit trying."

She looked up at Charlie and smiled, the light-up-a-room smile that told him she wasn't angry anymore. "Charlie, down here, if you're lucky enough to even *find* someone to love, you got to hold on to that tight as you can, you know? So that's what I'm doing, holding on, hoping it comes out right, and enjoying my daydreams in the meantime." She raised her eyebrows. "Okay?"

Charlie smiled with resignation. "Okay," he said.

"Should I call you if I hear anything?" She gestured off toward Redemption Mountain.

Charlie thought for a moment. "No, probably not. Safer if you don't. I'll find out soon enough."

"Charlie, if you hadn't warned us—and I ain't sure what Bud and Petey can do, anyway—but if you hadn't come out here, then that would have been it for Redemption Mountain, right? Bud'd have no choice but to give it up."

Charlie shrugged. "Yeah, most likely."

"So if they find out . . . find out it was you who told us—"

"Natty," he interrupted, "don't worry about it. I'll be okay."

Natty nodded. She wanted to go to him and hug him tightly, but she was afraid. Then Charlie backed away and turned to head up the trail.

"Hey, you coming to our soccer game tomorrow?"

"I wish I could. Going up to New York for a while. Closing on the house," Charlie answered.

"You coming back?"

Charlie smiled at her. "I'll be back," he said, starting down the path.

FROM BACK UP on the boulder, the sun was clearly visible, rising over the Alleghenies, igniting the tops of the mountains to the south. And closer, to the southwest, rising out of the hills still gray with shadow, a well-defined plume of dark smoke reached up to a cloud of wispy haze suspended over Redemption Mountain.

CHAPTER 21

CHARLIE WAS CERTAIN THE STORE WAS ON LEXINGTON AVENUE somewhere in the high Forties. It had been years since he'd been there, but he was a fairly frequent visitor when the kids were younger. It was hard to find, on the second floor over a luggage store and a camera shop, the kind of team sporting-goods store that Charlie thought must be unique to Manhattan. The store was more like a warehouse than a retail store, a labyrinth of high-ceilinged rooms connected by ramps, each piled high with brown boxes.

Even at 11:00 A.M., the store was busy. The clerks—hunchbacked old men who all acted like owners—were busy shepherding customers to the various sections of the store designated for each sport. Charlie found his way to a huge room stacked high with soccer equipment and got the attention of a salesman.

"Need uniforms for a soccer team," Charlie said.

"Little late in the season, aren'tcha?"

"We're starting over," said Charlie with a smile. "Red shirts, black shorts, and red socks. Under-fourteen team, fifteen players."

"Eighteen players," said the clerk, motioning for Charlie to follow him. "That's the package."

"Okay, eighteen," said Charlie. "And some black warm-up jackets."

"How about some matching pants? Look real sharp," said the salesman.

"Why not?" said Charlie.

The clerk pulled down several large boxes and showed Charlie the two shirt styles they had in stock. Charlie chose the more expensive of the two, a solid blood-red silk from Nike, with a black collar and stripes running down the sides. The lightweight black nylon shorts also had a red Nike swoosh. "Comes with numbers on the back," said the salesman, "and for only five bucks more you could put the team name on the front of each shirt."

"The Bones," said Charlie.

The salesman smiled. "Got just the thing for you," he said, leading Charlie over to a huge old book of logos and insignias. He leafed through the heavy book until he found the page he was looking for. There it was—a ferocious-looking silver skull and crossbones with red fire in the eyes. Charlie laughed, imagining the look on Pie's face when he saw it.

"Put it on the back of the jackets, too," said Charlie.

The salesman raised an eyebrow. "Getting a little pricey now, but I'll see what I can do."

Charlie smiled. "How about the pants?"

"Team must have rich parents," said the clerk.

"Yeah," said Charlie. "They're all in the energy business."

The order came to $3,500. "Take about two to three weeks—"

"I need it all in Red Bone, West Virginia, by next week," said Charlie, pulling out his American Express card. "Make it an even four grand if you can get it all there by Monday."

The clerk smiled as he took Charlie's credit card. "Red Bone. Must be a real ritzy town."

"Yeah, it's quite a place," said Charlie.

THE NOON RUSH hour was in full flurry when Charlie returned to the sidewalk. The revolving doors of the office buildings were spinning out the clerks, managers, and CEOs headed for lunch, shopping, or simply to enjoy the crisp fall air and a brisk midday walk in the world's greatest city.

Charlie walked up to 48th Street and headed west. He felt good about the uniforms. The kids would really appreciate them, and there was no reason why Natty's team had to look like the poorest team in the league. Charlie glanced at his watch and saw that he had plenty of time until his two o'clock meeting with the OntAmex and Kerns & Yarbrough people back at DD&M's office on Park Avenue. He'd take a walk through Rockefeller Center, over to Broadway, and back down through Times Square before heading to lunch at Nathan's. A hot dog with everything on it and a root beer would complete the quick dose of New York that he badly needed before heading back to Red Bone that night.

Leaving Nathan's, Charlie glanced across the street and something caught his eye. If he hadn't seen it on the bulletin board in the alcove between Barney's General Store and Eve's Restaurant, he would never have noticed the trademark icon of *Les Misérables*, the haunting image of the waif that had decorated New York for so long it had become invisible to the locals. He wondered if Natty would be on the Red Bone Baptist Church trip to New York, and a glimmer of a plan began to form in the back of his mind.

His thoughts of Natty were dispelled as soon as he began the walk back to the office, replaced by anxiety over the afternoon meeting. When Lucien had reached Charlie in Mamaroneck, he'd sounded worried.

"Torkelson and Tuthill are coming to town on Wednesday, and they want you to stick around for a meeting. Torkelson was pissed over that Redemption Mountain fiasco, and they're bringing that lawyer up from Charleston to find out what went wrong. You have anything to do with that, Charlie?"

Charlie considered the question for a moment before he replied. "No, Lucien," he lied. And that would be his story. *Screw 'em. If they wanted to act like gangsters, then he'd play clueless.* He smiled as he recalled his conversation with Terry Summers about the Redemption Mountain raid.

Even though it was obvious that Summers had a vested interest in the OntAmex side of the Redemption Mountain issue, the junior engineer was in good humor over the debacle at the farm. *Charlie, you had to be there,* said Summers. *Yarbrough's at the picnic table out in front of the house, sitting across from DeWitt, ready to close the deal. And the feds and that county cop are all standing around, drinking lemonade. So Yarbrough says to the farmer, "Now, we know you got something illegal growing in that cornfield up there." DeWitt looks up toward the field, then all of sudden, whump, the damn field is totally engulfed in flames. We could feel the heat a hundred yards away. DeWitt looks back at Yarbrough and says, "What cornfield?"* Summers laughed. *Oh, man, Charlie, it was funny. 'Course, Yarbrough didn't get much of a kick out of it. We all went up around back of the field, where there's a barn with this thousand-gallon*

*gasoline tank and a two-hundred-foot hose. And Petey, the son, he's stand-
ing there smelling like a gas station, watching it burn. They had to get
tipped off, Charlie—thirty minutes, at least—to give the field a good soaking.*

Charlie glanced at his reflection in the polished copper panel of the
elevator as it rose to the sixth floor of the DD&M building. He noted
the difference in his appearance from the thousands of times he'd ridden
this elevator during his tenure at the firm. His hair was longer, curling
over the top of his ears, and his face was tanned from the hours in the
sun at the construction site. He was also dressed more casually, in chinos, a white cotton dress shirt, and blazer. If he was going to take a pum-
meling from Torkelson and Tuthill that could end his career, he was
going to be comfortable doing it.

The conference room was more crowded than Charlie had expected.
He immediately got the feeling that there was more at stake here than an
inquiry into the Redemption Mountain incident. At the far end of the
long table, in his usual position, sat Jack Torkelson, a bottle of water and
a glass of ice in front of him. Tuthill, who would direct the meeting, sat
near the middle of the table. To his left were the OntAmex lawyers.
Across from Tuthill sat Yarbrough and another lawyer from his firm.

As Charlie acknowledged those he knew around the table, he couldn't
help focusing on the individuals who seemed out of place. Seated between
the Charleston lawyers and Torkelson was Warren Brand, the ambitious
vice chair of the DD&M executive committee. Across the table from him
were two younger members of the executive committee, shills of Brand.

At the near end of the table, closest to the door, Lucien stood to offer
his hand. "Nice to see you again, Charlie," said Lucien, a paragon of cor-
diality in all circumstances. Charlie took a chair a space away from Lucien, trying to spare his friend the appearance of being too closely aligned
with him, as Tuthill started the meeting.

"Now that Charlie is here, we can get to these two West Virginia
items." Tuthill looked down at his notes. "Charlie, first of all, let me say
that the Red Bone project is going extremely well. Under budget and
ahead of schedule. But we've got a couple of issues we need to discuss.
First off is the issue of the planning-board meeting and how we went
from putting a new roof on a little library to building a brand-new struc-

ture, along with some kind of athletics-field megaplex, that we never discussed." Tuthill stopped and looked over at Charlie.

"You said you had two issues, Larry," said Charlie. "What's the second one?"

Yarbrough slapped the table with his open palm. "You know goddamn well what the second issue is!" he exploded. "I used up a lot of valuable capital last week. Called in some big markers—sittin' there ready to close the deal, and, *whoosh,* the damn field goes up like a fucking napalm strike in the Mekong Delta. And, goddammit, Burden, you're the only one who could have tipped them off."

As Charlie moved his chair closer to the table to address those present, his eyes met those of Warren Brand. Brand stared at Charlie with a furrowed brow, looking more serious about this issue than he was entitled to be. Charlie was stumped as to what Brand's interest was, and it was the one thing about the meeting that worried him. He could take care of OntAmex, because in the end all they cared about were results, and he was building their power plant much faster and cheaper than they'd expected. That was worth a lot more than the reputation of some hillbilly law firm. And they'd get the Redemption Mountain coal through eminent domain, which is how it should have been done in the first place. But Brand was a puzzle.

"Now, Vernon," said Charlie, "let me tell you a couple of things about your raid on Redemption Mountain. First of all, you had too many people involved—too many possibilities of a leak—which is what happened. Did you know that the local cop was a high school sweetheart of Natty DeWitt? And that he's still got the hots for her?" Yarbrough looked up, startled. "Dammit, Yarbrough. Didn't you do any background checks on those people?" Charlie turned to Tuthill. "Larry, I don't know what you guys were thinking, okaying such a harebrained scheme." Tuthill winced. "You go up there like the Gestapo . . ." Charlie shook his head in exasperation. "What a disaster you guys almost caused."

Charlie stood up and moved around the table slowly, knowing he had the group's full attention. "Let me tell you what would have happened," he continued. "The DeWitts would have gone to jail. And they'd never have sold you the farm. They're too proud," he added. "They're proud, and it's all

they've got to show for a lifetime of hard work—and for all the heartache they've suffered." Alice DeWitt's voice flashed through his mind.
"Their whole family's buried up there on that mountain." He shook his
head slowly. "It was lunacy to think they'd sell.

"So you bring in the DEA, and the state police, and you show 'em a
field full of marijuana, and you're all done, Vern, you've shot your wad.
Now, the cops do their part and arrest the farmer and his son. And then
what happens, Vern?" Charlie moved around the end of the table to have
a more direct view of Yarbrough, who offered no response. "You should
know, Vern. Two men in jail. Next thing that happens is they get a lawyer. Maybe a sharp criminal lawyer from Charleston. And the lawyer
listens to the pig farmer's story, and the first thing he says is, 'What the
hell was a corporate lawyer representing Ackerly Coal and the OntAmex
Corporation doing on a drug raid in McDowell County?'"

Tuthill grimaced at the mention of OntAmex and stole a quick look at
Torkelson, who sat motionless, concentrating on Charlie.

"Then the story gets out and *The Charleston Gazette* puts it on the
front page, all about OntAmex trying to extort a local family out of their
farm, like it was the late 1800s all over again.

"Worst of all, Vern, we've got a pretty important PUC hearing this
spring on the merger with *Continental Electric*." Charlie emphasized the
magic words that made even Torkelson shift his weight in his chair. "But
now, instead of worrying about a dirt-poor farmer or his hillbilly granddaughter, you've got a big-time criminal attorney—one of your own,
Vern—with his fist around your client's balls and a multibillion-dollar
merger at stake." Charlie walked back to his chair, shaking his head. "It
was an asinine plan, Yarbrough," he said, as he took his seat again. "And
you're lucky it turned out like it did."

Vernon Yarbrough didn't seem too anxious to debate Charlie's
synopsis. "Well, we didn't see it coming out that way," Yarbrough offered
with unaccustomed meekness. "But you never know what might've
happened—"

"Okay, Vern," Charlie cut him off. "Let's talk about the library. We got
lucky there, too. Hankinson, the chairman of the planning board, has
become a friend of mine. He lives next door to me in Red Bone." Charlie
leaned back in his chair in a more relaxed position for the easy part of the

meeting. "We play cribbage almost every night," Charlie said with a smile. "So, at the beginning of the meeting, he pulls me aside—you saw him, Vern, right?—and tells me we've got some trouble with the other planning-board members. They're going to okay the pond relocation, because Hank got their commitment, but they don't think much of OntAmex or the roof project, so they're going to sock it to us down the road by making us apply for permits for everything we want to do."

"Like *what*?" Yarbrough asked, trying to regain a leadership position with his client.

"Like a permit for bringing in the turbines over town roads," Charlie shot back quickly, "or cutting the right-of-way through the forest—"

"They can't—" Yarbrough began.

"Or for flying helicopters over the town, or for taking water from the Heavenly River, or for having *Porta Potties on the site*! They can do anything they want, Vern, and they're a couple of miserable pricks, according to Hank. If they're not happy, they can shut us down anytime they want."

"C'mon, Burden, there's laws and statutes that—"

"*Oh, Vern, don't tell me about statutes!* You know the way those backwoods boards operate. They can destroy you with red tape and delays, and by the time you get 'em into court, you're *two years* behind schedule."

Tuthill flinched at the mention of a two-year delay.

"So I had to improvise," Charlie continued. "We build them a new building and some athletics fields, and we get the permanent cooperation of the planning board. Now we own them," he added, knowing the kind of words OntAmex liked to hear. "Plus," he leaned forward onto the table to play another trump card, "when the PUC hearings come around, we've got a showpiece of community involvement to put on display for the media. And we get it all for under a million bucks."

"Less than a million?" Tuthill asked. "And we've got the board on our side?"

"Larry, the crowd stood and cheered."

"They cheered?" asked Tuthill, looking over at Yarbrough. "Vern, is that what happened?"

Yarbrough nodded grudgingly. "They loved it."

"When's the last time OntAmex got a standing ovation at a town meeting, Larry?" Charlie asked, pressing his advantage.

At the end of the table, Torkelson stirred, drawing the group's attention. "Okay," he said, "let's put this all behind us. Charlie, go back down there and keep the plant on schedule. Build the town its library and baseball field. Take care of the planning board, and keep an eye on the DeWitt granddaughter. Spare no expense, but make it clear to the girl that everything stops if she causes trouble."

Torkelson turned toward the Charleston lawyers. "Yarbrough, get started on the eminent domain proceedings, like we discussed. Get the judge and everyone else on the same page. Spend whatever you must to keep it quiet, but get the job done."

"Already in the works, Jack," Yarbrough replied confidently.

"Then we're done here," Torkelson announced.

CHARLIE CLOSED THE door to his office and took a deep breath. He'd lied and bluffed his way through the inquiry and come away in a stronger position than when he'd started. But he had no illusions about what had just taken place or about his career at DD&M. His days were numbered. He'd survive just long enough to finish the job in Red Bone. They needed him there, but once the turbines were in, Torkelson and Tuthill were going to put a bullet in his head, and he'd be finished at Dietrich Delahunt & Mackey.

His thoughts were interrupted by a soft rap on the door. Lucien entered, shut the door behind him, and stood close to Charlie. "Nice job," he said with a thin smile. "You handled that beautifully. We live to fight another day."

Charlie looked his friend in the eye. "What's going on, Lucien? What's up with Brand?"

Lucien dropped into one of the low leather chairs next to the window. He looked drawn as he pointed to the other chair, indicating that Charlie should take a seat. "My time is about up here, Charlie. They're going to squeeze me out, Brand and the rest of the committee."

"That's impossible, Lucien." Charlie was shocked. "There's no way they can—"

"Times have changed," Lucien interrupted. "The young guys will eventually have the votes. They'll move the company out of New York, seek out a profitable merger, sell the building, and the remaining partners will reap the financial windfall."

"C'mon, Lucien. You've made it clear that you'd never move the company, and you've always had more than enough votes—"

Lucien held up his hand. "Brand has OntAmex now."

"How the hell did that happen?" asked Charlie. "How did Brand get—"

"It's not Brand, Charlie," Lucien interrupted. "He's not capable of managing something like this; we both know that. It's Torkelson. He's behind it all.

"Torkelson's star is rising fast," Lucien continued. "He *is* OntAmex now that Duncan and Red Landon are so far removed from operational matters. He's been a huge part of their growth strategy and their success, and this Red Bone plant will be his crown jewel. He brings this one in— the biggest, most efficient, most profitable non-nuclear plant ever built in North America—and there will be no stopping him. He'll have the power to do whatever he wants."

"Maybe I should dump some ball bearings into the electrical conduits," Charlie offered.

Lucien smiled. "Not the way we do things, heh, Charlie?"

"So Torkelson and Brand have a deal, is that it?"

"My spies tell me that Torkelson's going to use his leverage to back Brand. I'll be voted out and handed a golden parachute, and, I'm afraid, so will you, my friend."

"And he'll have plenty of leverage," Charlie responded. "Next year we stand to make, what, thirty million in fees from OntAmex?"

"And Torkelson will have the power to take it all away."

"What does Torkelson get?" Charlie's voice had dropped into the lower tone that men use to discuss the darker issues of business transactions.

Lucien leaned forward with his hands locked in front of him. "My guy tells me that Brand had a couple of belts with him one night and let it slip that Torkelson gets five mil out of the deal, and something a little short of that for Tuthill, too, all on the quiet, after Brand takes over."

Charlie shook his head. "He's a crook. A cheap fucking extortionist," he said bitterly.

"You'd never be able to prove it," said Lucien. "That's the way it is now, Charlie. The world's changing. *Everything's* about money and the power to make more money. And having it all *today.*"

Charlie suddenly thought about the China project, Lucien's dream and his passion. He would never see it completed—and Charlie wouldn't see it at all. *Why not just pack it in now and forget about China and West Virginia?* Then he thought about Ellen and her new house and noticed the stack of architectural drawings of small libraries and athletics fields on his desk. *Yes, he still had things left to do in West Virginia.*

"I've got a company to run." Lucien's words jarred Charlie from his thoughts. "And you've got a power plant to build." Lucien stood. "The barbarians are at the gate, Charlie."

"We'll find a way to fight them off, Lucien. We always do," Charlie said, gripping his friend's hand.

"We'll find a way," said Lucien, putting on his self-confident smile, but Charlie could see that his eyes didn't agree.

CHAPTER 22

THE YELLOW SCHOOL BUS LURCHED AND SWAYED ALONG THE winding road as the gray-haired woman struggled with the oversize steering wheel. Sitting in a front seat across the aisle, Natty kept a wary eye on the driver and on the road, her left hand squeezing the top of the seat as they went into each turn. Geneva Gunnells had been the elementary-school bus driver for nearly forty years, but Natty was always ready to leap across the aisle and grab the wheel.

In the backseat, Zack Willard held court. Sitting next to Zack was Paul, whom Zack had adopted as his "main man" and had engaged in a season-long project to teach him some English swear words. Paul laughed along with the others, although Natty knew he probably had no idea what they were saying.

There seemed to be some extra enthusiasm in her team today, and while none of them would admit it, Natty knew it was because this was the first game they would play in their new uniforms. That today's game was against their biggest rival only added to their excitement. Natty had to admit that she couldn't wait to see the look on the face of the Welch coach when her team filed off the bus.

She looked over at Emma, two seats behind Geneva. Her shiny black warm-up jacket was zippered all the way up. The matching black pants had a red stripe running down the seam, which Natty had to concede looked sharp, although she would've preferred red warm-ups rather than the ominous-looking black. But the kids loved them.

Natty had a tough time believing it when she discovered the six boxes piled just inside the children's library. She'd gone in to get the soccer balls before Wednesday's practice, and there they were. A note taped to the top box read, *Mrs. Oakes—A gift from the OntAmex Company.* It wasn't signed, but the boxes all had white shipping labels from New York City.

Natty's mouth fell open when she realized what the boxes contained. Then she found an envelope with a form letter from the salesman, thanking Charlie, along with a packing slip and a pink copy of the invoice. Natty gasped when she saw the total cost—four thousand dollars! *My God!* She'd gotten this year's T-shirts for less than a hundred dollars for the whole team.

Natty looked back toward the rear of the bus, toward her four-thousand-dollar team. They had quieted down a little as they got closer to Welch. Then Sammy Willard moved to the side and she could see Zack, talking earnestly now. Natty knew he was talking about today's game and he was getting the Bones ready. That was good, because this was going to be a tougher game than when they took Welch by surprise in their first meeting this season.

CHARLIE SKIPPED DOWN the flight of stairs between the store and the restaurant. He was looking forward to an enjoyable afternoon with Hank. He wandered into the restaurant to say hi to Eve. It still bothered him that she'd obviously cooled toward him.

In the first booth, he recognized the unmistakable form of Mabel Willard. Across from her sat Ada Lowe and a white woman they introduced as their travel agent from Bluefield. Mabel's huge smile brought Charlie to their booth. Taped to the side of the table was a hand-lettered poster stating: NEW YORK CITY TRIP! SIGN UP TODAY! Mabel slid over to leave just enough room on the bench for Charlie. "Come sit down with us here, Mr. Burden. Need to talk to you 'bout somethin'."

"I've only got a few minutes," Charlie explained, as he settled into the booth. "Going over to Welch with Hank to watch the soccer game."

Ada Lowe smiled. "Oh, that's nice, Mr. Burden. I'm too old to be traveling to all them games, but that's nice that you boys are going."

"Now, then, Mr. Burden," said Mabel, "I'm thinking that you might be interested in going on our little trip. We only got fifteen out of the twenty bodies we need to get the special group rates."

Charlie listened politely, wondering why *anyone* had signed up for the trip—a ten-hour bus ride each way, with a stop for lunch at a Bob Evans in Pennsylvania, two nights at the Milford Plaza, and, of course, the trip's salvation, a Saturday-matinee ticket to *Les Misérables.* And all for just $321, which, Charlie had to agree, was a pretty good value.

"What do you say, Mr. Burden?" Mabel was all business, slapping the fingers of her right hand on the table for emphasis. "Can we sign you up and get a small deposit today?"

Charlie knew he wouldn't be taking a ten-hour bus ride or staying at the Milford Plaza, but he wanted to make sure the trip came off and that Natty Oakes was on it. If anybody in Red Bone deserved to go, it was Natty, and the prospect of meeting up with her in New York was irresistible. He smiled and shook his head. "No, ladies, I'm sorry, but I won't be able to make your trip, much as I'd love to see *Les Misérables* again."

Mabel sighed and patted Charlie on the arm. "That's all right, Mr. Burden, we'll find some others somewheres."

"How about Natty?" Charlie asked. "Is she going?"

Ada Lowe shook her head. "No. She'd love to, but she's feeling real bad 'bout owing Gus money for repairing her car, so she really don't have the money to spend."

Charlie pulled out his wallet and platinum American Express card and handed it to the travel agent. "Okay," he said, "here's what I'll do. Put the last five trips on this, courtesy of OntAmex Energy. Then find five more people who want to go but can't afford it." He smiled at Mabel. "Just make sure Natty's one of them."

Mabel grinned from ear to ear. "Why, Mr. Burden, that girl goin' to have a *wonderful* time in New York City!"

THE CHRYSLER NEW Yorker was actually a very comfortable ride when it hit a stretch of road without any bumps, ruts, or potholes to challenge the ancient car's suspension. Charlie leaned back into the once-soft leather seat, stretching his legs out in front of him. "They don't build cars like this anymore, Hank," he said, looking over at the old man hunched over the chrome and wood-trimmed steering wheel.

"And a good thing, too," Hank replied. "An environmental disaster is what it is, burning too much gas and fouling the air." He looked over at

Charlie with a glint in his eye. "If I didn't love it so much, I'd feel guilty."

Charlie laughed and rolled down the window. He was enjoying himself, riding along with his friend on a beautiful fall day, the workweek over and things going well at the plant. And to top it off, he was on his way to watch the Bones in action. Plus, he had to admit, he was looking forward to seeing Natty again. Charlie hadn't seen her since he'd returned from New York. He told himself that he wasn't avoiding her, just being prudent. But he did get her note, pushed under his apartment door that morning: *Mr. Burden, Please thank the OntAmex Company for the new uniforms. The kids love them! Game tonight in Welch, 5:00 P.M., if you want to see how they look. Sally and me will be at the Roadhouse later. Buy you a beer. Nat.*

It was a hard invitation to pass up, and Hank was happy to let Charlie buy him dinner afterward at Moody's, although he warned Charlie that the place could get a little raucous on a Friday night.

"Well, Hank, I'm about due for another fight," Charlie said, laughing. "It's been a couple of months."

Hank had insisted on driving, as the big Chrysler needed some exercise. He also wanted to show Charlie a spot he might find interesting if they had some extra time. On Cold Springs Road, they came to a stop as a long flatbed trailer, loaded with freshly cut tree trunks, strained to pull itself out of the logging road. Hank edged the Chrysler forward a few yards, to where they could see down the newly carved dirt road. A long white trailer sat up on blocks. A sign on the side door read GARVEY LUMBER.

Charlie could see a flurry of activity down the road and hear the big chain saws. He breathed in the heady mixture of sawdust, pine scent, and exhaust from the gasoline engines and envied the men working down the road.

"That's a good day's work they're putting in there, eh, Charlie?"

He turned back to Hank and nodded. "You earn your money when you're cutting trees. Kind of work that lets you know you've accomplished something."

Along both sides of Cold Springs Road, a dozen cars and pickups were parked at haphazard angles in the tall grass. A white pickup caught Charlie's eye. It was the truck he'd seen on this same road, the day he and Pie rode the bulldozer around the site. The same truck that Natty had reluctantly climbed into when they were walking up the hill from the library.

When the log hauler finally pulled out, they made good time. Hank would point out things of interest along the road, mostly things that *used* to be—a closed elementary school; a derelict factory; a drive-in movie theater with dozens of rusted speaker pipes pushing through the high weeds; an old Dairy Queen.

As they approached Welch, Hank again broke the silence. "First thing you need to understand about where we're going is that, if there was ever an industry that cried out for a labor union, it was coal mining. Back in 1890, when the United Mine Workers of America was formed over in Ohio, and then for a good part of the first half of the 1900s, coal mining was about as close to chattel slavery as anything we had in this country since the Civil War.

"The coal companies owned the towns and the houses and paid the miners in scrip, which could only be used at the company store at inflated prices. The miners were systematically cheated by the clerkweighmen on the amount of coal they were credited with, and the working conditions in the mines were lethal. Between 1890 and 1920, West Virginia had twice the mine death rate of any other state. The opportunity for organized labor was ripe, but it wasn't that easy back then. Didn't have the labor laws we got now. When the union finally started to send organizers down here, the coal companies got together and formed the Kanawha County Coal Operators Association. Then they hired the infamous Baldwin-Felts Detective Agency in Bluefield to provide *mine security*." Hank glanced over at Charlie to see if he recognized the name. Charlie shook his head.

"For years, Baldwin-Felts was just an army-for-hire of thugs and gunmen—leg breakers used to intimidate miners and union organizers. And they were effective. Baldwin-Felts made these southern counties, McDowell, Logan, and Mingo—*bloody Mingo*, it came to be known as— hazardous duty for organizers and union men. Just the name filled miners with terror. They operated like some kind of law-enforcement agency, 'cause the coal companies owned the politicians and most of the sheriffs.

"The result of all this oppression," Hank continued, "was violence, in the form of the famous West Virginia Mine Wars. It all started in April 1912, with a strike up in Kanawha County, and didn't end until September

1921, at the battle of Blair Mountain, when the miners gave up rather than fight the federal troops that President Harding sent down here to stop the *insurrection*." Hank shook his head ruefully. "That was the end of the union down here for many years," he said. "And the miners paid the price for a long, long time." He paused in his story to point out the Tug Fork, which ran along the western boundary of the town. "Lot of history in that river, Charlie. Lot of history. But that's a lesson for another day."

Hank turned right onto Court Street. "Mine wars were interrupted by the First World War, when everyone more or less put their own problems behind them for the sake of the war effort. Country needed the smokeless coal, wages improved a little, and there was plenty of work for everyone."

Hank pulled the big car into a small parking area in front of an old gray stone building that sat atop a hill. A sign at the bottom of the stairs read, WELCH COUNTY COURTHOUSE. He turned off the car and got out, pausing for a moment to lean back and look up at the imposing structure. He started toward the stairway, motioning for Charlie to follow. "When the war ended," he resumed, "the country went into a recession, miners got laid off, and the violence started up again."

They reached the top of the stairs, and Charlie examined the building for activity while Hank caught his breath. There were a few lights on inside, but no sign of anyone coming or going. Charlie was curious as to what Hank wanted to show him. But instead of walking toward the front door, Hank eased himself down on the top step of the staircase. He pointed to a spot across from him. "Here, Charlie," he said. "Sit down right here." Hank gazed out at the town laid out below them before continuing. "I'll skip some of the background, but in the spring of 1920, the non-union miners over in Mingo County went on strike, which got the coal companies pretty agitated. In May of that same year, a couple of courageous union men, Fred Mooney and Bill Blizzard, came down and spoke to an assembly of three thousand miners in a little town down on the Kentucky border called Matewan." Hank looked over at Charlie for a sign of recognition.

"I've heard of Matewan," said Charlie.

"The result of that rally was that fifteen hundred miners joined the United Mine Workers of America, which was bad news for the coal operators. So Baldwin-Felts was called in to take care of the situation, and on May nineteenth, twelve *detectives* got off the train in Matewan, wearing pistol belts, and a few carrying satchels containing Thompson subma- chine guns. The gang was led by Albert and Lee Felts themselves.

"What made Matewan different was that, while the coal company owned the housing, Matewan was an independent town. It had its own mayor, fellow named Cabell Testerman, and its own sheriff, a young man named Sid Hatfield. No relation to the Hatfields you're thinking about." Hank paused for a moment, then squinted at Charlie as if he were looking back in time. "Can you imagine the guts it took for a young fellow like that to stand up to a gang of professional thugs like the Baldwin-Felts men?

"But that's what happened. Along with Testerman, Sid Hatfield con- fronted the Baldwin-Felts men at the train station and told them he wouldn't stand for any miners being put out of their homes in his juris- diction. 'Course, Albert Felts ignored him. Took his gang out to the Stone Mountain coal camp and evicted six families of miners who'd joined the union. Threw all their belongings outside in a cold, drizzling rain. Made an example of them and said they'd be back for more.

"By the time the Baldwin-Felts men got back to Matewan, word had spread about the evictions and that Hatfield planned to arrest Albert Felts. Dozens of miners armed themselves and headed into town. What hap- pened next was probably what you've heard about or maybe saw in the movies—the battle of Matewan, sometimes called the Matewan massacre."

Hank shifted his weight, spit some tobacco juice onto the grass, and wiped his mouth with the sleeve of his suit jacket. "Young Hatfield, along with the mayor and a few deputies and miners, marched right up to the Baldwin-Felts men in front of Chambers Hardware Store. Told them he was arresting the lot. So Albert Felts drew out his pistol and, at point- blank range, shot and killed Mayor Cabell Testerman. The battle was on."

Hank looked over at Charlie with a gleam in his eye. "But that was a bad day for Baldwin-Felts, 'cause they didn't know who they were deal- ing with. Sid drew his guns and killed Albert Felts and a few of the other *detectives*. Hundreds of shots were fired, and when it was all over, the street was littered with bodies. Seven Baldwin-Felts men were dead, including Albert and Lee Felts. Two miners had been killed, and four others wounded. That was an important day for the union, because the

miners *finally had a hero*, a lawman who was tough enough to stand up
to the mine operators and their hired thugs."

Charlie could see that his friend's eyes were filled with tears. He
remained silent while Hank took a few moments before continuing.

"Tough time to be a hero, though," Hank said softly. "Tom Felts, the
last brother, swore revenge. He used his contacts to have Sid, along with
twenty-two other townspeople, indicted for murder. Case went to trial in
January 1921, at the Williamson Courthouse in Mingo County. Charges
were dismissed against most of the accused, and the rest, including Hatfield, were acquitted.

"But Felts wouldn't give up. He had Sid and his friend, Deputy Ed
Chambers, who was also a union supporter, indicted on a trumped-up
charge of shooting up a town over here in McDowell County. The sheriff
told Sid that nothing would come of it and that he'd guarantee their
safety." Hank took out his pocket watch and saw that it was almost five
o'clock. He started to push himself up. "Don't want to be late for the
game." Charlie stood and reached over to help Hank up.

For several moments, Hank stared down the long stairway, lost in
his thoughts, while Charlie waited. Hank's voice was subdued again
when he resumed. "It was a beautiful day in August, too hot to be wearing wool suits and starched collars, but that's what Sid and Ed wore for
their court appearance when they walked up these stairs here that we've
just come up.

"But the sheriff wasn't around that day, nor any of his deputies. They
weren't anywhere near this town when Hatfield and Chambers—both
of 'em unarmed—walked up these stairs with their wives that beautiful
summer morning. And when they got to the top of the stairs," Hank
looked over toward the front door of the courthouse, "out of that door
come a fellow named C. E. Lively, a Baldwin-Felts assassin, along with
two other gunmen. They murdered Hatfield and Chambers right in front
of their wives. And then, to finish the job, Lively walked over and put one
more bullet in Sid's head, while his wife watched in horror. Then the
murderers walked down these stairs and drove off. They were never
brought to trial." Hank stood with his hands in his pockets, staring
down. Charlie got the impression that his friend was saying a prayer.

Finally, Hank looked up. "Sid Hatfield was a handsome young man,

Charlie, tall, with a strong jaw and clear eyes, and the look of a good man about him." Hank smiled. "Reminds me a lot of you."

Charlie laughed. "Don't try to make me into a modern-day Sid Hatfield. And nobody's gonna shoot me, either. Times have changed, Hank." Charlie looked at his watch.

"*Dammit*, Charlie, I keep tellin' you, *nothing's* changed here in a hundred years. The coal operators are just big companies now, like Ackerly and OntAmex, and Baldwin-Felts is a law firm in Charleston or Washington, but it's all the same, and when it comes to takin' coal out of the ground, you'd better stay out of their way." Hank leaned a little closer to his friend. "I know what you *did*, Charlie," he said, "on the Redemption Mountain thing."

Charlie couldn't hide his surprise. "How did you—"

Hank interrupted him. "Not much happens around here I don't find out about. The point is, Bud DeWitt would've lost his farm, and he and Petey both'd have gone to jail, weren't for you. And Ackerly Coal would be getting ready to start blasting off the top of Redemption Mountain."

Charlie stared at Hank, wondering if he should confirm the story. Finally he gave in. "Hank, it's not that big a deal. C'mon, let's go," he said.

Hank reached out and held his arm. "Charlie, if *I* know what you did, *they* know, too," he said quietly. "You need to be careful now."

Charlie's instinct was to laugh it off, but he respected Hank too much to ignore his words. He nodded and put his hand on his friend's shoulder. "Okay, Hank," he said. "I'll be careful."

CHAPTER 23

THE WELCH TEAM WAS USING THE ENTIRE FIELD FOR THEIR warm-up when the yellow bus from Red Bone pulled into the parking lot. Natty got off first, caught the eye of the opposing coach, and made a show of looking at her watch to show that they'd arrived in time. Standing next to the coach was Kyle Loftus, the commissioner of the league, talking to his friend Wayne Lester.

The blue-clad Welch team stopped to stare at the Bones in their new uniforms, trotting toward their side of the field. Charlie and Hank watched their arrival from the far end of the field, sitting in folding chairs that Hank had stored in the trunk of the Chrysler.

"Take a look at this," Hank said. Charlie quickly picked out the Pie Man, whose warm-up jacket reached down well below his waist. He had his Yankees hat on backward, the brim tipped up at a jaunty angle. You could see how proud he was from all the way down the field.

"Now, where do you suppose Natty got them flashy new suits? Looks a little rich for a team from Red Bone." Hank eyed Charlie with suspicion. "More like what teams from New York might wear, don't you think?"

Charlie winked. "Maybe they had a bake sale."

The Bones quickly took the field without benefit of a warm-up, but when Natty noticed that the referee hadn't arrived, she called out to Zack to lead the team in a quick jog around the field. On the sideline, Kyle Loftus was busy on his cellphone, trying to locate the missing official. A moment later Loftus strode toward the two coaches. "Wife says he must have forgotten about the game."

The Welch coach shook his head. "Asshole." He spit tobacco juice on the field in front of Natty. "Well, let's find somebody to ref," he said, looking back toward the bleachers.

"Should be somebody ain't got a kid playing in the game," Natty offered.

"Good luck with that," said the coach.

Natty spied Hank and Charlie sitting by themselves. She'd been wondering if Charlie would take her up on her invitation, and her heart skipped a beat when she saw him smile back at her. "I got somebody," Natty said, starting off toward the sideline.

"Say, Hank . . . Charlie," she called out. Charlie smiled, knowing what was coming. "Got no ref for the game. I, uh, was wondering if either of you boys think you might be fit enough to run up and down the field with these kids. That is, if you know something about the rules." Neither man moved. Natty fidgeted. "'Cause they'll find somebody on their side of the field, and that won't be—"

Charlie saved her, pushing himself out of his chair. He pulled his sweater off and started to walk toward the center of the field. "For this, you'll have to buy me a *pitcher* of beer," he said, as he passed Natty.

"You're going to need it." She laughed, turning to jog back toward her bench.

"Here you go, ref," said Natty, tossing Charlie a whistle on a rawhide cord.

"Thanks, coach," he said, walking backward. "Love the new uniforms," he added.

Natty wrinkled her nose. "Santa Claus brought 'em."

The opposing coach met Charlie at the center of the field. "Now, you done any of this before, fella?" He didn't wait for an answer. "What you need to watch for with this Red Bone team is the offsides. Team's famous for being offside, 'specially that girl, so you gotta watch her." Charlie bent over and rolled his chinos up a few inches over his running shoes. "They can get rough, too," the coach continued. "Gotta watch them black boys. Like to throw their elbows and hips around, know what I'm sayin'?"

Charlie stood up and reached into his pocket for his sunglasses. He put the whistle in his mouth and blew a loud blast, startling the Welch coach. "Let's go, then. Keep the time on your side, and let me know when there's two minutes left in the half."

Being on the field was different from sitting on the sideline, and Charlie was surprised at how fast the kids moved. In the past he'd always reffed younger kids' games. He also quickly realized that a few of these players were exceptional for their age. Emma and Paul, Natty's midfielder from Poland, were obvious superstars. And the Willard brothers dominated whatever sector of the field they were in.

But the blue team also had an exceptional soccer player. It was the tall, blond-haired boy named Gabe, whom Charlie had followed down the hill before the first game in Red Bone. Gabe was playing midfield opposite Paul and was proving every bit his equal. He was always in control, with a powerful kick from either foot, and was an excellent passer. He was also a fine sportsman—several times after inadvertent rough contact, he'd reached down to help one of the Bones players to his feet.

After a few frenetic trips up and down the field, Charlie was winded, but once he got accustomed to the pace and remembered that the ref's chief responsibilities were to keep the game from getting too rough and to stay out of the way, he began to relax.

The Welch team was getting the better of the early play. Their strategy was to keep the ball in the Bones' end of the field. The second part of the blue team's strategy was revealed the first time the Bones were able to get the ball up to Emma. One of the Welch fullbacks, a short, rugged-looking boy they called Rudy, quickly jumped in front of Emma with minimal effort at going after the ball. It was probably a foul, but Charlie let it go because it was marginal, and he didn't want to show any favoritism to Natty's team or to Emma as a girl.

"Gotta call that one, ref," Natty said calmly, strolling slowly along the sideline. It was the first thing he'd heard her say since the game began. In contrast, on the Welch side of the field, the coach was moving up and down the field with the flow of the action, his foghorn voice calling out instructions to his players. His players seemed to tune him out, and Charlie tried to do the same.

NATTY HEARD THE coach yelling, Charlie's whistles, and the usual shouts of encouragement and criticism from the spectators along the sideline.

But as the game settled in, she began to lose her concentration and indulged herself by focusing completely on Charlie Burden. *There he was, this rich, beautiful man from New York, running up and down a shabby soccer field in West Virginia, volunteering to be a fill-in ref—a job that nobody ever wanted—in a game in which he didn't even have a kid playing. And he was there because of her—sure, because of Pie, too, but mostly because she was there—and that amazed her. And it frightened her. She thought about what he'd said to her up on the boulder, the words she'd never forget.*

The ball scooted across the sideline, rolling directly toward Hank, who reached down, too late to stop it. One of the little kids patrolling the sidelines ran after it. "Hey there, you in the chair," the ref called out. "Gotta be quicker going after those balls." Hank laughed and waved at Charlie. *And look at the joy he's brought into that old man's life, just by being his friend. Hank, who'd been wallowing in loneliness since Alva Paine died, sitting there now at a kids' soccer game, enjoying the low sun and the smell of wood smoke in the fall air.*

Then Natty noticed Pie moving up and down the sideline, following the action. But it wasn't the ball he was watching. It was Charlie, a proud happy face revealing his excitement at having his adult buddy on display for everyone to see. *How much Pie had changed in the few months he'd known Charlie! The little boy she so desperately loved was finally developing some self-esteem and confidence that he could do things, be something, and that he wasn't so different from the other kids. All he needed was an adult male to treat him like a regular kid—and show him some love.*

Natty thrust her hands into the pockets of her jeans, straining to see Charlie through the swirl of players. She swallowed hard, fighting the empty feeling that rose inside as she thought, for the first time, about Charlie disappearing from their lives for good. *Why couldn't she accept the fact that Charlie Burden was the man she'd been daydreaming about for most of her life?*

A roar from the opposite sideline brought Natty's attention back to the game. She looked up to see the blue team high-fiving one another as they headed back toward the middle of the field. A disgusted Brenda Giles flung the ball angrily out of the Bones' goal. Natty was embarrassed. Her team had given up a goal and she hadn't even seen it. She clapped her hands together hard. "C'mon, Bones. We'll get it back." It was the first time they had been behind all season.

After a few minutes of even play in the midfield, Zack gained control of the ball with some room to move upfield. He raced it over the center-line and sent a perfect feed through to Emma. But just before Emma reached the ball, from her blind right side, Rudy hurtled himself into her, sending her crashing into another Welch player. Her mouth smashed into the second player's knee. It was as vicious a tackle as Charlie had seen in kids' soccer, and he blew his whistle loudly as he raced over toward Emma, who lay on the field, blood flowing from her lower lip. Then he heard the Welch coach from the sideline.

"Atta boy, Rudy. Way to watch her. Good clean tackle."

Charlie felt his jaw muscles tighten. A rough play on the field was one thing, but an irresponsible comment from a coach was another. He watched Natty help Emma to her feet. She was still dazed, and a small towel pressed to her mouth was red with blood. He headed for the Welch coach. "That's a yellow card for that kid," said Charlie. "And a yellow card for you, too."

The coach smirked at Charlie incredulously. "Don't get carried away, buddy. You're just a sub here," he said loudly. He pointed out toward the field. "And if that *little girl* out there can't take it, maybe she shouldn't be playing in a boy's game."

"One more irresponsible comment out of you and you're gone," said Charlie. "Now, start acting like a coach. These are kids out here."

The coach crossed his arms. "Screw you, asshole. C'mon, get out there and get the game going, or we'll find someone else to ref."

Charlie strained to control himself. "You've been warned, coach." It was then that Charlie noticed two men staring at him from the sideline. One was the insurance man who'd given Natty a hard time at the game in Red Bone. But it was the other man who got Charlie's attention. He was tall and heavy, with a pencil-thin mustache and a toothpick between his puffy lips. Charlie was certain he'd seen him before.

Without Emma to watch, the Welch team became more aggressive, moving up the field to press the attack. A minute before halftime, they scored again. Angered by the incident with Emma, Zack had been trying to do too much by himself and lost the ball to a good tackle in front of his own goal. The Bones trailed 2–0.

At the half, Charlie walked over and sat down next to Hank.

"Rough game," said Hank.

"That's my fault," admitted Charlie, pulling his sweater on. The sun had dropped behind the nearby hills and the air had become cooler. The field lights had come on automatically.

Natty walked over and tossed Charlie a plastic water bottle.

"How's Emma?" Charlie asked, unscrewing the cap of the bottle.

Natty looked over at her team. "She's got some bruises, and her lip is swollen, but she's okay." Natty waited while Charlie took a long drink from the bottle. "Hey, Charlie, I'm sorry about the coach. Wouldn't have asked you to ref, if I'd known."

"It's okay." Charlie smiled at her. "I can handle him."

Natty frowned and exchanged a look with Hank, then she started out toward her team. Charlie looked at Hank.

"He's a tough customer," said Hank. "Used to be a cop but got a little too rough, one time too many." Hank turned and spit his tobacco juice in the dirt next to his chair. "Drives a truck now for the teamsters."

The second half started much like the first, with the Welch team lofting the ball down toward the Bones' end of the field every chance they got. On defense, Rudy stuck close to Emma wherever she went. Her lower lip was swollen, and she still had some dried blood on the front of her new red jersey and a smear of blood on her right leg just above the knee. She also appeared to be limping slightly.

From the beginning of the half, Rudy took every opportunity to bump Emma and to cut her off roughly when she attempted to get into the play. Charlie called several fouls on him, but most of Rudy's rough play occurred when they were away from the ball and Charlie wasn't watching. Rudy became more emboldened by the Bones' frustration and began to taunt Emma, quietly at first and then, as his confidence grew, more loudly, to entertain his teammates.

"Hey, whatcha got on your leg there, Emma? That blood from your period? Emma's having her period! Watch out, she'll get some on you." Rudy was enjoying himself. "How long you been havin' your period, Emma? Think you'd have bigger tits by now. That is, if you're really a girl."

Emma tried her best to ignore Rudy and move away from him, but he shadowed her relentlessly and kept up a nonstop patter of taunts. Several times Emma looked to the sideline, and Natty could see her trying to fight back the tears. Natty tried to smile some encouragement to her, but she knew that Emma's shyness was paralyzing her on the field.

Rudy soon found a new sensitive spot. "Hey, Emma, nice lip you got there. You got big lips, anyway, Emma. How come your mama don't have them big lips?"

Charlie could hear snatches of what was being said, and he could see the smiles on the faces of some of the blue defenders, but he was too busy to tell who was saying what to whom. As he blew the whistle for a blue throw-in directly in front of the Welch bench, Charlie was surprised to hear someone on the field call out, "Ref, hey, ref. Time-out. Time-out."

Charlie looked up to see Gabe, the blond Welch midfielder, making a T with his hands as he walked up the middle of the field. Uncertain about the rules, Charlie nudged Matt Hatfield, standing next to him. "You get time-outs?" he asked softly.

"One each half."

Charlie blew the whistle loudly. "Time-out, blue," he called out, pointing to the bench.

"What the *fuck*?" The bewildered Welch coach walked out onto the field to find out what was going on. Gabe ignored his coach and continued walking up the field. He looked angry and was headed directly at the still-smirking Rudy. The stocky fullback was taken by surprise when Gabe fired two hands into his chest, knocking him off his feet.

"You cut the shit right now, Rudy. You play soccer, and you shut the fuck up! You hear me?" Rudy bounced up quickly, but it was evident that he wanted no part of a fight with the stronger Gabe, who pushed him backward again, a finger in his face. "And you leave her alone. You stop talking to her, you stop talking shit, and you stop fouling her! You got that, Rudy? Just play soccer!"

The Welch coach got to the boys ahead of Charlie and grabbed Gabe's elbow, dragging him off the field. "How about you mind your own *damn* business, kid. I'm the coach of this team, not you. And you can rest your mouth on the bench for the rest of this game."

Gabe picked up his sweatshirt and kept on walking as the coach sent a sub onto the field.

When the blue team called time-out, Natty had started onto the field to console Emma. As the Welch team's best player gave himself up for Emma, Natty backed quietly off the field. This was a situation she would let Emma deal with on her own.

"C'mon, ref! Let's get this game going!" the Welch coach bellowed from the sideline. With a 2–0 lead, he was eager to get the clock started for the last ten minutes of the game. But Emma now played with a renewed determination, motivated by the gallantry of Gabe, a boy she knew only from the soccer games in which they'd competed over the years—both of them too shy to ever say anything to each other—and by her anger at Rudy.

The Bones controlled the action with a tempo that the blue team couldn't match without Gabe in the midfield. After keeping the ball in the Welch end of the field for several minutes, Sammy sent a blistering cross into the center of the field, where Emma knifed through several Welch defenders and, leaping high in the air, took the ball on her chest. The ball went softly into the air, but Emma never let it hit the ground. She left her feet for a vicious sidewinder kick, rocketing the ball past the startled goalie.

The Welch coach was incensed. As his team walked back upfield for the restart of play, he screamed at Rudy, "She's your responsibility! Don't let her run free like that, boy. Stop playing like a pussy, or you'll be on the bench, too!"

Charlie glared at the coach as he screamed at his players and was an instant away from blowing the whistle and tossing him out of the game, but there had already been enough anger on the field without another confrontation. He hoped that the rest of the game would play out without incident.

"Two minutes!" called out the gray-haired woman keeping time on the home side of the field. Charlie turned to her and nodded with a quick smile as he trotted toward the Welch end of the field.

The Bones quickly gained possession after the restart, and Paul brought the ball over the centerline. He waited as long as he could before lofting it high toward the right corner in front of Emma. As she approached the bouncing ball, calculating her angle to the goal, she could sense an ominous movement at her blind side. Flashing back to earlier in the game, she turned just in time to see Rudy coming straight at her, full speed. Emma refused the natural instinct to slow down and lose the race to the ball, choosing instead to fire her right arm out in a rigid stiff-arm, the hard base of her palm smashing into the bridge of Rudy's nose, knocking the unsuspecting boy cleanly off his feet as she hurtled past him to the ball.

The blue sweeper was positioned between Emma and the goal, his feet dancing nervously, a look of abject fear on his face as the league's best player bore down on him. Emma danced quickly around him, juking left, then right, and back to the left again, as the sweeper's feet went out from under him.

Welch players were sliding through the grass, trying to poke the ball away, while the goalie moved out to cut down the angle, but Emma could do whatever she wanted with a ball on her foot fifteen yards from the goal. At the left post, Sammy was wide open and waiting for the pass that Emma normally would have made. But this time she drove the ball home with a blistering shot, tauntingly placed inches over the goalie's left shoulder. She ran into the goal and grabbed the ball to get the game restarted quickly.

The Welch coach was out on the field, running down Charlie. "That was a foul. A foul, *goddammit*! What are you looking at, buddy?" he screamed, a few feet away. "That's no goal. She hit my guy in the face!"

Charlie pointed to the center of the field as he turned toward the incensed coach. "Tie game," he called out loudly. Then, softly, he added, "That was a good clean stiff-arm."

"One minute," called out the timekeeper.

"Emma, you *fucking whore*! I'm going to get you for that," yelled Rudy, as he trudged upfield like a bull, oblivious to the blood that flowed freely from his nose.

Players were still trotting back into position when Charlie blew the whistle for the restart. He wanted to give the Bones one more chance to score and win the game. The ball caromed around in midfield for a few seconds before Zack came across the centerline like a freight train. He dribbled through a pair of defenders and raced toward the goal. With time running out, Zack fired a powerful low shot that the Welch sweeper dove for, heading the ball across the end line.

"Corner," Charlie called out quickly, running across the field.

"There's no time left, you asshole!" the Welch coach screamed. Charlie looked over at the timekeeper. She put her palms up, not knowing
what to do.

"Ten seconds left," Charlie yelled. "Corner kick."

"Paul," Natty called out. Paul raced to the corner and readied himself
for the kick. Just before he took his long stride to the ball, he looked up to
find Emma.

The instant they made eye contact, Emma nodded, made a quick
feint, and sprinted toward the mass of players in front of the goal. Paul
stepped into the ball and sent it high and hard toward the box. Emma
sprang into the air, her head three feet over the scrum, and pounded the
ball with her forehead past the flailing goalie and into the net.

As Emma was coming down, Rudy was going up in the other direction. Rudy led with the top of his forehead and caught Emma just above
the right eye with a sickening smack, sending her backward in midair.
Charlie was still pointing into the goal when Emma got hit. He blew two
quick bursts to signal the end of the game as he sprinted toward Emma.
Rudy stood over her. "How'd that feel, you cunt?" he yelled.

Before Rudy could say another word, Zack drove his shoulder into
the Welch player's stomach, carrying him through the air and into the
goal. Zack got off several hard punches to Rudy's face before Charlie
wrapped his arms around him. As he struggled to pull Zack away, Charlie saw Natty on the ground, hunched over Emma. Then next to him
appeared the legs of the Welch coach.

"I want that nigger suspended for the season!" The coach's red face
was inches from Charlie's as he struggled to restrain the now-frenzied
Zack.

"Who you callin' a nigger?" Zack spat out angrily, trying to kick his
way out of Charlie's arms.

Rolling on the ground with Zack, Charlie saw that several other skir-
mishes had started on the field. It was turning into an all-out brawl. Suddenly a loud voice cut through the chaos.

"All right! That's enough!" It was the voice of authority that Hank had
developed in his fifty-year career as a schoolteacher and principal. "That's
enough," he repeated. "It's all over." In a few seconds, the fighting had
stopped, and the teams were drifting away from each other.

Charlie pulled Zack to his feet. "Okay, it's all over," he said. "You did what you had to." He was relieved to see Emma back on her feet, walking slowly toward the sideline with Natty, a towel pressed to her eyebrow. "Go see how Emma is. I'll take care of the coach. Okay?"

Zack's muscles relaxed and he seemed to slump in Charlie's arms. "Okay," he whispered. But Charlie could feel the boy's tears dropping onto his forearm. He released his grip from behind but kept his arm around Zack's shoulders, which developed into a hug as he came around to look into the boy's face.

"Hey, Zack," Charlie said to make eye contact. "He shouldn't have said that. He shouldn't have said what he did. But all I can tell you is there are a lot of ignorant people in the world, and he's one of them. So don't worry about somebody like that. Okay?"

Zack grunted, then wiped his eyes with the bottom of his new shirt, now torn in the middle. Charlie walked him up the sideline to where the Bones were packing up their gear. Natty saw them and walked their way. "How's Emma?" he asked.

"She's okay," Natty said. "Going to have another good bruise. Probably going to need a couple of stitches, but she'll be okay." Charlie nodded. "Going to take her to the clinic when we get back. Then I'll stay with her for a while. Make sure she doesn't have a concussion."

"Good idea," said Charlie.

"Gotta cancel on the Roadhouse tonight." Natty smiled briefly.

"That's okay," Charlie said, as he started to walk away. "Going to have a word with the coach here."

"Charlie, be careful with him," Natty said.

Charlie eyed the coach in the parking lot behind the bleachers as the man tossed a bag into the trunk of his car. The coach saw Charlie approaching and put on the wry smile he'd used when Charlie first confronted him during the game. He crossed his arms defiantly. Charlie hadn't decided what he was going to do until he saw the smirk on the coach's face.

He walked straight up to the coach and drove his right fist as hard as he could into the man's stomach. The shorter man gasped, doubled over, and vomited into the gray cinders of the parking lot. While he was still gasping for air, Charlie yanked his hair with his left hand, pulling the coach's head up against the top of the car. He stepped forward and drove his right knee up between the coach's legs, and the man's whole body shuddered with pain. Tears came to his eyes, and he heaved again down the front of his shirt.

"Remember this feeling," Charlie forced out between clenched teeth. "This is how a young black kid feels when an adult calls him a nigger. Now you're going to apologize to Zack, but I don't want a good kid like that anywhere near a piece of scum like you, so you'll apologize to me, and I'll pass it on to him." Charlie took a menacing step backward with his right leg. "Let's hear it, or you're going to need a fucking colostomy bag before you get out of this parking lot."

The coach, his eyes closed, tears and vomit running down his face, held up his hands as he struggled for air. "No, no," he managed weakly. "Sorry. Sorry, Zack," he whispered hoarsely. Charlie released his grasp of the coach's hair, and the man slid down the side of the car to the ground. As Charlie walked back across the field, he noticed a Cadillac pull up quickly behind the coach's car. Kyle Loftus and the man with the thin mustache got out and hurried over to the still-gasping coach.

NATTY HAD STARTED toward the bus with Emma. The girl held an ice bag to her eye, and a butterfly bandage covered her swollen lip. "Looks like you had fun today, Em," Natty said.

"Did we win the game?" Emma asked softly.

"I'm not sure. You got the goal, but I'm not sure what the league is going to do after all this. Doesn't matter," she said, putting her arm around Emma's shoulders. "That was one hell of a game you played."

As they walked past the goal, Natty noticed someone sitting on the grass on the home side of the field. Emma saw him, too. It was Gabe, sitting with his arms on his knees, watching them. Emma looked over at Gabe, then at Natty. Natty smiled at her and nodded. "Go ahead, Em. We'll wait for you."

Emma limped toward Gabe. She held the ice bag to her right eye and moved slowly. Gabe jumped up and began to walk toward her. They stopped about ten feet apart, unsure of what to say. Finally, Gabe spoke.

"Emma, I, uh, wanted to apologize for my team. They shouldn'ta treated you like that and said that stuff to you." He looked at the ground and scowled. "That ain't the way to play soccer." He thrust his hands into the pockets of his sweatshirt. "Anyways, that's all I wanted to say. Good game you played. *Real* good game." His voice and his eyebrows rose with enthusiasm. "*Damn!* Three best goals I ever saw!" Then he went silent, afraid he was talking too much.

It was Emma's turn to say something, but she wasn't sure if her voice would work. "Thanks," she squeaked out softly. Then a little more loudly, "Thanks for helping me. Hope you didn't get in trouble."

"Naw, that don't matter."

Emma glanced back at the bus. "I gotta go," she said, taking a step backward.

"Listen, Emma, I, uh, was wondering if you were going to play for Red Bone High next year. You and the Willards and that Polish kid—you think you'll all be playing?"

Emma shrugged. "I guess."

"'Cause I was thinking, I got an aunt lives in Red Bone, and I could, you know, live over there and transfer to Red Bone High to play soccer." Gabe couldn't hide the excitement in his voice. "So we could play on the same team, me and you, the Willard boys, and that new kid."

Emma smiled through the pain of her lip and her rapidly swelling eyebrow. "*That'd* be a pretty good team."

"*Hell,* state champions four years in a row is what *that* team'd be!" said Gabe proudly. "Go up there and kick the *crap* out of them teams from Charleston and Morgantown!" They both laughed, enjoying the idea of playing together on what would assuredly be a powerhouse high school soccer team.

The loud blare of the school-bus horn startled them. "Gotta go," said Emma again. "Thanks, Gabe, for helping me today."

"That's okay," he said. He held out his fist to her. Emma smiled nervously as she brought her left fist up slowly and pressed her knuckles into Gabe's. The feel of the boy's cool skin against her own sent a shiver up her arm.

"I'll see you, Emma," Gabe said, taking a step back. "Can't wait for next year."

On the bus, Emma surprised Natty by squeezing in next to her in the front seat, her aches and pains replaced by a giddy excitement. As the bus pulled out of the parking lot, Emma leaned forward to watch Gabe jogging down the street.

CHARLIE WALKED BACK across the soccer field to where Hank stood leaning against the Chrysler.

"Feel better?" Hank asked.

Charlie avoided Hank's eyes. "Feel like shit." He gestured toward the car. "C'mon, I need a drink."

CHAPTER 24

Moody's roadhouse sat a few feet off the dusty shoulder of South County Road. Bigger than it looked from the outside, the tavern was actually three buildings that came together in an
L-shape: an old clapboard house at the corner; a long shedlike structure
that housed the restaurant and bar; and, around the corner on the
unpaved side street, a smaller, flat-roofed house, topped by a neon sign
that blinked out FAT CATS, underlined with smaller letters promising
ADULT ENTERTAINMENT. The gravel parking lot was already half full,
mostly with pickups, when Hank and Charlie arrived.

Inside, Charlie recognized a few faces, but Hank knew everyone.
Charlie ordered a pitcher and two Jim Beams. After a couple of rounds,
they ordered sandwiches, before the kitchen closed. They could hear a
bluegrass band warming up in the large room off the bar. While they ate,
they watched the people passing through the bar. Charlie recognized
Natty's sister-in-law, Sally, who appeared to be a regular, chatting with
everyone she saw. Charlie saw Eve Brewster, too. Their appearance quick-
ened Charlie's pulse, in anticipation of the chance that perhaps Natty
had changed her mind and would come out after all.

"Gonna go drain the monster," Hank announced, rising painfully.
There were two choices for the men's room, he informed Charlie—a
small one upstairs, or a larger one out behind Fat Cats, accessible by a
long wooden deck out the back door of the bar. Hank, like most of the
men, would use the john at Fat Cats. "Easier than climbin' the stairs.

Might sneak a little peek at the main stage while I'm over there," Hank said with a wink.

Charlie nodded. *Fat Cats—where Hugo Paxton had his fatal heart attack. He'd have to go over later and check out the talent.* Charlie smiled to himself. He could see why the Roadhouse was a favorite spot of Hugo's. A steady stream of women in tight jeans, bare midriffs, and too much makeup made their way to the crowded room where the band was now in full swing.

Then, across the room on the other side of the bar, Charlie saw the man with the pencil-thin mustache, from the soccer game. He stared back at Charlie with a menacing scowl, a toothpick dancing nervously between his puffy lips. The bartender placed three longneck Budweisers on the bar in front of him. Charlie turned away, trying to recall where he'd seen him before. When he looked back, the man was gone.

"Hey, Charlie. Looking for someone?" Eve asked playfully, as she eased herself into Hank's chair.

"Hi, Eve. How are you?" Charlie smiled.

"I'm okay, Charlie," she said with a weary smile. She looked around the Roadhouse. "Don't come here much anymore. Used to come a lot, in my younger days."

"Interesting place," said Charlie, looking back toward the bar.

"Only reason I came tonight was that Natty said she and Sal were comin' out."

"Me, too." Charlie watched Eve closely for a reaction. She stared at him with tired eyes, then reached for a cigarette. Charlie noticed Hank seated at another table, engaged in conversation with an older couple. "You know, Eve," said Charlie, "up until about a month ago, I thought we were pretty good friends. Then I think you got the wrong idea about something." Eve smiled briefly and shrugged her shoulders. "But, Eve, you have to believe me when I tell you there's nothing going on with me and Natty. We're just friends. That's all it is, and that's all it's going to be."

A smile spread across Eve's face. "You and Natty. That's what you think this is about?"

"Well, I know you've seen us running together a couple of times, and—"

"And you've been going to her soccer games and become the best friend her son's ever had. And, of course, you let her drive your car around for a week, when hers was tore up." Eve shook her head and laughed. "Shit, Charlie, everyone in Red Bone's seen the sparks flyin' between you two since you landed here. Then you get up there at the planning-board meeting when Natty's at the podium, and you're telling everyone how you're going to build us a brand-new library, but you're lookin' right at Natty, and your eyes are locked like two kids at the junior prom. All we needed was some violin music."

Charlie was taken by surprise. "But, Eve, there's nothing going on," he protested. "That's what I'm telling you. We're just—"

"Charlie." Eve cut him off. She smiled, and her eyes were as soft as her voice. "Let me tell you something. There isn't a woman in McDowell County, including myself, who isn't hoping and praying that you'll fall mad in love with that girl and take her and her two kids away from here."

It took Charlie several seconds to grasp what Eve had said. "But what about your brother?" he finally asked.

Eve leaned back in her seat. "Buck's an asshole. He's my brother and I love him, but he ain't never deserved one second of that girl's companionship, let alone the mindless adoration she's had for him for the last twenty years." Eve took a long drag on her cigarette and shook her head. "Don't worry 'bout Buck. He's too dumb to know how lucky he is. Natty goes, he just finds some big-titted hillbilly girl, and he's happy as a clam." Eve looked at her watch. "Never given them kids any fathering, anyway," she added bitterly.

Charlie was starting to feel the effects of too many Jim Beams and a long day. He needed to use the men's room, but he needed to get things straight with Eve. "Okay, Eve," he said, "if it's not about Natty, then what is it?"

Eve exhaled a cloud of smoke. "It's the coal, Charlie. The surface mine on Redemption Mountain." She leaned forward again in earnest. "Don't you see, Charlie? The men have suffered too many years trying to make a living around here. Going from one meaningless low-pay job to the next, or more likely no job at all. After a while it beats you down, and you start to lose your self-respect, your sense of humor, any ambition you ever had." She took a long drag on her cigarette, turned her head, and blew a cloud of smoke toward the ceiling before facing Charlie again. "There's a sadness comes over a place. You see it here, Charlie, I know you do. Hell, all you got to do is look around at the men in this room." Eve gazed around her.

Charlie glanced briefly toward the bar for the man with the toothpick. He didn't have to examine the crowd to know what Eve was talking about. He'd felt it since he first came to West Virginia—the quiet resignation, along with the latent anger the men seemed to share. The inability to hold your eye for long.

"That mine is like a miracle," said Eve, "a huge power plant and a big mine coming here, with local men getting preference for the jobs. That's about all any of these fellas ever wanted out of life. Now they got a chance." She snuffed out her cigarette while Charlie waited for her to continue. "And you're trying to stop the mine on Redemption Mountain," she said quietly. "Don't ask me how I know that, but I know it's true."

Charlie looked around at the people in the bar as he wondered how he could explain it to Eve. *She wouldn't understand anything about the deck being stacked in favor of the big corporations, or how the state and federal bureaucracies were in the pockets of the multinationals, their lobbyists, and lawyers. How Charlie was sick of being on the wrong side for so many years. She wouldn't understand how it felt to be a professional lackey—a man who'd become successful far beyond his talents and promoted to a social class he never belonged in. Nor would she understand his empathy for Bud and Alice DeWitt and their mountainside farm, symbols in the struggle that felt like his last chance at redemption.*

Charlie smiled. "It's complicated, Eve, but the DeWitts don't deserve to lose their farm, and the environment doesn't deserve to be wounded by another mountaintop-removal mine. That's about as simple as I can make it."

Eve stared at him for a few seconds before flashing a smile. "Okay, Charlie," she said, looking at her watch. "I don't understand, but you're a good man. And I hear it's a done deal, anyway. Going to court in a few weeks, and they'll be taking the farm by eminent domain." She gathered up her cigarettes and lighter. "Union's already taking the names of men want to work on the mine." She held out a hand to Charlie. "So, still friends?"

Charlie took her hand. "Friends, Eve, whatever happens."

Eve left, and Charlie got up from the hard wooden chair. His body ached, his bladder was ready to burst, and his eyes were having trouble focusing. It would be good to settle into the big, cushy seat of the Chrysler for the ride back to Red Bone. He stopped next to the booth where Hank was now seated with three elderly men, all at least as old as Hank. Charlie noticed they were all drinking coffee. "I'm just going out back for a second, Hank, then I'll be ready to go."

Charlie made his way through the bar to a windowless wooden door, held closed by an antique thumb-latch handle. The door slammed behind him with the familiar crack that he'd been hearing all evening.

The night air was cooler than he'd expected, with the scent of autumn that reminded him of Halloween. The rear of the Roadhouse was in darkness, save for a spotlight on the back wall of Fat Cats. Pointed toward him, the spotlight served less to illuminate the wooden deck than to blind Charlie as he tried to find his way through the darkness.

A door opened under the spotlight, and two figures emerged. Charlie watched as the two men made their way around the corner of Fat Cats and pulled open the rear door of the bar. Loud voices and shrill catcalls escaped through the opening, along with the familiar strains of "The Hustle." The door closed, leaving the building in darkness, but now Charlie had his bearings. While he couldn't see the wooden walkway just a few feet in front of him, he knew where he needed to go. His left hand found a wooden railing. He passed the corner of the kitchen and felt the gravel of the parking lot under his feet.

Suddenly there was a flash of light in front of him. It was a lighter, held by a man seated on the railing twenty feet ahead. The man's head was down as he lit his cigarette. In the darkness, the flame cast a wide circle of illumination. Grateful for the light, Charlie took a few more steps, then the man turned toward him. The Zippo was extinguished with a sharp *clank*, but the instant of illumination was enough for Charlie to recognize the thin mustache and the puffy lips of the man from the soccer game.

Charlie stopped in his tracks. This didn't feel right. Then it came to him, along with the realization of the trouble he was in. The morning of the raid on Redemption Mountain. The man had been standing next to the white sheriff's cruiser in a police uniform—Deputy Sheriff Wayne Lester. No, this wasn't a good situation, Charlie told himself, as he tightened up both fists.

Then the spotlight disappeared, and Charlie's face felt as if it had exploded. As the world spun around him, he saw a hundred spotlights, on his hands and knees at first, then on his knees and one shoulder, as he tried to determine which way was up. He could taste the blood as he fought for balance, the top of his head pushing at the ground. Then he felt a powerful jolt across the middle of his back, and the pain came in waves, the lights growing dimmer as they circled away from him.

Charlie fought for consciousness. He pushed himself up on all fours and spit out a mouthful of blood, grimacing from the excruciating pain. There was a hot breath next to his ear. "Remember this feeling, boy. This's what it feels like when a big-shot New Yorker comes down here and fucks with the wrong guy." The voice took a step back on the gravel. "And here's one for your nigger pal."

The foot came through the darkness up into Charlie's stomach. He had to swallow repeatedly to keep from vomiting. But in spite of the pain, or perhaps because of it, Charlie regained his consciousness, and his head was clear enough to understand the seriousness of his situation.

Charlie saw the coach's black soccer cleats, but when he reached out to grab a foot, his arm just pawed the air.

"All right, boys, get him on his feet. Let's mess up his face a little."

Two new sets of shoes shuffled across the gravel. Rough hands grabbed hold of his arms and pulled him up. Charlie knew that, if they pulled him to his feet, he'd be defenseless. But when he tried to fight off the hands, his back felt like it was on fire. Unable to resist, he went slack against the arms that held him up for the beating to come.

Then he heard the sickening smack—a sound he knew well—of fist against flesh and bone. And then again, and once again in rapid succession, and feet shuffling quickly around in the gravel. Then the hands released him. Charlie turned his head in time to see the coach land heavily on the ground a few feet away, his cleats scraping slowly against the dirt. And he heard Wayne Lester speak for the first time. "Ain't your fight, Buck. This boy's got it comin' to him."

"Three on one ain't much of a fight, Wayne." The deep voice was confident and strong. Charlie was immediately glad that the voice was on his side. "Plus a two-by-four." Charlie heard the hollow sound of a piece of wood hitting the ground. "What's the matter, Wayne, you forget your nightstick?"

"That wasn't me, Buck," Wayne Lester pleaded. "I didn't know he was going to use a board on him."

"Bullshit. Just your style, you and these little girls you hang out with. Beat it, Kyle, less you want to be next, after Lester and I settle an old score."

"Hold on, Buck," said Lester. "We was doin' you a favor. This guy's been red hot after your wife since he got here. Been thick with Natty all over town, and pallin' around with your kid."

"Fuck you, Lester." Buck cocked his right arm.

"It's true, Buck," said Kyle Loftus, taking a hesitant step toward the two men. "How do you think you got that loggin' job with Garvey?"

"That's bullshit. What's this guy want with Natty?"

"Garvey told me himself," said Loftus. "Said Burden called him up and told him to put you on."

"Why else you think Garvey'd give a loser like you a job?" Lester added, feeling bolder. "And he's trying to kill the Redemption Mountain mine 'cause Natty's been whispering in his ear."

"That ain't true . . ." Buck sounded less sure of himself.

"I was *there,* Buck. When they torched the field. Burden tipped 'em off. The lawyers in Charleston got his cellphone record for that morning. Shows Burden called the farm right after we headed up there." Charlie groaned as he pushed himself to a sitting position. He tried to speak, but his mouth was full of blood.

"Wake up, Buck, and see what's going on," said Kyle Loftus, as he bent over to pull the coach to his feet. "Come on, let's get out of here."

Two headlights lit the men from across the parking lot. As the Chrysler slid through the gravel, stopping just short of Charlie, Hank leaned on the horn. Buck took off up the ramp toward Fat Cats, while Wayne Lester went back into the bar. Kyle Loftus pulled the groggy coach through the dark parking lot to a brown Cadillac.

THE CEILING FAN was turning in the wrong direction, Charlie was certain of that. Then he moved, not much more than a twitch, and the shooting pain in his back reminded him that he wasn't in his apartment. Without moving his head, he could see the light-green curtains hanging from an aluminum halo around the bed. He was in a hospital bed. Charlie labored to lift his left arm and look at his watch, but it wasn't on his wrist.

"Almost two-thirty. 'Bout time you woke up. I was about to pull the sheet up over your head and call a priest." Charlie turned to see Natty rise out of a metal folding chair. Next to her, the Pie Man jumped up to follow her to the side of the bed.

"Hey, Pie Man. How's my best bud?" Charlie held up his palm for a more-gentle-than-usual high-five. He held on to Pie's hand as the boy stood next to the bed for a better view.

Pie pointed a finger at Charlie's face. "Charlie look like a raccoon."

Charlie grimaced as he laughed. "That's what a broken nose does to you." He reached over to feel the gauze bandage that covered the bridge of his nose. "Fourth time for me, or maybe the fifth—I can't remember."

"Were you in a fight, Charlie?"

"It wasn't much of a fight," he replied, trying to be vague for Pie's sake.

"Doctor says you'll be all right," said Natty. "Took X rays of your back. A gash and a deep bruise."

Charlie recalled the excruciating pain of the two-by-four as it dug into the flesh of his back. He reached down to feel the tight bandage around his torso.

"'Course, you won't be getting any modeling jobs," said Natty.

Charlie smiled. "Did he say when I could leave?"

"Tomorrow. You have a concussion. Hank said he'll pick you up. He left a little while ago. Been here all night and all morning."

The word *concussion* reminded Charlie of the incident at the soccer game. "How's Emma?"

"Fine. A lot better than you are. Just some stitches."

Natty watched Charlie for a few moments, then reached into her pocket. "Pie, why don't you go out in the hall and get a soda from the machine?" She pulled a crumpled dollar bill out and squeezed it into Pie's hand.

"Okay, Mama." He slapped Charlie a high-five before exiting.

Charlie raised up the bed so he could look directly at Natty. He let out a deep breath at the pain. "I must look like hell."

Natty smiled. She leaned in closer to examine the bandages, the professional caregiver unable to resist her natural instincts. She touched his forehead to see if he was running a fever.

Her hand felt soft and cool, and he longed to touch her fingers, but Natty seemed to realize she had crossed a line. She took her hand away and folded her arms in front of her.

"I was in this same bed a couple of years ago." She motioned briefly toward her left eyebrow. Charlie watched her without comment. He waited until Natty met his gaze with a troubled look on her face.

"Hank says he saw Buck there last night," she said quietly. "He said that when he drove the car up, he saw Buck run off, along with Kyle Loftus. . . ." Her voice trailed off. "Charlie, did Buck do this to you?" she whispered. "'Cause if he did, that would—"

"No, Natty, no." Charlie tried to shake his head. "Buck saved my life, or at least my pretty face."

Natty smiled, but she still looked worried. "Buck didn't come home 'til real late last night, 'bout three in the morning. And he was pretty drunk. Slept in the living room." She rocked nervously on the balls of her feet. "Ain't the first time for that, o' course, but he's been pretty good since he started working. Buck loves that job, cuttin' trees, and he's been a lot better."

"Natty, some things were said last night that may be a problem for you. Buck was about to go after that deputy, Wayne Lester—"

"Buck's had it in for Lester for years now, but I was hopin' he'd let it go. It's probably why he helped you in the first place, just to have a go at Lester."

"Probably. But Lester didn't want to fight Buck, so he started to talk his way out of it and said some things about us."

"Us?"

"Well, more about me than you, but stuff about *us*."

"Oh, shit."

"Told Buck that I've been after you since I came here, and how we've been together a lot, and how I'm trying to stop the Redemption Mountain project because of, you know, how I feel about you, that kind of thing." Charlie sounded embarrassed.

Natty rolled her eyes. "Damn, how does he come up with shit like that?"

"And Loftus told him I called Pat Garvey about the job."

"That ain't good." Natty shook her head dejectedly. "Things were going okay. Buck still don't pay no attention to the kids, but least he was coming home."

"Natty, I'm sorry about all this." He reached out and touched her hand. "But if he does anything to you, you've got to get out of there, and you've got to call me right away."

Natty looked at his fingers on her hand, and recalled the empty feeling she'd had at the soccer game, when she thought about Charlie leaving for good.

"No, I'll be okay. He ain't like that anymore." Natty scowled and shook her head. "Damn Wayne Lester. What's he got to go shootin' his mouth off for?"

Charlie took his hand away. "That may be my fault," he said. "When I was in New York last week, we had a meeting about the raid on Redemption Mountain, and I had to do a little tap-dancing around the truth."

"So what'd you tell 'em?"

"I blamed it all on Lester. Said that you two went to high school together and that you were very close." Natty scrunched up her face. "It gets worse," he said, wincing. He smiled sheepishly. "I kind of implied that you two were still seeing each other, and that's why he tipped you off about the raid."

"Aw, jeez, Charlie!"

"I couldn't think of anything else."

After a few moments, Natty smiled, then she giggled. "You really told them that?"

Charlie nodded. "And there's something else I need to apologize to you for. At the meeting, I, um, referred to you as a *hillbilly*," he said sheepishly.

Natty laughed and smiled at him. "Charlie, I *am* a hillbilly, and proud of it, too. I'd never take offense at that, and I won't ever stop being a hillbilly." Then she scowled. "I guess Lester must be pretty pissed off."

"I'm sure he is. But they know about the call on my cellphone that morning, so he's probably off the hook."

"Then OntAmex knows it was you. Does that mean trouble for you, Charlie?"

"I don't think so. They want me to keep the plant on schedule and they plan to take the farm by eminent domain, anyway. Do you know what that means?"

"Grandpa Bud explained it to me. Says he got some legal papers from the sheriff last week about a hearing or something at the high school. Says he talked to a lawyer but most likely he'll lose the farm."

"Looks that way," said Charlie with a sigh. He reached out and took her hand. "I'm sorry, Natty, but I don't know if there's anything anyone can do to stop it now. I'm going to make one last try, but it's probably not going to help." Charlie gently rubbed the back of her hand with his thumb.

"Okay, Charlie," she whispered. "You did what you could." Finally she pulled her hand from his and glanced around the curtain to see if there was any sign of Pie. "Got to go," she said, taking a step backward. Natty felt as if she'd stopped breathing, and her heart pounded in her chest. She came forward quickly, leaned over, and kissed Charlie on the lips, softly, but a telling moment longer than a thank-you kiss. Then she turned and went out through the curtain.

CHAPTER 25

C HARLIE LOOKED UP FROM THE DRAWINGS SPREAD OUT ON THE hood of the Navigator to watch the truck dump a load of stones for the new soccer field. A small bulldozer stood by, ready to spread the load. It was an extravagance, to improve the drainage, but he was going to build a library and athletics complex in Red Bone that the town of Mamaroneck would be proud of.

This was quite possibly the last project that he'd have control over for some time. He was certain that his career at DD&M was over. The intel about the call was the one good thing to come out of the beating he took at Moody's Roadhouse. At least he knew where he stood.

Envisioning the new library reminded him of the books they'd need to fill it. A library wasn't a library without books. And he was reminded of the phone call to Ellen he'd made earlier in the week, the first phone call to her in which he'd substantially distorted the truth. He'd called about the annual October weekend that they spent at the house in Vermont to enjoy the incredible foliage and one last round of golf at Sugarbush.

This year Ellen had invited Dave and Linda Marchetti, which was fine with Charlie. Dave and Linda were both golfers and good company if the weather was bad. Two weeks ago Charlie had confirmed his plans to fly up to New York on Thursday night, so they could be on the road early Friday morning.

Not long ago, he'd have looked forward to a weekend of spectacular scenery and gourmet dining in the Green Mountains, but now it all seemed trite to him. What he really wanted to do this weekend was go to the Bones' soccer game and spend some time with the Pie Man, and, of course, Natty was never out of his mind. She was, if he had to admit it, the biggest reason he wanted to stay. Their paths hadn't crossed since the hospital, and though he ached to run with her in the mornings, it was probably too risky for Natty. But he missed her, and he wanted to see her.

He told Ellen a poor version of the truth. *He'd been involved in an altercation in a bar, and had his nose broken by a wild elbow. He'd gone to the hospital for a quick resetting—nothing serious—but he would be uncomfortable flying, and he also wasn't up for a five-hour drive to Vermont.* The silence on her end of the phone was palpable. She halfheartedly proposed putting off the trip to the following weekend, which Charlie quickly rejected with a fabricated schedule of meetings rather than the real reason—the Michigan–Ohio State game that Saturday and the lobster and beer party he'd planned with Pie. Ellen hung up with a curt "Fine, Charlie. Take care of yourself. Call me next week."

It started to rain. Charlie pulled up the hood of his windbreaker and looked at his watch. Six o'clock, time to call it a day. He'd see if Hank wanted to have a beer, play some cribbage on the porch, and have a late dinner down at Eve's.

THE HONDA'S OLD windshield wipers chattered madly against the sudden downpour. As Natty drove slowly along Cold Springs Road, looking for the turnoff for the power plant, she noticed water flowing over the right edge of the road. In the mountains, building anything always rerouted running water, but she was surprised to see it washing over the sandy shoulder.

The rain had turned to a sprinkle by the time she reached South County Road. Natty hesitated at the turn, with thoughts of just heading home to spend some time with the kids before falling into bed. It had been a hard week and she was tired. But Woody and Mr. Jacks were expecting her, and Woody needed his legs wrapped. She also needed to check Mr. Jacks's meds and make sure he'd been eating enough. And they both needed their Friday night glass of Jack Daniel's. Natty sighed as she took a left and headed toward Old Red Bone. *Maybe it's better to have such a simple life that a can of beer and a shot of Jack Daniel's is the high point of your week.* She laughed as she realized that it would be the high point of her week, too.

The store was closed, so Natty tracked down Eve in the back of the restaurant and got the key. She would leave the money on the counter and return the key to the inside stairwell when she was finished. Eve told her that Woody and Mr. Jacks had been over for lunch and had eaten a hearty meal of meat loaf and mashed potatoes.

Natty pulled out a six-pack of Budweisers, a pint of Jack Daniel's, and a carton of Marlboros. Then she tossed a tin of Red Man chewing tobacco into her bag. After counting the bills in her wallet, Natty sighed, put the carton of cigarettes back, and took down five single packs. Coming out from behind the counter, she grabbed a large bag of pork rinds and stuffed it into the bag.

"Want some company?" The voice, just a few feet away, almost made her drop the bag. Natty turned to see Charlie leaning against the door frame. He was wearing an old flannel shirt and his running shoes.

"Charlie, you scared the shit out of me."

"Sorry." He gestured toward the Pocahontas Hotel. "Saw your car coming up the hill. Figured you were on your way over to see your friends across the street. Can I tag along?"

"Sure," she said. "Woody and Mr. Jacks'll get a big kick out of that." She held out the bag. "Here, you can carry this."

Just as Natty was about to lock the door, she stopped. "Forgot something." She went behind the counter and slid open the glass door to the small selection of cigars that Eve kept on hand. She pulled out two Macanudos in short white sleeves and pushed them into the front pocket of her jeans. She'd pay Eve for them next week.

There was no sign of life on Main Street as they walked down the wooden steps toward the Pocahontas Hotel. "How's your nose?" Natty asked.

"Prettier than ever." Charlie chuckled. He felt like he was in high school again, carrying a book bag for a girl he had a crush on—the feeling he always had with Natty.

"Oh! I almost forgot," she said. "Mabel told me about the New York trip. *Jeez*, Charlie, you shouldn'ta done that. That's way too generous of you."

"Not my money. It's OntAmex's, and they can afford it. You going to be able to make it?"

Natty started to walk again. "How can I not go? Free trip to New York." She turned to Charlie. "You going to be there?"

"If I can, I will. I'd love to show you *my* favorite running trail."

"Sounds great," said Natty. "Be nice if you could be there."

"How's the team doing?"

Natty smiled. "Wow, what a season. Only a few games left, and I don't think anyone's going to beat us this year. Emma's really drawing a crowd. We got people comin' from all over to watch her play, and we'll probably be invited to the tournament in Charleston. They always ask the best team in our league. That would be a treat for the kids."

They reached the entrance of what was once the Pocahontas Hotel. Charlie stopped. He needed to ask Natty a question before they went in. "Did Buck say anything about the fight?" Charlie asked, examining her face in the dim light.

Natty shrugged. "He asked me about the woodcutting job. Just told him I'd mentioned that he needed work. He's okay with that."

"How 'bout Redemption Mountain?"

"He asked how come you were against it, and I told him I wasn't sure you *were*." Natty turned toward the door.

Charlie stopped her. "Did he ask you about us?"

Natty smiled. "Didn't say a thing about that." She shrugged. "Never been worried too much about me."

They went into the cavernous lobby. The silence was broken only by a soft scurrying sound behind the counter. "Rat or a cat," said Natty. "Plenty of both living here." She led him down a wide hallway toward the back of the building. They passed the cage of an ancient elevator before Natty took a left onto an open staircase dimly illuminated by a bare bulb on one of the upper floors.

They climbed the stairs to the third floor and walked down a long hallway. The wood flooring sagged in the middle and creaked with each step. Since they'd entered the building, Charlie had thought about the fire hazard the ancient structure posed. He looked for signs of a sprinkler system and found none.

At Room 310, Natty rapped on the door and gently pushed it open. "Hey, boys," she announced. "Nurse Ratched here for your weekly lobotomies." Charlie followed her into a large room filled with the unmistakable odor of men's bodies and stale tobacco smoke. The room was dimly lit by a small reading lamp on a table next to an iron-framed bed and by a TV set on a stand placed in the center of the room. *Wheel of Fortune* blared from the TV.

"Lookee here, Mr. Jacks, we got us some company." A large black man pushed himself laboriously out of an ancient leather recliner. Beyond him, a small, wiry black man with patches of gray fuzz on his head and wearing thick bifocals was seated at a wooden table, his back against the wall.

"Boys, this is Charlie Burden," Natty announced. "Charlie's the big mule down at the new power plant. For some reason, he was interested in meeting a coupla beat-up old coal miners." The larger man held out a massive hand. "Charlie, this is my friend Mr. Woodrow Givens."

"*Wheehee*, Charlie," the man said, taking his hand. He reminded Charlie of an old prizefighter. "You must be somethin' *real* special, 'cause Miz Natty knows we only allows the best kinda people to visit us here in the palace."

"And this is Kermel Jacks," Natty added, as the smaller man turned off the TV.

"I's pleased to meet you, Mr. Burden," said Mr. Jacks, holding Charlie's hand in both of his. He had the deep, raspy voice of a longtime smoker. "It is truly an honor . . . for us to welcome you to our home."

"Thank you, Mr. Jacks," said Charlie. "I'm glad I finally had the chance to meet you fellows. Natty's mentioned you many times."

Taking the bag from Charlie, Natty placed it on the kitchen table and put the beer in an old Amana refrigerator. "Only had enough for five," she explained, bringing the cigarettes over to Mr. Jacks.

"Tha's okay, Natty, I got enough." He handed Natty a tattered envelope. She counted out the bills she needed and put the envelope in a drawer. Then she tossed the can of Red Man to Woody.

"Thank you, Natty, but don't you think, in honor of our guest, we should have a visit with Mr. Daniel's?"

"Later, Woody. You know the rules. Business first. Now take off them pants."

"*Wheehee*." Woody grinned at Charlie. "If she don't sound like a workin' girl from Cinder Bottom."

Natty pulled a wooden chair from the kitchenette and opened her case on the bed. She removed a plastic bottle and two rolled-up bandages, then carefully unwrapped the old bandages from Woody's legs, which were painfully swollen at the ankles. Rubbing lotion into her hands, she began to massage Woody's legs, starting with his feet. Her hands were small but strong, and she squeezed his flesh vigorously enough to make Woody wince. After a few minutes of hard work, she stopped, pulled her sweater over her head, and tossed it on the bed.

Under her sweater, Natty wore a plain gray T-shirt. The short sleeves revealed her thin arms, moist now with sweat and bulging with sinew as she strained to knead some life into the large man's legs. Breathing deeply, she ignored the hair that had come loose from her ponytail and hung over her face. She looked over and flashed Charlie a dazzling smile that lit up the dark room and made his heart race. He thought she was the most beautiful woman he'd ever seen.

Natty turned back to work on Woody's right leg, and Charlie couldn't take his eyes off her. He thought about her coming to do this every week, caring for these old men, bringing them a bit of comfort in their last days—not as part of her job but as a friend. It was something she wanted, she needed, to do.

"Why don't you boys tell Charlie a little about coal mining?" Natty suggested, with a quick smile at Charlie.

"Coal minin' . . ." Woody murmured softly. "Now, that's a life." The old man looked down at his hands in his lap and nodded. He held his hands up to Charlie and smiled. "This is what a life o' coal minin' gets ya." The fingers on his massive hands were crooked and gnarled. One pinky bent outward at the knuckle, and the thumb of his left hand was missing. He dropped his hands to his lap with a sigh. "Weren't a bad life, though. Early times was hard, before the union got some changes. Then, when things got better, the Negro miners could only work in the dog holes, where they was still bustin' stone by hand, skimpin' on the shorin', and cheatin' on the count."

"Don't get all worked up, Woody," said Natty, as she rewrapped his left leg. "Look at the life of luxury you're living now."

Woody burst into a huge white smile and laughed. "*Wheehee*, you're right about that, child. Got the good life now. Did I tell you Mabel Willard brought us up a turkey pot pie t'other day?"

"Tell Charlie about the Red Bone mine, Woody. He'd be interested in that."

"Best mine I ever worked in. 'Course, by that time I wasn't a nigger anymore. I was *Mister Givens*, shift foreman." The old man laughed. "That's what forty-four years o' workin' underground gets ya. A little bit a respect, after all. Yep, this was a good mine," he said. "Slope mine safer and easier than the deep mines."

"A slope mine?" Charlie was unfamiliar with the term.

Mr. Jacks was eager to join the conversation. "Slope mine is how you mine a seam o' coal tha's up in a mountain," said Mr. Jacks. He stopped to cough and spit a mouthful of black liquid into a can on the floor.

Charlie was curious. "So how do you get the coal out?"

"Why, the oldest way there is. You get up to where the coal is and you tunnel right into it. Called a drift mouth. Then you go in and bring out the coal."

"Do they still do slope mines?" Charlie asked.

Woody shrugged and shook his head. "Naw, hardly ever see a slope mine anymore, lest it's a small operation. Now they just blast away the mountain, bring in the big shovels, and push it all over the side."

"Mountaintop removal," said Charlie.

Woody scowled. "Ain't even minin', usin' dynamite to destroy a whole mountain. No skill, no engineerin' at all in that."

"Could you still get the coal out with a slope mine?"

Natty looked at Charlie as she took Mr. Jacks's blood pressure.

"Well, o' course you *could*," said Woody, pulling his pants back on. "Problem is, it costs more—'bout twelve dollars a ton, I always heard. That's a lot a money. 'Course, some of it goes into miners' pockets, which ain't all bad. But a man's labor costs more than dynamite."

"Twelve dollars a ton," Charlie repeated. "That is a lot of money," he said, as he did the math in his head. Thirteen million a year. More than 250 million over the life of the mine. A significant amount, even to a company as large as OntAmex. But he needed to learn more about the feasibility of a slope mine for Redemption Mountain.

The sound of a flip-top snapping open jarred Charlie from his thoughts. Natty handed him a Budweiser and brought one over to Woody. She went back to the refrigerator and returned with one for herself and for Mr. Jacks.

"Okay, boys, workday's over," she said, sounding tired. She took a long pull on her beer and set it on the kitchen table, then grabbed four small juice glasses from a cupboard, took the bottle of Jack Daniel's from the bag, and filled each glass. Charlie stood to help her, taking the glasses to Mr. Jacks and Woody.

"Why, thank you, Mr. Burden," said Woody. "Let's have a toast to the Red Bone power plant."

Natty held up her glass and smiled. "To Charlie's power plant," she said, and took a sip of the whiskey.

"That's about the best sippin' whiskey there is," declared Woody, savoring his Jack Daniel's. The room was hushed for a few moments, as everyone enjoyed the warmth of the liquor.

Natty finally broke the silence. "Almost forgot," she said, reaching into a front pocket of her jeans for the cigars. She handed one to Charlie as she moved over to the table next to Mr. Jacks.

"You think of everything," said Charlie, sliding the Macanudo from its tube.

Natty cut the tip of her cigar with a small penknife, then handed the knife to Charlie. He clipped off the tip of his and watched Natty light up. He could see that this was not the first cigar she had ever smoked.

"How 'bout this, boys? Cold Bud, a shot of Old No. 7, a good cigar, and great company." Natty smiled and winked at Woody.

"You said it all there, child," he said.

Charlie leaned back in his chair and smiled. "This is probably what heaven is like," he suggested, taking a pull on his cigar. Woody grinned.

For another hour, Charlie basked in the company of Natty and the two old miners as they joked and reminisced about Old Red Bone, the Pocahontas Hotel, and its former residents. They finished the Jack Daniel's and shared the last two Budweisers. Sitting in the dark, musty room, in a hidden corner of Appalachia, Charlie felt as warm and contented as he had in a very long time.

As he and Natty were leaving, Charlie invited Woody and Mr. Jacks to his lobster party the following Saturday. In spite of their trepidation at seeing a lobster for the first time, the old miners were thrilled by the invitation.

THE COOL, DAMP air of the street was refreshing after the closeness of the smoky room. Charlie and Natty walked down Main Street, making a detour around a huge puddle. Natty's voice was amplified in the thick air. "Thanks, Charlie, for doing that. You got no idea how much that means to them. Don't get many visitors."

"I enjoyed it. Enjoyed watching you help them."

"Those boys, they ain't got much time left. Kermel ain't got long at all, way he's goin', and Woody, pretty soon they'll start cuttin' his legs off little by little, and he'll have to live in one of them old residence hospitals in Charleston or Beckley." Natty sighed. "God, I'm going to miss them. Hey," she added, touching Charlie's arm. "That was real nice, inviting them to your football party. They'll enjoy that."

"I'm glad they want to come. You know, you're invited, too."

"Lobsters, huh? Where you getting lobsters around here?"

"My son's shipping them down from Boston. They pack them in ice and send them anywhere you want."

Natty nodded. "Yeah, that shouldn't cost too much."

Charlie laughed. "So you'll come?"

"Never had a lobster. Suppose I shouldn't miss the chance." They walked the last few yards to Natty's car without speaking. A nervous tension surrounded them, made more acute by the stillness of the night. Natty wondered what time it was, but she didn't want to check her watch and risk Charlie thinking that she was in hurry.

Charlie took a deep breath and swallowed back the nervousness in his throat as they walked through the darkness. The street was illuminated solely by an old-fashioned streetlamp on the far side of Main Street. It reminded him of the streetlamps of his youth; his gang would throw stones at them to see who could pop the little bulb and send a shower of sparks to the pavement.

They reached Natty's car and she opened the back door of the Honda. Charlie put her case on the backseat. "Thanks, Natty, for letting me come along," he said. "It was a very enjoyable evening."

Natty put her hands in her pockets and leaned back against the

Honda. Charlie studied her delicate face in the dim light and wondered if there was another woman anywhere like Natty. Natty spoke first. "Charlie, I been thinking a lot lately about you leaving here—going to China, like you said." She gazed up into the darkness across the street, as if she needed to avoid his eyes. "Gives me a real empty feeling," she nearly whispered.

"I've got some time left here, Natty. Won't be before—"

"Charlie," she said, turning back to look into his face, "what I'm saying here is . . . if you were to ask me to go upstairs, for a beer or something, well, I'd probably go."

Charlie swallowed hard. He needed to get this right, because he knew that Natty had made a decision that was probably as difficult as any choice she'd ever made. But he needed to say no to her, to deny himself what he'd been aching for all evening, aching for since he'd come to Red Bone. He took a deep breath, stalling for time.

"Nat, we can't do that," he said finally. "Not tonight."

Natty pressed a little harder against the side of the car and blew out a deep breath. "Well, that's a relief," she said. "I ain't too sure I got clean underwear on, anyway."

They both laughed. They seemed to laugh a lot, thought Charlie, as he smiled at her. He reached out and gently pushed back the shock of hair that fell over her eye. "Earlier this week, Nat," he continued, "I had to lie to my wife about you, and I didn't like how that felt."

Natty squinted up at him. "What'd you have to lie about, Charlie?"

"Wasn't about you, directly. It was about why I couldn't go up to Vermont with her this weekend. I made up some stuff about my broken nose and too much work, but it was about you. You're the reason I didn't want to go. I wanted to stay here and see you, do what we did tonight, and go to the soccer game tomorrow. To see the kids and Pie."

Natty looked down at her feet.

Charlie knew that he was embarrassing her, but he had to continue. "And I wanted to be alone with you," he said, "and hear you say the words you just said."

Natty sniffed. "So, *what*, Charlie?"

"Nat, last winter my wife had an affair—an old friend of hers. Didn't last long, couple of months, I guess, but I found out about it from someone else. I can still remember how that felt . . . when I found out." He winced at the memory. "I don't know which felt worse, her having an affair or having someone else tell me."

"I know what that feels like, Charlie," Natty whispered.

"I can't do that to her," he continued. "Whatever happens with us, I want it to be different. I need to tell Ellen how I feel . . . before anything happens."

Natty wiped her eyes with her sleeve. "Jeez, Charlie, you goin' for husband of the year or something?"

Charlie laughed. "Hardly," he said, looking away. "Nothing like that."

"What are you going to tell her, Charlie?"

"I don't know. I haven't gotten that far."

They both chuckled. He looked across the street and paused for a few seconds. "First I'm going to tell her that I love her," he said. "We've been married for twenty-six years, and for twenty-five of those years, Ellen was as good a wife and mother as a woman can be. One mistake, one . . . experiment, doesn't wipe all that out." He squinted into the streetlight.

"Plus, it wasn't all her fault. You remember how you told me it wasn't all Buck's fault that day he hit you?" She nodded briefly. "Well, Ellen's thing, that wasn't all her fault, either."

"What'd you do, Charlie?"

He saw the curious look on Natty's face. "I changed," he said. "We had a nice life together. Then, after the kids left and my job changed, then I changed. We were living the life that Ellen always wanted, and I realized I didn't really want that life. So I made some decisions without thinking about her. I abandoned her. Not physically, but socially and emotionally, and I pretended that it shouldn't matter. It's hard to explain."

Charlie paused for a moment. "I also have to tell her that I met this woman in West Virginia. A remarkable woman. The nicest, kindest . . . funniest, most selfless person I've ever met." He looked up from his feet and met Natty's eyes. "A woman who has no idea of how beautiful she is or how special she is."

Natty turned away to hide her face.

"I probably won't tell Ellen about how my palms get sweaty and my heart beats like a drum every time I see this woman—that wouldn't be fair—but I have to tell her that I can't get her out of my head and I'm not sure I ever will, and that, when the time comes to leave West Virginia, to leave her . . . I'm not sure I'll be able to do that."

In the darkness, Natty tried to blink away the tears as best she could. After several moments, she brought her sleeve up and pressed her eyes to it. She sniffed and sighed as she turned back to the light.

"You okay?" asked Charlie. "You're not going to throw up on me, are you?"

Natty smiled. "I'm okay. Just never been called *remarkable* before." They both laughed softly. "Gotta go," she said, turning to find the door handle. Charlie watched until the Honda, sending up white clouds of exhaust into the cool night air, disappeared around the corner.

CHAPTER 26

CHARLIE ZIPPED HIS WINDBREAKER AGAINST THE MORNING CHILL as he walked up a short hill to the soccer field in Princeton. The sky was a slate gray, threatening rain. The referee was carrying a ball to the center of the field, and Charlie could see the Bones on the far sideline, huddled around Natty for a last-minute pep talk. He began to feel the gnawing in his gut that he always experienced now when he saw her, made more acute by the shared intimacies of the previous evening.

The Princeton team, outfitted in sharp purple shirts, dominated the early game. But it didn't take long for the Bones to settle down to their game and for the Princeton team to lose their confidence. After Emma unleashed a bullet into the top corner of the net, she jogged back up the field, taking a wide detour toward the visitors' sideline for an enthusiastic high-five from a tall boy with blond hair, wearing blue jeans. Charlie recognized the Welch midfielder Gabe and smiled, realizing why Emma seemed to be playing with a little extra flare.

A few minutes later, Sammy scored off a corner kick and Natty called a time-out. She put Emma and Sammy on defense and put the Pie Man in the game. The boy scurried around the middle of the field, always a few steps late to the free balls. But he also was playing with extra determination today. Charlie watched as a long ball went past the Princeton defenders with Pie and the other forwards in hot pursuit. The ball went over the end line and Pie bent over to catch his breath.

"Hey there, Pie Man, good job!" Charlie called out. Pie straightened up with a smile. He raised a hand for their usual high-five wave.

"Hello, Charlie," he said, still short of breath. He looked as if he was about to say something else, but he stopped and, for a fleeting moment, shifted his gaze to the hill beyond Charlie. Charlie pointed as the goalie sent a long goal kick back upfield. Pie whirled and raced off to join the action.

When the play was down in the Bones' end of the field, Charlie would steal a glance along the sideline to watch Natty—and think about last night and what they had come so close to. She turned to follow the ball up the field and saw Charlie. Her hands were in the pockets of her black warm-up jacket, and the bill of her hat was pulled down low over her eyes, but her smile made Charlie's heart thump and forced him to draw in a cold breath. Then she quickly turned her attention back to the game.

Charlie watched Natty come to a stop and rock back and forth on her tan construction boots, her thin legs and small waist camouflaged by the baggy jeans. He envisioned her up on the boulder, lying back on her elbows next to him, gazing out at the mountains, telling him her stories, giggling, smiling, laughing at herself, her T-shirt pulled tightly around her breasts, her smooth legs splayed out lazily on the curved rock, having no conception of how alluring she was. Then he saw her kneading the cold flesh of the old black man's legs, the muscles in her arms and hands shining with moisture in the dim light of the smoky room, and then sitting on the bed, laughing and sipping Jack Daniel's with the three men and enjoying her cigar.

When Natty turned abruptly to move back up the field, Charlie felt a cold chill as he realized that he'd made a horrible mistake the previous night. If he'd taken her upstairs and they'd made love, today would have been the first day of a giddy, glorious minefield of a future that they would be exploring together. Charlie ached for that feeling—to share that with Natty—but he knew the opportunity was lost.

The Bones carried their water bottles out to the spot in front of the goal where they would sit and listen to Natty's halftime instructions. Charlie took a few steps onto the field to catch Natty's eye, then stopped as two men approached her from the home side. Natty shook hands with the men. They seemed to be having a lighthearted discussion, before one of the men got a little more serious. Natty listened intently, nodding several times with a few words in return, then smiled broadly as they shook hands again. They turned to cross the field and Natty started toward her team in front of the goal.

When she saw Charlie, Natty seemed to hesitate before ambling slowly toward him. Charlie stood still, his hands pushed down into the pockets of his windbreaker, watching her approach. When she was still twenty feet away, he nodded toward the two men. "Good news?"

"I guess it *is*," she said. "Invited us to the Thanksgiving tournament in Charleston. First time ever for Red Bone. Kids are going to be thrilled." There was something distant about her, about the way she spoke, the way she avoided his eyes, and the same feeling of emptiness that he'd experienced earlier swept over him again. Then she turned toward him and squinted with a wrinkled-up nose. She adjusted the strap of the athletics bag on her shoulder and let out a sigh. "Charlie," she breathed out, "Buck's here."

It took Charlie by surprise. "Where—" he started, but Natty cut him off.

"Up on the hill, in back of you. With Sally." Charlie could feel the eyes on the hill trained upon them.

"That's good that he came to watch Pie play," he said, trying to sound sincere.

"First time ever Buck's come to one of our games. Seven years, and he finally comes to a game," she said, almost to herself.

"Charlie, last night . . ." She hesitated. "Last night, that was like the best date I ever had. Thank you for going over and seeing Woody and Mr. Jacks with me. That was real nice." She let out another sigh and looked up. "I gotta go, Charlie." Her eyes darted almost imperceptibly up the hill behind him, then back again. "Okay?" she said softly.

"Sure, I understand, Nat." Charlie made a show of looking at his watch. "I've got to get going, anyway."

Natty gave the Bones the news about the tournament, and Charlie heard their excited shouts as he walked toward the parking lot.

* * *

Woody givens's description of slope mining ran through Charlie's mind as he waited for his office computer to warm up. *Easiest way there is to mine coal . . . twelve dollars a ton . . . puts more miners to work.* Charlie glanced out his window at the power plant. The project was now well ahead of schedule, with no major problems on the horizon, which also meant it was beating budget, too.

But Redemption Mountain was a disaster, for him personally and for DD&M. He not only failed to secure the purchase of the DeWitt farm, he'd declared his allegiance to the enemy, and, worse than that, he'd been exposed. That was a mortal sin, and when the timing best suited OntAmex, Torkelson would administer an ignominious end to his career. Of that, Charlie had no doubt.

DD&M would survive without Charlie or Lucien. Warren Brand and his lieutenants would move the company to some class-B space in Fort Lee, sell the building in Manhattan, and divide up the assets. In a year they would sell what was left of the company, at an inflated price, to one of the midsize engineering firms blinded by the prospect of acquiring some big-time OntAmex contracts.

For some, it would probably be a blessing. He and Lucien would be fine. Their professional reputations and their balance sheets would take a hit, but they'd survive. But Bud and Alice DeWitt would not. Nor would their son Petey or Natty's mother. They would lose their farm, their livelihood, and, more important, their heritage—the familial bond to the land that came from four generations of DeWitts born and buried on Redemption Mountain. And Redemption Mountain was going to disappear. *Hard to feel close to a piece of land pulverized by a thousand tons of ANFO and turned into valley fill.*

As his computer tinkled out its familiar welcome, he rolled his chair closer and let out a sigh. The economic advantage of mountaintop removal had already been proven at scores of mines throughout West Virginia and Kentucky over three decades, and nothing in his research would change that.

Yet in the back of his mind was the immeasurable cost of mountaintop removal. Hank's angry accusation reverberated in his head. *If Redemption Mountain was in California . . . or Vermont . . . in the Catskills . . .*

Of course, Hank was right. You could never obliterate a mountain, covering over streams and wildlife habitat, anywhere outside of Appalachia.

He started with a query to Nina Matlin, the DD&M librarian. He requested everything she could find on the economics of mountaintop-removal coal mining. Then he launched his own search, which yielded dozens of articles and files devoted to the horrors of mountaintop removal. Charlie read for several hours, then changed into a sweat suit for a run, anxious to punish his body and numb his mind with a hard five-miler before it got too dark. Whatever it took to avoid thinking about Natty Oakes.

After four laps around the power plant, Charlie decided to push himself with a mile-and-a-half sprint back to the apartment. He ran past the windowless hulk of the old elementary school and an abandoned trailer being swallowed by the ubiquitous kudzu vines. Farther up the road was the concrete rubble of a long-decrepit motel and another deserted building with boarded-up windows.

Hank's words echoed in his mind: *You see any great wealth, see any old money, around this town? After more than a hundred years of coal production, what did West Virginia and McDowell County and the town of Red Bone have to show for it? Crumbling roads and derelict buildings . . . Monongah, Farmington, Buffalo Creek, and dozens of monuments to thousands of dead miners . . . streambeds stained orange with ferrous oxide . . . homes and towns sinking into abandoned mines . . . drinking water that ran brown . . . too many children living in poverty . . . a town that couldn't afford to patch the roof of its library . . . Woody and Mr. Jacks squatting in an abandoned firetrap to live out their final days . . . Bud and Alice DeWitt, who hadn't suffered enough with the deaths of their sons and granddaughter, now soon to lose everything . . . and Natty Oakes, the most incredible woman he'd ever met.* Charlie stumbled to a ragged stop in the middle of the dark, deserted road. He'd had enough. He bent over, hands on his knees, gasping for breath, sweat running off his forehead. He thought he might throw up.

NATTY WALKED SLOWLY across the field under the weight of her athletics bag. Far ahead, she saw Emma and Gabe walking together. They would take a seat a little farther back in the bus from where Emma normally sat. Natty smiled to herself. She'd never seen Emma happier.

"Hold on there, Miz Oakes." The voice came from behind Natty. She knew who it was before she turned to face Kyle Loftus. "Understand you got the invite to the Thanksgiving tournament up in Charleston."

"You *know* we did, Kyle. So what?"

"Had a league meeting other night 'cause of that ugly incident at the game in Welch, and I got to inform you that you got two players who is suspended from any sort o' postseason play."

"*What!* What kind o' shit are you trying to pull, Loftus?"

"You heard me," he replied firmly. "The Willard boy, Zack Willard. Suspended for starting a fight. And the girl, too, Emma—flagrant foul. Broke that kid's nose."

"You go *fuck* yourself, Loftus. You can't do this!" Natty whirled around, nearly hitting him with her bag as she made her way to the bus.

"Can do it, and did do it," Loftus called after her. "Those two are out."

Natty spun around briefly. "You put it in writing," she yelled, not knowing what else to say.

"Already in the mail."

"I can appeal it," Natty yelled back.

"Be my guest."

THE BLINKING RED light on the Hewlett-Packard printer called for another black ink cartridge. Charlie looked over the stacks of pages on his kitchen table, the text marked with red circles. In front of him was a yellow pad, a dozen pages filled with notes.

He tossed the pad and his pen onto the table, sending another dozen sheets to the floor, where a small pile already resided. He reached over to his laptop, clicked on ABORT PRINT, and grabbed the bottle of Heineken on the corner of the table. He didn't have another ink cartridge, and he didn't need it, anyway. It wouldn't help. None of it would help.

Charlie looked at his watch. For nearly eight hours straight he'd been reading downloads and studying charts. He stood up and took his beer out onto the back porch. The air was cold, but after a long night inside the apartment it felt good. The best he could do was to reduce the differential to around ten dollars a ton, and even that required a great many assumptions. *Too many assumptions. Too much bullshit. Companies like OntAmex don't make decisions based on bullshit.*

Charlie took a swig of his beer and looked over at the cigar box on the table. Hank had put a piece of hard plastic over the box with a rock on it to protect it from the wind. Charlie moved the rock and the plastic and opened the ancient brown box. From under the two decks of playing cards, he extracted the appointment book Hank used to record their winnings and losses. He leafed through the first two-thirds of the book, which recorded the years of games between Hank and Alva Paine.

Charlie compared his measly part of the book to the scores for Hank and Alva. *Twenty-one years' worth of cribbage games—now, that was a friendship.* He looked at the last page. He was down $407. *How the hell does he do that?* Charlie'd won about an equal number of games, but Hank always seemed to win a little more money in his wins and lose a little less in his losses. *It's all in the pegging,* thought Charlie, resolving to improve the next time they played.

Charlie went back inside to the kitchen table. *One more thing to do. One last try for Bud and Alice DeWitt.* He sat down in front of his laptop and searched through his address book for Duncan McCord's personal email address, reserved for a few friends and old teammates, because they understood that it was not to be used for business-related correspondence. Charlie was about to break the rule.

Duncan—In a few weeks, through an eminent-domain proceeding, the Ackerly Coal Company and OntAmex are going to destroy a family living on a small farm on Redemption Mountain, West Virginia. Within weeks of the displacement of the DeWitt family from Redemption Mountain, the destruction of the mountain will commence with the beginning of a mountaintop-removal surface coal mine. Mountaintop-removal mining is an environmental catastrophe that would be inconceivable anywhere outside Appalachia, where the population is thin, the people voiceless, and the politicians are owned by the coal-mining industry.

Charlie reread the last sentence. *So, what's the problem? Duncan would say.*

It's clear to me now that the plan for Redemption Mountain was made long ago and is the main reason that the plant was sited in McDowell County. I learned recently that Jack Torkelson and Larry Tuthill, along with the president of Ackerly Coal, visited Redemption Mountain two years before the final selection process began. Very soon, you'll own the plant and the coal company, along with the mineral rights to Redemption Mountain and the contract to supply the coal to the Red Bone generating facility. With all this integration, is it possible to do the right thing for the environment and for an elderly couple who don't deserve one second of the harassment they've already taken from your lawyers and the coal people down here?

Charlie scowled, reading his own words. Duncan would probably hit the DELETE key and conclude that Charlie had lost his mind. He decided to press on, even if it was pointless.

There is at least one alternative to mountaintop removal. It is admittedly more costly but, considering the environmental impact, an alternative worth considering. A slope mine could harvest the coal at a premium of eight to ten dollars per ton over a surface mine.

Charlie grimaced at the lie and inserted a few links to some inconclusive studies of the cost differential.

Duncan, this isn't how we should be acting down here. This is how corporate interests have been treating Appalachia for a hundred years—crippling the workers and leaving behind poverty, heartache, and ecological ruin. Maybe it's time for us to cut it out.

Looking forward to an old-fashioned Big Ten ass-kicking of OSU this weekend. Go, Blue!—Charlie

He briefly considered deleting the whole letter and starting over when he was less tired. *No, Duncan would easily see through the economic bullshit. Anyway, he'd wasted enough time on the whole thing already.* He hit the SEND button. *Sorry, Bud, Alice. It's the best I can do.*

A few seconds later, he received an auto-reply from Duncan. *I'll be out of the country until the 10th of November, attending conferences in*

Switzerland and Belgium, followed by a vacation in the Canary Islands. Will respond to your email when I return. Duncan McCord

Charlie stared at the message and laughed. *Switzerland, Belgium, and the Canary Islands—a long way from the topless bars in Detroit you used to love, Dunc.* He turned off the computer and went to bed.

CHAPTER 27

WHEN THEY PRIED OFF THE LID OF THE FIRST PACKING CRATE, Charlie was glad he'd invited Eve to the party, too. The lobsters were three- and four-pounders, much too big to cook in his small kitchen. Pie's eyes went wide with amazement, and he took a tentative step backward when he saw the brown lobsters in the plastic bag of ice. Eve reached in, pulled out one of the monsters, and placed it on the restaurant kitchen's floor.

"Charlie, the lobthter is very ugly. Do you really eat it?" Pie edged forward for a better look.

"Pie Man, you're going to love lobster," said Charlie, taking two more out of the ice and playfully thrusting them at the boy, who retreated with laughter. With a dozen huge lobsters, they'd have more than enough. Charlie broke out two Stroh's and handed one to Eve.

"Little early for this, isn't it, Charlie?" asked Eve, taking the beer.

Charlie held his up for a toast. "It's the Michigan–Ohio State game, Eve. Gotta get tuned up." He helped Eve retrieve a huge dust-covered pot and put the lobsters in the walk-in cooler. Then he and Pie went upstairs to get the apartment ready. On the way, Charlie stopped in the store for a fifth of Jack Daniel's, a large bag of pork rinds, and some cheese curls for Pie.

They rearranged the living room, moving the overstuffed sofa and love seat around to face the TV set. It would be a little crowded, but they'd manage.

"C'mon, Pie, let's go over and get Mr. Jacks and Woody," said Charlie.

Hank was coming in as they left, carrying an armload of snacks and a clear bottle of something that looked suspiciously like moonshine. Eve followed with a huge bowl of salad, a basket of bread and rolls, and two large bottles of wine. *Jesus*, thought Charlie, *we'll be lucky if anybody's still awake at halftime.*

With Charlie helping Woody, and the Pie Man holding on to Mr. Jacks, they slowly made their way down the stairs of the Pocahontas Hotel and across the street. Hiking up the four flights to Charlie's apartment proved to be a challenge, especially for Woody, who needed to rest at each landing. Finally, they made it to the fourth floor. Charlie settled the two old miners on the couch, put a bowl of Stroh's on ice on the coffee table, and turned on the TV.

Eve and Hank had been busy during their absence. The kitchen table was crowded with plates, silverware, a pile of napkins, and bowls for the butter, which Eve had brought up from the restaurant. She even had small lobster forks and a few shell crushers, which Charlie never would've remembered. Hank sat on the love seat and visited with Woody and Mr. Jacks. Pie was busy with the cheese curls. Hank had a beer, as well as a small glass of the corn liquor he'd brought. Eve poured herself a glass of Chablis, and after preparing two loaves of garlic bread for the oven, she stepped out the back door to take in the view.

Charlie pulled a Stroh's out of the bowl and followed her. Eve was leaning on the railing, gazing off into the distance.

"Forgot what a great view you get from up here. I should charge you guys more."

"No question about that," said Charlie. "Thanks for all your help, Eve, you've been great."

Eve lit a Merit 100. "C'mon, Charlie," she said, gesturing to the soccer field below. "You make a new library and ball fields for us. I make garlic bread." They both laughed. Charlie glanced at his watch. It was nearly game time. "Don't worry, she'll be here," said Eve with a smile.

"Maybe," he replied. He thought about the last time he'd seen Natty, a week ago at the soccer game in Princeton.

"Heard that Buck was at the soccer game. That he saw you there, talkin' to Nat." It was as if Eve had read his mind.

"That was a surprise," admitted Charlie.

Eve took a sip of wine and squinted into the sun. "Don't mean nothin',"
she said quietly.

"What do you mean?"

"It don't mean a goddamn thing, after all this time Buck finally showing some interest in them kids, in his wife." Eve shook her head angrily.
"Imagine, beatin' that sweet girl way he done and thinkin' he'll always be
the love of her life."

"Well . . . it means something to her," Charlie said.

Eve turned and grabbed his Michigan T-shirt. "It's too late for Buck
now, that's what I'm telling you, Charlie. That girl's so dippy over you."

"C'mon, Eve, how do you know if—"

"'Cause I know," Eve said. "Women know about these things." She let
go of Charlie's shirt. "Important thing now is how *you* feel." She eyed
Charlie warily. "So how *do* you feel about her, Charlie? And don't give me
any of that bullshit about nothin' happenin' 'tween you two, like you
were peddlin' that night at the Roadhouse."

Charlie crossed his arms against his chest. *There it was—the question
he'd been dodging for months. How did he really feel about Natty?* He
thought about their conversation in the dark a week earlier. He'd tried to
tell Natty how he felt about her then, but what had he said? Did he actually tell her anything? He told her that she made his palms sweat and his
heart beat faster and that she was *remarkable*. And that he still loved his
wife. *God, what an asshole.*

Eve studied his face intently. Charlie sighed and gave up the fight. "I
think I've been in love with Natty since the first moment I saw her, in your
store that night I arrived," he said softly. "I've never felt like this before."

Eve smiled, giddy at finally hearing Charlie say what she'd hoped for.
"I knew that, Charlie, but tellin' me ain't doin' anyone any good. You
gotta tell Natty. And you gotta tell her soon. Else you two could end up
makin' a mistake'll haunt you the rest of your lives you keep waitin' for
life to be perfect, where nobody ever gets hurt."

Charlie recalled the sick feeling at the soccer game when he sensed
Natty slipping away. "I know, Eve. I just haven't had the balls to admit it
to myself, I guess."

"So tell her tonight, Charlie," Eve said emphatically. "Tell her tonight.
Will you?"

"C'mon, Eve," he pleaded. "Give me a break here—"

"I'll have Pie sleep at my place. You do what you have to do." Eve took a sip of wine. She lowered her voice to a whisper. "You tell that girl how you feel, and then you make love to her like she ain't never been made love to before—which won't be too goddamn difficult."

Charlie heard the crowd noise from inside, signifying the opening kickoff. He looked down the hill just as the red Honda came speeding into view. "We'll see, Eve. We'll see."

Eve scowled at him. "Charlie, you may never get the chance again."

NATTY BREEZED INTO the apartment with a twelve-pack of beer and a bottle of wine. "Woo woo, go, Michigan!" she called out, flashing a smile to Charlie in the kitchen. "Game start yet?" She hugged Eve and Hank, then went over to the couch and put an arm around the old miners. "How you boys doin'?" she asked, looking them over carefully. She cuffed Pie playfully, put an arm around his neck, and pulled him close. Pie grinned, his mouth half full with cheese curls.

Natty turned around just as Charlie brought two chairs in from the kitchen. It would've been natural for Natty to hug him as she had the others. But when their eyes met, they both hesitated, and the moment passed. The crowd noise from the TV grabbed Charlie's attention as a Michigan runner broke free for a long gain.

"Yeah!" Charlie shouted. "Go, Blue." He offered up a high-five to Natty. She smiled and slapped his open palm.

"Okay, let's get this party going," she said, wedging herself between Woody and Mr. Jacks. She reached into the bowl of ice and pulled out a Stroh's. "Go, Michigan!" she yelled, punching the air as the Wolverines got another first down.

It took a while for the group assembled in front of the small TV to embrace the Michigan cause, but, led by Charlie's enthusiasm and supported loudly by Natty and Pie, they gradually got caught up in the spirit of the game, cheering at every positive Michigan play. This was, after all, Charlie's party, and it was his team. They would do their part.

Hank—aided, no doubt, by the occasional sip of his moonshine— quickly became a Michigan fan, firing pork rinds at the TV, while Pie screeched with laughter whenever Michigan was penalized. And the

level of enthusiasm was raised noticeably when Charlie brought out the
bottle of Jack Daniel's and a shot glass for each of the adults to toast each
Wolverine score. Natty took control of the bottle and won a brief argument with Charlie that the extra point after a Michigan touchdown
required another toast.

It was a good half for Michigan, and a good party. From his chair
behind the couch, Charlie looked around the room at his diverse gather-
ing of friends. It was definitely a strange group. But was there a nicer,
more agreeable bunch of people anywhere? Charlie felt a rush of satisfaction as he thought about his buddies from Michigan watching on wide-
screens in sumptuous family rooms or members-only lounges at exclusive
country clubs, none of them having as good a time as he was.

At the end of the first quarter, Eve slipped away to turn on the stove
and get the water boiling in the huge pot. A little while later, Charlie and
Pie went down to put the lobsters in. Natty and Eve set out the garlic
bread and melted butter.

Just before the second half got under way, Charlie and Pie made their
triumphant entrance, carrying platters of steaming red lobsters. Charlie's platter was piled high with several of the huge lobsters, while Pie,
beaming with pride, carried the champion of the bunch, a five-pound
behemoth that Charlie'd selected just for him. Charlie held his platter
around for everyone to select a lobster, then took a seat on the floor next
to Pie. Eve spoke. "Hank, you want to do the grace here?"

"I'd be honored to, Eve." Everyone joined hands. "Lord," Hank started,
bowing his head, "we thank you for these gifts that you've bestowed on us
this day, but, my goodness, Lord, I think you gone a little overboard in
the bounty department." They all laughed. "We'd all be real fortunate to
have a slice of Eve's meat loaf tonight, never mind this incredible meal we
got here." Hank nodded his head several times. "But we *are* thankful,
Lord, and we want you to know that, for this and all your blessings. We're
thankful to have another day with our old friends Woody and Mr. Jacks,
and all our friends. And, Lord, we also got to offer up some additional
thanks for visitin' upon us a few months ago a special friend, someone
who's done a lot for us all . . . someone we know's going to be leavin' us
soon . . . and we're all gonna miss him when that day comes, particularly
those of us winning considerable amounts of money at cribbage." Every-

one laughed again. "So we thank you for sending us Charlie for a little while," Hank looked up and winked at Charlie, "and we all thank Charlie for this wonderful dinner. Amen."

"Amen," everyone said.

"Thank God!" Eve exhaled. "Drag that out any longer and the damn football season'd be over."

The feast was on. Charlie helped Pie with his lobster, while Natty, Woody, and Mr. Jacks watched Charlie, learning how to eat a lobster as they went along. After cracking one of the huge claws, Charlie dunked the succulent meat in Pie's butter dish, and everyone watched as Pie tried his first bite. Charlie laughed with pleasure as the boy's face lit up. "Oh, Charlie, lobthter is very delicious!"

They turned the volume up on the TV to hear over the clatter. Pie was especially animated in his enjoyment of this newfound delicacy. Michigan scored a touchdown, and they finished off the Jack Daniel's. Hank raised up his bottle of moonshine from under the table for toasting subsequent scores and was met with unanimous approval.

Glancing at a close-up of a Michigan cheerleader, Charlie suddenly jumped to his feet. "Oh, jeez, Pie Man, I completely forgot!" He started toward the bedroom and returned with a white plastic bag, which he tossed to Pie. "Been holding on to this for today's game." Pie reached into the bag and pulled out the dark-blue shirt. His eyes grew wide as he unfolded the shirt to reveal the yellow MICHIGAN lettering. He held it out in front of him.

"Look, Mama, Univerthity of *Michigan!*"

Natty stood up and reached for the shirt. "Let me see it, Pie," she said. She quickly pulled it over her head.

"Mama!" Pie protested.

"How's that look?" asked Natty, smiling at Charlie. "Look like a cheerleader?"

"Maybe the mother of a cheerleader," Eve squawked, clearly feeling the afternoon's liquor. By the time the game ended, everyone was stuffed, Hank's moonshine was gone, and Mr. Jacks was sound asleep, snoring loudly. They sat around the table for another hour, sipping wine and coffee and talking in the low-key, relaxed way of good friends. They talked about food and sports and joked about growing old.

Eventually the conversation came around to Natty's soccer team and the incredible season they were having. A troubled look came over Natty. "Don't know if we'll be going to the tournament after all," she said, describing her run-in with Kyle Loftus after the game in Princeton. "No point going up there without Emma and Zack. Wouldn't be fair to them or the rest of the kids. Real good teams get invited to that tournament. Better than us, anyway, even with Emma and Zack."

Charlie listened while the others voiced their outrage. "Going to get an appeal hearing," explained Natty, "but that ain't going to do any good. Be at Loftus's office, with him and his buddies who run the league, so I'll probably just skip that."

"Keep the appeal hearing, Nat," Charlie suggested. "I'll go with you. May be some way to get him to change his mind."

"Going to beat him up for me, Charlie?"

"Not a bad idea," he responded. Everyone laughed.

THE TABLE AND a good part of the floor around it were covered with bowls filled with red lobster shells, leftover salad, bread crusts, beer cans, and used napkins. Darkness arrived through the tall windows, and Eve busied herself packing up the extra lobsters.

"I'll come to clean up after I take this down to Mabel and the boys," she said, heading for the door. "Pie Man, you'll sleep down at my place tonight, special treat." She winked at Natty as she left the apartment. Hank excused himself to visit the bathroom and clean his shirt, soiled with drawn butter, and Natty forced herself up from the couch to start clearing the mess from the coffee table.

At the kitchen sink, Natty felt Charlie move behind her, then his hands grabbed her biceps and shook her playfully. Natty laughed as he passed through the screen door and disappeared into the darkness of the porch to have a cigar. She stood still for a moment, savoring the tingly feeling she had in her arms where Charlie had briefly held her, and felt a stirring deep inside. Everyone would be leaving soon, and she'd be alone in the apartment with Charlie.

Pie sat on the couch, his eyes half closed, his head resting on Woody's arm. A golf tournament played on TV. The boy's face was covered with butter grease, bread crumbs, and other residue from the meal. He still held on to several pork rinds, as if he'd forgotten they were there. Natty smiled down at him. It had been a big day for the Pie Man, one he'd remember for a long time.

She was leaning over to pick up another load from the coffee table when she heard a light rapping at the door. She listened again, trying to tune out the sound of the TV, and there it was, three polite taps on the door, so soft that no one else could hear them. She pulled open the door and saw an apparition, a vision from another world, because the last thing she expected to see was a stranger in the hallway.

Natty stood mute from her surprise, staring at what had to be the most beautiful woman she'd ever seen up close. The woman was taller than Natty, with lustrous black hair that fell just shy of her shoulders. She stood with her hands in the pockets of an elegant long black leather coat with a high collar and a pair of high-heeled black boots. Her makeup accentuated her dark eyes, and her lips were painted a deep red. She wore delicate diamond earrings.

The stranger smiled pleasantly at Natty's surprise, and her eyes fluttered briefly to the yellow Michigan lettering across Natty's chest. She pulled a gloved hand from her right pocket and held it out to Natty. "Hello," she said, "I'm Ellen Burden."

Natty reached out and tried to think. "Oh, Charlie's wife," she managed softly. *Holy shit! Charlie's wife's standing here in the fucking hallway!* She attempted a smile, unaware if her facial muscles were working properly. "Natty . . ." she whispered hoarsely. She cleared her throat. "Natty Oakes," she said louder. *Oh, jeez, this isn't going to look good for Charlie.*

Ellen Burden smiled as she looked at their still-clasped hands. "It's a pleasure to meet you, Natty. This is Charlie's apartment, isn't it?"

Natty let go of her hand. "Why, yes, ma'am, it sure is," she said, adding a little extra drawl. "C'mon in here, ma'am, and welcome to West Virginia!"

Ellen entered the room and found herself standing next to a coffee table. She took a quick glance at the couch, where an old, wiry black man with white hair was asleep, his head on his chest. Leaning against the arm of a second black man was a little boy, who also looked to be asleep. A curious concoction was smeared across the boy's face. Ellen turned to smile at Natty, who'd shut the door behind her, then she gazed at the lobster shells littering the table. "Oh, yes," she said, almost to herself. "The Ohio State game. I'd almost forgotten."

"Yes, ma'am, and it was a beauty: 31–17, Michigan."

Ellen smiled again at Natty, and her eyes moved again briefly to the blue T-shirt.

Woody finally noticed the newcomer and pushed himself up slowly from the couch. "Miz Burden, this here's Woody Givens, lives across the street," introduced Natty. Then she pointed to the end of the couch, where Mr. Jacks had just awakened. "And over there is Kermel Jacks, his roommate. Boys, like you to meet Miz Ellen Burden, come all the way down here from New York to visit Charlie." Woody held out a big paw. "*Wheehee*, sure is a pleasure to meet you, ma'am." Ellen nodded.

On the couch, Mr. Jacks squinted through thick bifocals as he tried to understand what was going on. "What? What's that?" said the old man. Ellen smiled pleasantly while Natty grabbed a used napkin from the table. Holding Pie's head with her left hand, she rubbed the napkin over her sleeping son's greasy face.

"And this little pecker here," she said, standing up and tossing the napkin back on the table, "is my son, the Pie Man." Ellen looked at the boy for a few moments, then turned to Natty.

"He's . . . what, twelve or thirteen?"

"Yeah, 'bout twelve, close as we can figure," said Natty. Out of the corner of her eye, she saw Hank approach from the bedroom. "And look who's comin' now," she announced, redirecting Ellen's attention. Hank had removed his stained shirt and pulled his suspenders up over his naked torso. The pale folds of his liver-spotted flesh jiggled as he entered the living room.

Natty scooted around the coffee table to intercept him. "This old show dog here's my boyfriend, Pullman Hankinson," she said proudly. Before Hank could react, she added, "Hank, this beautiful lady's Charlie's wife, Miz Ellen Burden."

The afternoon's liquor may have slowed Hank's reaction, but it hadn't dulled his wits. "Why, Miz *Burdan*, it sure is a pleasure to meet any wife of Charlie's," he said with a deep laugh. He turned and nuzzled Natty's ear. "Could be I'll be gettin' me another 'fore too long." Natty put her arms around Hank's neck and kissed his cheek, while he, enjoying his new role, put his hand on her back.

"Aw, Hank, you need to stop teasin' me now." Natty was startled to see Charlie standing behind his wife, enjoying the show, a wide grin on his face.

"Hello, Ellen," he said. Ellen tilted her head and smiled at her husband as she examined his face.

"Darling," she said warmly, "how *is* your nose?"

"Much better," he said, moving forward to hug her. "This is a surprise."

"Duncan made all the arrangements—the helicopter from Charleston. Then a nice man, Mr. Hicks, the security guard, drove me up here."

"You've met everyone?" asked Charlie.

"Yes," said Ellen. "I've met all of your friends."

Hank and Natty nodded, while Woody stared wide-eyed in confusion. A moment of silence filled the room. Finally Natty announced, "Charlie, Eve and me'll come and clean up this mess tomorrow. We'll all be gettin' out o' here now." She leaned over the couch and shook Pie awake. "C'mon, Pie Man, time to go. Let's go, Mr. Jacks." Hank thanked Charlie for dinner and left, followed by a perplexed Woody. Natty herded Mr. Jacks and Pie—still half asleep—out the door. "Thanks, Charlie," she called out over her shoulder as they left. "Hank and me had a great time."

Hank slipped quietly into his apartment while Natty helped Woody and Mr. Jacks down the stairs. Pie was asleep on his feet, so Natty deposited him in Eve's apartment. In the vestibule at the bottom of the stairs stood a green paisley-patterned suitcase with brown leather trim. Natty stopped for a moment and gazed at the expensive-looking bag. *Jeez, even her suitcase is beautiful.* After getting Woody and Mr. Jacks safely home, Natty left the Pocahontas Hotel and walked down the middle of Main Street. She suddenly felt the chill of the night and remembered that she was still wearing Pie's new Michigan shirt. She'd left her sweater on the floor at Charlie's.

Eve was just back from Mabel Willard's when she saw Natty enter the dim circle of light in front of the store. She held her palms up. "What happened to the party?"

Natty smiled. "Charlie had company." She paused, to let Eve suffer a bit. "His wife dropped in."

Eve's jaw fell open. *"No shit?"*

Natty nodded. "Flew down from New York today."

"Aw, Nat," Eve said, shaking her head. She started to say something else, but Natty cut her off with a wave as she pulled open the door of the Accord.

"You got Pie on your couch. See you tomorrow." Natty got in the car and pulled the door closed. Tomorrow she'd get up early and go for a long, hard run.

CHARLIE AND ELLEN seated themselves in a booth at a front window of Eve's Restaurant. The place was busy, with a half dozen customers seated at the counter and the tables. After ordering blueberry pancakes, Charlie walked over to the store to get a paper.

Most of the restaurant patrons used Charlie's absence to steal another look at the stunning wife of the power-plant boss, down from New York. She was clearly in a different league from the women in Red Bone, wearing a gorgeous lavender turtleneck and tightly pressed designer jeans. Charlie returned to the booth with the Sunday *Charleston Gazette.*

"No *Times?*" said Ellen.

Charlie laughed, pulling out the sports section. "No *Imus in the Morning,* either."

Ellen rolled her eyes. "How do you stand it?" she said, smiling.

"It's pure hell," he answered, as he searched for the football news to see who the Giants were playing. They were drinking their coffee when Hank entered and took a stool at the counter. Ellen smiled brightly and gave him the friendly finger wave she used for acquaintances whose name she couldn't remember. Charlie turned to see who it was. "Hey, Hank, how you doing?"

"Morning, Charlie, Miz Burden," said Hank with a nod.

Charlie turned back to Ellen for a second, then twisted around again to face Hank, his arm on the back of the booth for support. "Natty sleeping in this morning?" Charlie had a mischievous twinkle in his eye that was hidden from his wife.

Hank coughed, and his eyes darted around the restaurant to see if anyone else had heard. He dabbed his mouth with a napkin, though he hadn't eaten anything. "That's right, yeah," he said quietly. "She, uh, got a little tired out last night."

Charlie had to stifle a laugh. "She's quite a girl you got there, real live wire."

Hank's whiskers bounced up and down nervously, while his eyes circled the room. "She's somethin', all right," he mumbled.

The waitress arrived in front of Hank with a coffeepot, sparing him further torture from Charlie, who turned back to his wife. Ellen eyed Hank for a moment before peering through the front window.

"Oh, look, there are your friends, Mr. Woody and Jack," she announced. Charlie spotted the two elderly miners helping each other across Main Street. "This really is a small place," said Ellen. "Everyone probably knows everyone else in town."

"Pretty much," said Charlie, as their pancakes arrived.

When they were nearly finished, Ellen looked up and smiled.

"Hello, Miz Charlie, I am the Pie Man," he said, stopping next to the booth. Pie held his hand up to Ellen for a high-five.

"Good morning, Pie Man," she said, touching his hand lightly with her palm.

Pie stared at her for a moment, then turned to Charlie. "Hello, Charlie." They exchanged a high-five, and Charlie pulled the front of Pie's Yankees cap down over his eyes, making him laugh.

"Thomeday I will become a engineer like Charlie," Pie said proudly.

Ellen touched the boy's shoulder. "That's wonderful, Pie Man. I think you'll make a terrific engineer."

"C'mon, Pie, your pancakes are ready," Eve called from the kitchen. Pie ran off.

Ellen eyed Charlie as he looked out at the street. "He's delightful."

"Yes, he is." Their eyes met for a few seconds, but neither one spoke.

Finally, Ellen broke the silence. "Let's take a walk, Charlie. Show me your baseball field." They left the restaurant and walked slowly down the hill toward the athletics fields, now under construction.

"You really have to go back to New York tonight?" Charlie asked.

Ellen nodded. "I have a luncheon tomorrow. I'm joining the board of the Westchester Arts Council."

Charlie smiled. "That's great, congratulations." Ellen's new position as the president of the country club was already paying dividends. "How's the house?" he asked.

"It's coming along," she said, with a tone that told Charlie it was going to cost them another fifty thousand before she was done. "Planning a Christmas party for the club people and the neighborhood. And, of course, any of your friends you want to invite."

"Sounds great," said Charlie, quickly pushing the idea out of his thoughts. They stopped at the site of the children's library, and Charlie walked Ellen around the footprint of the new building. His excitement was palpable as he described the activity rooms with their skylights, the computer room, and cozy reading nooks.

"Maybe we can get some books from the Westchester Library Association," Ellen offered. "I'll bring it up at the next board meeting. Could be a nice charitable project." They crossed the new soccer field as Charlie pointed out the features of the athletics complex. Between the soccer and baseball fields, they mounted the wooden steps of the newly constructed gazebo, while Charlie described the landscaping that would eventually complete the parklike setting. Ellen sat down on a bench inside the gazebo and gazed out at the site. "You've been busy here, Charlie. This is quite an undertaking. Is this normal? A project like this for such a small town?"

He joined Ellen on the bench. "Well, we owed this town something, and we needed some good PR. . . . It'll be a nice park when we're done."

"That's good, doing something nice for these people." Ellen's voice fell away as her eyes drifted out toward the surrounding hills. They sat quietly, enjoying the morning sun as it warmed the air. Then she spoke again. "So, Charlie—have you slept with her yet?"

Charlie stared out at the field. One of the things he loved about Ellen was her perception. While she loved to talk, Ellen was one of the world's great observers and listeners. She could sit quietly in a room full of people and, minutes later, tell you everything about them. There was no sense in trying to mislead her. Charlie squinted briefly, with a twinge of emotional pain, and looked over at his wife. "No." He managed a weak smile.

"But you plan to?"

Charlie shrugged. "I don't know. It's a little complicated."

"Because she's married?"

Charlie chuckled. "Because *I* am."

Ellen turned away, staring up at the red stone buildings at the top of the hill.

Charlie wondered whether she was thinking about the prospect of losing him or about opportunity. He had no doubt that, in the circles in which she now traveled, Ellen—with her looks, intelligence, and sophistication—could easily bag one of Westchester's upper-tier, old-money scions and move effortlessly into a life of wealth and leisure that would make the Dowling Farms house look like servants' quarters. That was another thing he loved about Ellen. She could always take care of herself.

Finally she turned back to Charlie. Her face showed no anger or jealousy. "She's a lovely girl, Charlie."

"She's *different*, all right."

"May want to rethink the hairdo, though," Ellen deadpanned.

Charlie smiled and got to his feet. "I guess you didn't buy that act she and Hank put on."

Ellen laughed, rising from the bench. "Not for a second." Her eyes narrowed as she took a step closer to Charlie. She crossed her arms and looked out at the field. "I knew the moment she opened the door . . . that I'd be losing you to her."

"Ellen," Charlie protested softly, "That's not—I don't know what's going to happen. We haven't even—"

"Charlie, Charlie," she interrupted, coming closer. She put a hand on his chest and paused to compose her thoughts. "Listen, Charlie. You've been a wonderful husband and a perfect father, but just because our children have grown up doesn't mean we have to shrivel up and die." Her eyes were slightly moist. "I love you, Charlie, and I always will, no matter what happens. But you need to find out . . . what you want, what you need in your life. And God knows . . . you need *something* different, Charlie." She touched his arm briefly. "So you need to explore this thing with, um . . ."

"Natty," he said.

"If you don't, you'll always wonder, and it'll never be right with us again." She looked into Charlie's eyes and smiled. "Believe me, Charlie. I know."

* * *

AFTER AN EARLY dinner in Welch, Charlie and Ellen drove back to the plant. The OntAmex helicopter was waiting, ready for takeoff. Charlie stowed Ellen's Louis Vuitton bag while she buckled in. She'd removed her cellphone and a copy of *Town & Country* from her shoulder bag and placed them on the seat next to her. As the large blades began to turn, Charlie leaned over and kissed his wife goodbye.

"Good luck, Charlie," she said. "See you at Thanksgiving." Charlie nodded and squeezed her hand before leaving. He stood next to his car and watched the helicopter lift a few feet into the air before spinning around to the north. Through the window, Ellen waved, the cellphone already at her ear.

CHAPTER 28

THE GROUND FOG CLUNG TO THE LOW SPOTS LIKE THICK SMOKE, hiding the pavement in front of the Lexus. Charlie crept along Cold Springs Road, peering out the passenger window for the turnoff to the lumber camp. Finally he started to see cars and pickups parked in the weeds on the shoulder of the road. He found a spot for his car and took his athletics bag from the trunk.

He was fifteen minutes early, but a dozen men were already waiting in groups of two and three, talking, smoking, and sipping coffee from Styrofoam cups. He could feel their eyes on him as he made his way down the steep dirt-and-stone road.

Charlie entered the equipment shed and introduced himself to the foreman, a big, red-faced Irishman named Devine. "All ready for ya, Mr. Burden. Got ya teamed up with some of our best boys." He looked down at the roster on his clipboard. "Mr. Garvey said to just make sure you don't get hurt out there, so we got ya with some real good woodcutters." He handed Charlie a plastic-wrapped package of chaps. "C'mon, I'll introduce you to the boys."

They walked around to the side of the shed, where several battered utility vans were being loaded with equipment. Two men were carrying large chain saws, which they deposited on the floor of the van. "G'mornin' dere, boss," one of the men said, in the heavy French Canadian accent that Charlie had become familiar with in his college hockey days.

"Frenchy, Dogface." Devine gestured to Charlie coming up behind him. "This is Mr. Charlie Burden, fella I was telling you about. Charlie's going to cut some wood with you today. Your job is to make sure he don't get hurt."

Charlie winced a little at Devine's warning as he shook hands with the two men. Frenchy was at least six foot six and had the physique of a world-class weight lifter. His neck, shoulders, and arms rippled with muscles, and his huge hand felt like it was made of iron. His dark hair was pulled back into a short ponytail under a red bandanna.

Dogface was a foot shorter and looked a little older, but he had a similar physique on a smaller scale. He had a long, bony face with a long nose and sunken cheeks. His massive forearms were covered with tattoos. Both men glanced at the brand-new chaps Charlie carried under his arm, then back to Devine.

The foreman avoided their eyes, studying his clipboard. "You boys'll be limbin' and buckin' today out at pole eight."

Both men frowned. "Aw, c'mon dere, boss," said Frenchy, "don't be wastin' us on dat baby stuff. We got a lot a da big trees to bring down out dere." Dogface shook his head and went back to loading the truck.

"We got a mess o' logs at pole eight to get ready for the helicopters, so that's where we need you." Devine rapped his pencil on the clipboard, indicating that the discussion was over.

Frenchy grinned and put his huge hand on the foreman's shoulder. "Okay, boss man," he said, winking at Charlie. "We have a good time prunin' da bushes today. And, Mr. Charlie, we take good care of him, Dogface and me and Bucky. We bring him back tonight, good as a shiny new penny dere, aye?" Frenchy pulled an old canvas duffel from his shoulder, tossed it into the truck, and headed for the driver's seat.

Charlie wasn't sure if he'd heard Frenchy correctly, but Devine confirmed his fear. "Where the hell is Buck, anyway?" the foreman asked.

"He's bringing the water, boss," said Dogface. It all clicked in Charlie's head. *Of course Pat Garvey would've told Devine to put him with Buck. He'd made the call for Buck to get him his job, so Garvey would naturally think there was some sort of relationship.*

Then Buck Oakes was standing next to Devine. He put a heavy plastic water bucket down at his feet and stared coolly at Charlie.

"Buck, guess you already know Charlie Burden here. Says he knows how to use a chain saw." Devine looked over at Charlie. "That right, Burden?"

"I've used a chain saw," said Charlie, holding out his hand. Buck took his hand briefly. Up close, he looked bigger and more powerful than he'd appeared when Charlie saw him in his truck. He had the neck and shoulders of a football player, and his black mustache, goatee, and small dark eyes projected an ominous aura. Standing this close to Buck, Charlie could feel the anger and violence lurking just below the surface.

Frenchy stuck his head out the window. "C'mon dere, let's go, aye, Bucky?" He banged the outside of the door with a huge hand. "Got us some wood t'cut."

Dogface took a seat up in the cab with Frenchy, while Charlie and Buck climbed into the back. They sat facing each other on benches that ran along both sides of the van. Stuffed under the benches were chains, pulleys, coils of heavy rope, boxes of various tools, and a large first-aid kit. On the walls hung a selection of handsaws, pry bars of various lengths, and two very old two-man crosscut saws. Charlie noticed the ancient saw behind Buck. "You still use those?" he asked.

"Naw, not really. Frenchy and Dog like to take down a tree with it once in a while. For the *art o' lumberjackin'* and that kinda shit. They're both fuckin' nuts." Buck busied himself adjusting the tension on one of the saws, making it clear that he wasn't in the mood for any more idle chatter.

After a rough ten-minute ride through the woods, the truck lurched to a stop in a clearing covered with piles of logs awaiting the mill. Looking around, Charlie could see hundreds of stumps scattered on either side of the path and tried to imagine the labor needed to cut down that many trees on this kind of terrain. This was clearly work for rugged men who knew their trade, and Charlie started to feel guilty for thinking that he belonged out here, even for a day.

Frenchy and Dogface were at the back of the truck before Charlie could untangle himself from the equipment at his feet. They unloaded all of the equipment, and only then did Charlie survey the job ahead of them. Up the slope, on the high side of the gully, a sea of brown, gold, and green foliage covered an area about the size of a football field. It was impossible to tell how many trees were down.

Frenchy and Dogface strapped on plastic leg protectors that looked as if they'd been through the First World War. "Okay, Bucky, why don't you and Charlie go down the end dere, and me and Dog'll start up here," said

Frenchy, looking up the slope. "We'll meetcha in the middle," he added, smiling at Charlie. The incline was steeper, and the trees a little bigger, where Frenchy and Dogface would be working.

Buck shouldered his bag, grabbed a saw and one of the gas cans, and started for the far end of the field of fallen trees, leaving Charlie to carry the other saw and the oilcan. By the time Charlie reached the top of the slope, he could hear the high-pitched whine of the other chain saws. Buck walked Charlie up to the top of the slope between the first two trees and showed him how to cut a limb lock. Then it was Charlie's turn. He had to pull the starter rope a few times to get his saw running. "Good," said Buck. "How's that feel?"

"A little lighter than I thought it would be."

"We'll see how light it feels about three o'clock," Buck said. He pointed out a twisted limb for Charlie to cut. After a couple of tentative incisions, Charlie managed to shear off the limb without any pitch back. Buck nodded, put his ear protectors in place, and moved over to another, larger tree.

Charlie watched as Buck methodically cut through some large limbs, working steadily along one side of the fallen tree. While Buck didn't have much going for him in terms of people skills, he was a true craftsman when it came to cutting trees, moving the powerful saw like an extension of his arm, with no wasted motion. Down at the other end of downed trees, Frenchy and Dogface moved through their work at a similarly efficient pace.

Charlie went to work on his tree, clumsily at first but quickly gaining confidence. Soon he was ripping through the limbs, some a foot wide. After an hour, the sun had risen high enough to reach them, and Charlie was sweating profusely. He stopped to take off his sweatshirt, then saw Buck coming toward him with his own two-liter water bottle and Charlie's little Dasani bottle. He tossed the small one to Charlie. "You're gonna need more water."

"Think you're right," Charlie agreed, drinking most of it. Buck took the small bottle from him and filled it from his.

"That'll last you to the break," he said, handing it back.

"Thanks," said Charlie, but Buck had already started off toward his saw. They each limbed several trees before the ten-thirty break.

"Union rules, no exceptions," Buck said, as they walked toward the van and the orange water bucket. Frenchy and Dogface were already at the truck, eating apples. Frenchy reached into a bag and tossed one to Charlie. The Canadian grinned.

"Hey, Charlie, you cut da wood like an old-time logger up dere. I watch you sometime and you do some good work. First day and you keepin' up okay dere wid Bucky, for sure." He looked over toward Buck with a wide grin. "'Course, Bucky ain't a real logger, though. More of a painter or a sheetrocker maybe, when he gets da work, aye, Bucky?" Dogface laughed.

Buck ignored the Canadians, reached into the bag, took out two apples, and sat down on an old stump. Charlie slumped onto the back bumper, drinking water and wondering if he was going to last all day.

Frenchy laughed. "You'll be okay, Charlie. We cut seven, eight more trees before lunch, and den afternoon be much easier. We get done early. Maybe have some fun," he said, with a wink to Dogface. "Hey, Bucky, how's dat soccer team of your wife's?"

Buck scowled to hide his enthusiasm, but his voice gave him away. "Won again last night. Eight-nothin' ass-kickin'."

"So when do they go to dat tournament in Charleston?" asked Frenchy.

Buck shook his head. "Nat don't think they're goin' now, 'cause o' their two best players got suspended. She got a meetin' next Tuesday to try to appeal, but it ain't gonna do no good."

"Where's the hearing going to be?" asked Charlie.

Buck eyed Charlie warily for a few seconds before answering. "Kyle Loftus's office in Welch. Prick scheduled it for two o'clock, just to make it tougher for Nat to be there."

Charlie wondered if Natty would even go to the hearing now, but for what he had in mind, it almost didn't matter. He tossed his apple core into the weeds and filled his small bottle at the water cooler under the amused eyes of the loggers.

"I need to check in with the plant," said Charlie, starting out toward the hill. "See you up top," he called to Buck. Charlie unzipped the pocket on the side of his bag and took out his cellphone. He found several numbers for Vernon Yarbrough. He chose the lawyer's cellphone—he didn't have time to leave voice-mail messages.

"Yarbrough," the lawyer growled.

"Hello, Vern; Charlie Burden. I need a favor."

"Uh-huh, a favor." Charlie could hear a door close as Yarbrough paused. "Now, Burden, why don't you remind me just why it is that I should give a flying fuck about anything you might want?"

Charlie had expected the response. "C'mon, Vern, you're more of a team player than that. Plus, you're forgetting how I saved your ass on the Redemption Mountain thing."

"Saved my *what*?" Yarbrough said loudly.

Charlie moved into the woods to stay out of Buck's earshot. "Okay, Vern, listen. You're still on retainer to OntAmex, and when I'm here, I speak for my client. Plus, this concerns DeWitt's granddaughter, and it could help in the eminent-domain hearing."

After a few seconds, Yarbrough gave in. "Okay, Burden, what's it about?"

Charlie explained about the Charleston tournament and the suspensions. "The hearing's next Tuesday, in Welch, at this guy Loftus's office."

"Not much time to get ready," said Yarbrough.

"I know. I just found out about it."

"So what do you want me to do?" asked Yarbrough.

Charlie smiled. "Do what you do best, Vern. Show up at the hearing and plead Mrs. Oakes's case. Get Loftus to lift the suspensions."

"And all this has what to do with the eminent-domain hearing?"

"Vern, you do this, and I'll see that Natty Oakes doesn't testify at the hearing."

Yarbrough laughed. "Burden, that girl can get up and dance naked on the judge's bench, for all I care. She can testify 'til she's blue in the face—come December, we'll still be makin' footballs out o' them pigs and havin' a nice chicken barbecue up on that farm."

"Well, Vern, you're probably right," said Charlie, "but the PUC might not like some of the things she says." The threat sat between them like a lit firecracker, while Yarbrough quickly reviewed everything that Charlie Burden could possibly know.

They both knew which side Charlie was on, so the propriety of his passing information on to Natty Oakes for her to make public was a moot point. Finally, in the face of uncertainty, which all lawyers detested, Yarbrough chose the path with the least risk, as Charlie knew he would. Showing up in Welch to stare down a small-town insurance man wasn't heavy lifting for Yarbrough. It would be a day's worth of billable hours, plus some inflated travel expenses. "Okay, Burden, okay," he conceded. "I don't need anything you're sellin' today, but I'll help you out. Can't promise anything, because we don't have a lot of time."

"See you Tuesday." Charlie put his phone away and went back to work.

Like Buck one tree over, Charlie fell into a productive rhythm, proceeding steadily down the tree trunk, the rest of the world blocked out by the noise of the saw. He was beginning to understand how the solitude and closeness with nature made loggers love woodcutting to the point that all other work was unsuitable.

At lunchtime, Frenchy and Dogface laughed when they saw Charlie's tiny peanut butter sandwich. Frenchy insisted that Charlie take half of his second roast beef sandwich, and Dogface tossed him an orange. Charlie sat on a warm boulder, enjoying the stillness of the woods. The cloudless sky had turned a dark blue, and the sun cut through the cool autumn air, soothing his aching thighs and shoulders. He lifted his face to the sun, the sweet smell of fresh sawdust and tree sap in his nostrils, and wondered if this wasn't the best occupation in the world.

It was three o'clock by the time Buck and Charlie finished limbing and went back to where they'd started, to begin bucking the logs in half. This felt more like lumberjacking to Charlie. Even as his arms began to shake with fatigue, he reveled in the satisfaction of what they'd accomplished. It was a feeling he hadn't experienced in a long time. Just after four o'clock, they met Frenchy and Dogface in the middle. "Hokay, Charlie," said Frenchy, turning off his saw. "Das a good job you do today."

"We all done for the day?" asked Charlie, his arms aching for rest.

Frenchy hefted his bag over his shoulder and picked up his saw. He looked toward Buck, who was already halfway to the truck, then up to the pine forest farther down the ridge. "Well, Charlie, maybe we still got some fun ahead of us before we go back." He turned and grinned at Dogface. "Aye, Dogman?" Dogface shook his head. Frenchy laughed.

When they reached the truck with the equipment, Buck was sitting on a stump, waiting. "Bucky, you do some good woodcutting today," said Frenchy.

"Great," said Buck. "Now let's get the fuck outta here. I got a beer waitin' for me down the Roadhouse."

Frenchy dropped his saw and duffel in the sand. "Hey, what's the hurry dere, Bucky? Still is early, and maybe Dog and me, we got a little proposition for you and Charlie, aye?"

"I don't want to hear it, Frenchy. Let's go."

Frenchy walked down the road in front of the truck. "C'mon, Buck," said Frenchy, "I want to show you something you don't see so very often."

Buck sighed, but his curiosity was piqued, and he followed Frenchy down the gully, trailed by Charlie and Dogface. Frenchy walked about fifty yards down the road, then started up the slope toward the ridgeline, stopping halfway up.

"What's the deal?" asked Buck.

Frenchy looked up the hill. "See dem two big firs, side by each up dere, Bucky?"

Charlie looked up to where two magnificent firs, each over one hundred feet, dominated the ridgeline. At their base, they looked to be at least three feet wide. Both wore red spray-painted X's, marking them for removal.

"We'll cut 'em down tomorrow," said Buck, turning to go back.

Frenchy grabbed his arm. "Bucky, dem two trees is like identical twins. Same size each one, same wood. And look how *big* dey are," he said, pointing up. "Bucky," he implored, "we may never get da chance again to take down such a tree by hand." He clapped a big hand on Buck's shoulder. "Like dey did in da old days, aye?"

"None of that shit today, Frenchy. I ain't in the mood." Buck shook his arm free and started to walk away. "Plus, Burden ain't a woodcutter."

"I tink Charlie must be more woodcutter den you, for walking away from a tree-cuttin' contest."

Buck stopped in his tracks.

Frenchy held up a fifty-dollar bill. "Fifty bucks for da first tree down, me and Dog, you and Charlie, wid the two-man saws. Pick your tree."

Buck wasn't used to backing down from a challenge. His eyes flickered for a moment up toward the big trees, then back to Frenchy. "That's stupid," he spit out quietly. "Burden ain't a woodcutter," he turned again and started down the hill.

"We'll do it," said Charlie loudly before Buck could leave. "You got a bet."

"Hokay, Charlie. Attaboy!" Frenchy looked at Buck and pointed at Charlie. "You see dere, Bucky? Charlie, he's a real woodcutter, he is."

Buck strode over to Charlie and pulled him far enough away from the others so as not to be overheard. "Burden, you don't know what the fuck you're gettin' into here. You ever take a big tree down with a crosscut saw dull as a butter knife? Halfway through, you'll think your back is on fire and your arms are gonna fall off." He didn't wait for an answer. "Listen, Burden, these guys, they're pros at this. This is what they *do*, Frenchy and Dog. They enter lumberjack contests. Shit, they been on *ESPN*."

Charlie took a deep breath and glanced at the Canadians, who smiled back. "So what?" said Charlie. "Fuck 'em. We can beat these guys." He whirled away from Buck and went back toward Frenchy and Dogface. "You're on," said Charlie, reaching for his wallet. "But it's two hundred—a hundred bucks a man," he said, pulling out two hundred-dollar bills.

Frenchy grinned broadly and clapped his hands together loudly. "Das why you da big mule, Charlie!"

Buck pushed past Charlie and moved up the slope, eyeing the two big trees. "One condition," he said, turning to Frenchy. "Gotta hit the water bucket with the trunk."

Frenchy laughed and threw away his apple core. "Whatever you want, Bucky," he said, starting off down the hill with Dogface. "We land dat tree smack on Charlie's little bitty water bottle, if dat make it better for you," he called back. They laughed their way down the slope.

At the truck, Buck and Frenchy threw several iron wedges, a maul, and an ax in their bags, then pulled out the long two-man saws. They sprayed them with oil and examined the teeth and handles, finally agreeing that there was no advantage to either saw. At the orange water bucket, Buck filled his plastic bottle, then put the two-liter bottle to his mouth, drained half of it, and handed it to Charlie. "Drink it all," said Buck. "You're going to need it."

Buck kicked over the water cooler, sending the remaining water into the sand. He tossed his bag to Charlie, hefted the saw over his shoulder, picked up the empty water bucket, and started up the hill.

The two fir trees were twenty yards apart, and, to Charlie, they were even bigger than they looked from the bottom of the hill. Buck took his time examining both trees before he chose the one on the right. Buck and

Frenchy hiked down the slope to position the water cooler. They maneuvered a loose stump to a spot where the falling trunk of either tree would hit it without interference from the high branches. They negotiated a position equidistant between the two trees and placed the orange plastic cooler on top.

Buck jogged back up the slope. "Let me see your hands," he said to Charlie, rummaging in his duffel bag. Charlie took off his gloves and displayed his palms. Buck pulled open a jar of Vaseline and smeared Charlie's hands with it. "You'll be bleedin' through your gloves in ten minutes without this." Buck showed him how they would cut a notch centered on the line to the water cooler. He kept his voice low. "Frenchy won't bother with a notch. He'll figure he can hit it without one, but this's real stringy wood."

Buck explained how they would cut on a slightly downward angle about a foot into the tree, then hammer the wedges in, to keep the saw from binding. "Tree settles down on the saw, you're done." Buck picked up a handle of the saw to show Charlie how to grip it. "Lean into the tree and pull hard, don't push, and don't stop. Use your legs, your back, and your arms, all together."

"I'll learn as we go," said Charlie, with a quick smile.

Buck leaned in a little closer. "Listen, Burden, I got to tell you . . ." He lowered his voice further. "I ain't got a hundred bucks on me, so . . ."

"We're not going to lose," said Charlie. "I guarantee it." Buck shook his head as he stood up, pulling his gloves on.

Frenchy and Dogface had taken their shirts off, though the air was cooling rapidly. Tying a fresh bandanna across his forehead, his orange gloves tucked into the front of his pants, Frenchy walked over to Charlie. He looked like a professional wrestler.

"Okay, Charlie," he said, pointing to a spot ten yards away. "When she starts to go, you move quickly to way back here. Don't go directly behind the stump, and don't wait. When you hear it crackin', you go quick, aye, Charlie? And you watch overhead. Dese trees be bringing down some limbs." Charlie looked at his escape route and nodded.

"Okay," said Frenchy, as he went back to his tree. "You say when."

Charlie and Buck started in front of the tree with a horizontal cut for the notch. With their first few strokes, Charlie realized how difficult a task it would be. When they completed the notch, it seemed to Charlie that they were already too far behind to catch up. With his back to the other tree, Charlie could hear Frenchy and Dogface stroking their saw at a faster and more powerful tempo than Buck and he.

Buck glanced toward the other tree. "We're okay, Burden. Just lean into the cut." Gradually they settled into a powerful rhythm, with Charlie trying to copy Buck's technique. He was impressed with Buck's strength, as his shoulder and neck muscles bulged with each stroke. He also admired Buck's focus and drive, as his eyes burned with the flame of competitiveness. It occurred to him that Buck was having his first enjoyable moment of the day. He was a match for either of the Canadian lumberjacks. Now if only Charlie could hold up his end.

After ten minutes, Charlie's hands and arms were burning. He tried to use more leg and back, but he could feel the fresh scar tissue across his back protesting. He was having trouble catching his breath, and sweat was pouring into his eyes, but he couldn't let go of the saw. "Doin' okay, Burden," Buck encouraged. "Stay strong. Long, strong pulls. You got it."

Charlie set his jaw and ignored the pain, concentrating on each pull. They were about a foot into the tree when they heard Frenchy and Dogface hammering in the wedges. It wasn't a good sign. Charlie looked over at Buck, who shook his head.

They cut hard for another few minutes before Buck stopped. "Wedges," he said breathlessly, scrambling behind the tree, picking up the ax and the big wedge for the center of the cut. Charlie welcomed the moment of relief from the saw but found he had trouble making his arms work. Finally he got a wedge into the cut and managed a feeble hit with the maul just as Buck landed a massive blow to the big wedge with the back of the ax.

"Watch out," said Buck, taking a step toward him while bringing the ax back for another swing. Charlie had barely moved when Buck brought the ax through the air with a powerful swing, landing a loud, metallic blow dead on Charlie's wedge, sending it well into the cut.

For the next ten minutes, they leaned into the saw with long, powerful strokes. Charlie's hands, arms, and back were beyond hurting, and his long-sleeved T-shirt was now completely dark with sweat. The wound on his back was burning, and he thought he could feel skin tearing apart with each pull of the saw. Liquid seeped down his back, but he couldn't tell if it was sweat or blood until he looked down and noticed the creeping ooze of dark maroon on the left side of his shirt at the ribs. Inside his right glove, he could feel the burn of torn blisters and the slippery combination of blood and loose skin.

"Doin' great, Burden. Doin' great," Buck spit out between breaths. "We're gonna beat these assholes."

Charlie squeezed his bloody right hand tighter around the wooden handle. They were halfway through the trunk when a cold wind started to blow. The sun had disappeared and the temperature was dropping quickly. Twigs and small branches rained down on them as the tops of the trees swayed menacingly in the darkening sky. Charlie could feel the chills and nausea of hypothermia as the wind blew against his sweat-soaked clothing.

"Dogface is crampin,'" Buck whispered excitedly. "Dog's crampin' up."

Behind them, the other saw had slowed its pace noticeably. Charlie turned his head for a quick glance and saw that Dogface had a look of excruciating pain. As he turned back to his own tree, Charlie vomited on his right arm, a milky liquid sprinkled with what looked like small pieces of apple skin. He spit repeatedly to try to break the long strings of saliva that hung down from his mouth to the front of his shirt, before deciding to ignore them.

As the big tree swayed, Charlie heard the trunk groan and felt the roots heave beneath his feet. The wind had knocked loose some large dead limbs, and one crashed through the branches above them, splintering into a shower of dead wood. Charlie realized the danger they were in. These trees weren't going to go quietly.

"C'mon, Burden, don't let up!' Buck yelled. "We're almost there."

Then the wood popped like a firecracker next to Charlie's ear. The cut had widened several inches, and when Charlie looked up, both trees were leaning slightly downhill. Buck was in front of the tree now, driving the ax violently into the notch to adjust the fall angle. "She's goin', Burden, move back!" he shouted.

Charlie pried his hands off the saw and tried to run back to the spot Frenchy had pointed out, but his legs gave out at the knees. He scrambled slowly over ground now littered with twigs, branches, and pine needles, feeling the earth heave under him as the roots strained to keep the old trees upright.

Then an ungodly explosion of cracking wood made Charlie spin around to watch the violent ending. He was amazed to see Buck standing next to the tree, watching as both trees began their long, final trip to earth. Frenchy, also oblivious of the danger, stood between the two trees, hands on hips. The trees crashed thunderously down the slope, sending a cloud of dust high into the air and illuminating the area around them with daylight, as if the window shades of the forest had been thrown open.

Charlie watched the two men for their reaction. They both stood motionless for several seconds. Then Buck bent at the knees and sprang into the air, letting out a mighty whoop. He jumped on top of the fallen tree, arms raised in the air. "Yeah, baby!" Buck strutted down the log, bobbing his head like a turkey. "Direct fucking hit is what I'm lookin' at here, woodcutters." Buck was grinning from ear to ear as he came back up the log. "Hey, c'mon, Burden!" He waved a hand, motioning Charlie forward. "You gotta see this!"

Charlie struggled to his feet and limped toward the fallen tree. He was beginning to feel his arms and hands again and barely managed a smile. Buck disappeared once more, dancing down the trunk of the tree. Frenchy met Charlie at the top of the slope, his hand extended. "When was da last time you have dat much fun, aye, Charlie?"

Charlie laughed. "Yeah, been a while." He looked down the slope and saw Buck standing next to the flattened water cooler. Charlie realized it was the first time he had seen Buck smile all day.

Frenchy clapped his hands. "Hokay, boys, good job." He handed Buck two hundred-dollar bills and winked at him. "Next time we don't give you Charlie for a partner."

Charlie sat down on the stump, exhausted, watching Frenchy and Dogface walk down the hill. Behind him, Charlie heard Buck drop his bag on the ground. He turned his head just in time to see Buck pull out a long hunting knife. The blade glistened in the dim light. Charlie glanced downhill for the other men, but they were nowhere in sight. He instinctively tightened his back muscles.

"Hold still," said Buck, gingerly peeling up the bottom of Charlie's bloody shirt. The razor-sharp knife sliced easily through the middle of the wet shirt. "Shit, Burden, little grunt work and you city guys fall apart."

"It's an old wound," said Charlie. Buck handed him a clean long-sleeved shirt from his bag and a bandanna to wrap his hand in. The shirt felt warm and dry. Charlie put it on but stayed on the stump, too tired to move.

Buck reached into his front pocket and pulled out the bills that Frenchy had given him. "Here's your hundred." Charlie took it and stuffed it into his back pocket. "Buy you a drink down the Roadhouse, if you're goin'," said Buck.

"No," Charlie said. "I think I'll get my hand wrapped and go soak in the tub."

Buck looked down the hill at the flattened water cooler and laughed. "Well, I got three days off and a paycheck, plus a hundred o' Frenchy's dollars in my pocket, so I'll be goin' on a little toot myself."

"Maybe you should just go home, Buck." Charlie tried to sound friendly.

"Yeah? What do you know about my home, Burden?" Buck spit out angrily.

Charlie didn't want to get into it with Buck, and he shouldn't have said anything, but now he had no choice. "What I know, Buck," he said calmly, "is that one of these days you're going to be my age, and your kids will all of a sudden have grown up, and you'll have missed out on the most enjoyable thing there is in life. Being a father. Being a father to great kids, like you've got." He frowned with disgust, because he knew that Buck didn't get it. "You're going to miss it all, Buck, and you'll never get those years back." Charlie pushed himself up from the stump to try to end the conversation.

Buck had an angry, confused look on his face. "Maybe you'd like to be goin' home in place o' me. Like those boys was sayin' at the Roadhouse that night? All that stuff about runnin' with Nat and pallin' around with the kid." Buck's voice was getting louder, and he was inching closer to Charlie as he spoke. "And who knows what else you been doin'!"

Charlie wanted to let it go, but he wasn't going to back down. "Nobody's been doin' anything, Buck. The Pie Man was the first person I met down here. He's a great kid, and I like him a lot. Natty showed me her running trail, and I ran with her a couple of times. That's it, Buck." Charlie reached down for the crosscut saw.

Buck wasn't ready for the conversation to end. "Yeah, well, maybe you oughta just stay away from my family," he said, "and keep the fuck out of my business."

Charlie threw the saw down, moved in front of Buck, and put his face up close to the younger man's. "Buck, you can go on being a shitty father and your kids'll do all right, anyway. And you can keep on being a shitty husband, and someday you're going to lose Natty, whether I got anything to do with it or not." He pushed his finger into Buck's chest. "But," he lowered his voice, "you ever hit that girl again, I'm comin' after you. You understand me, Buck?"

Buck swallowed hard and glared at Charlie, but he didn't move for several seconds. Finally, the loud horn of the truck blared from the base of the hill. They both looked down to see that Frenchy had turned the truck around to head back and had his head out the window. "C'mon, dere, girls," he yelled. "You can fuck echudder up de ass all daway back now. Let's go, aye?"

They rode without speaking. As they neared the foreman's shed, Charlie said, "Listen, Buck, thanks for all your help today. I enjoyed it a lot, even pukin' all over myself." Buck couldn't help smiling. Charlie held out a gloved hand. "You're a great woodcutter, Buck. I'd cut down a tree with you anytime." Buck took his hand briefly and nodded almost imperceptibly.

The truck stopped at the shed and Buck started to get out. Charlie spoke again. "Do me a favor, Buck, will you? When you do get home, tell Pie about how we beat those two lumberjacks. How we cut that tree down and landed it right on top of that water bucket. Pie will get a real kick out of that."

Buck hesitated for a second. "Yeah, sure," he grumbled. "I'll tell him about it."

CHAPTER 29

THE ROAD TO WELCH WAS DESERTED WHEN NATTY REACHED TOWN at nearly 2:00 P.M. It wasn't always like this, she recalled. When she was a kid, it seemed like the huge coal trucks were always coming and going—straining and belching black smoke in one direction, banging and rattling their empty bins on the return.

Natty thought she knew where the Loftus Insurance Agency was, but as she drove down Main Street she began to get anxious about being late. *It would be just like Kyle to cancel the hearing if she was a minute late.* She sighed as she remembered the futility of the whole thing.

Then she saw the blue Lexus parked in front of the insurance agency, and her heart raced. She hadn't expected Charlie to show up after his wife had come to town, but there was no mistaking that car. She pulled in, leaving a few spaces between her car and Charlie's.

Out of habit, she arranged the shock of hair a little lower over her left eyebrow. She leaned forward and looked in her visor mirror at her eyes, then lifted her chin to see her mouth, before slumping back in her seat. Natty recalled Ellen Burden standing in the hallway outside Charlie's apartment, looking so perfect, her silky hair shining, eyes made up like a model's, her lips painted an elegant dark red. She wondered if she should start wearing a little eye makeup and maybe even some lipstick once in a while—as she did for a time in high school, before Buck came back. Before she got too busy with so many other things. She pushed the mirror away and reached for the door handle.

Through the insurance agency window, she saw Charlie seated in a waiting area, surrounded by green plants. He was wearing a black blazer, a white shirt, and a silver tie. His professional attire seemed strange to her, as if he were a different man from the one she knew.

Entering the office, she saw several women behind a counter, busy on their phones. A man stood waiting with a handful of papers and a license plate. Natty felt intimidated by the professional look of the office. She was also nervous about seeing Charlie for the first time since she'd met his wife and realized what a charade this fantasy of hers was.

An open door revealed a wood-paneled conference room. Suddenly Kyle Loftus appeared in the doorway. "Mrs. Oakes, we'll be with you in just a minute," he said pleasantly. Then he saw Charlie in the waiting area and the smile left his face. "He with you?" he asked, as Natty turned and saw that Charlie was on his feet.

"Yes, I'm with Mrs. Oakes," Charlie said. "I reffed the game in question—remember? So I thought I should be here to make sure the facts are straight." He brushed past Loftus and entered the conference room without offering his hand. Loftus hesitated, then followed.

Charlie introduced himself to the two men already seated at the table and handed out business cards. "I'm in charge of the new power plant over in Red Bone," he said, to make sure they knew who they were dealing with.

Loftus took a chair on the far side of the table and introduced the other members of the committee as Walter and Gary. Natty recognized one as a coach of one of the Welch Little League baseball teams. The other was Loftus's brother-in-law and an employee of the agency.

Charlie moved to the middle of the table and sat down. Natty took a seat next to him. She smiled briefly at Walter and Gary across the table and waited for Loftus to start the meeting.

"What we got here is real simple, 'cause, as you may recall, I was at the game and saw everything that happened." Loftus glanced at Walter and Gary and gestured toward them with his left hand. "We discussed it a couple of weeks ago and agreed, unanimously, that suspension of the two players from any postseason play was completely warranted under the rules and bylaws of this association." Walter and Gary nodded in agreement. "So, there it is," Loftus said, slapping the table lightly with the palms of both hands. He flashed a toothy smile at Natty and then at Charlie and raised his palms to invite a response.

"Well," Natty said, clearing her throat. "It ain't fair, 'cause it was the other team's fault. That coach and that kid Rudy, they started all the trouble, and you know it, Kyle."

"Doesn't matter," said Loftus. "The coach has been dealt with, and their season's over, anyway." Loftus looked at his watch.

Charlie leaned forward. "It does matter," he said firmly. "You're penalizing two kids unfairly, and a whole team will be punished because"—he looked directly at Loftus—"you and your buddy got your egos bruised."

Loftus sat back in his chair with a wry smile. "Seems like somebody else took a little bruisin' that day." Walter and Gary smirked knowingly.

"This isn't about me or anything that happened after that game," Charlie said angrily. "I want you guys to do the right thing and let those kids play in the tournament."

Loftus shook his head. "Ain't gonna happen, my friend," he said, pushing his chair away from the table. He pointed an index finger at Natty. "You take that girl and that black boy up to Charleston, they ain't gonna let your team on the field."

Loftus was startled as Vernon Yarbrough filled the doorway of the conference room. "Help you with something there, fella?" Loftus asked.

Yarbrough ignored him, moving to the edge of the conference table and tossing business cards down in front of Loftus and then Walter and Gary. He turned to Natty and held out his hand. "Mrs. Oakes, how nice to see you again." Natty remembered him from the pond hearing. "Charlie," he said, reaching past Natty, "how's everything at the Red Bone project?"

"Everything's great, Vern," Charlie replied, relieved that the lawyer had finally appeared.

Yarbrough remained standing. "I'm here to represent Mrs. Oakes and the two juvenile victims in this matter, Emma Lowe and Zachary Willard." The lawyer opened his briefcase and took out three packets. He placed one in front of Loftus, then gave the others to Walter and Gary. Yarbrough sat down next to Natty.

After a few moments to allow the men to glance at the documents, Yarbrough leaned forward and put his arms on the table. "What you're looking at here, gentlemen, is a million-dollar civil suit against each of you for the irreparable harm you're causing my clients with this discriminatory and, I might add, racially motivated ruling. I'm sorry, I should have asked earlier—are you men represented by counsel today?"

Walter and Gary looked at each other nervously. Loftus forced a thin smile and tossed his packet to the middle of the table. "This is bullshit," he said, glancing at his brother-in-law. He sat back in his chair and crossed his arms defiantly. "It's all bullshit," he repeated.

Yarbrough rubbed his palms together slowly in front of his face. "*Bullshit*, that's an interesting word," he said. Charlie suppressed a smile as he awaited the coming eruption. "So, Mr. Loftus," the lawyer continued, "it's your contention that I left my very comfortable office in Charleston, for a ninety-minute flight down here to godforsaken McDowell County, to present to you gentlemen a professionally prepared legal document, which is, in fact"—he slammed the tabletop as he shouted—"just *bullshit*?"

Yarbrough's face was flushed with anger. His voice was deep and loud, uncaring if they were overheard in the outer office. "Gentlemen, let me tell you about that pile of bullshit sitting in front of you! What you have there is a minimum of two years of litigation and one hundred thousand dollars in legal fees for each of you—I shit you not—and in the end we may not get the million but we'll get six *goddamn* good figures, and I'll be going after your houses and your cars and your wives' little pinky rings, just to cover my fee. And when you're done with my personally guided tour through the West Virginia tort system, you hillbillies will be riding fucking mules around these mountains, sellin' long-term-care insurance to dyin' coal miners!"

Natty sat unmoving, trying to grasp the idea that this monster of a lawyer could actually be on her side. "Now, Mr. Loftus," said Yarbrough, with slightly less volume, "in your best interest, sir, you and I need to caucus in private."

Loftus, his face locked in a nervous scowl, stood and followed Yarbrough from the room. They entered a corner office behind a smoked-glass wall. Yarbrough noticed a floor-to-ceiling curtain along the wall and pulled it closed. The insurance man took refuge in the tall leather chair behind the desk and motioned for Yarbrough to take a seat. Yarbrough ignored him, walked behind the desk, and stood menacingly at

Loftus's side. He tossed a file down on the desk and spoke softly. "Now, Mr. Loftus, what you got to do right now is pick out which one of those pictures in there you'd like us to send to your wife."

Loftus opened the file and groaned. The first picture was an eight-by-ten black-and-white shot of an overweight but very buxom woman, in her midtwenties, descending an outside stairway from a second-floor apartment. The next picture showed Kyle Loftus following her. The third picture showed Loftus and the girl locked in an embrace on the landing. "Aw, *fuck*," Loftus moaned. "You put an investigator on me over this bush league crap?"

Yarbrough closed the file and leaned in close to Loftus's ear. "Brother Loftus, in the next few seconds you need to fully embrace the idea that this issue is a lot more important to some very powerful people than it is to *you*. Then you need to go back into that conference room and make it right with that woman in there, or, believe me, I will make *fucking you over* my number-one hobby well into my retirement years."

NATTY LEFT AS soon as Loftus returned to the room and announced, to the obvious relief of Walter and Gary, that the appeal was accepted and the suspensions were lifted. Out in the street, she walked quickly to her car. As she reached for the door handle, she heard Charlie behind her. "Good luck, Nat," he said.

Natty turned and walked slowly over to the side of the Lexus, then looked down through the glass roof. "I used to have a car like this. For a week." Charlie smiled. "Thanks for doin' this today."

"You're welcome," he replied, his eyes locked on hers.

After a few moments she looked off toward the hills. "Redemption Mountain—that's a hopeless case now, right?"

Charlie sighed. "I'm afraid so, Nat. There's no stopping it at this point. The hearing's just a formality."

"That's what Bud says."

"I'm sorry, Nat. I tried . . ."

"Anyway, the kids'll be happy when I tell 'em they can play. Felt kinda good, for a change, bein' on the same side as the big boys with the expensive lawyers."

"It helps," admitted Charlie. "How's Pie? Haven't seen him in a while.

Haven't seen you around, either," he continued, spreading out his fingers on the moon roof. "So, what happened, Nat?"

She didn't want to have this conversation. "Aw, Charlie," she said softly, "moment I saw your wife standing in the door, I knew what a jerk I'd been . . . for thinkin' about us . . . for dreaming stuff."

"Natty—" Charlie protested.

She shook her head. "Woman like that don't come all the way down to Red Bone less she's really . . ."

"Nat, you've got that all wrong," he said firmly.

"Charlie, what are you doin', sayin' all that stuff to me, when you got a wife like that at home?" She slowly lifted her eyes up to his.

"Natty, I fell in love with someone else." Charlie inched his left hand forward, and their fingertips touched. "And I've never lied to you about anything. I told you how I felt, that night we went over to see Woody and Mr. Jacks. That was the truth."

After a few seconds, Natty asked, "Did you tell her . . ." She hesitated, afraid to say the words. "You know, what you said you would?"

"I didn't have to. She said she knew the moment you opened the door that I was in love with you," Charlie replied.

Natty looked at her feet, stalling for time. She hadn't been ready to hear Charlie say the words. "That night, when I was standin' there lookin' at her in the hallway, all she had to do was say *boo* and I woulda peed in my pants."

Charlie laughed, and watched Natty for a few moments. "I met Buck last week," he said. "We cut down some trees."

"I heard," said Natty, grateful for a change of subject. "He told Pie all about it. It was real nice, Buck tellin' Pie a story. How you two beat some professional loggers, cuttin' down a big tree. Pie was so proud."

Charlie laughed again. "We had a good day."

Natty made a face. "Damn, Charlie, couldn't you and Buck just have a fistfight, like in the movies? You know, *fightin' over the girl*, instead of becoming pals? Now Buck's in love with you, too." She looked up quickly when she realized what she'd said.

"Well, we didn't exactly part company as best friends." Then he remembered the trip to New York that weekend. "You still going on the New York trip?"

Natty smiled. "No reason not to, I guess."

"Good. We'll go for a run. I'll meet you in front of your hotel, Saturday morning, six-thirty."

Natty nodded, then looked at her watch. "Got some old people I still need to tend to. I'll see you in New York." Charlie watched her get into the Honda and drive off.

As CHARLIE AND Natty were driving away from Welch, a gray Nissan Sentra—the cheapest rental car available at the Charleston airport—labored slowly up Redemption Mountain Road. The car passed the DeWitt farm before backing up and pulling in under the huge oak tree that covered the driveway with a thick layer of leathery brown leaves.

The driver made a note in a tattered spiral notebook before getting out of the car. He was a tall, gaunt man in his late sixties with a protruding Adam's apple, a deeply lined face, and a permanent squint. He wore an old gray suit, a rumpled khaki raincoat, and a gray fedora that had obviously served its owner for many years. He glanced at his watch and shook his head, angry at himself for being late. He should have started out earlier.

He moved slowly up the wooden stairs onto the porch. An observer might guess that he was an insurance agent, or maybe a process server, but not the owner of the largest private investigations firm in Toronto. At the front door, he removed his hat and introduced himself to Bud and Alice DeWitt. He'd called a week prior, and he and Bud had chatted for a while.

For some reason, Bud trusted him—maybe it was his reference to growing up on a wheat farm in Manitoba—and answered his questions about the farm and the recent attempts to buy it. The stranger was particularly interested in the day the cornfield burned—who was there, how many vehicles, what kind of uniforms the men wore. He didn't ask what was growing in the field or how it burned, just about the men.

Later, he walked around the charred remains of the field and around the perimeter of the farm. In the failing light of early evening, he drove up to the top of Redemption Mountain, stopping first at the cemetery and the high pond. He returned to the farmhouse for dinner with the DeWitts, listening attentively to the family's history on Redemption Mountain. But he offered little about himself or his mission. After refusing repeated offers to stay the night, he made the four-hour drive back to

Charleston, took a room at a Quality Inn near the airport, and rose early the next morning for a seven-thirty flight to Toronto.

A FULL CREW was at work on the library—two men finishing up the shingling, and several others installing windows on the second floor— trying to get the outside of the building finished before the cold weather arrived. As he pulled into the parking area, Charlie could hear the staccato bang of carpenters' hammers, the satisfying sound of real work being accomplished.

Charlie thought about the meeting in New York to which he had been summoned on Friday. The message had come from Larry Tuthill, to meet with a committee of OntAmex and DD&M people to review Charlie's projects.

Once, it would have seemed like a fairly benign meeting, but the fact that Terry Summers and Warren Brand would be attending was a clear warning. Friday afternoon was typically when high-level management coups were orchestrated, to give the company the weekend to clean up the mess and manage the spin. With the power plant on schedule and the eminent-domain taking of Redemption Mountain in less than two weeks, Charlie knew he was now expendable. There was a good chance that, after tomorrow, he'd have little reason to return to Red Bone.

Walking up the wide stairway of the new library, Charlie smiled at how beautifully the light streamed in from the skylights. The small partitioned reading nooks would be cozy spots for the children of Red Bone. Charlie heard the crackling footsteps and muffled voices of the roofers overhead.

He sat on one of the low benches, which would eventually have padded seats, and looked around, imagining the final result. He thought about Natty's daughter, Cat, the tiny girl with the long, silky blond hair, who was always paging through a picture book whenever he saw her. *Cat will love this spot, up on the top floor of the library. It'll be her special place . . . like Natty's boulder.* Charlie closed his eyes. He ached to hold the little girl in his lap and read *Charlie and the Chocolate Factory, The Dragons of Blueland,* and *The Indian in the Cupboard* to her, as he'd done with his own children long ago.

He heard a creaking sound on the stairway, and a backward Yankees cap appeared. The boy turned and saw Charlie smiling at him. Pie climbed the last step and jumped in front of Charlie, both palms raised for a high-five. Charlie laughed as he raised his hands to the boy. "Hello, Pie Man," Charlie said. "I've missed you."

Still holding Charlie's hands, Pie said, "I went to your office, but they say Charlie gone to New York."

Charlie let go of the boy's hands and knocked his cap down over his eyes. "I'm going to New York tonight. C'mon, Pie Man, sit down," he said. "Tell me about school and the soccer team. I understand the Bones are going to a tournament in Charleston."

Pie sat next to Charlie, but he had something else he wanted to talk about. "Charlie?" he asked in a small voice. "Will you tell me the story about you and my papa cutting down the big tree?" Charlie smiled and nodded, as the boy, wide-eyed with anticipation, folded his legs underneath him on the bench.

"Your dad and I were out in the woods, way down where some of the trees are over two hundred years old. We were cutting trees with two lumberjacks named Frenchy and Dogface, two of the best loggers around," said Charlie, beginning the story that Pie would cherish for the rest of his life.

CHAPTER 30

THE BUS WAS UNLIKE ANYTHING NATTY HAD EVER RIDDEN ON. IT was purple and silver with dark-tinted windows, and it towered over the road as it pulled out of the Red Bone Baptist Church parking lot. A five-hour trip would get them to the motel in Pennsylvania, then another five-hour drive on Friday morning would bring them to New York. Natty was anxious about the trip, but a free weekend in New York, with two nights in a hotel and a ticket to *Les Misérables*, was too good to pass up.

She felt uncomfortable about leaving the kids—she'd never been away from them overnight, except for her hospital stay—and she was uneasy about missing her patients on Friday. But the real cause of the gnawing in her stomach was Charlie Burden. He was definitely going to be in New York now, and they even had a kind of date set up, didn't they? And if anything was ever going to happen between them, she had a strong feeling that it would have to happen this weekend.

Mabel Willard put a soft hand over Natty's, positioned on the armrest between them. "You okay, girl?" she asked, sensing Natty's unease.

"Ain't even out of Red Bone, and I'm already homesick," she said with a laugh. "Ain't been out of West Virginia since high school."

Mabel patted Natty's hand. "Been a long time for me, too," she said. "Twelve years. Since Lorena was havin' her troubles, and I had to go up to Detroit and bring the boys home."

Natty squeezed Mabel's hand. "I remember. I was pregnant with Pie when Lorena died." Natty recalled Mabel's beautiful, talented daughter, two years ahead of her in school. She was so self-confident and ready for the world, she couldn't wait to leave McDowell County to seek her fortune in the big city. A year later, she was living in a Detroit tenement, the mother of twin boys, and a year after that she was dead from an overdose.

"Took those babies away from that awful man, one in each arm, and took the bus back down here." They were quiet for a few minutes, each woman lost in her thoughts.

"Mabel?" Natty whispered. "Do you still miss her . . . after all these years? I mean, do you think about her a lot?"

Mabel sighed. "Zack and Sammy are a handful, but, yeah," Mabel's voice cracked, "I think about Lorena every day, first thing when I get up in the morning, last thing at night. Mother never stops missin' her child."

After a few moments, Natty said, "How about a father? Think they miss their kids like that?"

Mabel sniffed and straightened up a little in her seat. "Well, men are *scum*, o' course, so they don't miss nothin' for too long but their drinks and their pussy and their TV sets." Both women burst out laughing.

Then Mabel lowered her voice to make sure no one could overhear. "But, child, if you're asking me what I think you're asking me, well, then, I'm going to tell you one time and then zip up my fat mouth forever. Whatever you end up doin', ain't no one in McDowell County, including myself, will ever say you shouldn'ta done whatever you chose to do. 'Cause, child, you earned that right. Losin' your daddy, and then little Annie, bless her soul, and raisin' them kids by yourself, helpin' so many people all these years—my God, child. You earned the right to finally, one time in your life, do somethin' just for yourself and for them children!" Mabel looked up to see if anyone had overheard. Satisfied, she continued in a lower voice. "Now, you know Buck was never one of my favorites. Never could warm up to the boy or his daddy. And then he went and took advantage of you—"

Natty laughed and shook Mabel's arm. "Wasn't quite the way it was, Mabel. That was as much my doin' as it was Buck's."

"I know, child. You was in *love*," Mabel said, with an angry scowl. "And you was still in love the night he beat you and put you in the hospital for two weeks, when you couldn't eat solid food for a month." Mabel stopped abruptly and took a deep breath.

Natty rubbed the black woman's forearm. "That was just one time, Mabel. 'Cause of his drinking."

"That kinda thing ain't never a *one time*. Seen enough bruised women in my time to know," said Mabel.

Natty didn't argue. She already knew Mabel's opinion of Buck. After a long pause, Natty stretched her eyebrows up to look into Mabel's huge brown eyes. "So what should I do, Mabel?"

"Natty, child, you got to do what your heart tells you to, without caring about what Buck thinks, 'cause he don't deserve one more second of you feeling guilty about what happens to him." Mabel squeezed Natty's hand in both of hers as she looked past her out the big window.

"Charlie's a good man, Nat. Seen that first time I met him, on the porch in front of the store. And I seen Charlie was already moonin' over you like you was a couple of high school kids. The way he was watchin' you, and the look in his eye. He was a goner!"

They both giggled, and Natty pushed the black woman's arm playfully. "Go on, Mabel, you don't know nothin' of the sort."

"I knows what I knows," Mabel said quietly, "and that man loves you and them children, so it's all up to you, child, to make something out of it or don't."

"I think you're bein' a little overly romantic, Mabel," Natty said, half to herself. She turned toward the window. Mabel crossed her arms and rolled her head away to try to nap.

Natty gazed out the window, unaware of the scenery passing by as the bus struggled with the narrow road to the highway. In her mind, she saw Charlie standing next to the Lexus, as she put her arms on top of the car. She heard him say it again—the *L* word. *Said it twice, in fact.* Natty smiled and let the warmth of that moment, the sound of Charlie's voice, engulf her once again. *The first time in her life any man had said he loved her—least one not pantin' and humpin' up a hot sweat in the back of Buck's daddy's Blazer.*

THEY WERE NOW on the highway and the bus sped along, headed for Pennsylvania and the motel and, tomorrow, for New York City. *And then what?* After they checked in to the hotel, they would go on a bus tour and then to dinner at the fancy restaurant in Central Park.

Natty thought about the new-dark-blue warm-up suit she'd bought in Bluefield. She didn't want to look like a hick when they went running in New York. After their run, she would get her hair done, before the matinee. She felt her front pants pocket, where she'd tucked a small wad of money.

They had an extra ticket to *Les Misérables*, which they all agreed Natty would offer to Charlie. *After the play, that would be their time. Maybe they'd have dinner.* Natty smiled as she thought about the short black dress with the matching jacket she'd bought for the occasion and the silver high heels she'd borrowed from Sally. *Shit, I hope I can walk in them.* Natty tried to remember the last time she'd worn high heels.

She swallowed hard. So if something were to happen between them, it would be Saturday night. Charlie had already told her how *he* felt, so now it was up to her. She knew that this might be her last chance, because Charlie wouldn't be in West Virginia much longer. She sensed that he could be gone right after the Redemption Mountain hearing. Ten days, then Charlie might be gone, with nothing resolved, the opportunity gone, all the affection and feelings between them adding up to nothing. *Not even a kiss, unless you count that cheap little peck when he was in the hospital.* This weekend would be different.

THE FINAL LEG of the trip, as the bus passed through the Holland Tunnel and into Manhattan, was a blur. As it moved up Eighth Avenue, the buildings got taller and the noise louder. Soon they were surrounded by a sea of yellow taxis, all moving too fast and blowing their horns.

The bus came to a stop on the corner of West 45th Street, in front of the Milford Plaza. After the group claimed their luggage on the sidewalk, the travel agent led them into the hotel lobby jammed with tourists, where they waited to check in and get their room keys.

Natty and Mabel laughed when they opened the door to their room and saw how tiny it was. They laughed again when they saw the room rates posted on the door of the closet—and this was one of the cheaper hotels in New York! They unpacked and, with an hour to spare before their bus tour departed, they talked Ada and Emma's mother, Janice Lowe, into going out to find Times Square.

They were lost immediately. After a couple of blocks, they dug out the little map the travel agent had distributed, and after turning around several times while looking up at the street signs, they figured out which direction to go. At the Disney Store, Natty gawked at the price tag but bought a Mickey Mouse I LOVE NEW YORK T-shirt for Cat and a Yankees shirt for Pie. Stuffing her money back in her front pocket, she wondered if she'd have enough left to get her hair done.

When they found Broadway, they stopped to watch the street shows, a juggler, a rock 'n' roll duo, and three black teenagers break dancing. The music, combined with the roar of buses and trucks, produced a sound unlike anything the women had heard before. The aroma of sausage, onions, and fresh coffee drifting through the air reminded them of their hunger. As they passed several small restaurants, Mabel and Ada examined the posted menus and rolled their eyes at the prices.

On their way to the hotel, Natty pulled her three friends into Starbucks, where they bought the smallest coffee available. They found a table at a window and watched the passing parade. Then, mindful of the time, they headed back so they wouldn't miss the tour bus. They would have some sorely needed nap time later, before dinner at Tavern on the Green, a very special treat, the travel agent said, courtesy of Charlie Burden.

THE OLD ELEVATOR in the DD&M building moved slowly. Charlie figured he could've run up the six flights in the time it took. But he was in no hurry today. This was one meeting he wasn't looking forward to. His fears were confirmed when he glanced into the boardroom. He couldn't identify everyone, but there were too many people for a simple projects meeting. He saw Summers and Tuthill, and a couple of other DD&M executive committee members who were in Warren Brand's cabal. They had no real reason to be at a meeting about OntAmex business. So the meeting would be about something else.

Charlie strode purposefully down the hall. He wanted to see Lucien before he stepped into the wolves' den. His friend looked old and tired, seated in one of the black leather chairs in his office. "Hello, Charlie," he said without rising. Standing at the dry bar was Charlie's old golfing pal, Mal Berman, counsel to DD&M and Lucien's personal lawyer.

"Hello, Charlie," Berman said warmly.

Lucien spoke up. "It's over, Charlie. Brand's got the votes to take over."

Charlie sat down hard, surprised. "How could they vote? I'm on the executive committee!"

"Didn't need you, Charlie," responded Berman. "Had a solid majority. Called an emergency session on the grounds that an important client needed to address the committee on short notice."

"That's horseshit, and you know it. They can't do that!"

"They can," said Lucien, "and they did."

"They've got the votes, Charlie, that's the important thing," said Berman.

Charlie was quiet for a few moments, thinking. Things were moving awfully quickly.

Lucien offered Charlie a cigar, which he declined. "Torkelson made it happen, Charlie. He, Tuthill, and Brand visited a few board members in person and called the others by phone. They reviewed the size of the revenue stream that the current OntAmex projects provide for DD&M and gave them a preview of all the new business they would direct DD&M's way over the next ten years—hydroelectrics in Canada, half a dozen gas and coal plants, a new plant in Mexico . . . You know the numbers."

"Billions, if he can deliver them all," said Charlie.

"And the immediate payoff—huge bonuses from the sale of the building."

"Minus Torkelson and Tuthill's take," added Charlie.

"Never be able to prove that part. They're too clever by far," said Lucien.

Berman added, "Some of these guys will double their net worth in six months, plus there's the promise of an extremely profitable company for the rest of their careers."

"Pretty hard to pass up," said Charlie.

"Torkelson did a good job," said Lucien somberly. He waved his cigar at Charlie with a laugh. "You're half responsible for this, Charlie, that great job you're doing in West Virginia. With that Redemption Mountain coal, OntAmex will have the most efficient large-scale generator in North America. That's significant—to OntAmex, Wall Street, and the politicians."

"Which all helps the stock price," Berman interjected, "and makes the merger with Continental Electric a better deal all around."

"When you're flying as high as Torkelson, you have a lot of leverage," said Lucien, "and he's using it to take control of DD&M. Sure, Brand will sit in this office, but Torkelson'll be calling the shots." Lucien looked across the room to the picture of his father on the wall.

"Don't know what they have planned for you, Charlie," admitted Lucien. "Brand knows you're too smart for him, but he also knows you're close to Duncan. That's a problem."

Charlie smiled as he stood to leave for the boardroom. "That's a problem I'm not going to solve for him." He shook hands with his two old friends. "I'll let you know what happens."

Some of the men in the boardroom were having cocktails and had loosened their ties when Charlie finally made his appearance, thirty minutes late. He shook hands with Larry Tuthill, but he didn't bother to greet Warren Brand. He nodded to Terry Summers and took a vacant seat not far from the door. In the corner of the room was a secretary to record the minutes.

When everyone was seated, Warren Brand moved to his chair at the middle of the table. He stared at some notes in front of him before looking over at Charlie. "Thanks for coming in," he said. "This won't take long. You've met with Lucien," he continued, "so you know what's happening here. The executive committee met in emergency session this afternoon, and, as of December, I will be managing partner and Lucien will be leaving the company—with an excellent package."

Charlie's blood was boiling, but he sat calmly. Short of diving across the table and taking out some of Brand's cosmetically perfected front teeth, there was nothing to be gained from this meeting. Any grievance he had would have to become a legal issue.

"As for your own status," Brand smiled, "you'll be off the exec, but we *do* have some great news for you." He gestured toward Larry Tuthill. "Due to Larry's personal recommendation, we'd like you to wrap things up in West Virginia over the next few weeks, hand the project off to Summers, and then," he paused dramatically, "we're going to give you what you wanted back in the spring: You'll take over the second dam project in China."

Charlie stared blankly at Brand while he digested this new twist. He had to admit, he was surprised. Finally, he had to smile, forcing himself not to burst out laughing. *China! That's perfect. Brand gets him off the board and out of the country, and Torkelson gets him a world away from the OntAmex business and away from Duncan McCord.*

"Okay, Warren," he said, looking at his watch. "I've got some things to finish up in Red Bone. Then I'll think about China." Charlie stood up. "But before I leave, I've gotta tell you guys what you've done here today." He looked around at the other executive committee members. "Not Warren. This isn't new to him. He's always been a backbiting slug, whose only talent in this business was to find the right asshole to crawl up."

Brand closed his notebook abruptly and stood up.

Charlie ignored him. "Now he's Torkelson's butt boy, and you guys are turning this company over to them. It's the beginning of the end." Charlie put his hands in his pockets and looked around the table. "You've insulted and embarrassed Dietrich Delahunt and Mackey's greatest asset, the man who built this company." Charlie shook his head in disgust. "What were you guys thinking?"

THE NOVEMBER AIR was cold at 6:00 A.M. The forecast said it would warm into the fifties with rain in the evening, but right now it felt like snow. Charlie wore gloves and a wool New York Giants hat against the cold. In the pouch at the front of his sweatshirt, he'd stuffed cotton mittens and a wool OntAmex hat for Natty.

He crossed Park Avenue, enjoying the rare opportunity to saunter leisurely across the deserted street. Weekend mornings were a magical time in Midtown, when he felt as if he had the magnificent city all to himself. A few cabs trundled home the casualties of a Friday night gone on too long. A street sweeper moved toward him like some sort of wounded animal. There wasn't another pedestrian in sight.

Crossing Fifth Avenue at the library, Charlie jogged across 42nd Street and then up Broadway through Times Square. He entered the Milford Plaza on 45th Street and looked around the lobby. Natty was nowhere in sight. He went out the Eighth Avenue entrance and walked to the corner to see if she'd gone out that door. He glanced at his watch and saw that it was only six twenty-five. He was early.

"Hey, soldier. Looking for a good time?"

Charlie laughed and turned to see Natty a few feet away. She wore a dark-blue warm-up suit with the top zipped all the way up and the collar raised. Her hands were stuffed in her pockets. Charlie was right—she hadn't brought gloves or her Spider-Man hat.

"Hi, Nat," he said, pulling the mittens out of his pouch.

"Hey, Charlie." He handed them to her and stretched the hat over her head. Natty thought he might kiss her, but he smiled and stepped back.

"Ready?" he said.

"Gotta do at least five miles to work off that dinner from last night."

"C'mon," he said. "I'll show you what heaven is like for a runner in New York." They went north on Eighth Avenue, running at a slow pace to warm up and so they could talk easily. At Columbus Circle, they turned back down Broadway. Several joggers were headed into Central Park, but Charlie knew that wouldn't be as exciting for Natty as the streets of Manhattan.

As they ran through Times Square, Natty recounted Mabel's reaction to the New York prices, and Charlie laughed. They ran east on 39th Street, which was dark and cold, with no direct exposure yet to the morning light. Natty filled him in on their bus tour and was effusive in her praise for their dinner at Tavern on the Green. It was an experience the women would remember for the rest of their lives. Charlie was glad he'd added it to their itinerary. He knew that Tavern on the Green would make the women from West Virginia feel like high society.

Crossing Park Avenue, he showed her the Dietrich Delahunt & Mackey building on the next block south. He was staying in one of their corporate apartments.

"How come not in Manara . . ."

"Mamaroneck," Charlie prompted. "No sense going up there. Ellen's in Florida playing tennis, and I had a meeting here yesterday afternoon."

"Good meeting?" she asked.

Charlie hesitated, not wanting to get into it. "No, not really," he admitted.

"Anything to do with Redemption Mountain?"

"Not entirely. Things are changing in the company."

They ran up First Avenue so Charlie could show her the United Nations building, then he led her onto 48th Street headed west. "C'mon," he said, surging ahead of her, "let's work up a sweat." Natty responded easily, as he knew she would, settling comfortably into a more aggressive pace.

They turned right onto Lexington, and the wider avenue gave Natty the opportunity to see the height of the skyscrapers. By the time they reached 57th Street, they were both breathing deeply. They now had to dodge some morning dog-walkers and a few joggers wearing headphones. They ran down Fifth Avenue, slowing to a more leisurely pace so Natty could enjoy the stores and the opulence of the famous street. Charlie pointed out Tiffany's and Trump Tower, and Natty peered into several parked limousines to see if any celebrities could be seen behind the dark glass.

Suddenly Natty dashed across Fifth Avenue, dodging several cabs, and jogged down a side street. Charlie stopped and watched her slow to a walk in front of a basement shop. It was a chic beauty salon with a French name. He waited for her on the corner. "I just wanted to see when they opened," she said. "But they got a little sign that says BY APPOINTMENT ONLY." Charlie nodded, not wanting to tell her that a beauty salon off Fifth Avenue was probably a little out of her price range.

"I was planning on getting something done with my hair while I was here," Natty said, pulling off the wool hat.

"Your hair looks fine," said Charlie truthfully.

Natty laughed. "Yeah, like a mop somebody washed the gym floor with." She pulled the hat on again.

Charlie laughed as he reached into a pocket for his cellphone. He stopped walking and put the phone to his ear, smiling at Natty. "Hello, Carlos," he said. "I need a little favor." After another minute, he folded up the phone. "C'mon," he said to Natty. "I'll show you Rockefeller Center."

They walked down Fifth Avenue at a leisurely pace. "You've got a nine-thirty appointment at the Carlos Marché Salon. He's a good friend of mine. The salon is on the first floor of our building, the one I pointed out. A car will pick you up in front of your hotel."

Natty wrinkled up her nose. "A *car*?"

"The salon has its own limo for customers."

"I don't know, Charlie. It sounds a little ritzy. Maybe I'll just skip it."

"You know how hard it is to get an appointment there on a Saturday morning?" Charlie asked playfully.

"But, Charlie, I only got fifty dollars in my pocket. After that, I'll be walkin' around Times Square with a tin cup if I want another coffee at Starbucks."

"Don't worry about it," said Charlie. "Carlos owes me." He wouldn't bother to tell Natty that fifty dollars was about the minimum tip for a stylist at Carlos's salon.

"Oh!" said Natty, reaching into a pocket of her sweatpants. "I almost forgot. This is for you." She handed Charlie the extra ticket to *Les Misérables*. Charlie had planned to work for most of the day, then to meet Natty for dinner after the show. But it had been a couple of years since he'd seen *Les Mis*, and the thought of seeing Natty's reaction to the incredible show was too exciting to pass up.

"That's great," he said. "I can't wait to see it again."

"Again?" Natty squinted at him curiously. "How many times you seen this show?"

"This'll be the fourth."

"It's that good?"

Charlie smiled. "It's better."

They walked through Rockefeller Center, stopping for coffee and bagels to go, at a cost that Charlie refused to reveal. While they ate, he gave Natty a brief history of Rockefeller Center, pointing out the different buildings and the famous artwork on their façades. They stood at the railing of the ice rink, watching a lone maintenance man skate around the ice while pushing a wide shovel. He waved to them and did a graceful spin.

They walked by Radio City Music Hall and down the Avenue of the Americas to 45th Street. When they reached the corner of Broadway, Natty could see the awning of the Milford Plaza. She pulled off her mittens and hat and handed them to Charlie. "Here, save these for next time, okay?"

"How about tomorrow? Same time. We'll go downtown. I'll show you the Brooklyn Bridge, the most beautiful bridge in the world."

"Sounds great, but we're leaving at 9:00 A.M. Driving straight through going back." She looked at Charlie, thinking how nice it would be to spend the whole day with him on Sunday instead of going home.

He smiled and reached out to brush aside the ever-present lock of hair that fell across her forehead. "We'll have dinner, after the show?"

"Sure," Natty said, looking at her watch. "Uh-oh. Gotta get my shower, so I don't miss my *limousine.*"

"See you later," called Charlie, turning to walk back to Park Avenue.

Natty walked a few steps toward the Milford Plaza, then turned to watch Charlie trot east across 45th. She wondered if he had any idea of how special the morning had been for her. *Running the streets of Manhattan with this wonderful, handsome man, sharing coffee and bagels, talking, and walking through Rockefeller Center on a Saturday morning—a morning she would remember for a long time to come.* She spun around and started walking toward the hotel. *Nah, Charlie wouldn't know anything about stuff like that.*

CHAPTER 31

NATTY STOOD ON THE SIDEWALK AS THE LIMOUSINE PULLED away from the curb. She wished she had a camera to take a picture of it. The kids would never believe her! She wasn't sure she was in the right place until she saw the elegant silver lettering to the right of the main entrance. In small script it said *Carlos Marché Salon,* and, under it, *New York and Paris.* The large glass doors were emblazoned with black lettering: DIETRICH DELAHUNT & MACKEY, ENGINEERS, NEW YORK, SAN FRANCISCO, WASHINGTON, D.C., BEIJING. She looked at the sign and felt the familiar insecurity she often experienced when she thought about the life that Charlie led.

In the lobby, she spied an elegant wooden door with a polished metal plate identifying it as the salon. Inside, Natty thought she'd entered a museum. Colorful paintings adorned fabric-covered walls, and expensive-looking tables held elaborate wood carvings. To her right was a small waiting area with thick white carpeting and black furniture. A credenza held an assortment of beverages.

One of the two uncomfortable-looking chairs in the waiting area was occupied by a woman with long black hair, wearing large sunglasses, a suede jacket, and blue jeans tucked inside tall leather boots. Talking softly into a cellphone, she looked up briefly, then back at the floor. Natty was sure it was Demi Moore, who'd starred in her all-time favorite movie, *Ghost,* but, then again, maybe it wasn't. New York was filled with women who looked like movie stars.

To Natty's left, a thin black woman, her long hair cascading around her shoulders in tight braids, sat behind a wide mahogany table, with a telephone and a leather-bound appointment book. She smiled at Natty as she pressed a button on the phone. "Carlos Marché Salon," she announced. She began to speak French. Natty waited, wondering what she should do next. Her first instinct was to turn around and find her way back to the hotel.

Then, without a sound, a woman appeared from around a corner and stopped in front of Natty. She was attractive, in her late forties, with shoulder-length brown hair with gold highlights—*serious hair,* Sally would call it. The beauty of her face was accentuated by her makeup. Natty felt plain next to her. The woman wore tight black leather pants, a white blouse, and a tan vest, and had an air of authority about her.

"Hello, Mrs. Oakes," she said, "I'm Tina. I'll take you back to Mr. Marché's studio now." *Maybe Demi Moore* stopped talking into her cellphone and looked up again at Natty, this time with more interest.

They walked down a hallway, past several closed doors. From behind one door, Natty could hear the sound of a hair dryer. At the end of the hallway, Tina pulled open a heavy door. The floor of the room was covered in thick white carpeting, except for a small tiled area under a styling chair. A man seated at an antique pedestal desk spoke on a cordless phone. When he saw the two women, he hung up immediately and rose to greet them.

He was probably in his early fifties, Natty guessed, with closely cropped salt-and-pepper hair. Just a few inches taller than Natty, he had the physique of a gymnast. He wore a beige cashmere sweater that contrasted perfectly with the most beautiful light-brown skin Natty had ever seen. As he approached her, his mouth opened in a dazzling white smile that finally put Natty at ease.

"Hello, Natty," he said, with a trace of a Caribbean accent. "I'm Carlos Marché." He ushered Natty to the chair and stood a few feet in front of her, his eyes moving from her face to her hair. Finally, he reached out with both hands and held her hair away from her neck. "So," he said, letting her hair down again, "you're going to the theater this afternoon." He winked at Tina. "And then to dinner with our friend Charlie."

"First time I ever been to a show," Natty admitted. "First time in New

York. So I thought I'd get something done with my hair while I was here. Maybe just a little trim, you know, don't need anything fancy."

Carlos took a half step back, studying Natty's hair for a few moments more, a serious look on his face. "How much time have we got?" he asked softly, glancing at Tina.

Natty answered. "Well, the show starts at—"

Carlos came forward a step, shaking his head to interrupt her. He took both of her hands in his and looked into her eyes. "Natty, do you trust me?" he asked.

"Sure I do." She laughed. "You know this stuff a lot better than me."

"Okay, that's good," he said. He turned to Tina, who was already poking at her PDA with a metal stylus. "I'll need Javier for color, then Monica for nails." He smiled at Tina. "And you'll do makeup."

Tina smiled at Natty with raised eyebrows. It was apparent that she was getting the A-Team of the Carlos Marché Salon.

CHARLIE MADE DINNER reservations at a restaurant near the theater. It was classy without being stuffy and served a menu that Natty would be comfortable with. The reservations were for eight o'clock, which would give them plenty of time to head up to the atrium at the Marriott Marquis for a drink first. She would enjoy looking down at Times Square. At one o'clock, he pulled on a gray houndstooth jacket over a black wool jersey and started out for the Imperial Theatre. As he dodged the usual midday traffic, his cellphone vibrated.

"Hi, Charlie. Is this a good time?" It was Ellen.

"Yes, Ellen, your timing's perfect."

"I'm on the beach at the Boca Raton Club. Linda's gone back to the room. It's hot here. How's everything in New York?"

Charlie told her about the meeting with Lucien and Mal. She listened intently as he broke the news of the management coup at DD&M. Then he told her about his imminent posting to China. "They want me as far away as possible," he explained.

"Charlie, China was what we wanted all along, wasn't it?"

He had to smile at Ellen's use of the word *we*. "Yeah, China will be good," said Charlie absently.

There was a long pause before Ellen spoke again. "Is your friend in New York this weekend?"

Charlie hesitated. "Um, they're going to see *Les Mis* this afternoon and then to dinner at Tavern on the Green," he lied.

"So you won't be seeing her?"

Charlie stopped on the sidewalk. "I don't know," he said vaguely. "Maybe for a run tomorrow morning."

"Oh, she's a runner, too."

"Sort of."

Ellen waited a few seconds to see if he had any more to add. "Okay, Charlie, I'm going to go. Don't forget about Thanksgiving. We're all set for Vermont. Scottie and Jennifer are both coming."

"Wouldn't miss it," said Charlie softly.

"Good, okay. Love you, Charlie," said Ellen, before clicking off.

"Damn," Charlie said to himself, as he closed the phone. Lying to Ellen was becoming too easy, and he hated it.

THE IMPERIAL THEATRE was filling up quickly when Charlie walked down the center aisle to find his seat. The travel agent had secured a block of tickets center right. His seat was in the row farthest back, next to the travel agent.

He watched as the rest of the group filled in the empty seats in the two rows in front of him. They were smiling and enjoying themselves. Most of them waved to him as they found their seats. Before Mabel sat, she took a quick look at the back of the theater, then smiled at Charlie. There was an empty seat next to her.

The lights blinked and Charlie glanced at his watch. Natty was nowhere in sight. Charlie read his *Playbill* to see if he recognized any of the names in the cast. Then the houselights dimmed and the orchestra began to play. Charlie looked up to see an usher leading a slight figure to the one empty seat. The theater was dark now, with the curtain open and the spotlights trained on the stage. It was a woman—a small woman—or a girl, he was fairly certain, a little taller than Natty. Her hair was very short and cut like a man's, a golden—almost white—shade of blond.

Charlie's eyes kept darting back to the woman. As the stage lights came up, she turned to Mabel.

Charlie could see the delicate profile. He smiled to himself. He should have known. Carlos Marché wouldn't play it safe with Natty Oakes. He'd bring out every ounce of her beauty and put it on display for the world to see. That's what he did for a living. Charlie turned back to the stage and tried to focus on the greatest play in the history of musical theater.

The familiar strains of "One Day More" announced the approach of intermission. Charlie watched Natty and the women from Red Bone applaud vigorously as the houselights came up, then he rose to let a few women pass through to the aisle. "'Scuse me, Mr. Burdan," Mabel's cousin said hurriedly, "my bladder's about to burst, an' nat wouldn't be a pretty sight." He sat down again and perused his *Playbill* as the seats emptied.

Charlie shifted his gaze and noticed that Natty was still seated. He watched as she looked to her left, then down at her lap. She hesitated before turning around to face Charlie.

He rose from his seat slowly, his eyes transfixed on the woman before him. It was obviously Natty but so incredibly transformed that for an instant he thought it must be someone else. Her hair was shorn like a man's, in a long, ragged crew cut, and colored in a shade of light blond that seemed to glow in the dim light of the theater. But it was Natty's face—the first time he'd ever seen her with makeup—that made Charlie's heart pound.

The dark sweep of her eyelashes made her blue eyes sparkle, and her pale-pink lips shone with gloss. She wore a short black dress with a high neckline and a matching long-sleeved jacket. Then Charlie noticed that she was wearing earrings—small, dangling silver chains—as well as a thin silver choker. He took a breath as the realization hit him. *Yes, of course it was Natty. And she was absolutely stunning.*

She smiled nervously. "Hey, Charlie." She wrinkled her nose and shrugged her shoulders. "So, what do you think?"

Charlie furrowed his brow inquisitively. "You do something to your hair?" They both laughed. He motioned her toward the aisle and led her down to the empty orchestra pit. Standing next to her, he detected an alluring scent. "Perfume, too?"

She smiled shyly. "It's Tina's. You know, Carlos's assistant." Natty touched one of her earrings. "Her jewelry, too. I have to give it to you tonight, so you can give it back to her." She laughed. "At midnight I turn into a hillbilly again."

Charlie couldn't help staring at her. "You look . . . incredible," he said.

She smiled, embarrassed. "Thanks, it's just the makeup and the jewelry. It's still me."

Charlie looked down and noticed that she wore high heels and nylons for the first time since he'd known her. Her legs looked like a dancer's. "You're taller, too," he said.

"God, these shoes are killing me. Not easy, trying to be a woman."

Charlie looked up the aisle to see that some of the women were headed back to their seats. "How do you like the show?" he asked.

Natty turned to look at the stage and clasped her hands together. "Oh, Charlie, it's wonderful! Much better than I thought it would be. And I can't believe they're going to do the whole thing again tonight." She looked at him nervously. "Charlie, um, thanks; thank you for everything. This has been the best day of my whole life."

Charlie gazed into Natty's face and felt his heart race. "It's not over yet," he said, as the houselights blinked. As they arrived at Natty's row, Charlie pulled a handkerchief from his jacket pocket and handed it to her. She looked at him quizzically. "You're going to need it," he said.

FROM ACROSS THE narrow street, Charlie watched the orderly crowd flow slowly out of the Imperial Theatre. The lights from the other theaters on the street made it feel like daytime, though the November sky was dark at six o'clock. Leaning back against a smooth marble wall, Charlie wondered if it took longer for *Les Misérables* to empty out after a performance, with most of the women in the audience needing to visit the ladies' room to repair the damage done by tears and tissues.

Mabel Willard appeared with Ada and Janice Lowe, followed shortly by the rest of the group. The travel agent and a few of the other women headed toward Broadway, while Mabel, Ada, and Janice walked in the other direction. Probably heading back to the hotel for a nap before dinner, Charlie guessed. The crowd had dissipated to a trickle when Natty finally emerged.

Clutching Charlie's handkerchief, Natty started across the street. She still had the sophisticated, stylish look, but the slow, eyes-down walk in the obviously unfamiliar high heels gave her away. As she got to the curb, Natty looked up, and Charlie could see that *Les Mis* had definitely taken its toll on Tina's makeup job. Natty averted her eyes in embarrassment as she came up to Charlie. "Well," she said, with a sniffle, "I didn't think *that* was so funny." They both chuckled. She handed Charlie his mascara-streaked handkerchief. "You could have warned me."

"That would have spoiled all the fun."

"They didn't have to kill the little boy," she said, and her eyes welled up again. Charlie smiled and gave her back the handkerchief.

"C'mon, let's go have a drink," he said. They walked across 45th Street and down Broadway, enjoying the sights and sounds of Times Square and the feeling that comes from being surrounded by, yet completely invisible to, thousands of other pedestrians. It was a familiar sensation to Charlie but a new experience for Natty.

Charlie told her about his plan for a drink at the Marriott Marquis, but as they passed a crowded Irish-themed restaurant and bar, Natty stopped, took his hand in hers, and pulled him toward the entrance. "C'mon, let's go here." She pulled him through the crowded bar until they found two vacant stools. Charlie was disappointed when she let go of his hand to jump onto her seat. Natty ordered two Jack Daniel's and two pints of Harp. She put a twenty-dollar bill on the bar and looked quizzically at Charlie. "That enough?"

Charlie put another twenty on top of hers. "Just in case."

Natty rolled her eyes. "Be a tough town for an alcoholic." Their drinks arrived and Natty kicked off her shoes as she picked up her Jack Daniel's. "Okay, who should we toast?"

Charlie held up his glass. "To Woody and Mr. Jacks," he suggested.

Natty nodded. "To Woody and Mr. Jacks," she said, "sittin' up in their room in the Pocahontas Hotel." Natty looked out toward the street, her eyes unfocused. "Boy, that seems like a long way away from here, doesn't it?"

"It is," said Charlie. They drank slowly and talked for a long time. They ordered another round and soon forgot about the Marriott Marquis. They talked about their children, the upcoming soccer tournament, Redemption Mountain and the DeWitts and where they would go after the eminent-domain hearing. A third round arrived, and they talked about the library and the new soccer field. Then Charlie told her about China.

Natty nodded absently, mellowed by the liquor. "You going to go?"

Charlie drained the rest of his beer and looked at his watch. He stood up, his legs pressed against Natty's.

"I don't know," he said. "It depends."

"On what?"

He smiled down at her. "On how some things go in West Virginia. Now it's time to get to the restaurant. *You* need to eat."

"I need to pee." Natty stood up and was forced against Charlie by the crush of the crowd. He was an instant away from leaning over and kissing her on the mouth, but he hesitated. *Their first real kiss shouldn't be here in this crowded bar.* Charlie backed up to give her some room, and Natty looked down to find her shoes.

THE RESTAURANT WAS perfect, with subdued lighting and a candlelit table by a window overlooking the busy sidewalk. Natty smiled her approval. Charlie ordered a bottle of Chardonnay and told the waiter they were in no hurry.

The wine arrived and Charlie proposed another toast. "To the Bones and winning the tournament in Charleston."

Natty held up her glass. "To the Bones, the best-dressed soccer team in West Virginia." They clinked glasses just as something outside caught Natty's eye and made her smile. "Oh, God, Charlie, look."

Charlie twisted around, and there on the sidewalk, examining the restaurant's menu box, were the unmistakable figures of Mabel, Ada, and Janice, looking weary and cold.

Charlie grinned as he put his napkin on the table. "I'll go get them," he said. Charlie reached into his pocket for his money clip, peeled off a twenty, and pressed it into the waiter's hand. "We're going to need a bigger table," he explained.

"Not a problem, sir," replied the waiter.

After several minutes on the sidewalk, cajoling, begging, and finally threatening the three ladies, Charlie was able to coax them into the restaurant. Like the hostess of the table, Natty hugged each of the women and tried her best to make them relax and feel welcome. Charlie hung up their coats and came back to find himself sitting across the round table from Natty.

Mabel put her hand over Natty's on the table and grinned as she looked back and forth between Natty and Charlie. "What about our little girl here, Charlie? Cleans up pretty good when she wants to, huh?" The other women giggled.

"C'mon, Mabel," Natty protested.

The women had been wandering around for an hour and a half, trying to find someplace reasonable to have dinner. Charlie convinced them that OntAmex would foot the bill for dinner, which made them more comfortable than they would've been with the truth. After more cajoling, they relented and had a cocktail, with the understanding that nobody would be ordering that *fifty-two-dollar steak* they saw on the menu!

With the drinks and Natty and Charlie's hospitality, the women gradually relaxed and warmed up to the occasion. Soon, Mabel took center stage and had everyone at the table (and a few neighboring tables) in stitches with her observations about New York, New Yorkers, and New York prices.

They had another round of drinks, and Charlie ordered more wine for the table. The women were clearly enjoying themselves now. And, in spite of the change of plans, Charlie and Natty were enjoying themselves, too. Occasionally he would catch Natty's eye. She would smile reassuringly. When the ladies refused appetizers, Charlie ordered a selection for the table to share, and Natty confiscated the menus to keep the others from focusing on the prices.

For the next two hours, they enjoyed a wonderful meal, one of the best they'd ever had. Mabel eventually gave way to Ada, who fascinated them with her stories of growing up in the coalfields of Appalachia in the thirties and forties. Even Janice Lowe, as shy as her daughter, Emma, joined the conversation when it got around to the Bones and their star player. "All that girl talks about now is that boy Gabe from Welch," said Janice in her timid voice. "And he comes over and they go to kickin' soccer balls to each other for hours, they do!"

Natty laughed. "I think our little Emma's in love!"

"She sure is happy about *somethin'*," said Janice.

They had coffee and shared some decadently rich desserts, and before they knew it, it was eleven o'clock.

"You kids don't have to worry 'bout us," Mabel said as they left the restaurant. "We can find our ways to the hotel just fine."

"We'll take you there, Mabel," said Charlie. "Want to make sure you ladies don't sneak off and go out nightclubbing." The women shrieked at the suggestion.

"Was a nice dinner, Charlie," said Natty as she and Charlie fell behind the three women.

"Yeah," he said softly, "it was a real nice dinner. I think they enjoyed themselves. I did, too." Charlie thought about Natty and the ladies in front of them—poor women from Appalachia—and tried to remember when he'd enjoyed a meal more. Certainly not the dinners with Ellen and their friends at one of New York or Westchester's finer restaurants, with the conversation devoted exclusively to the art of living well. *Natty, Mabel, Ada, and Janice were people without egos or petty jealousies, without greed or pretensions, with no agendas or ambitions beyond being decent people. God, it was nice to be around them.*

It was eleven-thirty when they reached the hotel. The women thanked Charlie, hugged Natty, and quickly filed through the revolving door. A steady stream of pedestrian traffic entered and exited the hotel, even this late. Charlie looked at Natty and smiled. "Time for you to get to bed, little girl."

Natty nodded. "Yeah, I guess that's it for me."

Charlie kissed her lightly on the forehead, then backed away. "Good night, Nat. See you in the morning."

Natty folded her arms across her chest and squinted up at him. "You know, I get tired of thankin' you for everything all the time, Charlie, so I'm going to stop doin' that. But the ladies had a good time tonight, one they'll be talking about for years. Me, too."

Charlie watched her for a few seconds, not wanting to leave. "Go to sleep, Nat. I'll see you in the morning."

"Why don't you take a cab, Charlie?" she suggested.

"No, I'm going to walk and enjoy the air. It's not far," he said.

She waved to him and tried to smile.

A group of German schoolgirls crowded into the lobby while Natty waited for the elevator. She had to squeeze into a car that seemed to stop at every floor on the way up to twelve. She pulled out her card key as she padded down the carpeted hallway.

Standing in front of her door, Natty reached out to put the key in the slot, but she stopped. She looked down at the card and then up at the door, the door to safety and security. *The door to her same old life. The door back to Red Bone and Buck and hoping to make it through another night without a beating or an old, sick person dying on her. The door back to the same crummy trailer for her children—hillbilly kids with no future and no way out of the mountains. If she went through the door, then the night would be over, and when would she ever get another chance to be with Charlie? Shit, Charlie! What happened?* She squeezed her cheeks up tight to stop the tears, but they came anyway. Then she turned and ran down the hallway.

A man in the elevator asked her if she was okay, and she nodded and wiped away the tears. She worked her way through the crowd and out onto Eighth Avenue. Several empty cabs sat at the curb, but she didn't have any money left, and she didn't know the address, anyway. She ran back to the corner of 45th Street and began to get her bearings. She passed the hotel entrance and then the theaters, relieved to find Broadway. She couldn't believe the amount of traffic and the number of pedestrians still crowding the sidewalks. The cabs were bumper to bumper and the crowd a little more threatening than it was earlier.

She heard a few catcalls behind her—"Hey, baby, hey, mama, where you goin' in such a hurry?"—as she struggled to find the route she and Charlie had taken in the morning, which seemed like days ago. She should have paid attention to the route the limousine took to the salon, but all she'd looked at was the inside of the car.

She knew she had to cross Broadway, then go south for a few blocks, but how many? She had no idea. *And how would she recognize Charlie's building if she even found Park Avenue?* She edged along next to a huge herd of people crossing Times Square at a light. Then they stood, packed on a traffic island, waiting interminably for the sea of racing cabs to come to a brief stop. When the light changed, Natty moved across the wide expanse, hopeful that she was headed the right way. Then it started to rain.

God, she'd never catch up to Charlie before he got to his building. At the corner of 43rd Street, she kicked off her shoes and sprinted down the sidewalk. Her short dress was easy to run in, and she ran as fast as she could in her stocking feet.

Natty was thoroughly soaked by the time she darted across Fifth Avenue. The cracks in the cement tore at the soles of her nylons. At Madison

Avenue, she turned right and ran on the nearly empty sidewalk. As she passed a large bin overflowing with trash, Natty tossed her high heels onto the pile. She glanced at her watch. *Dammit! Charlie probably got a taxi as soon as it started to rain.*

She ran faster now, and her lungs and legs were starting to get the early burn that felt so good when she ran at home. The feet of her panty hose had torn away and now flopped around her ankles. Since 39th Street didn't look familiar, she ran on to 38th. At the corner, she stopped in the recessed doorway of an airline sales office, pulled off her panty hose, and rolled them in a ball. She deposited them in the trash container at the corner with a laugh. *They must find some weird stuff in the public trash in New York City!*

Natty jogged down 38th Street and was relieved to see she was nearing Park Avenue. She scanned the sidewalk on the opposite side of the street but saw no one who looked like Charlie. She was in less of a hurry now, realizing the futility of her chase. Charlie must already be in his apartment, fast asleep. Tomorrow morning, they'd go for a run. Then she'd get on the bus and head back to Red Bone. Maybe she'd see Charlie again, maybe not. Who knew, with the way things were going with his company. Maybe he'd just go to China without even returning to West Virginia.

Natty decided to walk one block in each direction, then walk back to the Milford Plaza and hope she didn't get mugged. The office buildings and storefronts on Park Avenue were dark. She was starting to shiver from the cold. The rain had abated, but the temperature was dropping, and her clothes were soaked. She could feel the sideways glances of the late-night walkers taking note of the barefoot woman, soaked and searching for something—like a lost dog—and she suddenly felt foolish and alone.

Passing a small shop, Natty noticed her reflection in the window. She'd forgotten about her haircut, and it looked strange to her, as if she were seeing someone else. The rain had matted down her hair, making it appear even shorter, but she had to admit that, even after running halfway across Manhattan in the pouring rain, she didn't look half bad. As she turned away from the window, she noticed the silver lettering for the Carlos Marché Salon.

"Natty?" Charlie's voice came from the shadows in front of the large glass front doors to his building. He stepped out into the light. "Nat?" he repeated. She stopped in her tracks.

"Hey, Charlie." He was without his sport jacket. He must have gone inside and come back out. She moved slowly toward him. "How'd you know I'd come?"

"I didn't. I was just hoping." He smiled. "I'm surprised you could find the building."

"Wasn't easy. Lost my shoes, then my stockings," she said with a laugh.

"You must be cold."

"Nah, I'm okay. Little wet, but . . ." She looked around her nervously.

Charlie watched her for a few moments. "You want to come up?" he asked softly.

Natty smiled at him. Then her eyes went up and her head followed, looking toward the lights visible on the second floor. She stared at the second-floor windows for a few seconds, then took a deep breath and let it out slowly. She looked at the sidewalk and squeezed her eyes shut. "Goddammit," she whispered to herself. "God*dammit,*" she repeated angrily, stamping her bare foot on the wet sidewalk. She looked up and Charlie saw tears in her eyes. He took a long step toward her and put his hands on her upper arms.

"Nat, what is it?"

She shook her head and took another deep breath. Tears ran down her cheeks. "I'm sorry, Charlie. I can't do this," she said. She looked up into his eyes. "I love you, Charlie," her voice squeaked, "but I can't *do* this."

"Natty—"

She dropped her arms, twisting away from Charlie. Then she stopped with her back to him.

He watched her shake her head in frustration. "What's wrong with me, Charlie?" she said, turning toward him. An older couple walking a small white poodle approached them. She opened her fists and waved her palms in the air. "People have affairs and jump into bed with each other all the time! Why is it so goddamn hard for us?" she implored.

The older couple smiled at Natty. She was embarrassed. "Sorry," she apologized. The man smiled and tipped his hat. Natty watched them move down the sidewalk, out of earshot. She sniffed and rubbed the tears from her eyes. "I'm sorry, Charlie."

"Don't be," he said. "It's okay, Nat, I . . ."

She shook her head again. "I came all the way to New York just to spend the night with you, Charlie, to make something happen, 'cause I love you, Charlie." The tears flowed again. "You're the most wonderful man I'll ever meet in my life—*shit*, Charlie, you're like the top ten all rolled into one—and I think you love me, too, but . . ." Natty blinked rapidly. "Now we're here, and I can't do it, Charlie." She squinted up at him pleadingly. "I can't do that to Buck."

"Natty, it's okay. I understand." Charlie wiped the tears gently from her eyes. "Remember that night we visited Woody and Mr. Jacks?"

"Yeah, I remember," she said, covering his hands with her own. "'Course I remember—the night you said I was *remarkable*." They both chuckled. They stood close together for a few seconds, then Charlie kissed her lightly on the forehead and took his hands from her face. Natty held his hands as they dropped between them.

"How come this is so hard for us, Charlie? What's the matter with us?"

He squeezed her hands. "There's nothing the matter with us, Nat," he said firmly. "I think we're just two moral people who find it hard to cheat on their spouses. And you're wrong—a lot of people do it, but I think most people are like us. Most people find it hard to do."

"Yeah, well, most people ain't married to Buck," Natty said. "So, what should I do, Charlie?"

"How about you go back to Red Bone and tell Buck that you're leaving him?"

Natty smiled. "How about *you* tell him?"

Charlie laughed. They were both silent for a few seconds, then the rain started again. "Sure you don't want to come inside and warm up?" he asked.

Natty peeked up at the second floor again. "Charlie, if I was to go in there with you, I'd probably never go back to Red Bone."

"What about your kids?"

Natty squinted. "What kids?" They laughed, then stood in silence for several moments. Natty took off her earrings and the silver choker. She looked at the jewelry in her palm for a few seconds as the rain dropped around the silver chains. She handed them to Charlie. "Tell Tina thanks, okay?" Charlie nodded. "Can you get me a cab, Charlie? I gotta go."

He moved to the curb with a hand in the air. A taxi pulled over much quicker than Charlie had wanted. He reached a twenty-dollar bill through the window and instructed the driver, "Milford Plaza."

As she entered the cab, Natty stopped, the open door between them. "Charlie, think we should probably skip the run tomorrow, okay?"

"Okay, Nat. You let me know what you want to do. I'll see you down in Red Bone. In about a week."

"Bye, Charlie." The cab pulled away from the curb and rumbled toward Eighth Avenue. Natty let her head fall back and closed her eyes.

CHAPTER 32

E**VE BREWSTER WAS STANDING IN THE RED BONE BAPTIST CHURCH** parking lot when the bus pulled in on Sunday night. She wore a long winter coat, buttoned up against the evening cold, and a sad, tired face. At her feet were a half dozen Merit 100 cigarette butts, flattened against the sandy pavement. Natty knew it was trouble as soon as she saw her. Through the window, their eyes met with no smile or wave or even a glimmer of welcome from Eve, and Natty knew that something bad had happened.

Her hands jammed into the jacket pockets of her new blue warm-up suit, Natty had tears in her eyes as she walked slowly from the bus. Eve laughed and cried at the same time when she saw Natty's new hairstyle. She hugged her and held her close. "Oh, God, you look sooo beautiful!" Then she sobbed, "I'm so sorry, Nat."

"It's Mr. Jacks, huh, Eve?"

Eve's voice quivered as she took a deep breath. "No, honey, it's Woody."

Woody Givens died in his chair in his room on Saturday night, about the same time that Natty, Charlie, and the ladies were having dinner in New York. Natty squeezed her eyes tightly for several seconds, then sobbed, "Aw, Evie, not Woody. He wasn't supposed to—" She pulled back to look at Eve. "Oh, God, what about Mr. Jacks?"

"We put him in Charlie's place. Hank and I brought him over so we could watch him," said Eve. "Didn't think Charlie would mind."

"No, he won't mind," Natty said, turning toward the bus. "Gotta get my bag and go see Mr. Jacks."

"They're going to move him to a home up in Beckley next week," Eve called after her. "Hank talked to someone."

Natty stopped. "Jeez, Eve, you'd think we could do better than that."

Natty left her car in front of the store and walked over to the Pocahontas Hotel. She found her way through the darkness of the first floor to the stairway and climbed the steps slowly to the third floor. *Maybe for the last time.* She wanted to get anything else that Mr. Jacks might need, but also she wanted to, in her own way, say goodbye to her friend Woody Givens.

For more than twenty years—since she was a little girl—Natty had known Woody, the huge, gentle black man who would call her over in the restaurant and give her a shiny quarter, no matter how poor he was. Sometimes he'd walk down the hill and push Natty on the swing when she was watching Buck and the other boys play baseball. He was one of her first true friends in Red Bone, someone she knew she could count on to always be her friend.

The room smelled the same as always—of tobacco smoke and men's bodies. Natty loved the smell of the room. She turned on the floor lamp next to Woody's chair and looked around. Mr. Jacks's drawer had been cleaned out and his dresser emptied. Eve and Hank must have taken it all across the street.

Natty sat on Woody's bed and looked at his empty chair in front of the small TV and, beyond it, at Mr. Jacks's straight chair against the wall next to the window. It was still cracked an inch to let the smoke out.

She thought about all the times that she'd come up here over the years. They'd tell her stories and enjoy their beer and never complain. Never a bitter word about the hard lives they were born into or the unfairness of working forty years in the mines, only to end their days in a dark, dingy room in Red Bone, West Virginia—the last residents of the Pocahontas Hotel. Natty always felt safe and warm in this room. She was going to miss it.

Going down the stairs for the last time, Natty couldn't hold back her tears. She stepped slowly, holding on to the banister, and sobbed for Woody, and for Mr. Jacks, who, she knew, wouldn't last long in a strange home in Beckley without his friend. Outside the front door, she wiped her eyes and walked slowly down the middle of Main Street, exhausted from the adventuresome weekend, tired of crying, tired of feeling so alone.

CHARLIE'S APARTMENT ALREADY reeked of tobacco smoke. Natty opened the door quietly and saw Mr. Jacks sitting next to the kitchen table, talking to Hank. "Hey, Mr. Jacks," she said, leaning over and kissing him on the forehead. She smiled at Hank, whose eyes were as bloodshot as she imagined hers were, and put a hand on his shoulder. "I'm going to try to call Charlie."

She went to the rolltop desk, where she'd seen one of Charlie's business cards. In the kitchen, she took the cordless phone off the hook. Charlie answered after two rings. "Hank?"

"No, it's me, Charlie. Natty," she said.

"What'd you do, break into my apartment?" he said with a chuckle.

Natty went out onto the porch, away from the open kitchen door. "Charlie . . . Woody died . . . Saturday night."

"*Aw, no.* Jeez, Nat. I'm sorry," Charlie said. "That's lousy. What was it?"

"His heart, they figure."

"What about Mr. Jacks?"

"Hank and Eve brought him over to your apartment."

"That's good."

"Eve says he'll be going to a nursing home they got for old coal miners up in Beckley."

Natty's sorrow was palpable, even over the phone, and Charlie didn't know what to say. "I'll be down there in a few days," he said. "For the eminent-domain hearing."

"Okay," said Natty weakly. Neither of them spoke for several seconds. Natty leaned on the porch railing and looked out at the black night. She swallowed hard. "Charlie?" she said.

"I'm here, Nat."

"Charlie, I've been thinking about a lot a things since yesterday." He remained silent. "Thinking about us and everything, you know . . ." Natty paused and heard only Charlie's breathing.

"Go on, Nat."

Natty took several deep breaths. She backed away from the railing and leaned against the wall. The bricks felt warm against her back. "Charlie, will you take me away from here?" she asked quietly. "Me and my kids? Take us somewhere else, somewhere we can be, you know . . . like a family?" Tears rolled down her cheeks. "That's what I want, Charlie." She wiped her cheeks, wondering once again if she was making a fool of herself.

"Natty, are you sure that's what you want?"

"I'm sure, Charlie," she said, sobbing softly. "I'm sure. I love you, Charlie, and I don't want to lose you, and . . . I can't *do* this anymore, Charlie. . . ."

"Nat, it's okay," he said, trying to calm her. "Nat, of course I will."

"You *will*, Charlie?"

"You *know* that's what I want. I love you, Nat. I love you, and I love the kids." Natty sniffed her tears back and smiled.

"Damn, Charlie," she whispered. "Been waitin' my whole life to hear someone say that to me, and now you're a million miles away and I can't even hug you or anything."

"Don't worry, you'll get your chance."

There was a long pause, then Natty cleared her throat. "Charlie, I'll tell Buck. When it's right, I'll tell Buck."

"Yes, you have to do that. Listen, Nat, I don't know what's going to happen after the hearing. I may not be working down there, so . . ."

"Charlie, I'd have to leave real soon, you know, after I tell Buck. I can't tell him and then stay around here for too long."

"Yeah, I know that. When do you want to leave?" asked Charlie.

"Can't be before the soccer tournament. Gotta stay for the kids."

"Okay," said Charlie. "Right after the tournament. When you get back from Charleston, have your stuff ready to go."

"Okay, where do you think—"

Charlie cut in. "I'll figure that out, Nat. I'll take care of it."

Natty smiled into the phone. "Okay, Charlie. I'm going to go now. I'm going to go see Mr. Jacks."

"Give him a hug for me, Nat. See you Friday."

CHARLIE WALKED ACROSS the high school parking lot, shielding his eyes from the brown leaves and dust that circled through the air on the cold wind of the gray day. *A lousy day for a lousy event*, thought Charlie. In a few minutes, Bud and Alice DeWitt would have their farm taken from them by a corrupt system of big business, influential lobbyists, and powerful law firms trampling on the rights of the poor and the disenfranchised. And the system was going to trample on him a little bit after the hearing, when Torkelson, Tuthill, and Warren Brand consolidated their power. Charlie had to smile when he thought of how little it mattered to him now, but that would be no comfort to Bud and Alice DeWitt.

He walked down the dark hallway and stood in the doorway of the gymnasium. The rows of folding chairs were set up facing him, and to his right, just inside the door, several uniformed men were busy carrying in what appeared to be a temporary judge's bench, a witness box, and a voice-activated stenography machine.

Two long wooden tables were placed at the front of the makeshift courtroom. Bud and Alice DeWitt sat at one of them, stoic looks on their faces. At the back of the room, a group of smiling men surrounded a red-faced Kevin Mulrooney. Charlie recognized the representative from the governor's office and the state senator who'd appeared at the cooling-pond hearing two months earlier.

A few yards away, Terry Summers and two other men Charlie didn't recognize stood listening intently as Warren Brand held forth on some topic, eyeing Charlie from across the room. He hadn't expected Brand. Perhaps his career with DD&M will be over sooner than he'd thought. As Charlie looked to the far corner of the gym, he saw Vernon Yarbrough in close conversation with Larry Tuthill. Staring at Charlie over Yarbrough's shoulder was Jack Torkelson. Charlie couldn't imagine why Torkelson was present, and wondered if he'd somehow underestimated the importance of Redemption Mountain to OntAmex.

As he walked over to the DeWitts, Charlie scanned the dozen or so spectators seated in the "public" section of the improvised courtroom. There were two groups of men, obviously miners with a personal interest in the hearing, an elderly couple, and a few individuals Charlie recognized from Eve's Restaurant. Then he noticed, in the center of the back row, an older man with short gray hair, who didn't seem like a local. He wore a rumpled khaki trench coat over a brown suit, a white shirt with a loose collar, and a thin black tie. He had a long, weathered face and a protruding Adam's apple.

Bud DeWitt took Charlie's hand. "Hello, Mr. Burden," he said quietly.

"Sorry it had to come to this, Bud." Charlie looked at Alice, who raised her eyes briefly, with a flicker of a smile. Charlie walked back to where he saw a few single folding chairs beyond the last row of seats. He wanted to be out of the way, just a fly on the wall, to observe the proceedings.

If it weren't for Natty, he would've skipped the hearing. But now that he was here, he'd have to suffer through the well-rehearsed performance of the insufferable Yarbrough and his troupe of actors and, afterward, face the open condescension of the victorious Torkelson and Tuthill and the sniffing superiority of Warren Brand. It was the price you paid for being on the losing side.

At least he'd get to see Natty today, and that would almost make it worth it. He wondered again how two people could be so in love with each other without having had any of the physical contact that leads couples to believe they're in love. But Charlie had no doubts.

A few more spectators straggled in, including Hank, who was frowning with disgust as he walked over to speak with Bud and Alice. He nodded briefly to Charlie, then took a seat behind the DeWitts.

The door clicked open again, and a pair of young professional-looking men in business suits came and sat in front of Charlie. They were lawyers, most likely, who, like every other suit in the room, saw an opportunity in the taking of Redemption Mountain.

Finally the judge took his place at the bench, shaking hands with Yarbrough on his way. Charlie eyed them with disgust. *These guys wouldn't even bother to hide their collusion.*

One of the court officers banged a heavy staff on the gym floor three times, announcing, "Hear ye, hear ye. The fourth circuit court of the state of West Virginia, now in session. The Honorable Winthrop Goodman presiding."

The judge briefly described the purpose of the hearing and explained that it was not a trial, that the rules were different, and that, at the end of the day, he would render a binding decision.

"As you can see," he said, "we've moved the venue of this hearing down to Red Bone for the convenience of the DeWitts and any witnesses they may wish to call." The judge turned to the other lawyers. "Mr. Callahan representing the state, and Mr. Yarbrough for the petitioners, the Ackerly Coal Company and the OntAmex Energy Company. Gentlemen, you have the floor."

A lawyer rose and introduced into evidence a dozen precedent-setting cases of eminent domain used by the state of West Virginia to seize private property to be used by the coal-mining industry. In a businesslike manner, he established for the court that this was a routine occurrence.

As the lawyer finished up, the gym door opened and Natty entered, followed by the Pie Man. They quickly took seats next to her mother. Charlie watched her, as did many of the other men in the room. With her new hairstyle, she couldn't hide anymore.

Yarbrough was launching into his opening statement. "This is a textbook case for the proper use of the eminent-domain statute," he began. Smiling and turning lightly on his feet, using his hands for emphasis while his deep voice filled the gymnasium, he had the attention of the entire room. "A huge, untapped asset, a major seam of low-sulfur coal, needed for the environmentally positive operation of our new power plant, putting hundreds of miners to work." Several of the miners in the audience voiced their approval, earning a smiling rebuke from the judge. "Bringing home union-wage paychecks and pumping new life into the economy of one of our state's most depressed areas." Yarbrough was playing every card in the deck.

The Pie Man got up and walked back to Charlie. "Sit down," said Charlie, squeezing Pie's arm. "Do you know what's going on here, Pie?"

The boy slumped in his seat. "Mama say Grampa and Mawmaw will have to move away from the farm. Mama was mad."

Yarbrough called several witnesses, including an engineer from Ackerly Coal, who testified that a Redemption Mountain surface mine was the only economically feasible method of supplying the new plant with local coal. Much of what was said was just technical jargon, but there was no way for the DeWitts' lawyer to refute any of it. Yarbrough introduced a document stating that his client, Ackerly Coal, was willing to assume the state's liability for just compensation for the property taken and would pay the DeWitts $100,000 for the farm, "well beyond the assessed

value of the property, as your honor can see from the certified appraisal,"
Yarbrough added. He turned and smiled at Bud DeWitt. "And, as a gesture of goodwill, we offer to include in the compensation any attorney's
fees incurred by the DeWitts in regard to this hearing, as well."

Then it was the DeWitts' lawyer's turn, and he stumbled badly. His
statement was disorganized and rambling. He tried to cite some precedent
in the DeWitts' favor but couldn't find the right notes. When he mentioned
mountaintop removal, he got a forceful objection from Vernon Yarbrough.
"No one has mentioned anything about mountaintop removal," the lawyer
admonished. Charlie smiled to himself. No, that would be a separate
closed-door hearing between the judge and Yarbrough, over cocktails at
their club. Charlie caught the judge looking at his watch. It was already five
o'clock, and the buzz level of the room was rising. It was almost over now.

Bud DeWitt settled into the witness chair for his futile statement. His
lawyer slumped down in his seat. This wasn't going to be pretty. As Bud
started to speak, Natty got up and went out the gymnasium door. Charlie could see from her hunched shoulders that she couldn't take any more.

Bud started with the story of his great-grandfather, an officer in the
Army of the West, who settled on Redemption Mountain after the Civil
War. But Bud was nervous and spoke in a halting, often unintelligible
manner, causing the judge to interrupt him to ask if he could *get on with
it*, making Bud even more nervous. No one in the room except Bud's
family paid any attention to his story—the only story at the hearing
worth telling, and the only testimony worth listening to.

Charlie had started to get up to go find Natty when one of the young
businessmen sitting in front of him turned and said something to his companion, and then, to Charlie's surprise, the first man looked over at the
older man with the Adam's apple. The younger man tapped his watch,
pulled out a black cellphone, and walked toward the back of the gym.
There was something going on in the room that Charlie wasn't privy to.

Pie heard it first. "Charlie," he whispered. "The helicopter is coming!"

He looked out the window, as did many others in the courtroom, to
see a flashing light reflecting off the row of green dumpsters in the alley.
Bud had stopped talking. All attention in the room was on the incredible
noise outside—all, Charlie noticed, but that of the man on the cellphone,
whose eyes were trained on the front of the room.

"Your honor, if we could continue?" Yarbrough was trying to regain control of the proceedings. The judge nodded and looked over at Bud DeWitt's lawyer.

"Is your witness about finished, counselor—" He was interrupted by the loud click of the gymnasium door and the entrance of a tall, powerful-looking man with a large round head on its way to complete baldness. The man strode to the front of the room, paying no attention to the judge or the other court officers, who glared at him inquisitively.

Charlie was unable to keep a smile off his face. He didn't know what was going on, but he knew it was going to be something very entertaining by the dramatic entrance of his old friend, Red Landon, the chief operations officer of OntAmex Energy. Landon was probably the sharpest utility executive on the planet, and, from the look on his face, he hadn't come to Red Bone on a social call.

Torkelson looked as if he'd seen a ghost. Then the gymnasium seemed to come alive. The young man with the cellphone had a brief conversation with Landon, who then started toward the back of the gym. The man with the protruding Adam's apple rose and turned to Torkelson and Tuthill. At the same moment, a stampede of loud footsteps came from the hallway.

Charlie sat up in astonishment as Lucien Mackey and Mal Berman came through the door, followed by the CEO of Continental Electric Systems, OntAmex's merger partner. The CEO and his two assistants headed straight for a red-faced Kevin Mulrooney.

The judge banged his gavel three times. "Order in the courtroom, please!" He raised his eyebrows to Yarbrough. "Could somebody tell me what's going on here?" None of the newcomers paid any attention.

Red Landon passed by Charlie without taking his eyes off Torkelson. He placed a heavy hand on Charlie's shoulder as he went by. Lucien made straight for Warren Brand and Terry Summers, and Mal went to the bench for a private conversation with the judge, handing him a packet of legal papers. The two young men who'd been sitting in front of Charlie now had rectangular plastic credentials hanging from silver chains around their necks. As one of the men passed by, Charlie was able to see his badge: SEC, it read in large, bold letters, and, beneath that, INVESTIGATIONS DIVISION.

*   *   *

IN A DARK section of the hallway just outside the gymnasium door, Natty sat on the shallow bench at the base of the portable bleachers. She didn't want to watch Bud DeWitt and his lawyer make a pathetic plea for some kind of leniency from the judge and all the lawyers and the big corporation men. None of them cared. All they wanted was their coal, and they weren't interested in family history or the sweat, blood, and heartache that the DeWitts had poured into their farm.

They didn't want to hear about all the DeWitt men who'd put down their plows to go off to fight America's wars or about those who never made it back to West Virginia. And they didn't want to hear about any DeWitt children or grandchildren buried on the side of Redemption Mountain.

Natty clenched her teeth in anger. Better for Bud to just stand up and give the judge and the rest of them his middle finger and walk out than to grovel through this pathetic, heroic, sad, wonderful story of the DeWitt family. But, no, Bud would never do that. Bud would be a gentleman to the end. Natty wiped the tears from her cheeks and wished she had a cigarette. She heard the roar of the helicopter overhead and knew the hearing would soon be over.

Then the outside door at the end of the hallway was pulled open, and she watched a large man with hunched shoulders move quickly down the hall. He didn't even look at Natty as he passed and yanked open the door to the gym. Then came a group of men who appeared to be lawyers or businessmen. They definitely weren't locals.

She didn't know what was going on with all these newcomers, but, from the look of them, it could only mean bad news. Natty leaned back against the surface of the wooden bleachers and closed her eyes while she waited for the hearing to end.

She heard the distant click of the outside door opening once more but ignored it, choosing to keep her eyes shut to the rest of the day's proceedings. *Just another latecomer to the lawyers' party*, she could tell from the sound of the hard, expensive shoes hitting the wooden flooring of the hallway. Forceful, confident, but walking more slowly than the others. Close to her now. And then the footsteps stopped. Natty waited to hear the gymnasium door open but instead heard a voice right in front of her. A voice that—even after two and a half years—she knew immediately. "Are you all right, miss?"

Natty opened her eyes and saw Duncan McCord standing a foot away, his arms in front of him, his fingers interlocked, leaning forward with a concerned look on his face. He wore the same suit he'd worn to the picnic the day the helicopters came. Natty smiled. "You gotta stop using that line on me. I'm sick of it," she said, looking up at the OntAmex president.

McCord stared at Natty for a few seconds, and a smile came over his face. "You've changed your hair, Natty, but you still have beautiful eyes."

"Thank you," Natty whispered, shocked that he remembered her.

McCord turned his head toward the gymnasium door. "What's going on here today, Natty?"

Natty frowned. "Oh, the lawyers and the coal men are taking my grandpa's farm away from him."

McCord looked slowly from Natty to the gym and back again. "Those *fucking* lawyers," he said, shaking his head.

Natty burst out laughing, then covered her mouth quickly, afraid that they may have heard her in the gym. It was the first time she'd laughed all week, and it felt good for a change.

McCord smiled and started off toward the gym. "Let's see if we can't do something about your grandpa's farm."

It took only a few seconds for the tumultuous buzz of the many furtive conversations in the gym to come to a complete halt. Duncan McCord stood inside the gym door, hands in his pockets, feet spread wide as he coolly scanned the room with penetrating eyes that missed nothing. The stillness of the room didn't hurry him. Even those who didn't know who he was knew better than to interrupt.

McCord looked at the judge and nodded. He walked over to the witness box where Bud DeWitt sat, dumbfounded. "You Bud DeWitt?" McCord asked.

"Yeah, uh, yes, sir," Bud answered.

McCord smiled and held out his hand. "Mr. DeWitt, I'm Duncan McCord, president of the OntAmex Energy Company, and I personally apologize for the troubles you've been put through over this. You can sit down now, sir. This is all over." McCord patted Bud lightly on the shoulder as the farmer passed by, returning to his seat. Then he walked past the judge's bench and stood in front of Vernon Yarbrough. "You our lawyer?"

Yarbrough rose, a practiced grin coming on like an involuntary reaction, his right hand pushing forward toward McCord. "Why, yes, sir. Vernon Yarb—"

"You're fired," said McCord, with no hint of a smile on his face, his hands at his sides. With his left hand, he made a fist with thumb extended and jerked it toward the door. "Get out!" he said angrily. "Now, before I kick your ass all over this room."

Yarbrough turned white and clumsily tried to find an escape route through the folding chairs. McCord turned to the room. "And that goes for the rest of you bums." He pointed two fingers at Torkelson and Tuthill. Red Landon, anger written across his face, stood between them, a firm hold on each man's arm, and ushered them forcefully toward the door, accompanied by several others and one of the SEC men.

Then McCord found Mulrooney, already on his way to the door between two Continental Electric Systems people and the second SEC man. Following close behind were Warren Brand and Terry Summers, escorted by Lucien Mackey.

At the front of the room, Duncan McCord didn't have to bang a gavel for attention. As soon as he started to speak, the room went quiet. "This hearing never should have happened. This is not the way the OntAmex Energy Company or its subsidiaries operates, and I apologize to the DeWitt family for the way some of our representatives have treated them. We have no intention of using our financial or political power to circumvent the laws or regulations of any state or government agency or to be a party to the environmental catastrophe of mountaintop-removal coal mining. It's not going to happen—in West Virginia or anywhere else.

"The miners in the room should know that our subsidiary, Ackerly Coal, will open a coal mine on Redemption Mountain and hire plenty of union miners to operate a slope mine to fuel the Red Bone power plant. We'll mine Redemption Mountain the old way, without destroying what God put down here to make West Virginia a special place." He looked back toward the DeWitts. "Without destroying the history and tradition of one of your state's great families."

Charlie followed Duncan's gaze and noticed Hank standing with his arm around Alice's shoulders.

"It'll cost us more," McCord continued, "but it's a price we'll pay." He crossed his arms and studied the floor for a few seconds. "You know, for a long time," he continued softly, "for most of the last century, big companies—coal companies and steel companies and utilities—have taken unfair advantage of coal miners and the coal-mining areas of this country, with West Virginia at the top of the list, I'd guess. So," McCord narrowed his eyes in thought as he gazed over the room, "now that the OntAmex Energy Company is getting into the coal-mining business, as an old friend of mine so eloquently put it not long ago, maybe it's time for us to just cut it out." McCord put his hands in his pockets, looked out at the crowd, and winked at Charlie.

When it was clear that McCord was through, Hank clapped his wrinkled old hands together loudly, and then again, and then the miners joined in. Soon, the entire room, which by this time was mostly local residents, was applauding this outsider, as many of them had done at a picnic two and a half years earlier. Charlie sat watching the Dewitt celebration, with the Pie Man at his side. Then something kicked his ankle hard, and he looked up to see Duncan McCord staring down at him, an angry look on his face. "You screwed up a good vacation in the Canary Islands, Burden."

Charlie smiled at his old friend. "That's tough."

McCord turned to Pie and smiled at his Michigan T-shirt, then held out a fist. "Go, Blue." Pie's face scrunched up into an instant happy face as he touched knuckles with the OntAmex president. McCord studied the boy for a few seconds, then looked back at Charlie. His thoughts were interrupted by the sound of Natty's voice.

"C'mon, Pie Man, we gotta go." She stood ten feet away, and Charlie came to his feet.

"Dunc, this is—"

"We've met," said McCord, turning to Natty. "A couple of times now."

Natty's smile returned as she watched Charlie's eyebrows rise in curiosity. She'd let him wonder. "Goin' out to the Roadhouse for a beer to celebrate," said Natty. "Love to have you boys join us."

McCord grimaced. "Nothing in the world I'd rather do right now, but I've got to get back to Toronto tonight."

"And I need to spend a few minutes with Duncan before he leaves," said Charlie. "Maybe I'll see you there later."

* * *

Mᶜᴄᴏʀᴅ ʜᴀɴᴅᴇᴅ ᴄʜᴀʀʟɪᴇ one of the short dark cigars he'd bummed from a miner in the parking lot. They stopped and turned away from the wind to light them, before starting out for a walk around the athletics field. In the center of the field, the helicopter hissed and whined as it began its warm-up sequence. They walked slowly to enjoy their short time together.

"This isn't done here, Charlie, you realize that, right?"

Charlie kicked a small stone on the track. "Yeah, I know that, Dunc. But you did what you could."

McCord blew out a cloud of smoke. "Another year or two, merger's done, we'll be selling off all this coal stuff. It's not our business."

"I know."

"Then Massey, or Consol, Arch—somebody else will own Redemption Mountain, and that'll be it for the DeWitt farm. That'll be it for the mountain. The economics kill you, Charlie."

"I know. But until then . . . What the hell happened here tonight?"

"It was all about money," said McCord. "Plain old greed and corruption and arrogance that, down here, nobody would care about what they did." He spit out a piece of tobacco and shook his head angrily. "It was all Torkelson. Lining his pockets, using his position to get rich quick. That's the trouble with hiring these fucking government bureaucrats. They work at shit jobs for years, then the first chance they get in the private sector, they figure the system owes them a fat bonus and a retirement home on Jupiter Island." They walked along the cinder track.

"Three years ago, Torkelson went to Ackerly and found a willing player in Mulrooney. He wanted five million to site the new plant in the heart of Ackerly's operations. Mulrooney knows that mountaintop removal is just about finished because of the environmentalists, so he offers Torkelson ten million for the coal contract, plus the help of OntAmex's political muscle to get a variance for Redemption Mountain. By the way, your numbers were a little off. It's about forty percent cheaper now to do a surface mine—about half a billion over twenty years. Makes ten million a pretty good investment up front."

"So how'd you get on to him?"

"Red figured it out," said McCord. "After your email, we started looking into the situation and realized that Torkelson and Tuthill were spending too much time down here. We put our investigator on it—the tall guy with the fedora—and he did some phone taps, broke into their emails, cellphones. All illegal, but we got what we needed. Mulrooney's got a big mouth, so we knew that's where the money was coming from. Then our guy got lucky and stumbled across Mulrooney's secretary, who he was tapping on the side. She spilled everything. Torkelson was getting the big dough, but he had to include Tuthill—he was getting two million—plus a million for that cocksucker lawyer. What's his name?"

"Yarbrough," said Charlie.

McCord stopped and turned to face him. "Yarbrough—that was his scheme, that raid with the cops and the DEA." McCord grimaced angrily. "Asshole. He's lucky nobody got killed that day."

"Could've been a tragedy," said Charlie.

McCord eyed him warily as he puffed on his cigar. "Understand someone tipped off farmer DeWitt they were coming."

Charlie flicked the ash from his cigar. "That's what I heard, too."

"Someone using your cellphone."

"Gotta stop leaving it lying around."

"Lucien told me you did a nice tap dance all over that lawyer in New York."

Charlie looked over and saw Lucien and Mal at the edge of the field. "Where does Lucien stand now?" asked Charlie.

"He was never out. Red went ballistic when he heard what Torkelson was trying to pull." McCord looked back toward the parking lot. "Red might be beating the shit out of Torkelson right now. I better find him."

"What about Brand?"

"He's done. Red's going to New York on Monday. Lucien'll call another executive-committee meeting, and Red will lay it all out for them. The other kid, too, the pretty boy—"

"Summers."

"He's gone, too. He was getting half a million. They brought him in after we announced the merger with CES and Hugo Paxton died. They sucked you into the scheme to keep me out of it. They wanted him in to keep an eye on you. They didn't think you would get so involved in things down here, and that Summers could represent DD&M."

"What about the judge? How much was he in for?"

McCord shook his head. "Judge was clean. He was just ready to do his country club pals a favor and get a variance for the surface mine. He was on the team but not on the take."

"So, that was just for my benefit, to get me to want the farm as much as they did, to protect you and the merger," said Charlie.

McCord laughed. "Nice job," he said sarcastically. "First chance you get, you screw me and go over to the farmer's team."

Charlie laughed, too. "They're nicer people."

McCord threw his cigar into the weeds and turned toward Charlie. "You took quite a chance sending that email, Charlie. Could have been the end of your career."

"Had to be done, Dunc. Hundred years is long enough."

"Good thing you did, or the merger probably would have blown up, once the SEC got wind of Torkelson's hanky-panky. And that would have been it for me."

McCord stopped walking. "You're doing okay, Burden, aren't you? Ellen told me all about your new house. She was real excited."

"Yes, Dunc, financially we're—"

"That's not what I meant, Charlie." McCord studied his friend's face. "You break your nose again?" He squinted to see better. "You definitely get uglier every time I see you."

Charlie shrugged. "Took a high stick in a bar one night. It's a rough town."

McCord scowled. "What's up with you and Ellen?"

Charlie guessed that McCord had received some information about Natty and him during the investigation. "Ellen and I are going to split up," he said. "We're . . . moving in different directions. Have been for a long time."

McCord nodded. "That's a huge break for Ellen. You've been holding her back for years." Charlie smiled and nodded in agreement.

"This have anything to do with the girl," McCord nodded back toward the school, "and the kid?"

Charlie gazed over toward the parking lot. "Yeah," said Charlie, "it's got a lot to do with them."

"Can't turn back the clock, Charlie. Can't make up for past mistakes," he said.

"I know that, Dunc. Not trying to. It's not about me."

McCord studied Charlie's face for a moment before he was satisfied. "So, what are you going to do?"

"I'm not sure yet. Think we might find some small town somewhere. Maybe Vermont or Wyoming. I was thinking about becoming a carpenter."

McCord stared pensively at Charlie for a few seconds, then glanced toward the helicopter. "I have to get going." He smiled at Charlie. "You're an idiot, Burden," he said, shaking his head, "but . . . Jesus, Charlie, I envy you." The two friends hugged before McCord turned and darted toward the helicopter. A minute later, it disappeared into the black sky, heading north.

CHAPTER 33

THE NEW FIELD WAS ALREADY FIRM, AND IF THE WEATHER stayed warm through the rest of November, it would need mowing soon. Natty couldn't help smiling as she recalled the uneven dirt and weed patch that they used to play on.

It wasn't lined, and the new goals wouldn't arrive until next spring, but the Bones didn't need them to practice for their opening game of the tournament on Friday. Natty watched her players dribbling balls from one end of the field to the other and back. Out in front, Emma was with the Bones' new assistant coach, Gabe, the midfielder from Welch. They always seemed to have fun when they were together, which thrilled Natty. It was a wonderful new experience for Emma.

Natty looked uphill and saw Charlie's blue Lexus coming toward her. She wandered over to the side of the road as Charlie slowed to a stop. She could see a small suitcase and Charlie's briefcase in the backseat. He opened his door and faced her over the car. "Looks like this is getting to be our regular way of meeting," he said.

Natty smiled. "Probably a good idea to keep a car between us at all times." She looked down into the car again. "Taking a trip?" she asked.

"I have to go up to New York for a few days—some meetings to sort the fallout from the hearing. Then we're going up to Vermont for Thanksgiving."

"Coming back?"

"Sunday night," said Charlie, watching her closely.

"Gonna miss the tournament."

"I know," said Charlie wistfully. He looked over at the Bones, who were running. "But my daughter and my son are coming up. . . ." He hesitated. "And I need to have some time with Ellen."

Natty drummed her fingers on the top of the car. "Charlie, you know when I called you after Woody died, well, maybe that wasn't real fair to you, and if you want to think it over some more . . ."

Charlie smiled and shook his head. "No, Nat, I don't have any doubts." He tilted his head slightly to look into Natty's eyes. "How about you?"

"God, no, Charlie," she almost whispered. "Best thing ever happened to me. Best thing ever happened to my kids, too. Hell, I've been dreamin' about this my whole life." She looked away as the excitement drained from her face. "Just that . . . I ain't said anything to Buck yet. Hasn't been a good time for that."

"How's he been?" asked Charlie.

"He's been, you know . . . okay. Different. Since he started working and the day he spent with you cuttin' the trees, he's been . . . better." She shook her head. "Don't change a thing." Natty chewed her bottom lip. "Just makes it, you know, a little harder, that's all. I'm going to tell him, Charlie," she said forcefully. "This week, before we go to Charleston on Friday."

Charlie watched her for a few seconds. Then he reached into the pocket of his jacket. He brought out a key ring with a small yellow plastic replica of a lantern on it and handed it to her across the car.

"This is for our company apartment in Bluefield. Nobody's in it." Natty took it and looked at the label. "Take the kids there when you get back from Charleston on Sunday night. I'll meet you there later, when I get back. Do you know where it is?"

"Sure," said Natty. "High-class place."

"Nothing but the best for you. Oh, and take this, too." He reached into his other pocket and brought out a thick black cellphone. "Turn it on when you're in Charleston, in case I have to reach you." He laughed as Natty studied the phone anxiously. "Just push the green button when you want to do something."

"Okay, Charlie," Natty said, taking a step away from the car. "Better get back to practice. See you Sunday night."

"I'll see you then, Nat. Good luck at the tournament."

* * *

THE PARKING LOTS were filled, so Natty had Geneva Gunnells stop the bus as close as they could get to the soccer complex. The Bones grabbed their equipment and started walking. Natty scowled when she saw that it was ten-thirty. They were supposed to report at least an hour before their eleven o'clock game. *That's all they needed, to be disqualified from the tournament after a three-hour bus ride!*

Natty trotted after her team. Carrying a heavy equipment bag, she was having a tough time keeping up. She ran through a boulevard of tents and concession stands lined up outside the main gate. Their new warm-up suits with the skull and crossbones on the back were attracting a lot of attention. *How proud the kids were of those uniforms! All thanks to Charlie.*

Natty swallowed back her anxiety about what she and Charlie were planning, made worse because she had yet to tell Buck. There was just never the right time. *And then Buck asking about the tournament, wishing her luck, giving Pie a pat on the back, and encouraging him to "give it everything you got, kid." Damn.* She'd call him from the motel that night.

At the top of the hill, Natty's anxiety turned to cold fear. There were several fields, and some of the games were already in progress. She had no idea where her team was supposed to play. Then she saw Gabe wave to her from a tent about fifty yards away. As she approached, he trotted over and took the equipment bag from her shoulder. "Register here, coach," he said. "We're on Field Three."

Natty registered and got the schedule and rosters of the other teams. There were eight teams in their division: four from West Virginia, two from Ohio, one from Kentucky, and one from Pittsburgh. They'd play one game on Friday, two on Saturday, and, if they got that far, the championship was on Sunday. The Bones could end up playing four games in three days with just one substitute—Pie. *Maybe the Bones had bitten off a little more than they could chew with this tournament.*

As Natty walked across the field, she saw the Bones going through their pregame warm-up under Zack's direction. At the end of the field, Gabe was kicking balls at Brenda in the goal.

Two other teams from their division were warming up on the next field. They looked formidable to Natty—bigger and stronger, and a little more organized. *One game at a time,* she told herself. *And try not to get embarrassed in the first game!*

An older man in a black referee outfit strode across the field, followed by a younger man and a woman carrying flags. A man and a woman seated themselves at a table on the sideline and set out some notebooks and a time clock. Natty smiled at the sight of all the officials. *This was real soccer!*

Just as the game was about to start, a photographer came to take the team picture. Some players sat on the grass while the second row knelt. Natty stood between Emma and Brenda in the middle of the back row, her arms around their shoulders.

A few minutes into the game, Natty's nervousness disappeared. She could tell from a few trips up and down the field that the team from Ohio was no match for the Bones. Their forwards weren't fast enough, and their fullbacks couldn't keep up with Emma and Sammy.

Natty could see the first goal coming, as Paul raced the ball across the midfield with an open field ahead of him. He placed a perfect pass out to Sammy, who faked a run up the sideline, then lofted a long high ball toward the far right corner. Emma streaked past the stunned fullback, tipped the ball to herself, and headed for the goal. She easily dribbled past one defender and spun through two others, with an electrifying move that had the spectators applauding before she calmly brought the ball past the helpless goalie and pushed a slow roller into the left corner of the goal.

"She makes it look too easy." The voice next to Natty startled her. She turned and saw a handsome young man in a shiny maroon warm-up suit and baseball cap. Natty smiled.

He introduced himself as the coach of the Charleston Chargers, who were playing next on Field Three.

"How's your team?" asked Natty, recalling that the Charleston team was seeded second.

"Oh, we're good," he said with a smile. "Like your team."

"Gonna win the tournament?" asked Natty.

The coach laughed. "No, not us. Not you, either. No one's gonna beat Pittsburgh. They're loaded. It's an all-star team, put together to win this tournament." He followed Natty along the sideline. "They could beat most any high school team in the state."

"Thanks for the encouragement," she said with a laugh. Out on the field, Paul ripped a shot that hit the crossbar and caromed twenty yards out to the middle of the field, where Emma took it in midair and sent a sizzling low skidder into the left corner of the goal.

"Wow," said the Charleston coach, shaking his head. "She's incredible."

Natty turned around to find the Pie Man, the lone figure on the bench behind her. "Pie, go in for Emma," she called to him. Pie jumped up from the bench and pulled off his Yankees hat before running over to the scorer's table.

"Where are your extras?" asked the coach, looking at Natty's empty bench.

Natty laughed. "That's him," she said.

"You know you can take up to three kids from other teams in your league, if you're short of fifteen players. Didn't your league commissioner tell you that? Four games in three days is a lot for these kids. You gotta have subs." As if on cue, the referee blew his whistle and waved Pie and four new players for the Ohio team onto the field.

"Too late now," said Natty, as she turned to see Gabe on the sideline giving Emma a high-five. "Hey," she said, grabbing the coach's arm. "I got one right here," she said, pointing to Gabe. "How do I get him on the roster?"

"Maybe they'd allow it, if you could get written permission from your league commissioner. If you get it faxed up here, they'd probably let him play. 'Course, I'll protest it when you play us." He nudged Natty and laughed. "Just kidding, coach," he said.

Natty looked up and smiled. She liked this handsome young man. "Thanks a lot. I'll look into it."

"Okay, listen, I'm going over to the tent to check on getting your other player on the team. See what I can do."

"Jeez, thanks," said Natty. They shook hands, and the coach disappeared into the milling crowd. Natty stole a peek at the end of the field as he reappeared, walking the end line behind the goal.

With the score 5–0 in the second half, Natty put Emma and Sammy back on defense and had Pie and the Steele brothers play the forward line. She couldn't tell the kids to stop playing, but if she left Emma and Sammy up front and the Ohio team got any more demoralized, the score would rise to double digits quickly.

"That's a mistake, trying to hold down the score," said the now-familiar voice next to her. "They use goal differential to determine the losers' bracket on Saturday." She turned to see the coach of the Charleston team holding a piece of paper in his hand.

Natty smiled up at him. "I'll remember that when we play your team." They both laughed.

"Here," he said, handing Natty the paper. "Have your league commissioner fill in your player's information, sign it, and fax it to the number at the top. Do it tonight and they'll let him play tomorrow."

"Hey, thanks, this is—"

"Gotta go find my team, coach," he said, backing away. "Good luck tomorrow."

"You, too, coach."

AFTER DINNER AT McDonald's, Natty and the Bones went back to the motel and she collected all the shirts and socks in a laundry bag. The shorts wouldn't need washing until Saturday night, if they weren't on their way home by then. Natty sat on the edge of the bed, an equipment bag at her feet, counting out the bills in the envelope marked *breakfast—Saturday*.

She'd already used some of it at McDonald's, and she needed a few dollars for the coin-operated laundry. She tucked the bills into the front pocket of her jeans, then transferred Charlie's cellphone to the pocket of her jacket. "Be back in about an hour," she called out to Geneva, who was reading on the bed. Emma and Brenda were sprawled on the floor, watching television.

She checked the boys' rooms to make sure nobody was killing anyone, hefted the laundry bag over her shoulder, and walked around to the side of the motel, where the laundry was. It had started to drizzle, and rain was forecast for the rest of the weekend. Natty stuffed everything into two washers and sat down on a bench near the dryers. She took out the phone but it was too noisy with all the machines going, and several women sat nearby, reading magazines. Natty needed privacy for this phone call.

She decided to sit in the bus. She didn't want to have to yell into the phone when she told Buck that she and the kids were leaving. After she talked to Buck, she'd call Sally to check on Cat and to see if she could track down Kyle Loftus in the morning. Heart racing, she punched in the numbers.

He picked up on the first ring, surprising her. "Buck," she whispered. "Buck, it's me, Nat."

"Oh. Hey, Nat. What's happenin' up there? How's the tournament?"

"It's good. We won our first game. Six, nothin'. Wasn't too good a team."

"See what I told ya? You'll be kickin' ass all weekend," Buck said enthusiastically. "Ain't no one gonna beat the Bones. Right?"

"I don't know. There's a team from Pittsburgh is supposed to be unbeatable."

"Hey, fuck that, huh, Nat? Them iron heads from Pittsburgh ain't never played against Emma Lowe and the Willard boys." He chuckled. "And they sure ain't played against the Pie Man before."

Tears welled up in her eyes. "Yeah, that's right, Buck," she managed.

"There you go," said Buck. "Can't beat 'em 'less you know you can beat 'em."

"How come you're home on a Friday night? Roadhouse burn down?"

"Nah, just tired from workin' all day."

"Yeah?"

"I got Cat here. Me and Cat are watchin' a tape."

"You and Cat," said Natty.

"Watchin' *Home Alone*. Stupid movie, but the kid knows every word of it," he said with a chuckle. "It's unbelievable."

"It's her favorite movie," Natty said softly. "She's seen it a hundred times." Natty bit her lower lip and squeezed her eyes tightly closed for several seconds.

"Nat? You there?"

"I'm here, Buck," she said, drawing in a deep breath. "Hey, Buck, listen, I need you to do something real important." She explained the situation with Gabe and dictated the information for Kyle Loftus to approve.

"I'll go into Welch tonight and drag that asshole out of bed. Don't worry, I'll get your kid on the team."

Natty looked at her watch. "Why don't you just stay with Cat," she said. "Watch your movie. Be better you go over in the morning, anyway."

"Okay. Probably right."

"Thanks, Buck." There was a long pause between them. "Okay, Buck," Natty said finally, "I gotta go now. Say g'night to Cat for me."

"I will, Nat. Good luck up there."

Natty turned off the phone and sat in the darkness for several minutes. She stared at the rain running down the window and then laughed
out loud, wiping the tears from her eyes as she pictured Buck sitting on
the couch next to Cat, watching *Home Alone*.

ON SATURDAY MORNING, the Bones beat the team from Kentucky, 5–0,
with slightly more effort than it took to win their first game. The Kentucky team had lost to Pittsburgh on Friday, 12–0. The rain had stopped
for the morning games, but it was sprinkling steadily as Natty made her
way toward Field One. The Bones were already on the field, warming up
again. Natty pulled her Spider-Man hat down tightly against the breeze
and started to jog. Then she heard a voice.

"Hey there, Miz Oakes, that you?" said a voice behind her. Natty turned
to see the tournament director. He pulled a piece of paper from under his
poncho. "Got your permit here to use the Miller kid, Gabe Miller. We
added him to your roster." Natty took the paper, unfolded it quickly, and
saw Kyle Loftus's signature at the bottom. Her face lit up with excitement,
but the director had already headed for the shelter of the tent.

Natty smiled as she pictured what would've been a very brief negotiation between Buck and Kyle Loftus. Digging through her equipment bag,
she found an extra uniform, still in its plastic package. Next she started
rooting through the kids' bags, looking for a pair of socks and shin guards.
She found some in Paul's bag, as well as a mouth guard that looked fairly
clean. Gabe was rolling balls out of the goal to a semicircle of shooters just
outside the box. Natty called him over.

Gabe's mouth dropped open when he read the rain-soaked fax. "Welcome to the Bones," she said, handing him his uniform. "Better get suited
up, game's about to start." She gathered the team around her and told them
about their new teammate.

Emma's eyes widened. "You mean Gabe's gonna play for us?" she
squealed. The rest of the team was excited, too, knowing that Gabe was one
of the best and toughest players in their league.

"Make a circle now, so Gabe can change," Natty said, as she saw the
referee crew walking across the field. "Hurry up, game's going to start.

Emma, you and Brenda turn your backs." Gabe would have to play in his sneakers, but Natty knew it wouldn't bother him a bit.

"Hear you got a new player." Natty turned and saw the handsome young Charleston coach walking toward her.

"Thanks to you," she said, as they shook hands.

"It's just a game." He smiled at her.

Natty looked out onto the field and noticed how many spectators there were. Field One was the only field with bleachers, and they were completely filled.

As soon as the game started, it was evident that the Charleston Chargers were a great team, easily the best team they'd faced all year. They worked beautifully together, dominating play for the first ten minutes of the game. But the Bones gradually raised the level of their game, as Natty had seen them do before. Plus, Gabe was a force in the midfield, and Natty could see right away that the Bones would have had little chance of beating the Chargers without him. The teams slogged to a scoreless first half, but not before Hardy Steele sprained an ankle, leaving the Bones with the Pie Man as their only substitute.

With ten minutes left in the still-scoreless game, the rain stopped, and it became windy and cold. After a long, sustained attack by the Chargers, Natty called a time-out. "Okay, we got five minutes left," she said, "and we're going to beat these guys, but we don't want to go to overtime, because we don't have as many subs. From now on, everyone, you get a shot at the ball, you kick it as far downfield as you can. Don't worry about possession. Okay?" She looked around at the exhausted yet attentive faces. "Then, if you get a good clear going, I want everyone rushing up the field. Forget about defending. Three players on the ball, and everyone else goes to the goal. We'll probably only get one chance, so when it comes, everyone move up fast."

Play restarted with a goal kick from Brenda that got knocked down by the swirling wind. The Bones battled valiantly, especially Zack, who seemed to be everywhere, but they struggled in vain to get the ball out of their own end. Just as the scorekeeper announced that there were two minutes left, a Charleston player took an open shot from fifteen yards out, which Brenda leaped for and punched straight up in the air. The ball hung over the field for an eternity, dropping ten yards in front of the goal, where both teams converged on it.

Natty held her breath, but Zack rose out of the pack and caught the ball with a perfectly timed header, sending it on a long, high arc toward the middle of the field. Paul beat two Chargers midfielders to the ball, and the stampede was on.

Ten yards short of midfield, Paul played the ball sideways and hit it as hard as he'd ever kicked a soccer ball—in America *or* Poland. Gabe, Emma, and a half dozen Chargers all raced up the field. The ball landed twenty yards beyond Emma, who was in an even footrace with a Charger. But Emma shifted to another gear and beat him to the ball. Just as she controlled it, a Charger slid into her, sending her sliding through the mud.

Lying in the mud, Emma turned in time to see Gabe hurdle over her on a direct path to the ball. Gabe and the Chargers fullback kicked the ball at the same time, but Gabe powered the ball through as he knocked the defender off stride with his shoulder, then chased the rolling ball toward the end line, twelve yards from the goal.

Two Chargers bore down on him. He looked back for Emma, but she was still on the ground. Then he spied Zack flying down the middle of the field. Gabe put his head down and calculated the spot where he would put the ball.

Right before the first Charger reached him, Gabe sent a high chip shot floating toward the penalty-kick spot in front of the goal. As the ball took off, two defenders crashed into him, sending him tumbling beyond the end line. He watched as Zack flashed by, heading straight for the goal at high speed, and made the silver ball disappear with a leaping, vicious header and an ungodly scream. The ball hit the netting in the back of the goal just before Zack's momentum sent him sliding on his stomach past the goalie. Then the ref's whistle signaled the end of the game.

From the mud, Gabe looked over at Emma again. She was still on the ground but was smiling back at him. He laughed and held a victorious fist up in the air. Zack held the ball out in front of him, raced to midfield, and did a fifteen-yard belly-flop slide through the deepest puddle on the field. When he stood up, you couldn't tell what color his shirt was. The crowd gave both teams a sustained ovation for what was truly an incredible soccer game. Natty watched her mud-covered, battered team come slowly off the field, too exhausted to celebrate. She couldn't believe they had to play again tomorrow.

NATTY CALLED BUCK again from the parking lot at the Laundromat. She left Emma and Gabe inside to watch the loads they had going. Tonight, everything had to be washed. They would look like a real team when they played Pittsburgh the next day. Pittsburgh had beaten Morgantown, 5–0, in the other semifinal.

From the dark school bus, Natty watched Emma and Gabe at the Laundromat. They sat on a bench talking, attentive, smiling, and polite to each other, with an occasional laugh, never running out of conversation. Natty loved watching them together. She pressed the last button on Charlie's phone and swallowed, unsure of what she would tell Buck, but this was it, time was up. Her breathing relaxed when no one answered.

Next she called Sally. "Cat's over here," said Sally. "Staying with us for the night, 'cause Buck went out. Don't know where."

"Oh, okay," said Natty softly.

Sally heard Natty's disappointment. "He spent the whole day with her, Nat."

"Yeah?"

"Took her up to Welch first thing in the morning, and they had lunch and went to the video store. Come back and watched a movie together, just the two of 'em. Cat had a special day."

Natty was silent. "Okay, thanks, Sal. Just tell Buck we won and we're playing Pittsburgh tomorrow." She clicked off and sat in the dark. She thought about Charlie, up in Vermont telling the beautiful, sophisticated Ellen Burden that he was leaving her for a mousy little hillbilly girl with a son named Pie Man and a daughter who had memorized the dialogue from *Home Alone*. Natty shook her head—and *she* was the one who couldn't tell Buck!

THE NEXT MORNING, Natty went for a three-mile run in the rain, then drove the bus to a Kroger and spent their last thirty dollars on five boxes of cereal, three gallons of milk, two large cartons of orange juice, and three bunches of bananas. That was all they'd have to eat until they got back to Red Bone that night. Natty kicked herself for not managing their funds better, because she knew that, win or lose, the Bones were going to be starving after the game. Natty let herself into the room and dropped the groceries on the bed. "Where's Em and Brenda?" Natty asked Geneva.

"Gone next door, I'd guess," Geneva replied, without looking up from her book.

Natty rolled her eyes. "Nice chaperoning, Neva," she said sarcastically.

"They be okay," Geneva said. "They good kids."

Natty knocked three times before the door swung open. She stood in the rain, dumbfounded, her mouth open in shock as she stared at four boys with their heads completely shaved, each one bald as a soccer ball, grinning from ear to ear. "*Oh, my God!*" she managed to shriek.

Then Pie squeezed through, his head shaved, too. Natty laughed as she hugged her son. Suddenly she stopped and the smile left her face as she remembered that Emma and Brenda weren't in their room. Then they emerged from the bathroom, their hair gone, followed by a bald Zack Willard still holding a disposable razor. His smile lit up the little motel room. Hand to her mouth, Natty shrieked, "Your mothers are going to *kill* me." Then she hugged the two girls and kissed the tops of their heads.

"Now, this's what I calls a team!" roared Zack, who was answered by a loud chorus of "Bones, Bones, Bones!" Natty stopped worrying about whether the Bones would be up for the championship game.

THE PITTSBURGH GOLDEN Knights were big and fast and strong, just as Natty had figured, but maybe they were a little too cocky. She wondered if the Knights hadn't had it a little too easy. They hadn't been in a tough game, as the Bones had against Charleston, and now, seeing that they were playing a real team, they were tightening up a bit.

Pittsburgh enjoyed an early territorial advantage, but they had few chances on goal as Zack skillfully directed the defense. The constant rain had slowed down both offenses. The field was becoming soggier and muddier by the minute, with puddles that stopped a rolling ball dead.

Just when it seemed that the half would end in a scoreless tie, Paul stole a careless pass in the midfield, dribbled easily around a Knights defender, and quickly advanced ten yards. Emma jogged lazily ahead of the play, as Paul waited for her move. As she closed in on the fullback in front of her, Emma faked her usual run to the outside, then spun back, cutting between the fullback and the sweeper, and Paul threaded her a perfect through ball, putting her one-on-one with the goaltender twenty yards out.

She tipped the ball with her right foot to slow it and immediately fired through the ball with her left foot, blasting it into the top left corner of the net. The Bones gathered around Emma and Paul and created a new goal celebration, with everyone rubbing the tops of their bald heads. The crowd cheered. It was only then that Natty noticed how large the crowd encircling the field had become. The bleachers were filled with umbrellas, and the opposite sideline and end lines were three-deep with spectators in rain gear. There were a significant number of little girls in soccer outfits along the sidelines at their end of the field, cheering happily for Emma's goal.

At halftime, Natty told her team to play good, solid defense and to wait for their openings. A team like the Knights, used to scoring a lot of goals, would become more and more frustrated and careless as the second half went on, and one more goal would win the game.

Ten minutes into the second half, her strategy was working perfectly. Paul and Gabe were hanging back and clogging up the middle of the field, forcing the Knights to try to go over them with long balls. But Zack was too fast, and he cleaned up everything that came into his zone. Natty's primary worry became her team's fatigue. Still, with the slow field, the game hadn't been anywhere near the war they'd had with Charleston, so she figured her players could hold up for another twenty minutes. Then Billy Staten sprained an ankle and she had to put Pie into the game.

Then Zack Willard broke his leg. He slipped in the mud while planting his foot to kick the ball, and he went down awkwardly. His leg twisted under him, and he didn't get up. The game was stopped for twenty minutes while the medics applied an inflatable cast and loaded him into an ambulance, which drove onto the field. It left deep tire ruts that quickly filled up with water.

Natty knelt on the field next to Zack, shielding him with an umbrella and holding his hand. All she could think about was whether the boy would be able to play football again. With Zack safely in the ambulance, Natty walked back to the rest of her team. Gabe came forward, his uniform soaked, his legs, socks, and high-top sneakers caked with mud. He had a nasty red welt over one eye from an errant elbow. "I'll play sweeper now, coach," he offered.

She nodded her agreement. "Good. Thanks, Gabe." The team huddled as the ref blew his whistle impatiently, anxious to get the game going again since the rain had increased in intensity. "Okay," Natty said, trying to sound positive. "Gabe's sweeper; Pie, you're in at forward; and, Sammy, you take Gabe's spot." She stopped as she watched the ambulance pull away, its red light flashing.

Before Natty could say anything else, Paul clapped his hands loudly. "Okay, now," he shouted. It was the first time some of them had ever heard the Polish boy speak. "For friend of mine, Sack, we play now like crazy motherfuckers to kick this ass of team we play, for Sack would want." He looked around the circle of faces. "Okay, my Bones?" Smiling, he reached up and rubbed the tops of the bald heads next to him. Natty and the rest of the team laughed and rubbed the tops of as many heads as they could on their way back out to the field. She was thankful. It was a far better pep talk than she could have given.

Gabe was an able replacement at sweeper, and Sammy was a solid midfielder, but there was no way to make up for Zack's dominating presence. Natty could feel the tide shifting, as Pittsburgh picked up their intensity in an effort to get the tying goal.

The Bones were hitting the wall. Four games in three days were catching up with them. At left forward, Pie was running as hard as he could, but he was barely a factor, usually sliding through the mud and out of the play as the Knights moved the ball upfield. Natty prayed for the clock to keep moving, but the talented team from Pittsburgh showed why they were undefeated. They ran hard and kept the ball in the Bones' end of the field. Natty forced herself to walk up to the scorer's table to check the time—just under five minutes. Gabe made a miraculous sliding save on a ball rolling into the open corner of the goal. The ball went over the end line for a corner kick.

The corner kick floated up in the wind and rain, then disappeared in a frantic group of jumping, kicking players in front of the goal. The crowd screamed in agony as the ball pinballed around the box, with no one getting a solid foot on it. A half dozen players lay in the mud, including Brenda, when the ball squirted free to a Knight with a clear path to the goal. He buried it in the netting, causing the entire Pittsburgh bench to race onto the field in wild celebration.

Just as the umpire placed the ball down in the center circle for the restart, the rain turned into a torrential downpour. Natty thought she could hear the sound of thunder off to the south. She knew there couldn't be much time left on the clock and was glad to see Emma take the back pass from Paul and blast the ball downfield toward the far left corner. Emma always knew the correct play on a soccer field. Then came two sharp toots from the ref's whistle, ending regulation play a minute early because of the weather.

The early whistle was okay with Natty, as was the ten-minute over-time. She was certain that her team, playing full defense for ten minutes, could kill off the overtime. Then they'd go into a five-man shoot-out, which she knew would be a pretty even match. They'd take their chances in the shoot-out. Natty huddled up her team and had started to give them the strategy when she heard her name called out.

"Say there, Miz Oakes." Natty looked up to see the referee at the scorer's table with the Pittsburgh coach and the tournament director; he waved her over. "Listen, Miz Oakes, what we're gonna do here, 'cause o' the weather, is just play the overtime and that'll be it. Not gonna go into a shoot-out."

Natty raised her eyebrows. "What if it's still tied?"

The director spoke up. "We'll just go by goal differential for the tour-nament."

"You can't do that!" Natty shouted. "They can play for a tie. That's like giving them the tournament."

"Well, that's what it's gonna be," the director declared, turning away from the group. The referee blew his whistle and jogged out to the center of the field. The thunder sounded closer, and the wind blew the rain side-ways as Natty trotted back to her team. She didn't like it, but she knew it was probably a good decision.

The Bones ran enthusiastically back out onto the field—everyone but Pie, who stood waiting for his mother's attention. Natty turned and saw him looking at her, a pained expression on his face. He needed to be at his position; the overtime was about to start. "Pie Man, what is it?" she asked, moving toward him.

"Mama," he said. "Papa's here." He turned and pointed across the field.

"What?" Natty sputtered, squinting into the rain at the spectators lining the field.

"He was here for the second half. He was yelling to me."

"Okay, go, Pie." She pushed him toward the field. The ball was already in play. Scanning the crowd, she saw Buck moving along the sideline, calling out to Pie. Then the cheering crowd grabbed her attention as the Knights moved the ball toward the Bones' goal.

The rain was pelting down, and it was hard to see the ball. Natty kept her eye on Brenda as she made a wonderful save on a hard, rolling shot. She punted the ball directly into the strong wind. Then Natty heard a shrill beeping sound from just behind her. It was Charlie's cellphone.

Reaching quickly into her equipment bag while trying to watch the action on the field, Natty finally located the cellphone. She looked down and pressed the green button. "Hey, Charlie," she said, her eyes on the field. "Where are you?"

"On the plane, coming into Charleston," he said. The noise of the rain made it difficult to hear him. "What's happening? Are you still playing?"

Natty laughed and half-yelled into the phone, "We're in overtime in the championship game. It's pouring and your phone's getting all wet."

"Don't worry about it." Charlie spoke louder. "Tell me what's happening."

Natty tried to give Charlie a shorthand version of the play-by-play. The Pie Man was scrambling frantically for the ball amid a circle of players. Natty saw Buck moving along the sideline, oblivious to the spectators behind him, staying even with Pie and calling out instructions, amplified every few seconds with a hand clap when Pie got his foot on the ball.

Then Paul kicked it farther up the sideline and Pie ran after it, encouraged by his father cheering him on for the first time in his life. Natty sobbed into the phone and the tears flowed down her cheeks. Thunder boomed overhead, as a Knights defender cleared the ball to midfield with a powerful kick that sent everyone racing in the opposite direction. Natty saw the timekeeper hold up two fingers.

"Two minutes left, Charlie. Ball's down in our end. Think we're probably out of time." A thunderclap drowned out his response.

"What, Charlie?" Natty yelled, trying to block her other ear. She saw

Buck across the field, staring at her, and they both knew it was obvious who she was talking to.

Then she heard the crowd roar and saw the ball flying from the Bones' end of the field, helped along by the swirling wind, headed at the Pittsburgh sweeper. He played it perfectly, bending slightly for a solid, low header that sent the ball in the other direction. But flashing across the ball's path, Emma took it straight in the chest at full speed. Without breaking stride, she pushed it ahead and raced straight for the sweeper. He moved to his left just as Emma moved to her left, and she was alone in the center of the field, thirty yards from the goaltender. There couldn't be more than a few seconds left in the game. Natty shouted into the phone. *"Emma's in alone, Charlie! She's all alone!"*

Five yards behind Emma, four Golden Knights raced after her as fast as they could, but Natty knew no one was going to catch her before she could get her shot off. The goalie was moving out, and the crowd roared over the deafening noise of the rain. A black umbrella flew across the field. "Hit it, Emma!" Natty cried out. "Hit it now!"

It was an easy goal for Emma, with either foot. She couldn't miss . . . from twenty yards, and then fifteen . . . but she didn't shoot. "Pull the trigger now, Em! Don't wait!" Natty yelled into the phone as she jumped up and down, moving out onto the field.

Then the goalie made his move, rushing out at Emma with the ball just a foot too far in front of her. But the ball wasn't too far in front of her—it was right where she wanted it. She waited for the instant the goalie started out and committed irrevocably to his slide. Emma took the long stride she'd been saving and tipped the ball to her right as the goalie slid. She regained possession and faced a wide-open net eight yards away.

Natty raised two arms in triumph, the phone held high in the rain, and watched in agony as Emma waited to shoot and the squad of pursuing Knights overtook her. They slid, tumbled, and dove through the mud to take Emma down, but not before she planted her left foot and, without even looking, swept the ball smoothly with the instep of her right foot on a path toward the left post.

Natty writhed in agony. "Emma! Emma, what are you doing?!" she screamed.

But Emma always knew what she was doing on a soccer field, and

Natty gasped as she followed the rolling ball. There, at the left end of the goal, all alone, was the Pie Man. She saw Buck, bent over with his hands cupped at his mouth, yelling. And she saw her son ready himself as the ball came toward him in the torn-up grassless dirt. Natty covered her mouth in fear that he'd slip or miss the ball entirely—as he often did—and she held her breath.

But Pie didn't miss it. He stepped into it perfectly, as he'd seen Emma and Paul and Zack do all season, and powered the ball into the back of the netting.

Natty screamed. "Oh, my *God*, Charlie! *Pie got a goal! We won the tournament!*" She ran out onto the field but stopped when she saw Buck holding Pie up high, hugging him against his chest with one powerful arm, the other lifted in triumph, spinning them both around in a circle.

Pie held his arms aloft, his face lit up with the biggest happy face of his life. The joy on her husband's face reminded Natty of the Buck of her youth, so long ago. She knew she was crying, but it was raining so hard, she wasn't sure. Buck put Pie down to let him run off and celebrate with his teammates. He stopped a few feet away from Natty and looked at the phone in her hand, then back at her face.

She rubbed her eyes with her right sleeve and smiled. "Thanks for coming, Buck," she said.

"I'm tryin', Nat."

She nodded. "I know you are, Buck. I know that."

CHAPTER 34

WHEN THE HEAT IN THE BUS FINALLY CAME ON, EVERYTHING started to smell like a wet dog. Some of the kids had changed out of their uniforms into dry clothes, adding their mud-caked uniforms to the mélange of towels and warm-up suits stuffed under the seats and piled in the aisle. Natty just sat in her wet warm-ups. Everything she had was damp, anyway. It was going to be a long, uncomfortable ride back to Red Bone.

It would have been worse if Buck hadn't had sixty dollars on him, which Natty borrowed for one last stop at McDonald's. At least the kids wouldn't starve. She thought about Buck driving all the way up to Charleston to watch their game. Good thing he came, too—to give her the money to feed the team and to bring Zack home from the hospital, after they put a real cast on his leg. No telling what time they'd be getting home if they'd had to wait for Zack.

Natty glanced over at Geneva, who was leaning over the steering wheel, trying to see through the pouring rain. "Let me know if you need a break, Neva," said Natty, knowing that the old woman thought she was the only one who could drive the bus. Geneva was too old to be driving, but she'd driven these roads for over forty years, and she'd get them home again tonight.

Natty twisted around to look at her team and saw the tournament trophy in its own seat across the aisle. It was mostly plastic—a silver soccer player with a ball at the end of his foot, standing on a round wooden platform held up by four foot-tall round columns. The plaque read *12th*

Annual Charleston Youth Soccer League Thanksgiving Tournament, First Place, The Bones, Red Bone, West Virginia. Natty thought that maybe there would be a good spot for it in the new library.

In the seat behind the trophy, Gabe and Emma, their bald heads almost touching, hunched together, talking quietly. Natty wondered what they were talking about. They'd said more to each other this weekend than she and Buck had all year. Behind them, the rest of the team was spread out around the bus, as the kids tried to find comfortable sleeping positions on the hard seats.

Natty closed her eyes, but she couldn't avoid thinking about the decision that lay ahead. After all the years up on the boulder, working on the dream that all little hillbilly girls dreamed, it was about to come true. But now she didn't know if she could go through with it. She was going to take the kids and meet Charlie in Bluefield. *But how could she do that now without having told Buck? And now he'd gone all the way to Charleston to watch their game and run up and down the sideline in the pouring rain, yelling out encouragement to Pie—words her son had never heard from his father. And after the game he'd picked up Pie and held him over his head and hugged him for what seemed like the first time. Pie had never been happier in his life.*

Natty chewed on her lip and felt the tears rolling down her cheeks. In the dark bus, no one could see the tears of joy she cried for her son. And for her husband. Before she could resolve her dilemma, Natty surrendered to the exhaustion of the long weekend.

CHARLIE PRESSED THE phone into the seat back in front of him and looked out the small window of the plane. Far ahead, a line of orange spread out in front of the plane. Beneath it, a blanket of dark clouds hid the rugged landscape of West Virginia. Somewhere below, Natty and the Bones were celebrating their victory and the winning goal scored by the Pie Man.

The flight attendant arrived with a large cup of ice and two small bottles of Canadian Club. Charlie lowered the tray in front of him and poured both bottles over the ice. He thought about his weekend in Vermont. It was like the old days. A traditional turkey dinner, a fire in the fireplace, the Detroit Lions on TV, and a game of Yahtzee afterward. There hadn't been enough snow for skiing, so the four of them took a long walk around the golf course, enjoying the crystal-clear air and spectacular views of Sugarbush.

He'd spent Saturday night alone on the deck with Ellen, while the kids went into Montpelier to the splendid old Capitol Theater for a movie. They bundled up and talked. Charlie filled Ellen in on the hearing in Red Bone and the China project, which he would take over not as an onsite engineer but as deputy superintendent, with complete responsibility for the second dam.

It would mean three years in China. Charlie told her that he hadn't decided what he was going to do, that he needed to think about it, although, he had to concede, it was a once-in-a-career opportunity. He left it at that, and Ellen didn't press him. She smiled in the dim yellow light that filtered onto the deck from the family room, reached over, and took his hand. "Okay, Charlie. You decide what you want to do."

Then, when all the talk about the company and China had been said, they sat quietly on the deck. The perfect opportunity had arrived to tell Ellen about Natty. But the words wouldn't come. They sat for a long time, watching the stars in the black sky over Lincoln Peak.

Was it cowardice or was it indecision, Charlie asked himself, gazing out at the thick clouds beneath the plane. He had the chance to tell Ellen, yet he let it pass. He even had the feeling that Ellen was *waiting* for him to deliver the news. But he couldn't do it.

Charlie took a large sip of his drink, closed his eyes, and leaned back in his seat. He saw Natty standing in front of the orchestra pit at the Imperial Theatre. He could smell her perfume and see her glistening lips, and he ached for her. He'd never met a woman like Natty, and he wanted to spend every waking moment with her. He hadn't changed his mind, only delayed the decision for a while. He'd meet her tonight in Bluefield, and they'd go from there.

The seat belt sign lit up. Charlie finished his drink and watched the curling snakes of water move across the small window at his shoulder. There was nothing but blackness below, down where Natty and the Bones were headed back to Red Bone.

THE BUS LURCHED with a noisy downshift of the gears. Natty struggled to go back to sleep, but after a few seconds a strange sound made her

straighten up in her seat. She twisted around to survey the interior of the
dark bus, but there was no movement anywhere. Across the aisle, Gabe
was asleep with his head on Emma's shoulder, while she was curled up
close to the window.

The bus swerved, and Natty looked out to see water running across
the road. In the yellow beams of the headlights, she could see the white
spray of foam where the water, flowing alongside the road, crashed into a
boulder or a tree. She got up and squatted next to Geneva. "Pretty bad,
Neva, huh?"

"Road's okay," said Geneva. "We'll be a little higher up soon." She
smiled nervously.

Natty stood and put a hand on her shoulder. "Okay, Neva. Let me
know if you need a break." But she knew Geneva wouldn't let her drive.
She never did.

Natty walked toward the back of the bus to inspect her sleeping championship soccer team—her *bald* soccer team, she realized again with a
start. She rolled her eyes as she thought of the reaction the parents would
have at the sight of the kids—including the two girls. She stepped gingerly
over the piles of wet clothing, gym bags, and empty McDonald's bags
and turned sideways to avoid the feet, elbows, and heads sticking out into
the aisle.

Everyone was still asleep, which was good, because the stink in the
back of the bus was wretched. She found Pie stretched out across the
second-to-last seat, his head and shoulders on Sammy Willard's lap.
Sammy was asleep against the window, his arm across Pie's chest. Pie
clutched his Yankees cap in both hands, settled comfortably on his stomach. Natty looked at her son and couldn't help smiling with pride. He had
grown so much this season. He'd made some real friends of his teammates
and had played an important role in a championship season that he
would talk about for years to come.

Natty returned to the front of the bus and slumped into her seat. With
her back propped against the window, she looked over at the tournament
trophy again and couldn't help smiling. The whole team had grown over
the season, and that made their victory even more sweet. She thought
about how much she'd changed, too. She had met Charlie and gone to New
York and become a woman and had felt—for the first time—what it was to

be loved by a man. But someone else had changed over the season, too, maybe more than anyone. Natty looked to the rear of the bus and through the back window, to see if Buck's truck might be following behind them. She wondered how long he'd have to wait at the hospital for Zack.

As she looked out the window, she realized that they were on Cold Springs Road, not far from the power plant. They were just minutes from the high school and her car, with the hastily packed bags in the trunk and the key to the apartment in Bluefield tucked into the visor. She swallowed back her nervousness.

Geneva slowed to make the sharp right-hand turn, whining in first gear to climb a short incline. The bus shuddered, and the engine raced at a higher pitch as Geneva tried to accelerate, but they didn't move. Natty instinctively reached for the pole in front of her as the rear of the bus slid to the right. Geneva gunned the engine, to no avail. She applied the brake, and the bus stood still, angled up the incline. Geneva shifted into reverse, but the rear of the bus began to slide toward the streambed thirty feet below. She tried first gear again, but it was too late. The roadway over the stream was collapsing under the weight of the bus.

Natty watched in horror as the bus slowly slid toward the stream and started to roll onto its left side. She screamed and stumbled toward the back of the bus when it rolled, losing her grip. She hit the edge of a seat, spun around, and landed hard on the side of the bus, hitting her head just above the window.

Natty wedged her forearms under her face for protection and held still, waiting for the bus to stop moving. She could feel liquid on her hands and knew that water must be coming in, but it wasn't cold, it was warm—and slippery. She tried to raise her head, to get up, but excruciating pain shot through her head, and the bus started spinning beneath her, around and around, as if they were in a whirlpool. She rested her face on her arms to wait for the bus to stop spinning.

Crashing noisily on the boulders that ripped at the sheet metal and cracked the windows, the bus careened down the streambed into the rushing water, until it came to rest on its side, thirty feet below Cold Springs Road. The headlights of the bus remained on, the left one visible a foot beneath the surface of the rushing water. Steam gushed out from under the hood like the last hot breaths of a dying dragon.

The icy water shocked Natty as it covered her mouth and nose, causing her to choke. She felt a searing pain in her head and another in her
ribs, now wedged tightly against the metal edge of a seat. She heard
someone groaning. Then she remembered what had happened and where
she was. *"Oh, my God! Oh, Jesus!"* She reached up to find the metal handle
on the top of the seat and finally pulled herself erect. The interior of the
bus was pitch black, but Natty could hear voices from the rear, where the
kids had been sleeping.

"Gilbert, you fat fuck! You're standin' on top of me."

"I lost my glasses," complained Gilbert.

"Hey, that was pretty cool," said George Jarrell.

"Man, it stinks in here," someone said, making Natty laugh. But the
movement brought a stabbing pain, and she reached up to discover blood
dripping into her left eye. Cold water swirled over her ankles.

"Okay, everyone, listen to me," Natty called out into the darkness.
"When I call your name, say *here,* and let me know if you're hurt. We'll
start with the defense: Brenda? Jason, Jimmy Hopson?" They were all okay.
"Georgie?" Okay. "Midfielders: Paul, Matt, Sammy?" Okay, okay.

"Think my arm's broken, coach," Matt Hatfield groaned painfully,
"but I'm okay."

"Hardy Steele? Pie?"

"Okay," said Hardy, then nothing.

"Pie Man!" Natty said louder. "Pie, where are you?"

"I'm okay, Mama," said Pie in a muffled voice. "But I can't find my
New York Yankees hat!" A loud clank came from the rear of the bus, and
a wave of cold air swept in.

"Hey, I got the back door open," yelled Sammy. "C'mon, let's get out
of here."

"Sammy, be careful—" Natty was distracted by a loud groan from the
front of the bus. *"Oh, Jesus,* Neva? Neva, are you hurt?" Natty moved forward, edging along the side of the bus.

She heard Gabe's voice up front. "I'm up here, Miz Oakes. Think Miz
Gunnells could be having a heart attack."

Natty saw a figure moving in one of the seats. "That you, Emma?"

Emma's voice was soft, as always. "I'm okay, Natty, just twisted around
a little. Go help Miz Gunnells."

Natty clambered over duffel bags to reach the driver's seat. Geneva moaned in pain. As Natty stood back to figure out how to get the old woman out of the bus, she noticed something silver behind the seat. It was Geneva's flashlight. Natty grabbed it and turned it on, shining it toward the rear of the bus just in time to see a bald head disappear through the emergency door. She couldn't tell who it was but guessed it must've been Emma. Sammy was standing outside, helping the others get out.

Natty turned around and saw that Gabe had pulled Geneva out of the driver's seat. She was still conscious, but her face was contorted in pain. "Think maybe my hip's broken," Geneva whispered, sucking in a painful breath of air. Natty shone the flashlight through the front windshield and saw that the torrent of water seemed to be increasing in volume.

"We can't keep her here," Natty said to Gabe. "Bus might get washed farther downstream." She turned the light toward the rear of the bus and shook her head. "Never be able to carry her through all that."

Natty pulled the lever for the folding door and was surprised when it opened directly over their heads. She looked up, perplexed as to how they would get Geneva up and through the door. But Gabe had it figured out. He told Natty to move into the stairwell, with her shoulders outside. She briefly shone the flashlight onto the steep embankment, where she could see her team picking their way uphill. She sighed with relief, knowing how lucky they'd been.

Natty laid the flashlight on top of the bus and reached down to grab Geneva under her arms as Gabe held the injured woman up to her. Then Gabe sprang up and suspended himself in the opening like a gymnast. He rocked forward slightly, pulling his legs up through the door. In an instant, he was standing over Natty, bending down through the door to take hold of Geneva and pull her out of the bus.

Natty scrambled out onto the fender, tucked the flashlight into her waistband, and helped Gabe lower Geneva over the side. Gabe jumped down and lifted Geneva after him. Natty held on to Gabe's arm to help him fight the current as he carried Geneva to shore.

Sammy and Paul came bounding down the slope when they saw Natty come out of the bus, and, with Gabe's help, they carried Geneva up to the road. It was a long, precarious hike, and when they finally reached the top, Natty felt a rush of relief and exhaustion. She was now aware of the pain that she'd ignored while escaping the bus. Gabe took off his wet sweatshirt and tucked it under Geneva's head.

Sammy's voice interrupted her thoughts. "Hey, Miz Oakes, how 'bout I run up to the power plant and get some help? Only 'bout a mile from here. They always got a security guard."

Natty looked up and down the dark road. "Okay, Sammy. We could be here all night waiting for someone to come along this road, and we need to get Neva to the hospital." She handed him the flashlight. "Here, take this so you can see where you're going. Gabe, why don't you go with him, just in case."

"Sure, Miz Oakes," said Gabe, glad to have a mission. The two boys jogged off, and Natty took off her warm-up jacket and wedged it underneath Geneva's back.

"Help will be here in a little while, Neva," Natty said, squeezing the old woman's bony hand. "You did a great job tonight. Nothing you could do about the road givin' out." Geneva scowled, angry at herself for losing control of the bus.

Natty stood up and looked down at their mortally wounded bus lying in the cold stream, and she felt a wave of sadness. The old bus had taken them to a lot of soccer games over the years. The water level had risen a little higher and now churned violently against the front grille, splashing up onto the windshield. The headlights had finally gone out.

She crossed her arms and walked a few steps up the road, trying to generate some warmth. All she had on now was a long-sleeved undershirt, which was wet, like everything else. She looked up to where the road had crumbled and thought about Sammy and Gabe. They'd be all right. They were tough, athletic kids and would probably be at the plant in a few minutes, the way they could run. *The way they could run.* Natty grimaced and squeezed her eyes shut. *The way they could run!* She felt her heart skip and was paralyzed by a shock of fear that racked her entire body.

Oh, God, no! She struggled to breathe and bolted toward the shadowy figures of her team sitting along the shoulder of the road a few yards away. Natty didn't have to count the bald heads to know. She felt the familiar stab of pain that was the memory of Annie. "*Oh, dear God, how could I do this again?*" she whimpered, looking frantically into the face of each of the kids—they were nearly indistinguishable in the dark with their bald heads.

"*Oh, my God!*" she gasped, leaping to the top of the guardrail to look down at the submerged bus. She screamed in anguish and despair. "*Em-ma!*"

Natty jumped out as far as she could, sliding, bouncing, and tumbling down the embankment, tearing her clothing and skin on rocks and roots. Halfway down, she fell and landed on her face, sliding over rocks and branches. She clawed her way over the large boulders at the edge of the stream and yelled again, "*Emma, I'm coming!*" before jumping into the icy water.

The current was swifter now, and she was immediately thrown against some boulders, smashing her left knee. She couldn't move her leg for a few seconds, so she floated with the current toward the rear of the bus, banging on the metal roof to let Emma know she was there. When she reached the back door, she pulled herself into the bus. "Emma? *Emma*, where are you?" she yelled over the noise of the water. She heard a small voice from the front.

"Here, *please*. I'm stuck," Emma managed weakly.

Natty made her way forward along the windows, holding on to the seats for balance. "Hold on, Em, I'm coming," she said, trying to sound confident. The water in the bus was now up to her knees. A few seats before she reached Emma, Natty's left foot went through a window. She could feel the glass as it cut through her warm-ups and thought she might black out from the pain. Her left knee was stuck in the smashed window, surrounded by razor-sharp shards of glass. "*Fuck. Shit. Goddamm it!*" Natty gritted her teeth to manage the pain that worsened with every moment.

"Natty?" Emma called out faintly.

She heard the girl coughing and spitting out water. *Oh, Jesus!* Natty gritted her teeth and pulled her left leg up through the broken glass. She was free. She took one tentative step with her left leg and knew right away that it was useless, so she hopped forward on her right, pulling herself along by the seat handles. Then she saw Emma's hand holding on to the top of the seat in front of her, to keep her head out of the water.

"Okay, Em, okay," said Natty, squeezing down into the seat beside her.

She thought about how long Emma had been alone in the bus, holding on for her life. She must be exhausted. Natty wrapped her arm around the girl, holding her above the water. Emma sobbed softly and Natty kissed the top of her bald head.

"My leg's stuck," cried Emma between sobs, "and it hurts. I thought I could get it out."

They sat huddled together in silence while Emma breathed deeply and relaxed her muscles. Then a familiar beeping came from over Natty's head. She and Emma both looked up. The sound was coming from Natty's athletic bag.

Stretching her arm out as far as she could, Natty was able to just reach an edge of the canvas bag and pull it down. She struggled to unzip the long bag. Charlie's phone glowed with a soft green light. "You expecting a call?" she asked. Emma giggled. Natty pressed the green button. "Charlie?"

"Hey, how's the championship, coach?"

"Charlie, listen to me. The bus crashed on Cold Springs Road and went down into the stream—"

"What? How did—"

"Charlie!" Natty yelled. "We need help! I'm on the bus with Emma. Her foot's stuck, and the bus is filling up with water. We're right near the turnoff to the power plant."

"Okay, the pilot's calling the plant now, and we'll call the state police. I'm on the helicopter. We're almost to Red Bone."

"Hurry, Charlie, I gotta go." Natty put the phone back into the bag and tossed it up over the seat. She could feel the cold water swirling around them and knew that she needed to get busy. "Hold on again for a minute, Em. I'm going to see if I can get your leg free."

Emma reached up and grasped the seat handle once again. Natty squeezed out from behind her, crawling along the sidewall to the seat in front of Emma. She took a deep breath and plunged into the water, running her hands along Emma's leg. She couldn't see anything in the dark water, but she could tell that it was hopeless. Emma's leg was wedged tightly into the small space.

Natty crawled back to Emma, who released her grip on the handle and fell back against Natty, exhausted. The water was now up to Emma's neck. "All right, Em, your leg's locked in there, but help should be coming real soon. Sammy and Gabe ran up to the power plant. We just gotta sit tight and wait, okay?" Emma nodded. Natty could feel the girl's body shiver. She pressed her cheek against Emma's head and exhaled warm breaths onto her skin. "We'll be okay, Em," Natty whispered.

Natty closed her eyes for a few moments, holding Emma tight. *Be calm,* Natty told herself. Then Emma coughed and struggled to pull herself upright. The water was rising quickly. Natty pushed forward and raised Emma's mouth another inch above the water, but she could see that it would be only a matter of minutes before Emma would be under. "Emma, pull yourself up, hard. I gotta find something for you to breathe through!"

Natty moved as quickly as she could, trying not to scream from the excruciating pain. She stood on her right leg and tried to think where she might find something for Emma to breathe through. Then she saw her athletic bag but found nothing in it that would work.

She stuffed the bag down behind Emma to help support her and hopped frantically toward the back of the bus. *Jesus, give me a ballpoint pen, or a straw, or something! A McDonald's straw! Shit, they should be all over the place.* Natty plunged under the water and swept her hands along the bus, searching for one of the discarded cups. But she came up for air, gasping and empty-handed, and pushed herself back toward Emma.

Emma's right arm was still locked on the seat handle, but her face was underwater. Natty lunged for her. She pinched Emma's nose shut with her right hand and covered the girl's mouth with her own, exhaling while the girl desperately sucked in Natty's air. Natty came up for another lungful of air, then pressed her lips tightly against Emma's again. She repeated the process three more times.

Natty had to come up for air and cough out some water she'd inhaled. She breathed in as deeply as she could but couldn't catch her breath. She felt Emma's hand pulling at her. Just as she prepared to plunge back into the water, a powerful beam of light entered the bus through the windows overhead, and she heard the roar of a helicopter.

The beam of light illuminated Emma's face underwater—she looked eerily pale. Natty gave Emma all of her air and came up panting. She struggled for breath, coughing, and then, out of the corner of her eye, she saw it. To her left, shining in the light of the helicopter's spotlight, was the tournament trophy. Most of it was underwater, but Natty knew it was the answer to her prayers.

She pulled the trophy from the water, holding on to one of the long plastic tubes that connected its base to the platform. She smashed the platform against the metal edge of a seat, sending the little soccer player flying. One of the plastic tubes she was after cracked open to reveal a metal rod. She grasped the underside of the base with her fingers and felt the tightly bolted nut and washer. *Oh, my God! Don't do this to me!* She tried to turn the small nut with her wet fingers, but it wouldn't move. Frantic, she smashed the trophy again and felt a little give in the plastic supports. Then she heard Emma's hand splashing the water again.

Natty dropped the trophy and lunged for Emma. She gave her air three more times, but it didn't seem to help much. Emma wasn't getting enough air from her. Natty reached down for the trophy as the light from the helicopter moved toward the back of the bus, forcing Natty to work in the dark. She pulled and twisted the trophy as violently as she could, then she felt Emma's hand grabbing her leg. But Natty was out of breath from her exertion, and when she went back down to Emma, there was no air left in her lungs.

Natty exploded out of the water, gasping for air and sobbing in despair. Over and over she smashed the trophy as hard as she could, until she felt it crack. Then she had one of the foot-long plastic tubes in her hand. She dove back toward Emma and pushed the tube between her lips. Emma coughed up through the tube. *"C'mon, Em,"* she pleaded, tears filling her eyes. *"You can do it, Em. Breathe, Emma, breathe!"*

Finally, Emma's coughing became less violent, and Natty could feel the girl's body expand as her lungs filled with air. With a deafening roar, another light moved over them, illuminating the entire bus. Natty looked up and could see another helicopter—bigger and louder than the first one, with two huge floodlights on its underside. Natty squeezed Emma's hand under the water and smiled down at her. Emma was several inches underwater now, but the end of the tube was far above the surface, and help was only minutes away.

Natty pulled herself up, trying to get a view of the road, now awash in red and blue flashing lights. Flashlights were bouncing down the embankment, and she tickled the back of Emma's head to let her know it was almost over. But, out of the corner of her eye, she saw something moving outside.

She stared through the right half of the windshield that was still above water, convinced it was a bad joke her oxygen-deprived mind was playing on her. She blinked her eyes, but it was still there, fifty yards away, higher than the top of the bus—a wall of black water, rolling toward them. Natty closed her eyes and put her cheek against Emma's forehead.

The wave, with its deadly cargo of stones, sand, and tree limbs, smashed through the windshield, filling the bus with muddy, boiling water. It picked up the bus and sent it screeching and banging over the rocks and careening down a ten-foot waterfall to deeper, slower water, where it rolled onto its top. It continued downstream another twenty yards until it hit the submerged trunk of a white oak and came to a stop, its tires just breaking the surface of the water like the paws of a drowned possum. The current slowly turned the bus sideways against the stream, and then it was still.

THROUGH THE RAIN, Buck could see the flashing blue lights far ahead. In his rearview mirror, he saw more flashing lights and knew something had happened to the bus. He pressed the accelerator to the floor. Then he saw the helicopters hovering over the stream. Buck parked across the road, left the engine running and the heater on for Zack, and jumped over the guardrail.

NATTY OPENED HER eyes, but she couldn't see anything and she couldn't tell which way was up. She floated slowly through the water, desperate for air, her lungs ready to explode. Then there was light from outside, dim at first, coming through the windows below her, and she could now see her bubbles rising to her left. She pushed off with her right leg and followed a bubble up toward the floor of the bus, overhead. Natty reached out and found the edge of something hard. She pulled herself up and pressed her face, her nose and mouth, against the hard rubber matting on the floor of the bus, tasting the grit but finding no air.

Natty floated down through the murky water and felt warm again. She smiled and even had to giggle, letting out small bubbles, when she saw her, finally, after so many years in her dreams. Annie reached down to Natty, her small fingers curved and still. Her chin was up and her mouth open slightly. She looked so relaxed and content, her dark eyes opened wide and unmoving, as Natty came closer, touching her hands, then kissing her softly on the forehead. Natty closed her eyes. *Oh, Annie, I've missed you so much.* Suddenly Natty was drifting away from her sister, down through the dark water, unable to stop herself. She reached out for Annie's hands, but she was gone.

Buck pulled natty through the door and thrust her lifeless body up to the waiting hands of the paramedics on top of the bus. They used Buck as an operating table, with him down on all fours in the water flowing over the bus. The medics pushed hard on Natty's back, then turned her over and pumped her chest while they forced oxygen into her lungs. Finally, she coughed, then coughed again, and the medics flipped her over. She gagged and vomited a stomachful of brown water onto the back of Buck's neck.

Two hours later, after all the children had been taken away, and the police cars and the TV truck had left, when the helicopters had gone and one ambulance and a fire truck remained, two firemen in scuba gear returned to the bus with an acetylene torch, cut away the iron stanchions of the seat, and removed Emma Lowe's body.

CHAPTER 35

Hank was seated on the bench in front of the store, waiting, when Charlie came out. The old man wore his brown suit and faded white shirt, the only suit Charlie had seen him wear. They presented quite a contrast, with Charlie in his expensive Joseph Abboud suit, but Charlie didn't care, and neither would Hank. They'd each dressed as finely as they could, to express as much respect as possible on a day when words would be difficult to come by.

They walked slowly up Main Street without talking. A cold autumn wind ruffled Charlie's hair and made his eyes water. Hank's white locks were pulled back into a tight ponytail, tied with a black ribbon that fluttered in the breeze. They walked past the Spur, the gin mill still dark at ten in the morning, and the United Mine Workers of America storefront.

They walked past Depot Street, its pavement cracked and crumbling, still laced with the brown weeds of summer, now waiting for the frost to finish them off. Charlie stopped and looked uphill toward the rusting hulk of the old coal tipple at the base of Red Bone Mountain. He thought about the thousands of faceless immigrants who had trudged up the hill for so many years to work in the mine and the poor black men like Woody and Mr. Jacks who had worked their whole lives in the mines and ended with nothing but broken bodies and tired minds.

Hank asked, "Whatcha thinkin', Burden?"

Charlie turned to Hank. "Thinking that Alice DeWitt was right: There *is* a lot of heartache in these mountains."

Hank was still for a second, then resumed walking up Main Street. "Had our share," he said softly.

Past Depot Street was the old-homes section of Main Street—the once-grand three-story homes built in the thirties for the mining-company managers, merchants, and professionals of the day. Today they were run-down relics, most in need of paint and new roofs, some needing quite a bit more. The oaks and sugar maples in the front yards were bigger now than when the children of the mine managers played under them, their old roots pushing up through the weeds.

At the next corner, Sammy Willard was seated on the front steps of one of the better-kept homes. He wore a suit jacket several sizes too small.

"Want to walk up with us?" asked Hank.

"Naw, gotta wait for Grandma and Zack. She makin' some pants for Zack to fit over his cast."

Hank nodded without comment, turned to his right, and started up Cornelia Street, Charlie at his side. The street went steeply uphill, as did all the streets on this side of town, and they walked slowly. Up ahead, a station wagon was parked in front of a white house, and a man carried two floral displays up the short walk. A small sign next to the door identified the building as a funeral home.

Charlie was surprised there wasn't a long line of people waiting at the door. A few cars were parked in the small lot next to the building. He thought about the traffic jam and the crowds of mourners that would attend the wake of a popular young athlete in Mamaroneck. But Red Bone was a small town in a sparsely populated county of Appalachia, so there was no waiting line for Emma Lowe.

Throughout the wake, the Lowes remained seated in the front row. Gus held his arm around Janice, who remained hunched over in anguish. Zack stood on his crutches next to Sammy, who knelt at their teammate's coffin until Mabel nodded that they could move away. Neither boy cried; they just looked scared. The black wig and Emma's sunken cheeks made her look much older than the girl they knew.

Hank sat down next to Ada, taking her hand while Charlie took a seat by himself in a middle row. He recognized most of the people filing past the coffin—people from the restaurant, members of the Red Bone Baptist Church Social Club, Emma's teammates.

Sally Oakes entered, and a few minutes later Bud and Alice DeWitt walked up the aisle, followed by Sarah DeWitt and Petey. Sarah noticed Charlie and came to sit next to him. She put her hand on his and spoke softly. "Natty's been taken to the hospital in Charleston for an operation on her leg. It's very serious."

Her eyes filled as she stopped to take a breath, and Charlie squeezed her hand. "She hasn't hardly said anything since the accident. She can't remember it . . . the accident . . . and she hasn't cried." Sarah seemed to drift off for a moment before speaking again. "Doctor says it's a . . . *fugue* state or something." She smiled briefly and patted Charlie's hand.

"Thank you," he said, although he'd already gotten a more extensive report from the hospital.

The funeral was in the afternoon—Janice Lowe insisted on getting it all done in one day, and the cemetery was in back of the funeral parlor— followed by a reception at Eve's Restaurant. About twenty people came, though there was enough food for twice that many. At one end of the counter, Eve had set up a bar, where most of the party congregated. Charlie had a Canadian Club and tried his best to comfort the Lowes, but there was too much pain in everyone's eyes for the usual well-meaning small talk.

He saw the glow of Eve's cigarette on the porch and joined her outside. They stood looking out at the dimly lit street, ignoring the cold wind. Charlie broke the silence. "I'd like to pay for this, Eve," he said, "for the reception. The Lowes don't need, you know . . ."

Eve flicked a half-smoked cigarette into the street and turned to Charlie. She put her palms on his chest and smoothed out his jacket. "Charlie," she said softly, "put away your checkbook. You're one of us now." He pulled her close and wrapped his arms around her, and they both cried their final tears for Emma.

CHARLIE WAITED THREE days, then drove to Charleston. The hospital was an ancient brownstone building in an old section of town. After circling through the only public lot for twenty minutes, he finally found a spot. He walked for what seemed like miles, through twisting, ramped, crowded corridors, before he found the psychiatric ward.

Natty's doctor was a gray-haired woman in her sixties, who studied Natty's file carefully before looking up at Charlie. "Natty can't remember anything from the last month or so, as best we can pin it down. *Traumatic amnesia.* She couldn't deal with what happened, so her brain blocks it all out and takes a little extra for good measure. Sometimes there's something deep in the subconscious that triggers it. Actually, it's a pretty common occurrence in traumatic situations. She doesn't remember anything about the accident. She also doesn't seem to remember anything about her soccer team."

The doctor stood up and closed the file. "It's a temporary condition, in most cases," she said, coming around the desk. "When she gets home, in familiar surroundings, she'll remember more and more. Come on, I'll take you to her. Try not to bring up recent events. We need to let her heal at her own pace." She walked Charlie down the hall toward Natty's room. They stopped outside the door and the doctor turned to Charlie. "Tell me, Mr. Burden, do you know her husband, Buck?"

"Yes, I've met him. Why?"

"Oh, I was just wondering why he hasn't been in to see her."

Charlie raised his eyebrows. "He hasn't visited her?"

"Not since the first day. He came up with her that day for the operation on her knee. But not since then."

"He's got some of his own issues," said Charlie.

"His presence could help her a lot." The doctor nodded toward the room. "On the right next to the window."

The room was cool and dark, illuminated only by the late-afternoon light coming through two large windows. Natty was sitting up with her head against the pillow, staring out the window. Her left leg, in a full cast, was elevated by wires suspended from a frame over the bed. A bandage covered her left eyebrow. Charlie watched her stare out the window, lost in thought. He cleared his throat, and she turned toward him.

"Hey, Mr. Burden," she said, instinctively feeling for the top of her robe. "This's a surprise. You shouldn'ta come all the way up here just to visit me." Charlie moved to a metal chair between the bed and the window. From there, in the light from the window, he could see bruises and abrasions on her face and hands. Her left cheek was swollen, and the skin under her eye was purple. Natty looked as if she'd been in a fight for her life.

"How are you feeling?" he asked.

Natty smiled without answering at first. It seemed to take more time to process the words now. "Won't be goin' runnin' for a while," she said, knocking her cast with her knuckle. "Depends on how the operation comes out. Knee was pretty messed up. Worst is the broken ribs, though. Hurts every time I breathe." Then she smiled again and pointed toward several flower arrangements on a table next to the curtain. "Thanks for the flowers. Yours is the biggest one."

Charlie glanced at the flowers without seeing them. "You're welcome."

"How's your power plant coming along?"

"Good. Ahead of schedule and under budget," he said, the standard answer.

"That's great," she replied. "So, you'll be going to China pretty soon, right?"

"China?"

"Like you told me. Said you'd be going to China soon."

Charlie watched Natty's face carefully. "Yes, that's right. I'll be leaving for China in another month or so."

A troubled look came over her face. "Think you'll be able to do anything about Redemption Mountain before you leave? Mama was in, and she didn't say nothin', but I could tell she's worried about Grandpa losin' the farm."

Charlie studied her face, still so incapable of concealment or duplicity. Even with the cuts and bruises and the thick bandage, it was the most beautiful face he'd ever seen.

"Mr. Burden?"

Her voice got his attention again. "Oh, no, you don't have to worry about the farm. It's all taken care of."

Natty looked surprised. "Wow, that's good news. Thank you, Mr. Burden."

"Thought we'd gotten over that *Mr. Burden* stuff."

Natty smiled and looked out the window again. After a few moments, she turned back to Charlie. "Sorry I threw up on your sneaker that day."

"You remember that?"

"'Course I do. Probably said some stuff we shouldn't've, huh, Charlie?"

"Maybe," he said, trying to make it easier for her.

"Then, that night we went over and saw Woody and Mr. Jacks," Natty said, "that was a good time. I can't wait to see them again. I miss those old boys. They may be the two best friends I got in the world." She raised her eyebrows to Charlie. "They okay, Charlie? You seen 'em around?"

Charlie's heart thumped. "Um, I haven't seen them in a while, Natty, so . . ."

"Charlie, you know I'm having trouble remembering stuff—mind's kinda fuzzy from an accident, they said." He nodded. "And Eve and Mabel come up the other day, and I was wondering, you know, what happened to my hair." She reached up and twisted a short lock. "Mabel told me all about the trip to New York, and gettin' my hair done at your friend's place, and going to the show and everything." Natty rolled her eyes. "God, what was I thinkin' about, goin' off to New York City for a weekend, leavin' the kids and Buck?!"

"It was a real nice weekend," said Charlie, his face lighting up. "We went for a run in the morning through Times Square and took a walk through Rockefeller Center. About the nicest run I ever had."

"And you and I went out for drinks, Mabel said, and ran into her and Ada and Janice Lowe and made them have dinner with us."

"The ladies enjoyed it. We all had a great time."

Natty was quiet for a few seconds, squinting her eyes in concentration as she composed her thoughts.

"What is it, Natty?" he asked.

"Charlie, since I can't remember nothin', I need you to tell me." She looked into his eyes. "I need to know if, you know, if anything happened between us in New York. If we—"

"Nothing happened, Nat. We had a nice dinner and I walked you back to your hotel. We said good night on the sidewalk. That was it." Charlie's heart beat faster as he recalled their meeting later, in the rain on Park Avenue, when he ached for her so desperately and wanted her to come inside and stay with him forever. Then he'd watched her leave in the taxi. It wouldn't do her any good to hear that part of the story. "It was a nice weekend, but nothing happened between us, Nat."

She nodded slowly and studied her hands in her lap. "Well, that sucks, huh, Charlie?" she said, looking up at him with a sparkle in her eye. They both laughed. "No, that's good, Charlie," she said softly. "That's good."

They talked about Pie for a while and how well he was doing in school. Natty didn't say anything about the soccer team, and Charlie didn't, either. There was a long silence, then their eyes met, but there was nothing left to talk about. Charlie looked at his watch.

"I need to get back down to Red Bone." He stood up next to the bed and Natty held her hand out to him.

"Thanks for everything. For helping Pie, and for Redemption Mountain, and, well, for everything you done for us."

Charlie took her hand and squeezed it gently. "Take care of yourself, Mrs. Oakes." He didn't know what else to say. "Take care of your family."

"I will," she said. "We'll be okay. Goodbye, Mr. Burden."

ON THE ROAD back to Red Bone, Charlie called Lucien's office on his cellphone. It was six o'clock, still early for Lucien to have called it a day.

"Hello, Charlie," Lucien said. "How is everything down there?"

"Been a hard week, Lucien."

"I can imagine," said Lucien, "a real tragedy." Neither man spoke for several seconds.

"Lucien, I've decided to take the China job."

"You're sure, Charlie?"

"I'm sure. It's time to go."

"Okay, Charlie. I think that's best for everyone. I'm glad you made that decision. I've got someone in mind for the Red Bone project. I'll send him down next week, and you can get him started. Then I'll make the arrangements for China."

"Thanks, Lucien. Like to be out of here in a few weeks."

"I can understand that, Charlie. I'll take care of everything."

"I'll be in Aspen for Christmas, with Ellen and the kids. Then, mid-January, I'll be ready to go to China."

"Sounds perfect, Charlie. I'll take care of it."

"Thanks, Lucien. See you soon, my friend."

THE YELLOW SCHOOL bus looked tiny parked next to the giant road grader in the equipment lot. Charlie had agreed to store it there, after the police and the insurance investigators completed their work on it. Yellow police evidence tape made an *X* over the space where the folding door had been. Charlie pulled the tape off and stepped up into the bus. It was damp and dirty inside. The windshield was gone, and most of the windows were smashed or missing. The key was still in the ignition.

Charlie tried to imagine what it had been like when the bus was upside down in the raging stream. He wasn't looking for anything specific, but he felt a need to see the inside of the bus before the salvage company towed it away. The kids' athletics bags and anything else of discernible value had already been removed, but the bus still looked like the inside of a dumpster. A thin layer of dirt coated the ceiling, walls, and seats, and two inches of mud, sand, and stones covered the floor, mixed in with a good amount of trash, dirty towels, and some unidentifiable pieces of clothing.

Charlie stepped on something and reached down to dig it out of the mud. It was a round wooden disc weighing several pounds. Charlie scraped away some of the dirt and saw the engraved brass plate: *12th Annual Charleston Youth Soccer League Thanksgiving Tournament, First Place, The Bones, Red Bone, West Virginia.*

He ran his thumb over the inscription and wondered if it wouldn't be better if he left the remains of the trophy on the bus. *No, it was an accomplishment for all of the kids, and someday they'll wish they had this memorial to their friend.* He held the trophy against his side and continued toward the back of the bus.

Something under one of the rear seats caught Charlie's eye—a small but unmistakable swatch of an embroidered logo. Charlie dug his fingers into the hardened mud and pulled out Pie's baseball cap. Charlie smiled, thinking how thrilled his little pal would be to get it back. Then he let out a deep sigh as he realized how soon he'd be leaving West Virginia for good. He quickly left the bus and headed back to the office. He had a lot of work to do to get the power plant ready for the next big mule.

At four o'clock, Charlie called it quits and drove to his apartment. He'd missed his run for several days, and he needed a good, long workout. He pulled on a gray sweatshirt and went out to the porch. The sun was disappearing fast, but he calculated that he'd have just enough light to make it to the end of the mountain trail. He could run the logging road and South County Road back up to Old Red Bone in the dark without a problem.

Charlie set out at a fast pace to beat the failing light. At the halfway point, he looked up to Natty's boulder. He had an urge to climb up to it, but it was getting dark, and what was the point of it now? He wondered if Natty would ever make it up to her special place again. Charlie began to run even harder, forcing himself to think about something else. He was glad now that he had only a short time left in Red Bone. *The sooner he left West Virginia, the sooner he could start to forget her.*

Charlie was winded and windblown by the time he reached the protection of the dense pines near the top of Oakes Hollow. He slowed to a jog and then to a walk over the soft covering of pine needles. The only sound in the woods was his breath. He stopped at the spot where Natty and he had their talk after she showed him the boulder. This would be his last visit to these woods. He closed his eyes and pictured Natty sitting on the stump.

Then Charlie's heart froze as he heard a metallic click, menacing and deadly and unmistakably not of the woods or of nature but man-made and just a few yards away. He peered into the shadows in front of him, from where the sound came. He blinked his eyes to see, trying not to move. A white speck flashed nearby, and a shape emerged—the eye, a head, hand, and forearm—followed by the dull glint of a crossbow and the silver tip of an arrow aimed at his face.

"Been waitin' for you, Burden." Buck's voice was angry and raw, barely louder than a whisper. He moved slowly out of the trees, the arrow trained on Charlie's face. "Shame how much you look like a doe, hoppin' through the woods in that sweat suit." Charlie could see Buck's face pressed against the bow's stock. "This distance, put one right through your left eye, arrow'd go halfway out the back o' your head."

Charlie backed away slowly. "Buck, this is stupid."

"Thought I told you to stay away from my wife."

"I haven't done anything with your wife, Buck," Charlie said, taking small steps backward toward the trail. Buck stopped, and Charlie thought he was getting ready to let the arrow fly. "Buck, don't do this. This is a mistake you'll—"

"This a mistake, too?" Buck snarled, tossing something shiny into the pine needles at Charlie's feet. He looked down and recognized the yellow plastic lantern at the end of the keys to the condo in Bluefield. Buck must've found them in Natty's car, along with the clothes she'd packed. "You know what them keys are, don't you, Burden? You was stealin' my wife, Burden. Stealin' my family."

Charlie looked at the key chain and thought about Natty and how close they'd come to a new life together. Now it was over—because of a tragic accident and the death of a young girl—and Natty was left with Buck. His jaw tightened with anger, and he took a step toward Buck.

"You don't have a family, Buck, 'cause you've never been a father. And you don't have a wife, 'cause you've never been a husband. All you've ever been is a drunken bully who beats his wife and ignores his kids, and Natty was sick of it. Nobody was stealing her." Charlie lowered his voice. "Natty'd been in love with you since the fourth grade. She tried as hard as she knew how, but after twelve years she'd had enough." Charlie shook his head. "She was tired of being alone, Buck. Tired of being unloved." He reached down and picked up the key chain. "You're not going to shoot me, Buck, 'cause you're a coward. Always have been. You've been afraid to be a husband, afraid to be a father. You've been afraid to admit that you're not a high school football star anymore. Afraid to become a man and do the things that men do." Charlie turned his back to Buck and walked toward the trail. Ten yards away, he heard the bow gun clatter to the ground.

"Burden, help me." Buck sounded as if he was crying. "I don't want to lose my wife. I don't want to lose my kids."

Charlie turned around. "Buck, don't you get it?" he nearly shouted. "Natty can't remember anything. She can't remember that she finally got up the courage to leave you. So you got a second chance you don't deserve."

"But I been tryin', Burden, since before the accident. Since I started workin'. I been tryin'," Buck pleaded.

Charlie sighed. "I know you have, Buck," he said.

"I ain't some wife-beatin' drunk. I'm just . . . Things never turned out like I thought they would. I never wanted to get married and have the kid . . . and then, ah, *fuck,* everything kept getting' worse all the time. . . ."

"Buck, it's time to be a man," said Charlie. "You want your family? Then be a father. You want your wife?" Charlie hesitated. "Then be a husband."

"What do I need to do, Burden? What should I do?"

Charlie took a few steps closer to Buck. "Tomorrow morning, you take Pie and Cat up to the hospital, and you walk into Natty's room holding their hands, and you make sure Natty *sees you* holding their hands. Then you tell Natty you love her and that you've always loved her, since that day you came back from Morgantown. You put that big Red Bone High football ring on her finger 'til you find something better, and you tell her that marrying her was the best day of your life. And that someday you'll buy her a little house with a white picket fence on a nice little street."

Charlie reached up and wiped the tears from his cheeks. "Then you'll be okay for a while, and you'll get your chance to keep your family. Afterward, it'll be up to you what happens next."

Buck was silent for several seconds, to make sure Charlie was finished speaking. Then he cleared his throat. "Okay, Burden. I'll do that. Tomorrow, first thing. I'll take the kids up there."

Charlie replied wearily, "Do it just like I said."

"Yeah, I will." Buck reached down and picked up the bow gun. "Sorry if I scared you. Had the safety on all the time."

Charlie turned to leave, but after a few steps he stopped. "Hey, Buck?"

"Yeah?"

"The tree cutting's about done out there."

"Yeah, I already got laid off."

"I got a job for you at the power plant. Permanent job, if you want it."

"'Course I do," said Buck, coming closer. "That's all I need."

"One thing, though: You can't drink anymore. I don't mean getting drunk. I mean you gotta give it all up—booze, beer, everything. Completely on the wagon."

"I can do that," said Buck firmly. "I ain't an alcoholic. I just drink 'cause . . . 'cause there's nothin' else."

"Well, now you got something else, right, Buck?"

"Yeah, Burden," he said quietly. "I got somethin' else now."

"Okay," said Charlie. "Come and see me next week at the plant." He turned and started to walk along the trail again.

"I will, next week," said Buck. "Hey, Burden, thanks," he called into the darkness, but Charlie was gone.

CHAPTER 36

CHARLIE WEDGED HIS LAPTOP CASE INTO THE OVERSTUFFED trunk of the Lexus and tossed his overcoat on top. He unzipped a pocket and withdrew a large brown envelope and a burlap sack before closing the trunk. Hank stood waiting for him at the corner. Charlie caught up with him, and the two men walked down the hill toward the new library. Hank looked up at the gray sky. "Supposed to get some snow later on. Hope it don't mess up your trip," he said.

"Should be okay," said Charlie. "Not supposed to come 'til tonight. Should be in New York by then." The library door was unlocked. The smell of fresh paint greeted them, along with the sound of someone moving a ladder on the second floor. Just inside were a half dozen computer boxes from Dell. "You'll have to find some high school kid to set these up," said Charlie. "It's beyond my capabilities."

"Mine, too." Hank laughed.

They sat at a long central table in the main room, surrounded by stacks of boxes from the Westchester Library Association. Charlie emptied the contents of the brown envelope on the table. There were three sets of shiny silver keys, which he passed over to Hank. Charlie thumbed briefly through two sets of legal documents. "This is to establish the Red Bone Children's Library Trust, with you as the trustee. Need to sign it in a few places and send it back to the lawyers. Keep a copy for yourself."

Hank grunted with a brief nod as he looked over the papers.

Charlie opened another envelope and took out a check. It was from

OntAmex Energy, made out to the trust. He pushed it over to Hank. "This'll keep you going for a while," said Charlie.

Hank viewed it through the lower portion of his bifocals. "Lot of money," Hank grumbled.

"Invest it in something safe; should last a few years."

Hank nodded again, continuing to stare at the check.

"One thing you'll have to do," said Charlie, "is hire a part-time librarian—fifteen, twenty hours a week. Someone who really cares about the kids."

Hank cleared his throat. "Got someone in mind. Soon as she's ready."

Charlie reached into the burlap sack and pulled out the remains of the Charleston tournament trophy. "See what you can do with this," he said, absently rubbing the small brass plate with his thumb. "The kids should be able to take pride in it." Hank took the heavy wooden disc without comment. Charlie picked up another envelope that Buck had given him. He handed the envelope to Hank without opening it. "Nice picture of the team from the soccer tournament." He didn't need to see it again, the image of a happy Natty Oakes, her arms around Emma and Brenda, laughing and proud, like the rest of the team around them.

They walked around the interior of the library, and Charlie pointed out the sprinkler and lighting controls in the basement. Charlie took a final look around the upper floor. He stood at the windows, looking down at the new soccer field, the gazebo, and the baseball fields beyond. With the beautiful green turf and landscaping, the project had turned out even better than Charlie had envisioned.

Hank wanted to spend some time in the library, so they said their goodbyes in the parking lot. Charlie said, "Left a check for you in the cribbage box."

Hank shook his head. "No need for that."

"Did better than I thought," said Charlie. "Better than Alva Paine."

"Had twenty-one years to work on him," said Hank, as he tried to smile. He turned to Charlie with his hand extended. "Better get going, Burden. You got a long drive ahead."

"Thanks, Hank. Thanks for everything."

"Burden," Hank looked up into Charlie's eyes, "you made a difference here. You made this a better place than it was when you came, and ain't many men can say that."

"I had a good teacher." Charlie gazed down over the soccer field and squinted with the pain of his thoughts. "Keep thinking, Hank, that maybe if I hadn't come here—"

"Can't blame yourself for any o' what happened," Hank said firmly. "Act of God, if ever was one. You did a lot of good things for a lot of people here."

Charlie looked back at Hank. "I just wish it didn't hurt so much." He stepped forward and the two men hugged. "Time to go," said Charlie, slapping Hank's back lightly. He trudged up the hill to Main Street for the last time. When he drove past the library, Hank was nowhere to be seen. On the seat next to him was Pie's Yankees cap. One more stop to make.

No one answered his rap on the metal door, and the inside of the trailer was dark. Charlie turned and looked up the hill. White smoke wafted from the chimney of the house, and two dogs observed him from under the porch. He thought about just hanging the Yankees cap on the door handle, but he wanted to see Pie before he left. Charlie hadn't seen him since he told him he was going to China. It was hard to tell if Pie was upset over the news. He'd become more reserved since the accident and, it seemed to Charlie, a little older, a little more mature. The accident had changed a lot of people.

A door slammed at the house across the road. Charlie glanced up to see two young children clambering onto pint-size plastic vehicles. Then Natty's sister-in-law Sally appeared in the front yard. She lit a cigarette and pulled a bulky sweater around her shoulders. At the sound of Charlie's steps, Sally squinted over at him.

Charlie stopped about twenty feet away, as one of the old coonhounds loped up and rubbed against him. He reached down and scratched the dog behind the ears. "What's his name?" he asked.

Sally stared at him blankly, then down at the dog, as if it were the first time she'd ever seen it. She took a long drag on her cigarette. "Hell, we got a hard enough time namin' the kids around here." With no makeup and her hair pulled back, Sally seemed older. She was beginning to develop the hard scowl and defeated look of the older women of McDowell County.

"I was looking for Pie," Charlie said, holding out the Yankees cap. "Wanted to give him his hat back and say goodbye."

Sally took the cigarette from her lips to speak. "Heard you were leavin'," she said.

"Job's done here. I'm on my way out."

"Pie ain't here. He's gone huntin' with his father. Buck and him are like best buddies now."

Charlie smiled. "That's good," he said.

"They'll be goin' up to see Nat tomorrow. They go up a lot," said Sally, watching Charlie closely.

"How's she doing?" he asked, though he'd spoken to Natty's doctor the previous day.

"Comin' home 'nother week or so. Still can't remember nothin' 'bout the accident or the soccer team. Don't remember Emma." Sally threw the cigarette butt down and ground it into the dirt with her shoe. "Ain't the way it was all supposed to . . ." She shook her head and frowned.

Large, lazy snowflakes began to fall. Charlie held his face up to the gray sky, inhaling the cold winter air of the mountains. "Looks like I better get going," he said. He held the Yankees hat out to Sally. "Would you give this to Pie and tell him . . . just tell him . . . thanks for being my best friend in West Virginia."

Sally took the cap without looking at it. "Sure, I'll tell him that."

Charlie backed the Lexus out onto the gravel road and pointed it down the hill. Sally stood next to the car. He lowered the window and looked up at her quizzically.

"Just wanted to tell you that Nat and Buck, they're doin' real good, like a couple of newlyweds." Charlie stared at her without comment. "So," she continued, "maybe some good come out of it all."

Charlie nodded. He raised the window and drove slowly down the hill. He wasn't sure what Sally meant by *it all*, but it didn't matter. None of it mattered anymore. He was leaving, and all these people in Red Bone would get along like they always had, and pretty soon they'd forget he was ever there. Just another outsider who'd come for the coal. *The way it's always been, for the last hundred years.*

EPILOGUE

Spring arrived earlier in Red Bone, West Virginia, than it did in central China, or even Mamaroneck. The grass of the soccer field was soft and thick underfoot and, with a few more weeks of sunlight, would explode with growth. Ellen's heels sank into the soft turf, causing her to lean on Charlie's arm to keep her balance. Up ahead, a publicist from Charleston, carrying large plastic scissors, and a photographer hefting several bags of equipment walked quickly to keep up with the OntAmex representative, who'd flown in for the event.

Charlie knew that the OntAmex man had drawn the short straw to fly down for the library dedication and couldn't wait to get it over with. The black helicopter hissed on the baseball field behind them, ready for a speedy departure. Charlie spied Eve Brewster, Mabel Willard, and several others from the Red Bone Baptist Church Social Club at the top of the stairway up to the library. Ada, Gus, and Janice Lowe would be there, too. Charlie took a deep breath. Four months in China hadn't been long enough.

The photographer and the publicist assembled everyone for the ribbon cutting. Zack and Sammy Willard, looking uncomfortable in suit jackets that were growing smaller by the minute, held each end of the wide red ribbon. Behind them, a plaque on the library wall displayed a reasonably good likeness of Emma holding a soccer ball, next to the inscription EMMA C. LOWE MEMORIAL LIBRARY.

Charlie, Ellen, and Hank stood at the back of the small crowd. Hank frowned and emitted a low growl, unhappy with the people chosen for the picture. Charlie didn't care. The OntAmex man delivered a sixty-second speech, and everyone made their way inside for sparkling cider and doughnuts. Hank took Ellen on a tour of the new library, stocked with the books she'd arranged to have donated by the Westchester Library Association. The new superintendent of the power plant walked over to Charlie.

"How's the new big mule?" Charlie asked. The engineer laughed. They talked for several minutes about the progress of the construction and the typical union problems that never seemed to go away. A brief pause allowed Charlie to change the subject. "So how's Buck Oakes doing? Job going okay for him?"

The superintendent was surprised that Charlie would know one of the security guards. "Oakes is doing okay, I guess. Haven't heard any complaints. Had a little beef with one of the other guards, but no big deal." He looked over Charlie's shoulder and smiled. "Speak of the devil," he said.

Charlie turned to see Buck's white pickup pull into the parking lot. Pie clambered out of the truck and trotted over to Charlie, followed by his father. Pie definitely seemed older, but the infectious look that Charlie would always remember him by remained. They gave each other a long high-five, then Charlie pulled him closer. "How's my best friend in West Virginia?"

"Charlie," Pie said excitedly, escaping the headlock, "Papa and me, we go hunting in the winter, and I shot a deer with my own rifle." Pie beamed.

"Wow, that's great, Pie Man," Charlie said, "getting a deer, that's really something."

Pie's smile disappeared. He put his hands in his pockets and shuffled his feet nervously. He glanced up as his father came over.

Charlie looked at Buck, then back at Pie. "What's up, Pie Man? What's the matter?"

Pie looked down at his feet. "Charlie, I am not Pie Man anymore. When I go to Univerthity of Michigan to be a engineer, like Charlie, they will laugh at me if I am called Pie Man." He shrugged. "Pie Man ith a baby name, and I am not a baby anymore. My name ith *Boyd*. Boyd Oakth."

Charlie looked at Buck for confirmation. "His idea," said Buck. "Kid's finally growin' up, I guess." Pie Man's happy face was back.

Charlie offered his hand. "I'm glad to meet you, Boyd Oakes. That's a fine name for an engineer." Charlie turned to Buck. He looked as if he'd put on a little weight since Charlie had last seen him. "How you doing, Buck?"

"Okay, Burden," Buck replied. "Good to see you again."

"Job going okay?" asked Charlie.

Buck turned toward the library. "It's all right," he said. "Good to be workin'." Charlie studied Buck's face for a second. He could still feel the anger lurking just below the surface. He started to ask Buck if Natty was coming to the open house, but Buck beat him to it. "Nat was going to come," said Buck, "but her leg's been hurtin' her some, and it ain't easy for her to walk. But she likes workin' up here at the library," he added. "Can't do her nursin' no more, so this is a good job for her."

Charlie smiled. "That's good." Then there was nothing left to say. "Well," he said, rubbing the top of Pie's head. The boy's hair had grown back in the months since the soccer tournament. "Better get some doughnuts and cider before the Willard boys eat everything."

They went into the library and joined the throng. Charlie lingered in the entryway, chatting with a few of the women from the Red Bone Baptist Church Social Club, until everyone left him to find the doughnuts. Alone, Charlie moved over to the trophy case hanging on the wall inside the front door.

On a tall pedestal sat the remains of the Charleston tournament trophy. It had been refinished in a deep brown. The inscription on the front gleamed. Against the back of the case was a huge photo of the Bones at the Charleston tournament, listing the players' names at the bottom. Charlie stepped closer for a better look, staring intently at the face of each boy in the front before he allowed himself to look at her, in the middle of the picture, with an arm around Emma's shoulders. Natty was laughing, with the smile that made his heart skip. He sighed deeply as he noticed Ellen and Hank walking toward him.

"Trophy looks great, Hank," said Charlie.

"Came out okay," Hank said, glancing at it briefly before heading for the door. The OntAmex man and the PR woman were herding people outside.

Ellen came over to Charlie. "Time to go," she said. Charlie smiled at his wife and nodded. Eve Brewster grabbed Charlie for the walk down to the field, while Ellen went ahead with Hank. They fell in behind Ada and

Gus and Janice Lowe, going down the long cement stairway. Up ahead, the women of the Red Bone Baptist Church Social Club were moving slowly down the stairs, holding up the procession. The OntAmex man and the PR woman were halfway across the soccer field.

Charlie smiled. *They'll just have to wait.* He would enjoy his last few minutes chatting with Eve. They walked arm-in-arm across the mushy sod of the soccer field, while she brought him up to date on life in Red Bone. Mr. Jacks had moved in with Natty and Buck after Natty visited him in Beckley. She took one look at the conditions, loaded him into her car, and brought him back to Red Bone, where they made a space for him in their trailer. Charlie laughed. He could picture Natty doing that. And the best thing about it, Eve added, was that Buck was okay with it.

The pitch of the turbines' whistle went up a notch as the helicopter's blades began to spin. Beside the gazebo, people were saying their good-byes. Charlie watched as Ellen hugged Ada Lowe. He turned and gazed up the hill, to the fourth-floor porch where he'd spent so many evenings with Hank. The rear of the building was bathed in late-morning sunlight. Charlie took a deep breath. "I loved it here, Eve. This is a wonderful place, with wonderful people."

Eve squeezed his arm and stared into space, a wry grin on her face. "Charlie," she said, "I'm going to go over and say goodbye to Ellen now." She nodded toward the street before starting off for the gazebo. Charlie turned and saw the orange Camaro roll to a stop at the side of the road. Sally had her arm extended out the window, a cigarette in her hand. She glanced over at Charlie and then toward her passenger.

Natty finally opened the door and stepped out. She held the seat forward to let Cat out of the back, and they both walked toward Charlie. Natty said something to her daughter, and Cat ran ahead. The little girl glanced nervously at Charlie and put her head down as she sped by. Natty moved slowly, with a noticeable limp, leaning on a cane. When she arrived at the field, her cane sank in the soft turf, forcing her to pull it out before taking her next step. She smiled at Charlie and put her head down to concentrate on the placement of her cane in the wet grass. He took a few steps toward her, conscious of the eyes watching them.

She stopped about eight feet away and looked around at the new turf.

"Used to have a nice field here, nice and hard, with a lot of stones. Easy to walk on." She looked up. "Hey, Charlie."

Charlie smiled. "How are you, Nat?"

She shrugged. "Knee ain't so good. Had to put some phony ligaments and stuff in there. Six months, maybe, I'll be fine, runnin' around again, all over the mountain." Natty's hair had darkened and grown out a little, with a shock starting to fall across her forehead once again. "I ain't complainin', though." She looked over at the gazebo, where Buck stood, his hands in his pockets, staring back at her. "Buck's been great, you know, since . . . since the accident."

Ellen waved, and Natty waved back. "Your wife still sticks out in a crowd, don't she, Charlie?"

He glanced over at Ellen. "She does that."

"How's she like her new house?"

Charlie turned back toward Natty. "We're selling it this week."

"She okay with that?"

He smiled. "She's got a bigger one to play with in China."

Natty continued to gaze over at Ellen. "I heard you were in China," she said. "Like you always wanted, huh, Charlie? Buildin' somethin' important."

"Yes, that's right. It's what I always wanted."

Natty watched Ellen climb into the helicopter. "Looks like they're waiting for you, Charlie."

He took a step closer. "I'm glad you came, Natty. I wanted to see you."

She flashed a brief smile. "Got most of my memory back now." She turned her face toward the library on the hill. "Not all of it, though. Don't remember *her* yet," said Natty. "I stare and stare at that picture up there, and sometimes I get these quick flashes of her, kickin' a ball or runnin' down the field, but they're gone in a second." She looked back at Charlie. "Remember 'most everything else, though, 'cept for the accident."

As Charlie watched her speak, surrounded by the green field and the forest behind her, his time with her suddenly flashed back to him—their runs along the mountain trail, the soccer games, their night at the Pocahontas Hotel with Woody and Mr. Jacks, the lobster party . . . falling in love with her. The helicopter whined impatiently on the baseball field.

"Hear some music once in a while from the show, and I think about New York." Natty laughed. "What a weekend that was, huh, Charlie?"

Their eyes locked for a moment, sharing the memory of what almost was, then Natty turned toward the gazebo, where Buck stood with Pie and Cat.

"Funny how things work out sometimes," she said.

Charlie looked down at her and stared into her eyes. "Yeah, it is," he said. Natty smiled at him.

Charlie turned toward the helicopter. "Time to go," he said.

Natty leaned on her cane and held out her right hand. "Thank you, Mr. Burden, for everything."

Charlie took her hand and squeezed it softly. "Goodbye, Mrs. Oakes." He turned and walked with long strides toward the helicopter.

Natty stood in the center of the field and watched as Charlie shook hands with Buck and Hank, hugged Mabel and Ada, and gave Pie a high-five and a long hug. As Charlie stepped into the helicopter, Natty walked back across the field toward the orange Camaro, her cane sinking into the soft new turf of the soccer field.

AUTHOR'S NOTE

Mountaintop-removal coal mining is an environmental, ecological, political, and social catastrophe that all of America should be ashamed of. We've allowed the coal industry to turn one of the most beautiful, biodiverse, and ecologically rich areas of our country—North America's oldest mountain range—into a national energy sacrifice zone. MTR has destroyed more than five hundred mountains and two thousand miles of streams. It poisons the land and it poisons communities and the people who live there.

Only in Appalachia, where the population is thin, powerless, and poor—where the coal industry has been systematically sucking out the wealth for the past hundred years while financing the careers of complicit state politicians and judges and members of Congress—could such a cancerous fissure in the integrity of our environmental consciousness take place.

Over the past fifteen years that I have been aware of mountaintop removal, there have been many optimistic signs that the movement to eradicate MTR was assuredly under way. In 1999, a courageous federal judge, the late Charles H. Haden II, ruled against the mining industry in an MTR suit brought under the Federal Clean Water Act. Environmentalists cheered this monumental ruling. Numerous websites documenting the destruction and desecration of MTR grew into voices for advocacy and activism. Volunteers marched on Charleston, Washington, and Blair Mountain. Celebrities like Bobby Kennedy, Kathy Mattea, Emmylou Harris, Sheryl Crow, Tim McGraw, Ashley Judd, and many others joined the movement. Great books were written, including *Coal River*, by Michael Shnayerson, and the epic achievement *Plundering Appalachia*, edited by Tom Butler and George Woerthner. Heart-wrenching documentaries like *Burning the Future: Coal in America*; *Coal Country*; and *The Last Mountain* delivered what had to be knockout blows. Prestigious environmental organizations, including the Natural Resources Defense Council and the Sierra Club, embraced the fight against MTR and brought their great organizational skills and marketing resources to the cause. And then the Obama administration, with a mandate for change, swept into power, saying all the right things about MTR. Surely the end was near.

Yet, in spite of all this outcry, and in spite of the competition from shale natural gas, the coal industry continues to blast away the mountains, forests, and streams of West Virginia and Kentucky. Dozens of new sites have been permitted, with dozens of applications awaiting review or appeal. The EPA heroically suspended the permits for Mingo Logan Coal Company's Spruce No. 1 MTR site in Logan County, West Virginia, and was hauled before a congressional committee to face the wrath of coal-friendly reps and their industry lobbyists. With the next Republican administration (as with the last one), the rate of mountaintop removal will again ratchet up to keep pace with our insatiable consumption of low-cost electricity, and destroying more Appalachian mountains will be a central component of our national energy policy.

To learn more about mountaintop-removal coal mining, and to perhaps add your voice to the outcry, start with the books and the documentaries mentioned above and the websites listed below.

iLove Mountains: www. iLoveMountains.org
Appalachian Voices: www.appvoices.org
Ohio Valley Environmental Coalition: www.ohvec.org
West Virginia Highlands Conservancy: www.wvhighlands.org
Coal River Mountain Watch: www.crmw.net
Natural Resources Defense Council: www.nrdc.org
The Sierra Club: www.sierraclub.org

GERRY FITZGERALD
August 2012

ACKNOWLEDGMENTS

Redemption Mountain is a work of fiction. The characters, their thoughts, actions, and words are entirely the creation of the author and any resemblances found to an actual person are coincidental and inadvertent. The corporations named in the story are also fictitious.

All of the places referred to in the story are real with the notable exceptions of the town of Red Bone, Redemption Mountain, and Hickory Hills Country Club. McDowell County is in fact the southernmost county in West Virginia, located in the heart of the Pocahontas Coal Field that powered America's industrial revolution and fueled the war machines that saved the world twice in the last century. Mamaroneck, New York, is a diverse city of seventeen thousand in Westchester County. New York, New York, remains the world's greatest city, and Warren, Vermont, is very close to Heaven.

The historical events referred to in the story are real, well documented from numerous sources, and are described as factually and faithfully as I can determine. Hank's personal account of the Buffalo Creek Disaster of 1972 borrows heavily from an enthralling and heartbreaking series of stories (largely the work of reporter Ken Ward Jr., mentioned below) published in the *Charleston Gazette* on the twenty-fifth anniversary of the tragedy in 1997. The December 6, 1907, coal mine explosion in Monongah, West Virginia, claimed the lives of 362 miners and remains this country's worst coal mine disaster. On November 20, 1968, a fire in the Consol Mine in Farmington, West Virginia, killed seventy-eight miners. The original New York production of *Les Misérables* closed on March 15, 2003, after a sixteen-year run on Broadway.

Hank's discourses on the West Virginia Mine Wars, the Matewan Massacre, and the subsequent fates of Sheriff Sid Hatfield and his deputy, Ed Chambers, are drawn from numerous sources, including: *American Heritage Magazine*, August 1974; *The West Virginia Mine Wars* by Cabell Phillips; "The Battle of Matewan," www.matewan.com/History/battle2. htm; "West Virginia's Mine Wars," West Virginia Division of Culture and History, www.wvculture.org/history/minewars.html; and "Matewan," *United Mine Workers of America History*, www.umwa.org/history/matewan.shtml.

For an understanding of the economics of the coal mining industry as well as what life was like in the coal fields during the last century, I am indebted to a wonderfully written book, *Coal: A Memoir and Critique*, by Duane Lockard (University Press of Virginia, 1998).

Throughout the writing of *Redemption Mountain*, I found myself continually referring back to and rereading parts of a wonderful book entitled *The Heritage of McDowell County, West Virginia, 1858–1999*, published by the McDowell County Historical Society and edited by Geneva Steele, Sandra Long, and Tom Hatcher. I came by this book through a chance online meeting of my friend Geneva Steele of Bradshaw, West Virginia, many years ago when I was just starting the book. She has supplied many helpful comments on the story over the years and I am in her debt.

The articles, columns, and blogs of Ken Ward Jr., of the *Charleston Gazette*, have educated me on the history of coal mining in West Virginia, coal mining safety, the attendant government bureaus and agencies, and the effects of mountaintop-removal coal mining in West Virginia as well as the machinations of local, state, and federal politicians who enable it to continue. Mr. Ward is an exhaustive reporter and a prolific, lucid writer whose style made every story enlightening, every paragraph a pleasure to read.

A great many people contributed to the publishing of *Redemption Mountain*. My agent, Loretta Barrett, was a rock and a great friend throughout a long process. My editors, Jill Lamar and Phyllis Grann, deserve medals for patience, as does Joanna Levine at Holt. My friend,

Carol Churchill, reviewed the entire, massive first manuscript many years ago and provided invaluable help and encouragement.

I am fortunate to have a number of good friends who took a great interest in the book and provided an incredible level of support and encouragement. They can't know how much their kind words and recommendations meant to me. I need to thank a few: Bob Page, Rich Dowling, Mike Aliberti, Pam Aronson, Kevin and Mary McCullough, Maryann and Fernando Goulart, John Skar, Dave Daniels, Joanne Carlisle, Debbie and Andy Okun, Donna Goff, Rolly Ciocca, Jay Hamilton, Gail Mathes, Korby Clark, Chris and Sue Mastroianni, Sheila Doiron, Tom Foley, and of course, Eddie Sheehan.

ABOUT THE AUTHOR

GERRY FITZGERALD has been in advertising for nearly thirty years, and owns an advertising agency in Springfield, Massachusetts. He holds a master's in journalism from the Medill School at Northwestern University and is a graduate of the University of Massachusetts at Amherst. He lives in East Longmeadow, Massachusetts, with his wife Robin, and has two children in college.